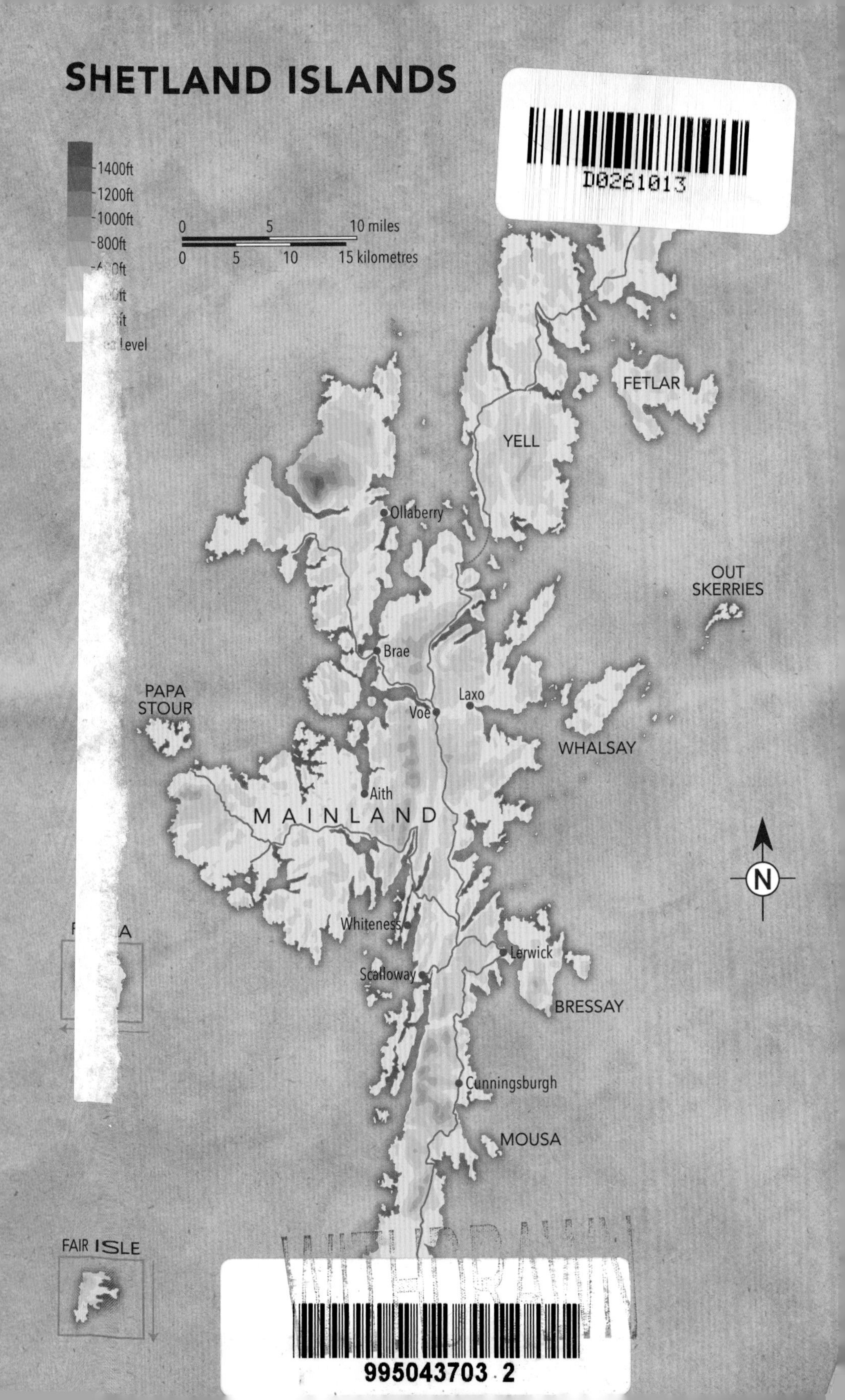
SHETLAND ISLANDS
1400ft
1200ft
1000ft
800ft
0
5
10 miles
0
5
10
15 kilometres
FETLAR
YELL
Ollaberry
OUT SKERRIES
Brae
PAPA STOUR
Laxo
Voe
WHALSAY
Aith
MAINLAND
N
Whiteness
Lerwick
Scalloway
BRESSAY
Cunningsburgh
MOUSA
FAIR ISLE

WILD FIRE

By Ann Cleeves

A Bird in the Hand   Come Death and High Water

Murder in Paradise   A Prey to Murder

A Lesson in Dying   Murder in My Backyard

A Day in the Death of Dorothea Cassidy

Another Man's Poison   Killjoy

The Mill on the Shore   Sea Fever

The Healers   High Island Blues

The Baby-Snatcher   The Sleeping and the Dead

Burial of Ghosts

The Vera Stanhope series

The Crow Trap   Telling Tales   Hidden Depths

Silent Voices   The Glass Room   Harbour Street

The Moth Catcher   The Seagull

The Shetland series

Raven Black   White Nights   Red Bones

Blue Lightning   Dead Water   Thin Air

Cold Earth   Wild Fire

Ann Cleeves

WILD FIRE

MACMILLAN

First published 2018 by Macmillan
an imprint of Pan Macmillan
20 New Wharf Road, London N1 9RR
Associated companies throughout the world
www.panmacmillan.com

ISBN 978-1-4472-7824-5

3 5 7 9 8 6 4 2

A CIP catalogue record for this book is available from the British Library.

Typeset by Palimpsest Book Production Ltd, Falkirk, Stirlingshire
Printed and bound by CPI Group (UK) Ltd, Croydon, CR0 4YY

In memory of Tim Cleeves,

husband and friend

Acknowledgements

This is the last Shetland novel and I'd like to thank all the people who inspired and supported me throughout the series. It's an impertinence for an outsider to write about a place that's so special, but Shetlanders have been generous throughout. My special thanks to Ingirid Eunson for her friendship and her stories.

Thanks to the Aberdeen support team – James and Nicola Grieve and Lorna and Robbie Dawson – for their kindness and for their willingness to share expertise with a scientific duffer. James, Nicola and Lorna get a mention in *Wild Fire*, but Robbie should be there too! Robert Moncrieff appears in the book through a generous donation by his wife to Bardsey Bird Observatory. Thanks to you both.

I have worked with a number of editors on the Shetland series and I'd like to acknowledge them all here. You've all contributed to the success of the stories: Sarah Adams, Julie Crisp, Catherine Richards, Vicki Mellor and Marcia Markland.

I've been published by Pan Macmillan for so long now that I feel like part of the family. There are far too many people to mention individually, but I'd like to thank you all for your kindness and your tolerance. Maura Wilding has become part of the team too; she's a friend and advisor as well as an extraordinary publicist. Thanks, too, to everyone at Minotaur in the US, especially Sarah Melnyk and Martin Quinn.

Last but not least, a huge thanks to my agent Sara Menguc, and to her associates around the world. A special mention to Moses Cardona in the US for arranging the best pre-awards party ever.

Chapter One

Emma sat on the shingle bank and watched the kids on the beach below build a bonfire. They'd dragged pieces of driftwood into a pile; it was something to do to relieve their boredom. Nothing much happened in Deltaness. It was too far from Lerwick for an easy night out, and the buses stopped long before the bars closed. The night was clear and still and the light drained slowly away. In another month it would be midsummer. Emma was there because she was bored too. When she was a child she'd longed for boredom, for quiet, normal days free from tension. School and homework, and meals with the family that didn't end in anger, shouting or worse. Now, she thought, she'd inherited a need for excitement, a longing to fill her days with action and challenge, to provoke a response from the people in her life. A need to make things happen.

She stared out towards the horizon, where the sea and the sky had blurred into one, and wondered why was she still here in Deltaness then, working as nanny? A voice in her head told her that she was still in Shetland because she was scared of the world away from the islands. Here she was safe, in a tight community where she knew her place. If she hadn't been so scared, she'd have stuck with Daniel Fleming, run away south with him, become an artist or a model or a designer. Emma closed her ears to the voice. She didn't like to think of herself as scared. Life here wasn't so bad. It had its own compensations. She took a bottle out of her bag. This wasn't her wonderful new bag that stood on her bed, reminding her of those compensations, but the one she'd made herself out of a scrap of leftover fabric. She took a swig of vodka and passed the bottle to the man beside her.

Magnie Riddell handed it back and slid his arm around her back. Soon he would try to stick his tongue in her mouth. That made Emma feel a little bit sick. She liked men, but on her own terms, and sometimes she thought sex was seriously overrated. Magnie was kind, and as different from her father as it was possible to be, but she still found it hard to be physically close to him.

The fire was lit now. She could feel the heat from the flames even from here, and sparks spiralled into the sky. Below them the kids were passing round cans of lager and cider. They were singing some chant she couldn't recognize, something about sport, or a verse stolen from the Up Helly Aa fire festival. Then she heard a sound behind her of pebbles shifting and rattling, and a small child appeared on the bank above them. He stared into the fire, apparently mesmerized. She recognized him at once. This was Christopher, Daniel Fleming's strange boy.

The group below caught sight of him and stared back. They began to laugh and shout. Magnie pulled away his arm and turned towards her. Obviously he expected Emma to intervene, to take care of the child. But she was off-duty and she was bored. She watched the scene play out below her and she smiled.

Chapter Two

Magnie Riddell was feeling old. He shouldn't be here with these kids; his mother would get to hear of it, because gossip spread through Deltaness even more quickly than it had when he was a bairn. Then, there might have been a chance of getting away with the occasional piece of mischief. Now even his mother was on Facebook, and it would just take one photo of him sitting next to Emma on the beach, his face lit by the flames and a bottle in her hand, for her to begin the old lecture. About how Magnie was all she had, now his father had left them for that foreign tart in Lerwick; about how he'd already caused her family disgrace: *No one has ever been in trouble with the police before. I couldn't show my face in the shop for a month. You need to grow up, Magnie. Settle down with a nice local girl and make me a grandmother.*

Magnie turned to Emma, who sat, prim and neat as his mother's Siamese cat, although she'd drunk as much as he had. That was what made her different from the local lasses who yelled and swore as much as the boys. She never lost control. She and Magnie were on the shingle bank, leaning back on their elbows, a little way from the fire and looking down on it. That was Emma too, always a little apart.

'Should we get back?' He thought perhaps she would allow him into the bedsit she had in the doctor's big house. She'd let him in once before and they'd lain on the narrow bed, and she'd let him touch her and kiss her, and he'd been wild with desire for her. Later, he'd slipped down the back stairs and out into the night without anyone seeing him. Scared and frustrated and excited, all at the same time. He'd hoped that might be the start of something, that it would make him her boyfriend and not just her friend. But the thing about Emma was that you could never be sure of anything. Even when they were kissing, when he'd unbuttoned her blouse and felt her skin against his, he'd felt that she was distant. An outsider looking in on what they were doing. Not exactly judging his performance, but not really engaged. He still didn't know quite where he stood with her and, for some reason that he couldn't work out, he was too frightened to ask her. Sometimes he wanted to lash out at her, to force Emma to take him seriously.

'I can't,' she said. 'Martha and Charlie are here and I need to keep an eye on them and walk them back.' Her voice was calm; there was something about her slow Orcadian voice that turned him on, drove him crazy. Just at that moment he would have done anything to possess her.

'I see. Of course.' Because what else could he say? She'd worked as a nanny for the doctor's family for years and though the two oldest were teenagers, she still felt responsible for them, in a way that he considered admirable. Even if it was frustrating tonight. Emma was more responsible, he thought, than the doctor and his wife, who never seemed to know or to care what their four children were up to. Without Emma, they would be allowed to run wild.

He looked down at the group by the fire to search for the Moncrieff kids. The only light came from the flames and so at first it was hard to make them out. He saw Martha first. She was sixteen, dark-haired. Since she'd started at the Anderson High, he'd never seen her wearing anything other than black. She was sitting cross-legged on the sand, brooding. The Deltaness gossip had her down as weird, attention-seeking. His mother tutted whenever she spoke of her: *That girl will come to no good. And why those piercings and the haircut that looks as if someone's been at it with a scythe? She'd be attractive enough, if she made something of herself.* He wondered, slightly drunk now, why his mother's words always seemed to appear in his head when he was least expecting them. He wished he could get rid of them, of her.

Charlie was fifteen, a year younger than his sister, blond, athletic. Magnie couldn't imagine him brooding about anything. Now he had his arm around a friend and they were singing. Maybe a football chant. Nothing musical, at least. From where he sat, Magnie couldn't hear anything like a tune. Just a beat. Charlie was waving a can of strong lager in the air. Soon he'd be sick. Magnie recognized the signs. *He'd* started drinking when he was a youngster too.

Behind Emma and Magnie, the shingle shifted. Magnie heard the clacking of smaller pebbles and felt them stinging his bare arms. He turned round. He hoped it wasn't one of the community elders, demanding that they keep the noise down or that they put out the fire. Then his mother would certainly get to hear he'd been on the beach with Emma. Recently, Magnie hadn't been entirely truthful when his mother quizzed him about the nanny. What business was it of hers, after all?

But a boy stood there. A young boy. He was dressed in a white T-shirt and white shorts, so it looked as if he was in his underwear, that he'd sleepwalked out of a dream. Magnie recognized him. His mother had pointed him out when he'd walked with her to the shop one morning: 'That's the daft child that lives in Dennis Gear's old place. They say he set fire to the school and he'll set fire to us all one day.' Magnie hadn't said anything. He knew his mother had had a soft spot for Dennis Gear – there'd been rumours about him and her having a fling at one time – and she hated the fact that the house had been changed so much. And maybe there was a touch of guilt about the way the old man died.

Now he felt sorry for the child, who looked so confused. The chanting around the fire, which had started as something to do with mocking a rival sports team, changed, became nastier. He made out the word and couldn't quite believe what he was hearing. 'Retard, retard, retard.' Magnie looked at Emma. She worked with children. Surely she would do something, take the boy into her arms and comfort him. They had to get him back to his family. But Emma made no move. She was still observing the scene below her. Magnie thought perhaps she was checking on Charlie and Martha. She wasn't looking at the boy standing above them. Magnie stood up and yelled at the group to stop their taunting, but his words were swallowed up by the noise. The chant changed. Now they were calling: 'Hangman, hangman, hangman.'

The boy had his eyes shut, his hands over his ears to block out the sound and the sight. Magnie couldn't believe that folk could be so cruel. He knew they weren't all cruel people. It was the drink and the fact that they were anonymous, part of the gang, changed by the flickering light into one monstrous, shouting whole.

Magnie scrambled up the bank to the child and picked him up in his arms. The boy didn't struggle. He felt very light, like a bird. There was no flesh on him. At the other side of the bank, out of sight of the fire and the teenagers, he set the boy on his feet. The chanting had stopped, as if the hidden kids were suddenly ashamed of what they'd done. Magnie took the child's hand. 'It's Christopher, isn't it? Come on then, Christopher, your mother and father will wonder where you are. Let's get you home to them.'

It was only when he turned back that he saw the shadow. A shape that he recognized, staring after him.

Chapter Three

They stood in the playground, waiting for the kids to be let out for the day. The biggest proportion were mothers, but there were two fathers, three grandmothers and the young woman who worked as a nanny for the doctor's family. Most afternoons they gathered into small friendship groups and the exchanges were desultory, light-hearted. After nine months, Helena Fleming knew what to expect. There was a little harmless chat, anecdotes about other children's antics and achievements. She never felt quite part of the group and seldom spoke of her own children, but was prepared to be a willing audience.

Today, though, there seemed to be more cohesion, more purpose to the conversation, and she hesitated for a moment before entering. The gate creaked when Helena pushed it open and the group turned towards her. She *knew* they'd been talking about her, waiting for her arrival. Suddenly they morphed in her head into something from a horror film, became more like a pack of hunting dogs than the neighbours she'd thought she knew rather well. They were greedy for gossip and for a moment she had a picture of them tearing her apart to get it, their heads thrust forward, slavering. She wanted to run, surprised at how frightened she felt.

She was a strong, independent woman, successful in her own right, and she shouldn't be feeling like this: numb, mindless, shaking. Shock and a residual pride kept her there, facing them. And really, she told herself, what could they do to her? They would be reluctant to make a scene. On the surface, at least, Shetlanders were a polite bunch. She turned her back and stooped, pretending to tie a shoelace, so she wouldn't have to look at them.

At that moment, the first class was released into the playground. Helena's children were older, but the waiting carers scattered to collect their offspring and immediately they became less threatening. They filled their arms with school bags and coats. Because this afternoon no coats were needed. It was May and warm for Shetland. The moment of tension had passed, at least for another day, and Helena relaxed, told herself that her reaction – the image of the hunting dogs – had been ridiculous. She should have faced the group, approached them and made conversation. How pathetic she'd been! How cowardly!

Ellie ran out soon after, elbows and knees flailing, socks around her ankles, chalk or paint on her forehead and down the front of her jumper. Talking. Sometimes Helena thought the girl had been born talking. Demanding attention, at least. Helena was used to listening with half her brain, nodding occasionally. It came to her, with a sudden dreadful moment of guilt, that she'd employed exactly the same tactics with her mother, when she was in the final stages of Alzheimer's. Helena bent towards her daughter and tried to focus, but she'd missed the beginning of Ellie's story and what she was saying now made no sense.

Besides, Ellie couldn't stand still for more than a moment and the girl was already bouncing away.

Christopher was the last to emerge, accompanied by the support worker. Christopher always came out last, always accompanied. Helena thought it would do him good to mix with the others, because how could he learn the rules of interaction if he was never given the chance? She still hadn't plucked up the courage to question the issue, though. She could understand why the school wanted to play safe, but she hated the way he was made to feel different. He was eleven, tall, dark-haired and dark-eyed. Beautiful. The support worker always insisted on feeding back any issues of the day. In London, the school had been too busy for that sort of service. There were too many children with problems. Then Helena would have been grateful to hear how Christopher had managed in class. She'd longed for information, for her child to be given the attention she felt was his due. Now the daily ritual depressed her. She didn't want to know that Christopher had sworn at one child or bitten another. She was exhausted by the pity and the understanding. She almost preferred the playground parents' hunger for information about her strange fire-setting child and her melancholic husband.

'Well, we've had quite a nice day.' The worker was a Shetlander, always cheery, even when passing on the most embarrassing news. 'Haven't we, Christopher?' She had at least learned that he disliked intensely being called *Chris*.

Christopher looked at his mother and rolled his eyes. Helena thought it was this arrogance that provoked much of the antagonism directed towards him.

He was bright – at least he had a fabulous memory, and the logic to solve maths problems – and because he thought he was the centre of the universe, sometimes he treated the adults around him, including his mother, as domestic servants.

'A bit of a temper tantrum at lunchtime, but nothing we couldn't handle.' Becky, the support worker, smiled. 'No messing about with matches today. See you in the morning, Christopher.'

He was wearing shorts and a T-shirt. Sandals. No jumper and no socks. His preferred outfit even in midwinter. He didn't seem to feel the cold, but hated the sense of fabric next to his skin, even natural fibres like cotton or wool. He never wore pyjamas and wandered round the house without any clothes at all, if he could get away with it. The school had got used to his scanty clothing now, but in the early days there'd been a daily phone call from the head asking why the boy had come in without a coat. 'We like them to get some fresh air, even when it's chilly.' Helena had tried to explain and then had sent Christopher to school with a coat and a jumper in a bag, muttering under her breath: *And if you can get him to wear them, let me know your secret.* Hoping, of course, that they wouldn't manage it, and *she* would be proved right. She had been proved right and the phone calls had stopped.

Christopher stood and waited while the exchange between Becky and his mother was taking place. He didn't fidget, like Ellie. There was a twitch occasionally, or he'd bite his nails or pick at his skin until it bled and formed a scab. This conversation between home and school was a routine that had to be gone through, and Christopher understood routine. By the time the meeting was over, the playground was empty. Helena shouted to Ellie, who was hanging by her legs from the climbing frame, to come down so they could go home.

They lived more than a mile away from the school, but unless the weather was horrendous they always walked. Christopher complained about not getting a lift, but, like the conversation with Becky, the complaint had become a ritual. He didn't enjoy being outdoors, and because he was eager to get home to his room and his computer, he walked quickly, with a strange, straight-legged gait that gave him the appearance of a robot. The road took them along the edge of a beach, with a couple of upturned ancient boats above the tideline along with the seaweed. A pebble bank separated the road from the beach, and Ellie scampered away from them to walk along its ridge, holding her arms out for balance. After a day of enforced inactivity, she was like a dog that needed a run. At the end of the beach there was a path across a low, boggy headland. At this time of year it was gaudy with colour: wild yellow iris, marsh marigold, campion and plants and flowers that Helena had no names for. She had decided, when they first moved here, that she would learn them all, but other events had taken over. From here they could see the house that had become their home. They called it Hesti, because that was what it had always been called. It was built into the hill that rose steeply from the flat marshland and there was a view from the front windows of the headland and the beach, all the way back to the settlement of Deltaness, with its school, shop and community hall.

Ellie ran ahead; they could see her ploughing up

the track towards the house, the incline hardly slowing her pace. Helena watched with envy and thought that once *she'd* had that much energy. She'd been able to dance all night and still be ready for work in the morning, still creative and fizzing with ideas. When had she lost all that? Not with marriage. Daniel had inspired some of her best work. They'd met at art school and married far too young, according to all her friends and her liberal parents: 'Why marriage, darling? Why tie yourself down when you're both still students?' But she'd loved the idea. The dramatic gesture. Perhaps they'd waited too long to have children. She'd been in her mid-thirties when Christopher had been born, nearly forty when Ellie had arrived.

She still hadn't reached any conclusion when they reached the house. Christopher was still marching with the relentless pace of an automaton, but she was slightly out of breath and paused for a moment and looked out at the wide valley that had been sculpted centuries ago by ice. She told herself that London might have cool bars and exhibitions and theatre, but it didn't have *this*.

By the time she went inside, Christopher had already disappeared into his bedroom. He would have shed most of his outer clothes and be sitting in his underwear in front of the computer screen. He'd be watching a totally unsuitable American cop show. Mesmerized, it seemed. He was obsessed with forensic details, and often he would need to be prised away from the screen for meals. That could result in silent sulking at best, and at worst a violent tantrum. Screams that once in London had resulted in the neighbours calling the police. Occasionally she relented and let him eat a sandwich alone in his room, knowing that this would set a dangerous precedent and the next day it would be even more difficult to persuade him to spend some time with the family, but feeling too exhausted to face the fuss.

Ellie was in the kitchen, foraging for food. She'd already peeled a satsuma and its skin lay discarded on the bench. She wandered past Helena and curled up on the sofa in the living room, calm at last, to watch CBBC. There was no sign of Daniel, though his car was parked in its usual spot behind the house. Perhaps he'd gone for a walk; it was a lovely day, after all, and he'd seemed very much brighter this morning. Helena was relieved. His depression came in waves and, like the sea, sometimes swamped him, washed away the man she knew and loved, leaving her with a bitter and angry stranger. It would be good to be in the house without him for a while.

The Shetland Times lay on the table. Daniel must have picked it up from the Deltaness community shop earlier in the day while she was working. Helena opened it, thought again how different it was from the local newspaper in the London borough where they'd previously lived. That front page had been Gothic in nature, with lurid tales of knife crime, assault, arson and shooting. This held details of a record haul of fish landed at Shetland Catch, sheep sales and a bairns' music festival. Her panic attack in the playground seemed ridiculous now. These were good people. She began to feel the stress drain from her body, got up to switch on the kettle and made a mug of tea, before returning to the paper.

Between the second and third pages there was a

piece of paper. It was small, precisely four inches square, neatly cut, possibly by guillotine. Graph paper. A design had been marked: dots in the tiny squares to form a stick person. It could have been the remnant of a child's game, because beside the person, the dots formed a crude gallows and the figure was already hanging. Hangman. Game over. But there were no letters, no lines where the letters were missing. And Helena had received images like this before.

Chapter Four

It was Saturday morning and Jimmy Perez was sitting outside his house – Fran's house – watching Cassie play in the small burn that separated their home from the croft where Magnus Tait had once lived. There was talk that it had been sold and that a man from Lerwick had bought it. He wondered if the man had a family; it would be splendid if a child moved in, someone to be company for Cassie and to boost the numbers in Ravenswick school. The sun was warm and he let his mind wander. Cassie was a self-contained girl of nine. He couldn't believe how the time had passed. She'd been four when he'd first met her, just starting school, and six when Fran had died. She turned occasionally to check he was there and then went back to her game. This was a piece of serious engineering; she was building dams and reservoirs to slow the course of the water. There'd been a lot of talk locally about experimenting with similar schemes to prevent another landslide. A huge slip had caused chaos in the islands three months before. Cassie was working on her own experiment. Her mother would have been proud of her efforts.

Below him ran the main road from Lerwick to Sumburgh Airport, but today the traffic seemed very far away, the noise a distant hum like summer insects. He watched as a red van he didn't recognize turned off the main road and climbed the narrow track towards the houses. He thought perhaps this was the new owner of Hillhead, the Tait croft, and that it might be a grand opportunity to meet him. But the van stopped outside his house and a woman got out. Perez struggled to guess her age. Late forties maybe: her hair was starting to grey. It was wiry, very curly. Unmanageable. She wore jeans and red leather boots, a hand-knitted cardigan in red and blue. Something about her style reminded him of Fran.

'Inspector Perez?' She was English. Rather intense.

'Yes.' He could tell that the visit would be work-related – it wasn't so unusual to be disturbed at home – and he continued quickly. Years of practice had got the words off pat. 'But I'm off-duty now, you know. If it's a police matter, you should go to the station in Lerwick.'

'Yes.' There was no argument. 'Of course. I shouldn't have come, and perhaps it's not so important. Probably not a police matter at all.' She waved at Cassie, who was still at work building her dam, and turned back towards the van.

Perhaps it was the wave to the bairn that did it. The wave and the fact that the woman seemed so sad. Sarah, his ex-wife, had called Perez 'emotionally incontinent', and Willow, his boss and occasional lover, said the description was just about right: 'You spread your sympathy and kindness too thin, Jimmy. Sometimes there's nothing left for the people who care for you.'

He called after the woman, 'I was just going to

make more coffee. Do you fancy one? We could talk informally. While you're here . . .'

'If you're sure. It does seem a terrible impertinence.' But she gave a quick, shy smile and he sensed her relief.

When he came back with the coffee she was playing with Cassie, helping to build a sandbank with a plastic spade, as serious in the task as the girl was. When she saw Perez, she put down the spade and walked back to join him. They sat together on the white plank that acted as a bench, their feet stretched in front of them.

'So why don't you tell me your name?' He sipped his coffee and looked out at Raven's Head. 'And what it is that's worrying you.'

'I'm Helena,' she said. 'Helena Fleming.'

'I've heard of you!' She'd arrived in the islands recently, nearly three years after Fran's death, but a few of Fran's arty friends invited him out occasionally to dinners and parties and he listened to their gossip. He'd been engaged to Fran Hunter, artist and mother to Cassie, but Fran had been murdered and he still knew it was his fault. He carried the guilt wherever he went.

Besides, he knew the woman's name because she'd featured in *The Shetland Times* and *The Shetlander* and had become something of a local celebrity. Helena was a designer; she used Shetland wool to create garments that were shown at London Fashion Week. People came from all over the world to commission her work. Rumour had it that the Duchess of Cambridge had bought one of her cardigans from a smart London store.

'We live at Deltaness.'

He nodded. He knew that too, in the way that information about islanders soaked into his consciousness. They'd bought Dennis Gear's house, and Dennis had killed himself soon after they finally moved in, shocking the community and somehow tainting the family. His sympathy for the woman increased.

'You'll have heard that a man hanged himself in our barn?'

Perez nodded and the woman continued.

'It was suicide. Your people investigated. There was a post-mortem. But somehow, it seems, we're to blame. According to the people in the community.' Her voice was bitter. 'They're making our life hell.'

'I'm sorry,' Perez said. 'That must be tough.' He knew all about the power of rumour and gossip. 'But I'm not sure it's a police matter. If you can stick it out, folk will soon find something else to chatter about.'

Helena Fleming continued as if he hadn't spoken. 'It's affecting us all. I have two children, a girl and a boy. Ellie's a bit young to notice what people are saying, though I'm sure she hears things at school. But my son, Christopher, is autistic. High-functioning, but still needing support. Sometimes his behaviour is a little strange, but he's not stupid. He's picked up on the hostility. He wants to know why they hate us.'

'Do they really hate you?' Perez thought that must be an exaggeration. Shetlanders weren't given to hate.

'Not all of them, obviously. We have friends. But we're considered odd, a bit dangerous. Christopher doesn't make things any easier.' She paused for a moment. 'He has obsessions. At the moment, he's obsessed with fire. He took matches into school and set fire to some waste paper in the playground. And Daniel, my husband, isn't the most sociable of people.' There was a moment of silence. He was about to prompt her to continue when she started speaking again. 'Daniel found the dead man. He still has nightmares about it.'

'I'm sorry,' Perez said again, 'but I still don't see how I can help.'

She was staring out towards Raven's Head. 'Someone's been coming onto our property. That must be a police matter.'

'You've had stuff stolen?'

She shook her head. 'Nothing's been stolen, but things have been left behind.'

She'd been carrying a green leather satchel and opened it to take out a plastic file. She unclipped the file and lifted out three small squares of graph paper, which she set carefully on the bench between them.

The first showed the frame of a gallows, the second had the gallows with a noose and the third included the hanged man. She pointed to the last image. 'That came yesterday, tucked inside *The Shetland Times*.'

'And the others?'

'The first came a month ago, a few days after Daniel found Dennis Gear. The second came last week. It was in my son's homework bag. Luckily I found it before he did.'

'Your son couldn't have drawn them?' Perez was feeling his way. He knew how he'd feel if anyone accused Cassie of creating bizarre pictures of hanged men, and he didn't want to upset his visitor. But this could be part of a game. Harmless. Perhaps the woman was overreacting.

'I thought it must have been him at first. I use graph paper to plot out my designs. There are piles of the stuff in my studio and he could have taken a few sheets. But Christopher said he hadn't made them, and Christopher doesn't lie.'

Perez said nothing. He'd never met anyone who hadn't told a lie. Even Fran, who'd been the most honest woman in the world, could lie when it suited her.

'Besides,' Helena went on, 'my son didn't have a chance to put this into *The Shetland Times*. My husband bought it while he was at school, and Christopher went straight upstairs when we got home. Really, I've been thinking about it and it couldn't have been him.' She looked at Perez, willing him to believe her.

There was a silence. Perhaps Cassie sensed a tension between them, because she turned away from her play and looked back at them.

'Do you have any idea who's behind this?' Perez thought this was a cowardly way to behave. He felt personal shame that a Shetlander could be so underhand and cruel. He knew the story of Dennis Gear well. The man had been forced from his home through a combination of bad luck and his own responsibility. His family had owned the croft for generations, but he'd never been much of a farmer and had sold off most of the land bit by bit, so there was only the house, the outhouses and some in-bye land left. When Gear's wife had died, he'd let things slide, got the sack from the waste-to-power plant in Lerwick. He'd owed money all over the islands and in the end the house had been repossessed. That had nothing to do with the Flemings from London, who'd bought it up and made it their home. Gear's final gesture – to kill himself on a property where children had lived, where a child might have found his body – had seemed selfish and mean to Perez, when he'd looked into the case.

'We didn't know Gear's history when we bought the place,' Helena said. 'And besides, we weren't responsible in any way for his problems. The house would have been taken away from him, whether we wanted it or not.'

'He was a popular man.' Perez could picture Gear at some fund-raiser in the Deltaness Community Hall. He'd been onstage playing accordion in one of the best dance bands in the islands, and Fran had dragged Perez onto the floor. Gear had been jolly, with a red face that suggested either a boozer or someone waiting for a heart attack. 'Member of the lifeboat crew; he liked a party.'

'And then we came along,' Helena said. 'Incomers. Different voices, different attitudes. With a strange, fire-obsessed son.'

Perez thought she was going to add more, but she stopped and he filled the silence with a question. 'How long has Christopher been obsessed with fire?'

Helena set her coffee mug on the grass. 'I think it started with Up Helly Aa. All that drama and the flaming torches. One night last week he wandered off and joined a group of teenage kids who'd lit a bonfire on the beach. They brought him back in a dreadful state.' There was a silence. Then the sound of a small inter-island plane overhead. 'I want to belong. I try.'

'You really think they're sending this stuff . . .' Perez nodded down to the scraps of paper, 'in the hope that you'll be scared away?'

'I don't know,' she said. 'I can't think of any other reason. They're wary of Christopher, they think I'm an arrogant cow from the south and that Daniel's just stuck-up.' There was a pause, and when she continued she was close to losing control. 'It's getting worse. As if someone's stirring up trouble, making up new stories about us. In the playground yesterday I could tell that things were different.' She gave a little shrug. 'Sorry, I know that sounds crazy.'

'I'm not quite sure what you'd like me to do. I'm not sure if any crime has been committed. If your doors were open, there's no question of breaking and entering . . .'

'I know,' she said, 'I should start locking up. But that was one of the reasons we came to Shetland. So we wouldn't have to live in some kind of fortress.' She was staring into the far distance, out to sea. 'I suppose I was hoping you might find out who was doing this stuff, talk to them, make them see that we just want to be a part of the community. I wouldn't want them charged. That would only make things worse. You're right, of course. It's not a police matter at all and I'm probably being paranoid. It could simply be kids.'

Perez wasn't sure how to answer that, so he fell back into the role of detective.

'Have you seen anyone hanging around the house?'

'Occasionally I've had the sense that someone is out there, watching us. But that was probably just me being hyper-sensitive.'

Perez thought that a dead man in your byre and strange little notes appearing in your house would make anyone sensitive. 'What about your husband? Has he seen anything unusual?'

This time the silence stretched even longer and, when she answered, she turned to face him. 'I haven't told Daniel, my husband, about any of this. He doesn't cope well with stress, and he was thrown by finding Dennis Gear. At the moment he seems a little better. Almost settled. I can't bear the thought of making him ill.' Another, shorter pause. 'Besides, Daniel wouldn't have seen anything. He was out yesterday afternoon, away from the house.'

Perez wondered how that might make a man feel – to have a wife who treated you like a child, who decided what was best for you. 'You must let me know immediately if you get any more of those notes,' he said. He was thinking that he would ask around. Deltaness was in the north-east of Shetland in Northmavine. It was a small community and if there were bad feelings – some individual who might want to scare off this incomer family – he could find out about that. He was already thinking of people he could ask. But he didn't want to raise Helena Fleming's hopes.

'I'm sorry,' Helena said. 'I shouldn't have come and disturbed you. It was a spur-of-the-moment thing. I didn't think it through.'

'Why did you come to me? Why not go to the police station about this poisonous stuff?'

'Because of your connection with Fran.'

'You knew Fran?' Hearing the name didn't hurt as it once had, but there was still the guilt and the ridiculous desire to put back the clock, rewrite the story of her death on Fair Isle three years before. Remove the knife that had flashed in the moonlight like blue lightning. *If I hadn't taken you with me to the isle . . .*

'She was the reason we came to Shetland. I met her a few times. Years ago, of course. At a party in London held by a mutual friend, at a gallery when she had her first exhibition there. She was a bit younger than me. But I loved her art and I watched her progress when she settled here. Daniel did too. That was what drew us here.'

Perez nodded towards the little girl playing in the water, damming the stream to form a pool. 'That's her daughter – that's Cassie. I look after her, though I'm not her biological father.' He paused for a moment and felt the need to explain. 'Duncan, her dad, is a bit flaky, and Fran kind of bequeathed her to me before she died.'

'I know,' Helena said. 'I heard.' She gave him a quick grin. 'Shetland's not the place for secrets, is it?'

'Ah, you'd be surprised.'

'I'll go,' she went on. 'I said I wouldn't be long. Daniel's great with the kids, but they're not the easiest.'

'You should bring them round sometime. Cassie likes having new folk to play with.'

She gave another quick grin and he saw how she and Fran might have been friends. 'They're both a bit bonkers. Not really house-trained.'

Perez nodded towards Cassie, whose arms were covered in mud as far as her elbows. 'I'm not sure that we're really house-trained, either.' He felt in his jacket pocket for a scrap of paper and a pencil and scribbled down his mobile-phone number. 'If anything else unusual happens – anything at all – give me a shout.'

He watched Helena walk down the bank to her van. She stopped on the way to chat to Cassie, who stood up. He couldn't hear what was said, but the conversation seemed animated and friendly. Once more Perez felt well disposed towards the strange woman; he didn't mind after all that she'd turned up on his doorstep.

Chapter Five

Helena didn't go to her studio on Sundays. When they'd first moved to Deltaness she'd worked every free second, desperate to build the business, to cement the contacts she already had with retailers in London and Europe. She'd been the main earner, of course, and while they'd had some savings, she'd known they wouldn't last forever. Daniel had been the person to collect the kids from school, to give them tea. For Helena, work had become an escape and an obsession. She'd never been a multitasker. One project at a time captured her imagination and filled her thoughts. She hadn't even noticed that Daniel was feeling so stressed until he'd burst into tears one evening, as they were preparing to go out for dinner with friends. She'd come out of the shower to find him in their bedroom sobbing. The door was open and both children were standing there looking in at him, while Helena dripped on the bare wooden floor.

'What's the matter?' Ellie had seemed most distressed. 'What's the matter with Daddy?'

Helena had sent them down to the kitchen with soft words, the offer of biscuits and usually forbidden fizzy drinks, and she'd taken Daniel into her arms. The towel had fallen to the floor and now she remembered the rough wool of his jersey against her skin. She'd made promises that she wasn't sure she'd keep: that she'd work less, spend more time with the children, more time with him. She'd still insisted that they go out for dinner with Robert and Belle that night, though. She'd been looking forward to the evening, to lively conversation and getting out of the house. To laughing again. She'd thought she'd go mad if she didn't have someone else to talk to. 'It'll do you good,' she'd said to Daniel, not really believing it, knowing even as she spoke that she was being selfish.

She *had* kept most of the promises. She tried to do much of her work while the kids were at school. She collected them at least a couple of times a week. She encouraged Daniel to follow his own interests. And she kept Sunday free for family time.

Today they decided they'd head out for a long walk in the morning. Belle Moncrieff had phoned the night before, asking if Helena would help with the Sunday teas, the community fundraising event, but that was the last thing she needed.

'Sorry, we've planned an expedition with the kids. Get them away from computer screens and out into the open air.'

Packing a picnic, she thought of Jimmy Perez, dark-haired and scruffy. Kind. She decided she'd take him up on his offer and visit him in Ravenswick again.

They trekked north, ignoring Christopher's complaints about the long walk. Daniel showed the children the otters at Suksetter and Helena skimmed pebbles and watched Ellie play in the sand at the edge of the shore. She was reminded of Cassie Hunter, and again of the detective with the Spanish name and dark good looks, felt a moment of lust and wondered how things would be if she were single. Then she thought that, without any responsibility at all, she wouldn't know who she was. The responsibility, like her anxiety about Daniel and the kids, gave her a role in life. She wasn't sufficiently brave to carve out her own identity. The work – the designs – were unimportant compared to caring for these people.

Back at the house, the children were tired and Christopher disappeared into his room. Ellie whined to be taken to the Sunday teas at the Deltaness hall, but Helena still couldn't face it. She had more important things on her mind. A family to protect. Daniel hid himself away in his office. He was probably transferring wildlife images from his camera onto the computer. They'd built big windows into the east of the house, and the sun drenched the kitchen with light and heat. Ellie wandered out into the garden to play. Helena, sitting in the rocking chair, felt herself drowsing. This was allowed, after all. It was Sunday, their day of rest. But she still had work to do, despite her promise to Daniel, and she made her way outside.

When she returned to the kitchen, she'd lost all sense of time. Sun still came through the window and it was warm in the room. Ellie was bouncing on the trampoline on the grass outside and Helena was reassured by the sight of her, but she felt a little dizzy and disorientated. She wasn't wearing a watch and the clock above the cooker needed a battery. She switched on the kettle, went out to the hall and shouted to Daniel to ask if he'd like tea. His office door was shut and there was no answer. She was about to go in when she heard a noise from outside the house, a strange yelping that she recognized immediately. It was the sound Christopher made when he was disturbed or excited. She thought Ellie must have persuaded him outside to join in a game.

Helena opened the door and looked out into the courtyard that was formed by her workshop, converted from some of the original croft buildings, and the house. Christopher was standing there, obviously disturbed, shaking. She went out to him. 'What's happened?' He didn't answer and she saw the panic still in his eyes. She went up to him and held him, very tight, against her body. Christopher hated light touches, arms around the shoulders, his hair being stroked, but sometimes he responded to a firm embrace. This time, though, it didn't work. He remained tense and pushed her away.

'Can you tell me what's wrong?' She kept her voice cool. Christopher didn't respond well to emotion of any sort.

He shook his head, took her hand and pulled her towards the byre. This was the only building they still hadn't renovated. When they'd bought the house, Helena had thought one day it might be converted into a self-contained home for Christopher, if it turned out he couldn't manage on his own in the big world, if he still needed their support when he was an adult. It stood a little apart, behind her workrooms. It was where Daniel had found Dennis Gear.

The double door that led in was rotten and had fallen on its hinges and it was left propped open. Inside, the only light came from the half-open door and one window high in the wall.

A body hung from one of the beams. The noose

was made of nylon rope. Helena didn't panic and was surprised at how calm she felt, how well she held things together. The scene was like one of the small anonymous drawings, brought to life, though this wasn't a replica of the dead Dennis Gear. It was a young woman, wearing a dress. She had bare legs. No shoes. Helena pushed Christopher away.

'Don't look. Stay outside.'

When he was gone, she went closer, touched an ankle. It was cold, lifeless. There was no point trying to get the body down, even if that had been physically possible, even if she could bear to do it.

She shifted position and looked up, so she could see the woman's face, and for a moment her stomach heaved and she thought she might be physically sick. It was Emma Shearer, the nanny who worked for Belle and Robert Moncrieff. She'd been one of the gossiping group who'd turned towards Helena when she'd gone to collect the kids the Friday before. Belle thought the world of her, but Helena had never taken to Emma, even on their first meeting. She'd been polite in the little conversation they'd had during those first encounters, helpful enough, picking up Ellie occasionally if Helena had been running late. But somehow knowing, superior, critical. *I didn't like her and now she's dead.* As if her dislike was to blame for the woman's death. As if that had been enough to kill her.

She heard a noise behind her and turned, thinking that Christopher had come back in, determined to send him away again. But Daniel was standing in the doorway, framed by the bright light outside. She could only see him as a silhouette, but she heard him gasp and thought what a shock this must be for him. He'd found Dennis Gear's body in exactly the same place. *What's happening to us? Why is our life here falling apart?*

She went over to him and pushed him into the sunshine. 'Where's Christopher?'

'I don't know.' He looked back into the barn. 'Shouldn't we try to get her down?'

'No point. She's dead. The police would want us to leave her there.' Helena knew because her guilty viewing passions, late at night, when the others were all asleep, were the true-crime shows on television. Just like her son.

She'd already put Jimmy Perez's number into her phone and she pressed the buttons now and waited for him to answer.

Chapter Six

Perez decided to go to the Deltaness Sunday teas. It would be something to do with Cassie; the weather was fine and he might pick up scraps of information about the Fleming family, some understanding at least of the tensions within the community. Often Cassie spent Sundays with Duncan Hunter, her natural father, but this week he was south on one of his mysterious business trips and she was resentful and moody, blaming Perez, not Duncan. Duncan spoilt her, let her stay up all night, then let her down. The overseas trips were becoming more frequent. Perez thought that unfettered access to cake, and the chance to meet up with other bairns, might lift Cassie's spirits. He decided it was unlikely the Flemings would be there; the teas would be full of gossip and he suspected Helena would make sure to keep well away.

In the car north, Cassie hardly spoke. It had been a battle to persuade her to come at all; she would have preferred a DVD and a lazy afternoon slouched on the sofa. She was plugged into a story tape and grunted occasionally when he asked her a question. He wondered how it would be when she was a teenager. The weather was still fine, sunny with a south-easterly breeze to keep away any fog. The car park at the community hall was already busy when they arrived. On the way into the building Perez nodded to a few people he knew – a woman he'd been to school with, and Robert Moncrieff, the GP who covered Northmavine. There were more familiar faces inside. He dropped cash into a bucket on the table near the door and queued with Cassie for home-bakes. They found space at a trestle table covered with a white cloth and a woman appeared as if from nowhere with a giant teapot to fill his cup. On the low stage, a couple of teenagers were playing the fiddle. Cassie saw Moncrieff's youngest daughter, a girl she knew from her gymnastics club, at another table and she ran off to join her. Perez sat and listened to the conversation that eddied around him.

Two women came to sit opposite him. He decided they must be sisters; they were both in their sixties, with the same square jaws; one was stocky, big-boned, the other slight with thin white hair. He thought perhaps the thinner sister was deaf because they spoke loudly, and their voices carried above the background conversation. But perhaps they just liked an audience. He didn't know them, but he thought he'd seen the bigger one before; she'd once worked in the bank in Lerwick. At first, he thought she was speaking about an ancient relative.

'I do think he'd be better off in a home, don't you, Lottie?' She paused then added: 'That Fleming boy.'

The sister had her mouth full of scone and could only nod.

'At the moment, he's a danger to himself and everyone else. Who knows what he might do next? They can't control him. They let him wander. He might burn us in our own homes.' Her voice was self-righteous, but Perez thought she'd probably be delighted if someone died as a result of Christopher's behaviour. It would provide a subject for conversation for years.

The sister had emptied her mouth. 'The mother seems a fine enough woman.'

'I'd say she was taking liberties. Coming to the islands and using our wool and our patterns to make her fortune.' The first speaker paused briefly to take a sip of tea. 'And not respecting the real traditions. If you ask me, I'd say she's just a user.'

Perez pictured Helena Fleming with her fierce determination to fight for her family. He wanted to break in and tell the woman that she was being unfair, but he thought that would only make things worse for the Flemings. He couldn't stand listening to the bile, so he got to his feet and looked for somewhere else to sit.

He'd been to school with Robert Moncrieff and remembered him as sporty, a bit aloof. Perez had been a loner when he first moved from the small school in Fair Isle to board at the Anderson High. There'd been low-level bullying and he'd been homesick. Robert's father had been a doctor too, working in the Gilbert Bain Hospital, at a time when most of the boys came from crofting or fishing families. Now, Perez thought it couldn't have been easy for the young Moncrieff to fit in, either. The inspector wandered over to the man, who shifted his chair to make room for Perez. The doctor was looking at the end of the hall, where Cassie and her friend were doing handstands against the wall.

'Look at those two monkeys.' Moncrieff's youngest

daughter, Kate, was a little younger than Cassie. 'They seem to get on fine, seeing as they only get together at the gym club.'

'Maybe it's easier to stay friends if you only meet up once in a while.'

'Aye, maybe.' The doctor paused. 'Little girls can be such bitches.'

'Not only little girls.'

'Ah,' Moncrieff said, 'I see you've just escaped the Deltaness witches.' He nodded towards the sisters. 'Lottie's not so bad, if you get her on her own, but Margaret Riddell lives on a diet of malice, gossip and rumour. Her husband left her because he couldn't stand it and has moved in with a Latvian waitress half his age who works at the Kveldsro Hotel in town.'

'So, she's become the subject of gossip herself?' Perez grinned. Even so, he found it hard to feel sorry for the woman.

'Indeed.'

'They were talking about the Fleming boy.'

'Were you involved in that business?' Moncrieff seemed surprised. 'Something and nothing, I'd have thought, setting fire to a pile of waste paper in the school yard. There was no damage done.'

'No,' Perez said. He only remembered then that Helena had spoken of the boy playing with matches at school. 'We weren't involved.' The teenage fiddlers finished a tune and there was a round of applause. Perez turned back to Moncrieff. 'Do you know the family?'

'Our younger kids meet theirs at school, and we've had Daniel and Helena round for supper a couple of times. We've been to their house for drinks, a family barbecue earlier in the year. You know what it's like in a place like Deltaness, Jimmy. Any newcomer is a source of interest and entertainment. Belle was delighted when they moved in. She thought they'd read *The Guardian* and we could have intelligent discussions about art and literature.'

'And did you?' Robert's wife Belle had grown up in England. Perez couldn't remember quite what she'd done for a living before moving to Shetland. Something in PR perhaps? Now she was a stay-at-home mother to four children and an active member of more voluntary organizations than Perez could list. Today she was in the hall kitchen, buttering bannocks. He'd glimpsed her as he came in.

'We did with Helena. Daniel's pretty hard-going. A bit intense and given to long and introspective silences.'

'He found Dennis Gear's body,' Perez said, though he was sure Moncrieff must already know that. 'Apparently it shook him up and he can't quite get over it.'

'Of course, poor chap. That might explain it then.' Moncrieff waved his cup at a young woman who was passing by with a teapot. 'I should be more sympathetic.'

'You're not his GP?'

'No, I think the Flemings signed up with the health centre in Brae. And of course even if I were his doctor, Jimmy, I wouldn't be discussing Daniel's condition with you.'

'What does the rest of Deltaness make of them?'

Moncrieff paused for a moment. 'Most of our neighbours are very tolerant people. We're used to welcoming strangers. From the Vikings on, there've been invaders in the islands.'

'Daniel and Helena Fleming are hardly invaders.' Kate and Cassie had moved outside and were doing backflips on the grass outside the hall. Perez watched them and wondered what it would feel like if *Cassie* were the centre of malicious gossip. He thought he'd feel murderous.

'Of course not. And Dennis Gear's house was in a dreadful state when they bought it, but they haven't had an easy time settling in. None of the locals wanted to take on the place – it was too much of a project. Which doesn't stop the muttering, now it's finished, about soothmoothers coming in and buying up all the best places.'

'And maybe there's a bit of guilt about the way Dennis Gear killed himself? Easier to blame the English family than to think they might have done more to support the man while he was alive.' Perez wondered if Gear had returned to Deltaness to kill himself as an accusation aimed at the community rather than the Fleming family. He'd probably never met *them*.

'You could be right. We all knew Dennis was having financial problems, but none of us saw that coming. And it's a constant reminder, isn't it, that grand new edifice on the hill, looking down on us? Daniel was an architect in London and he did make a terrific job of the house.'

'So, there's a kind of jealousy going on too?'

The girls had now collapsed into a giggling heap on the grass. The moody Cassie of the morning had disappeared.

'That's certainly the case with Helena's knitwear. Her work is famous because she's a brilliant designer, not because she's ripped off a few ancient Fair Isle patterns.' Moncrieff paused for a moment. 'And of course it helps that my talented wife is working on her publicity.'

'Belle's working for Helena now?'

'Mm, she started doing odd bits and pieces of local media, but she still has her old press contacts in London and now she does all Helena's PR stuff. She loves it.' Moncrieff paused. 'She and Helena are going to London in a few weeks' time for a special exhibition. God knows how I'll manage with all the kids on my own.'

'I thought you had a nanny! You won't be quite on your own.'

'Ah well, yes.' Moncrieff looked a little sheepish. 'Emma started with us when Sam was still a baby and Belle hadn't long given birth to Kate. She's fine with the little ones, but really not up to dealing with teenage tantrums. Did you know Martha is sixteen now?' He began a tale about his eldest daughter and the woes of standard-grade exams; how Martha was a member of the Deltaness rowing team and recently they'd beaten all-comers in the Whiteness regatta. 'We can't get her to take school work seriously, and Charlie's just as bad.'

Perez stopped listening very quickly. He was wondering why other people's children were boring, when Cassie was clearly fascinating. He shifted his chair slightly so he could see the girls outside. They were sitting on the grass chatting, but as he watched, their attention seemed to be caught by something outside Perez's line of vision. The hall door was knocked open and another child ran in. A boy stood just inside the room and started screaming. His hands were over his ears, as if his own voice was terrifying him. It took Perez a moment to make out the words – the boy was gasping for breath. Sweat was running down his face. The room fell silent and everyone was staring at him. The boy saw Moncrieff and ran towards him, caught hold of his hand and pulled him to his feet.

'Please come,' he said. 'You have to come.'

At the same moment, Perez's phone began to ring.

Chapter Seven

Jimmy Perez talked into his phone as he followed Christopher and Moncrieff up the hill.

'Inspector Perez, this is Helena Fleming.'

'If you're worried about your son,' Perez said, 'he's quite safe. He's here with me.'

There was a pause and she sounded confused. 'Christopher can't be in Ravenswick. He's only just left home.'

'No, no. I was in Deltaness for the Sunday teas. He turned up, rather distressed, in the hall. I think he was looking for Dr Moncrieff. We're both on our way to you.'

'Ah, oh good.' Her relief seemed so obvious that the words seemed inadequate, understated. Perez wondered if someone was listening in to the conversation. 'Yes, that makes sense. Thank you.'

'What's happened there?'

'Something terrible.' This time there was no emotion in her voice. 'There's been another death. Another hanging. A young woman called Emma Shearer. I'll be waiting for you as you approach the house. I'll show you then.'

Perez hadn't been to the house when Dennis Gear died. Sandy Wilson had been the officer on call and he'd taken charge of the case. The hanging hadn't been an unexplained death for long. Perez remembered now that Gear had left a suicide note, something self-pitying and very sad about how he'd loved the old house and felt a part of it, that something of him had already died with the renovation and it didn't seem worth living now.

Perez wasn't sure what he'd been expecting of the place. Perhaps he'd been afraid of something over-blown and tasteless, a simple Shetland croft house expanded until the original was unrecognizable, more suitable for Houston than Deltaness. After all, Moncrieff had described it as a 'great edifice'. As he turned away from the community hall and got a view of the building, he saw this was something altogether surprising and quite different. No attempt had been made to alter the original house – that was still there, virtually untouched and acting almost as a storm porch to one side – but the architect had used construction materials to reference the croft in a completely new two-storey extension. This was a modernist box, all clean lines, with the symmetry of the original and whitewashed in the same way. The flat roof was covered with turf and seemed to disappear into the hillside behind it. Perez wondered what Fran would have made of it and he thought it would have delighted her.

Helena was waiting for them. She knelt down and took Christopher by the shoulders. 'You did the right thing fetching Robert,' she said. 'Absolutely the right thing. But we'll take over now. You can go in. Dad's in the kitchen, if you need him, or you can go back to your room.'

Christopher nodded. He seemed calmer. Helena stood watching until she saw him go in through the door and then she turned back to them. 'Christopher found her.'

She led them across a paved courtyard, down a narrow path between the house and renovated outbuildings to a barn. Perez remembered the photos that had been taken here when Dennis Gear had killed himself. Then an ancient tractor had stood at one end. The man had stood on the wheel arch to throw a rope over a beam and then he'd jumped. The note had been left on the tractor seat.

Now there was no machinery left inside – presumably the Flemings had got rid of it, and the only indication that it had once been a working croft was a pile of hay bales at one end. They were too far away from the girl for her to climb them to hang herself. Perez thought of her as a 'girl' when he first saw her because she had the skinny, unformed look of someone very young, but he thought Fran and Willow would have called her a woman.

'She was already dead when I found her.' Helena seemed to feel the need to justify her failure to attempt to save the woman. 'I mean cold. Obviously dead. Besides, I don't think I could have got her down.'

'It *is* Emma.' Moncrieff was standing a little behind Perez and he was staring as if he needed time to process what he was seeing. 'Emma Shearer. Our nanny.' Perez turned to face the man and was surprised at how still and impassive he looked. Perhaps a doctor would be used to sudden death, but this woman had been almost part of their family. Moncrieff spoke again: 'Why would she hang herself?'

'This isn't suicide.' Perez had been certain of that as soon as he walked into the space. 'Not unless anyone has removed anything from the barn.'

Helena shook her head. 'Christopher found her. He was standing out in the yard when I saw him, making the noises he does when he's upset. He obviously hadn't gone anywhere else. He could scarcely move. I touched her leg, but nothing else at all. Daniel, my husband, only got as far as the door.' She closed her eyes briefly. 'It's like those drawings I showed you. A nightmare.' Meaning that literally. Perez thought she felt as if she was asleep, unable to wake up. He knew the feeling. He'd spent the first six weeks after Fran's death living in a terrible dream. Then she turned to him. 'But they can't be connected, can they? Nobody would be crazy enough to commit murder just to get back at us.'

'It seems unlikely,' he said, though he knew that some killers *were* crazy, that the motives for murder could be ridiculously flimsy. An angry gesture made from one driver to another. Hurtful laughter. A grudge held over years. 'I have phone calls to make. There are procedures. I'm sure you understand. I'll need to stay here until another officer comes to secure the scene. But you can go into the house and wait. I'll come and talk to you as soon as I can.'

'I'll have to phone Belle,' Moncrieff said. 'She'll be wondering what's happened, and Kate's still at the teas. The plan was that I'd take her home while Belle helped clear up.'

Perez thought about that. The Moncrieffs could be considered suspects. They'd employed the woman, lived with her. Even if they'd had nothing to do with her death, he'd prefer to talk to them individually before they had time to share their thoughts about the woman, to make up a story that would put them in the best possible light. That was what witnesses did. But it wouldn't be practical to keep them apart until the investigating team from the Scottish mainland turned up. He had to work within the reality of policing in Shetland; the Serious Crime team from Inverness took charge of any murder in the islands. He nodded. 'But please tell her to be discreet.' Word would get out soon enough. Gossip would spread like flames, licking at croft-house doors and windows, moving over kitchen tables, and bars and workplaces. 'And can you ask her to keep an eye on Cass, until I can get someone to pick her up?'

When he was alone, his first call was to his colleague Sandy Wilson. 'We've got a suspicious death. Dennis Gear's old place.' He wondered how long it would take before they started describing Hesti as *the Fleming place.* 'Will it take you long to get here? I can always contact Morag.' Sandy had a new woman in his life, and Louisa was a teacher in Unst. She lived on the island of Yell, a ferry ride away, and Sandy often stayed with her. And if he was visiting his parents, they lived in Whalsay, which would involve another ferry.

'I'm at home in Lerwick,' Sandy said. 'Half an hour.' Perez could tell he was already moving; he could hear the man's footsteps on the stairs. Just as well: Sandy would have to drive like a lunatic to get here in half an hour. Perez was about to replace the phone when he realized Sandy was still speaking. 'That's some unlucky house, huh?' Only then did the phone go dead.

Afterwards, Perez phoned Maggie, his neighbour. She was his first calling point to care for his daughter. There was no answer to her landline, but she picked up the mobile first time. He explained briefly that he'd been called out on a serious case. 'Cassie's at the Deltaness teas. I know it's a lot to ask, but could you collect her and keep her at yours? Belle Moncrieff is keeping an eye on her at the moment.'

'No problem, Jimmy. And we're only fifteen minutes away. We were up visiting my mother in Ollaberry. You know Cassie's bed's always made up in our house.'

Next, he rang James Grieve, the forensic pathologist based in Aberdeen.

'Any chance you can make it onto this evening's ferry? It's the direct one, so it leaves at seven tonight.'

'Is it really that urgent? We've friends coming for dinner and Nicola will kill me.' He seemed to reconsider. 'Though they're not the most entertaining of our friends. University people, and Nicola deals with them much better than I do.'

'It's a young woman. I'd guess she was strangled – and then the body was strung up from a beam. Maybe an attempt to make it look like suicide, though not a very convincing attempt. Maybe some sort of message. One of the witnesses has been getting strange anonymous notes.' Perez glanced through the rotten doors behind him at the corpse. It seemed to swing gently. 'There are young children here. The boy who found her is autistic. I'd like the body removed as soon as we can, so that the family can get their lives back to normal.'

James had four children of his own. 'I'm in town

anyway – Nicola sent me in to buy some decent wine. No problem about making the ferry. You'll get someone to pick me up and bring me to the scene?'

'Of course. It'll probably be Sandy.'

'And who will we have as SIO on this one, Jimmy?' The pathologist's voice was mischievous. Perez knew there'd been rumours about his relationship with Willow, the chief inspector of the Serious Crime Squad based in Inverness. 'Will it be the wonderful Inspector Reeves?'

'I'm not sure.' Perez could tell that he sounded defensive. 'It depends who's available.'

'Aye, well, let's make sure we get her, eh? She's the brightest spark of the team. And I know the two of you have a great working relationship. Now, I'd best be going if I'm going to make that boat. I'll call Nicola once we've started sailing. Then there's nothing she can do to stop me.'

Perez hesitated a while before making the next call. Willow Reeves was his senior officer, in effect his boss. He respected her skills as a detective. They'd worked together before, and she'd helped him when he was still grieving for Cassie's mother, Fran, first as a friend and more recently as a lover. The relationship was complex and ill-defined, and they'd made every effort to keep it secret. He didn't want to make demands or trade on her sympathy. Throw into the mix guilt – because he'd been responsible for Fran's murder and didn't think he deserved ever to be happy again – and the fact that Willow was his superior, and that meant he was confused. Except about one thing. Willow was the only woman since Fran who had moved him, who had filled his dreams. He wanted to be with her. Even now, debating which phone number to call her on, he felt a thrill.

He'd meant to be in touch with Willow many times since her last visit to the islands. Lonely nights when Cassie was in bed and he'd sat with a dram, remembering their last night together and trying to pull together the words. But never quite finding the courage to do it, in the end always thinking: *The way we left it, it's her responsibility to phone me.* Pride taking over.

He called her personal mobile. At this time on a Sunday evening she was unlikely to be at work. She'd be in her flat looking over the river in Inverness. He'd never been there, but she'd described it to him and he could imagine how it would be: big and light and messy. It took her a while to answer and he was preparing to leave a message when she spoke. 'Jimmy?'

'I'm sorry to disturb you at home.' Even after hearing just one word he thought she sounded tired, almost as if he'd just woken her. But the Willow he knew was indefatigable; she wouldn't have been sleeping at six o'clock in the evening.

'It's nice to hear from you.' Her voice was guarded.

'We've got a suspicious death.'

'Ah,' she said, 'so this is work, is it, Jimmy? And I thought it was me you wanted to talk to.'

He was surprised by the bitterness in her voice. 'I do. Of course.' He paused. 'I'm sorry. I suppose I wasn't sure if you wanted to hear from me. I didn't want to bring all that back. The stuff that happened when you were last here.' *The fact that you almost died, that I almost lost you too.*

'No, I'm sorry that I snapped. I'm just tired. Tell me about this case.' She almost sounded like herself again.

He told Willow everything he knew. 'Can you make it? Or are you tied up with other investigations?'

There was a moment's silence. He heard sheep on the hill and waves breaking on the beach below the house. Shetland sounds. He wondered if she could hear them on the other end of the line.

'You know I'm never too busy to spend time on the islands, Jimmy. I'll book myself onto the first flight in the morning.' He sensed there was something else she wanted to say and waited. Nothing. It seemed she was waiting for him to answer, because when she spoke again it was with a touch of impatience. 'Will you be there to pick me up, then?'

'Of course.'

'Good.' This time there was a shorter pause. 'Come by yourself, will you? There's something we need to discuss.'

The line went dead. He thought: *She's going to tell me that there's another man in her life. She's too classy to tell me on the phone.*

In the distance, he saw Sandy's car driving through Deltaness and making its way up the track towards the house.

Chapter Eight

When Perez turned away to make his phone calls, Helena led Robert Moncrieff into the house, into the big, light kitchen where the family spent most of their time. He looked around as if the place was strange to him, but of course he'd been there before. The Moncrieffs had been their first visitors after they'd moved to Deltaness. Helena remembered shared suppers at the long table that Daniel had found in a sale in Lerwick. According to Moncrieff, in the past it had stood in the dining room at the Anderson High and the staff had sat around it. One particular evening returned vividly: the meal over, she and Belle had been discussing their plans for the future over a sharp red wine, while Robert and Daniel had struggled to make any kind of conversation and they'd all drunk far too much.

After speaking to Perez in the courtyard, she'd asked Robert where he'd like to wait for the police, but he hadn't answered. He just wandered in behind her, not speaking, and now he sat on the small sofa and looked out into the garden. Helena had never known him be quiet for so long; she always had him down as one of those people who can't stand silence.

She and Daniel had agonized over where to put the

sofa, when they'd first moved in, and she still wasn't quite happy. It rested against one wall and made her think of the old people's home where her mother had spent her last months. It surprised her that the position of the sofa was so important to her, when a young woman was dead. She put on the kettle to make Moncrieff coffee and then, without speaking herself, she ran upstairs to check on Christopher.

'Are you OK?'

Christopher nodded, his eyes fixed on his screen, then turned to face her. 'She's dead, isn't she?'

'Yes,' Helena said. 'I'm sorry, she is.'

'I'm not sorry.' He paused. 'She was there that night at the bonfire on the beach the Friday before last.'

'What did happen that night?'

'No,' he said, 'I don't want to talk about it.' He shut his mouth tight, as he had when he was a small child and she'd tried to feed him the wrong food, using the wrong spoon. Still not looking at her, he spoke again. 'What's a hangman?'

The question made her freeze, but she knew she'd have to answer. If she tried to put him off, he'd only google it and come up with things that were even more horrendous.

'In the old days, when we didn't know any better, some killers were sentenced to death. They were hanged. The person who arranged that and carried it out was known as a hangman.'

He turned back to the computer, apparently satisfied, but she couldn't leave it at that. 'Emma wasn't sentenced to death. This was quite different. The police will find out who did it, and they'll go to court and then probably to prison for a very long time, but they won't be hanged. We don't do that any more.' *But perhaps a very long prison sentence would be worse.*

Now Christopher seemed almost bored. 'Yeah,' he said, 'I get it.' There was that arrogance again, which sometimes made her want to shake him.

Helena made her way back to the kitchen. It seemed her whole family was falling apart. She, Daniel and each of the kids might be living in the same house, but they seemed to occupy different worlds. It had been her role to hold them together and she'd failed. She handed a mug of coffee to Moncrieff. He muttered his thanks, but still seemed to lost in his own thoughts. Time seemed to be passing very slowly. There was still no sign of Daniel. Ellie, who had been watching television, came in to say that she was starving.

'How about pizza?' Helena said.

'Yeah!'

And that was something to do, while they were waiting for Perez to come back. Helena put a pizza in the oven, chopped up a few bits of pepper and carrot to give the meal the appearance of healthy eating, and offered Moncrieff more coffee. He must have phoned Belle, when she was upstairs with Christopher. Helena had heard the murmur of his voice but couldn't make out the words. When the pizza was cooked, she cut it into pieces and arranged it on two plates, took one up to Christopher and one to Ellie in the living room. An unheard-of treat.

Helena was desperate to talk to Daniel, but didn't want to do that while Moncrieff was sitting there, observing them all silently from his post at the end of the kitchen. When the detective had sent them all away from the barn, Daniel had immediately scuttled into his office, offering no explanation. If the situation had been less unusual, she would have been embarrassed by his rudeness in front of Moncrieff, but today that hardly seemed to matter.

It was still early, but she ran a bath for Ellie and put her to bed. It was something to pass the time, and she didn't want the girl still up when Perez did come back with his questions and explanations. Christopher slept very little, but he wouldn't come down now that he'd been fed.

There was the sound of a car on the track and then she heard it rattle over the cattle grid. Moncrieff had been looking at yesterday's newspaper and folded it on his knee. 'That must be the chap Perez has been hanging on for.' Only when he spoke did she sense how tense he'd been, waiting for something to happen. 'At last!' They couldn't see the yard from the kitchen. Helena was tempted to go upstairs to peer out and see what was happening, and probably would have done if she'd been here on her own. Instead, she continued to wait.

There was a tap on the outside door. Although she'd been waiting for it, the sound shocked her. She jumped to her feet to open it, but by the time she got there, Perez was already inside. 'I'm sorry to have kept you waiting,' he said. 'My colleague has arrived to secure the scene for me. And now, I'm afraid, I have some questions for you. I hope not to keep you too long. We can work on the detail tomorrow.'

'Robert's in the kitchen. Would you like to see him first? Then he can get back to Belle and the kids.' Helena thought that would give her a chance to talk to Daniel.

'That would be good, thanks.' Perez seemed relieved that she appeared to understand that he'd need to talk to them separately.

'There's coffee. It might be a bit stewed. I could make some more.' Why was she trying so hard with this man? Why did it matter quite so much what he thought of her?

'I'll just help myself,' Perez said. 'I'm sure it will be fine.' He went into the kitchen, closing the door quietly behind him.

Chapter Nine

When Perez walked into the kitchen, Robert Moncrieff jumped to his feet. His words came out in a rush, all bluster. 'This won't take long, will it, Jimmy? You know what Shetland is like. Word will have got out, and there are the kids to think about. They've known Emma for ages. Recently she's spent more time with them than Belle has. I want to be the one to tell them exactly what happened. I don't want them to find out about it on social media.'

'And what, exactly, do you think did happen?'

There was no reply.

'It's a suspicious death,' Perez said. 'None of us know yet how or why Emma died.'

'But it wasn't suicide, was it? There was no way she could have done that to herself.'

Perez didn't answer. Instead he asked his own question.

'Did the Flemings call you in when they found Dennis Gear?'

'Yes,' Moncrieff said. 'It was early one morning, before I'd gone out to work. I think the old man must have been hanging there all night.'

'Did you know him?' Perez wasn't sure where this was going. He was curious about Gear, though he couldn't see what relevance the man might have to Emma Shearer's death. Perhaps that was all it was. A Shetlander's nosiness.

'All my life. I used to play on this land when I was a kid. Help him out with the sheep sometimes.' Moncrieff smiled as if the memory was a pleasant one.

'Were you surprised when he killed himself?'

There was a pause. 'No. He was a proud man. He would have hated what he'd become.'

'I need to contact Emma's next of kin,' Perez said. 'I presume you can help with that.' It seemed a straightforward request and he was surprised when the doctor hesitated again.

'Her parents are both dead. Her father died when she was still at school. He'd been convicted of violence against her mother and died in prison. I don't know the details. Her mother passed away about a year ago. Cancer. A recurrence of an earlier illness. All very sad. Emma grew up in Orkney and her brothers are still based there. Emma went back to her home in Kirkwall for her mother's last few weeks.' He paused. 'Belle and I weren't sure whether she'd come back to us. We wondered if she'd want to stay in Orkney.'

'But she *did* come back?'

'Yes, it was a compliment, I suppose, that this was where she preferred to be.' Moncrieff stared out of the window at the lengthening shadow thrown by the house.

'How did she come to be working for you in the first place?'

'We put an advert in *The Shetland Times* and *The Orcadian* for a mother's help. I'm not sure what we were expecting really. Someone older and more experienced, perhaps. A grandmotherly figure who'd be as much a housekeeper as a help to Belle with the childcare. Then a GP colleague from Kirkwall got in touch to ask if we'd consider Emma. She'd pretty well looked after her brothers for three years, after her father was sent to prison and when her mother was first ill. He said it would do Emma good to get away from Orkney. The boys were older and her mother was in remission, so the family didn't need her so much. When no one else applied – Deltaness is bit out of the way for most Shetlanders – Belle and I decided to give Emma a chance.'

'So, Emma's brothers would be her next of kin?'

'Yes. Adam and David. Adam's away at university. Stirling. Emma was very proud of him. David's still in Orkney. He's the older of the two and he works in a hotel. Or a restaurant. I don't have a number or address for him. His number would probably be in Emma's phone.'

'We don't have that yet.' Perez had felt briefly in the pocket of the dress she'd been wearing, but had found nothing except a scrap of tissue. The dress was made of yellow-and-white cotton, colours that made him think of spring. With a fitted bodice and full skirt, it reminded him of the style of the Fifties, not a garment belonging to a young woman of today. But he knew nothing about fashion – perhaps that look was back. There'd been no jacket or bag in the byre. 'We'll need to search her room,' he said. 'That'll be later tonight. I'll send Sandy down, as soon as we can get a uniformed officer to relieve him here. Somebody is on his way. If you see Emma's phone anywhere else in the house, just leave it where it is and ask the family not to touch it.'

'Does that need to happen tonight?' Until now Moncrieff had been distant, almost disengaged. 'Can't it wait until tomorrow when the kids will be at school?'

'I'm sorry. This is a suspicious death. I have to treat it as a murder inquiry. We don't know yet where Emma was killed. It could have been in your home.'

'No!' The doctor's face was red now. 'You do realize that if people even start to think that we were in any way involved in her death, my position here would be untenable. At one time a GP would be above suspicion, but since Shipman . . .'

'We need to search Emma's room,' Perez said. 'And we have to find her phone. Everyone who knew her will be under suspicion until we find out what happened to her. Really, it's in your interest to help us.'

Moncrieff turned to face him and Perez saw the twelve-year-old schoolboy with his sense of entitlement, his boasting about the car his doctor father drove and the family's foreign holidays. 'You can't really think that Belle or I had anything to do with the girl's death?'

'I don't close my mind to anything.' A pause. 'When did you last see Emma?'

'Last night. Sunday is her full day off. She usually had a long lie-in. She had her own space – we turned the attic into a kind of bedsit with its own bathroom. There's a TV and she has her own laptop up there, a little fridge, a kettle and microwave. Usually she eats with us, but on Sundays she does her own thing.'

'Are you sure Emma stayed in her room last night? She couldn't have gone into Lerwick yesterday evening, stayed the night with a friend?' Perez thought he still didn't have any handle on the young woman. Was she the sort who'd party? To have friends of her own age in town? Had she dressed in the yellow-and-white dress because she planned to meet a boyfriend?

'She was definitely there last night. We sleep below her and I heard her television. She switched it off just as we were going to bed at about eleven.'

'But you didn't see her this morning?'

'No, I was in and out all day. Charlie had football practice, so I was into Brae with him first thing. Then I went and helped set up trestle tables in the hall. Martha's old enough now to keep an eye on Sam and Kate. There was no sign of Emma when I got back at lunchtime. I assumed she'd gone out by then.' Moncrieff looked at his watch. An expression of impatience.

'Any idea where she might have gone? Friends she could have visited?'

Moncrieff shook his head. 'Emma was very self-contained and I didn't pry. She was an adult and she'd lived in Shetland long enough to know her way round.'

'Did she have a boyfriend?'

The question seemed to surprise him. 'Oh, I don't think so. She never mentioned one.'

'Even though she'd been with you for seven years? No sexual relationship with a man?' He paused for a beat. 'Or a woman?'

'Really, Jimmy, how could I be expected to know?'

Perez thought Moncrieff sounded like a Victorian gentleman, who couldn't be expected to take an interest in the servant classes. 'Perhaps Belle would have more information about Emma's private life?'

The doctor gave a sharp little laugh. 'Oh, I very

much doubt that. Recently Belle's been busier than I have.'

'You said that she's doing the PR for Helena Fleming. Does that take up a lot of her time?'

'It's all she seems to think about just now. If she's not glued to her computer, she's swanning all over the country. Leaving me to hold things together. Well, I suppose Emma's death will cramp her style a little.' As if that was not entirely a bad thing.

They sat for a moment in silence.

'Would Emma have talked to Martha about where she was going today?' Perez asked. 'Or to one of the others?'

Moncrieff shrugged. 'Maybe. She saw more of the kids than she did of us.'

'And they might have seen her leave this morning? Have an idea where she might have gone?'

'Yeah, they might.'

But Perez thought Moncrieff would agree to anything now, just to get home.

'Did she drive? Have use of a car?'

'She had her own car,' Moncrieff said. 'It was Belle's idea. A gift for her twenty-first birthday. Not a new car, of course, and nothing flash. A little Clio. It's a nightmare in Deltaness without your own transport, and it was useful for us that she could get about too. She'd learned to drive when she first started with us, and then she used Belle's vehicle when she needed to. But often we were both out and then she was stuck. Having her own car, she could get to the Co-op for Belle's weekly shop, pick the older ones up from school in Lerwick if they needed to stay on after the bus had left. And it gave her a bit of independence on her days off.'

'Was her car still there when you got home from the hall at lunchtime?'

Moncrieff considered for a moment. 'I don't know,' he said. 'She usually parked it at the side of the house and I wouldn't have seen it when I went in, even if it was.'

'When you get home, can you check, and give me a text either way?'

Moncrieff seemed to see this as a form of dismissal and got to his feet. Seeing an end to the interview made him gracious. 'Of course, Jimmy. We want this cleared up as soon as possible.' He paused. 'We'll miss her.'

Perez thought that now the doctor would give some personal insight into the woman who'd worked with his family since she was a girl, that he would find some words to describe her character, pay a tribute to her personality, but he went on to say: 'I'm not quite sure how we'll manage in the house without her. I suppose we'll have to start looking for someone else.' As if Emma's death was nothing more than a domestic inconvenience.

Perez watched Moncrieff set off down the track towards Deltaness. A uniformed officer from Lerwick had turned up, and Sandy was talking to him. They were standing just outside the barn. 'I'm afraid it'll be an all-nighter,' Perez said to the new man. 'Prof. Grieve is on the ferry and we'll get him up here as soon as we can. Chief Inspector Reeves will be on the first flight from Inverness, and I'll pick her up from Sumburgh. But you'll be here at least until eight in the morning.

The family will stay in the house. I don't want to move them out because there's an autistic son who needs his own surroundings. I only met the husband when I turned up here and he seemed in a bit of a state. He might need careful handling. The woman, Helena, seems pleasant enough. I'll let her know you'll be here.'

'No worries, Jimmy. I've come prepared, with a flask and a mound of sandwiches.' The constable grinned. 'And if it gets chilly overnight, I'll just think of the overtime and that'll warm me through.'

Perez didn't know how to answer that. Through the rotten door, he could still see Emma Shearer's body. Instead he turned to Sandy. 'I want you to go to Moncrieff's house. Emma lived and worked there; she was a childminder for the four kids. The good doctor seems a peerie bit hostile about his family being disturbed on a Sunday night, but give him a moment to get home and let the children know what's happened, then get down there. He's going to text me to let me know if the victim's car is there, but you can check yourself. If it is, I doubt whether she's locked it. If not, we'll need the registration details. Seal her room first, though – apparently, she had a self-contained bedsit in the attic and they might have given her a key for it. I don't want to give Moncrieff time to meddle with her things and, after all, it could be the crime scene.' Looking into the valley, Perez saw Moncrieff climb into a large black estate car. 'That'll be Belle picking him up now. Off you go.' Sandy started off towards his car. 'And, Sandy?'

'Yes?'

'He can be a bit of a bully. Don't let him get to you.'

Sandy seemed surprised, and for a moment Perez

thought he would question the comment, but he only nodded and went on his way. Perez stood a little longer, wondering how best to tackle the Fleming family. He could see the husband and wife through the long, narrow window that looked into Fleming's study. Daniel was sitting at his desk, swivelled towards her, and she stood behind him, very close. Perez felt something of a voyeur; that he was intruding on a moment of intimacy.

He wondered if Helena had used her time there to tell Daniel about the strange messages that had appeared in the house and in her workshop. Perhaps he should talk to Helena alone first, to find out, so he wouldn't embarrass her by bringing up the subject. He found himself attracted to the idea. When Helena had come to his home in Ravenswick, he'd liked her. She was intelligent, and of course she'd admired Fran. He was still drawn to everyone who'd known Fran. Then he told himself that wouldn't do. He had to consider Helena as much of a suspect as everyone else connected to Emma Shearer. And just because *she* felt that her husband needed to be protected from the truth, Perez couldn't collude with her. He wouldn't play her games. Daniel might need careful handling, but he deserved to be told the truth.

Perez walked back into the house and tapped on the office door. 'Mr and Mrs Fleming, shall we talk now? In the kitchen, perhaps, where there's a bit more space.'

Chapter Ten

Helena had found Daniel sitting at his desk. She'd felt no connection as she walked in. It could have been a stranger leaning forward, his elbows on the table. He seemed not to hear her open the door or move into the room, and she felt a moment of irritation. How could he just ignore her, when she did so much to make his life easy? To protect him?

An unfamiliar car was parked in the courtyard outside the window and she had the idea that her life had been invaded, that everything was uncertain and it would never be the same again. Of course it had been hard to find Dennis Gear's body hanging in the barn, but this was quite different. Then she thought it was as if all the events of the previous weeks – the strange notes and the gossiping parents in the school playground – had been leading up to this moment. Like the low rumblings before a massive thunderstorm and torrential rain, they were all part of the same event.

She saw then that her husband was crying. He made no sound, but his skin was wet with tears. She stood behind him and stroked his hair away from his face and thought this seemed more than shock. It felt like personal grief. He turned and she held him tight to her, just as she'd done when Christopher was so panicky earlier in the afternoon. Daniel's body was lean and fit and she thought *that* hadn't changed so much over the years, though her response to it had.

'We'll get through this.' As she spoke she realized that she meant it. 'It'll be horrid – all these questions, that detective poking into our lives – but we've managed worse and it'll pass.'

'Have we? Have we managed worse? What can be worse than that?'

'She was never really part of our lives,' Helena said. 'It's so shocking because it's not long since you found Dennis Gear. Twice in the same place. Of course that's going to freak you out. But neither of them was close to us. We didn't even know the old man, and Emma was someone we bumped into in the school playground or at the Moncrieffs'. It's like seeing death and disaster on the TV news. I feel sorry for the starving children, but their pain doesn't touch me. Not properly. Not like Christopher's anger and distress when he can't tell us what he needs.'

He pushed her away slightly so she could see his face. 'I suppose you're right.'

She thought he sounded like a moody schoolboy. 'What's going on here, Daniel?'

'Look, you won't understand.' He paused. 'I suppose you'll find out anyway, when the police start digging. Her pain touches *me*.'

'That's how you are. Sensitive. No protective skin to stop the world getting in.' She was getting scared now, worried what he had to say, and she wanted to lighten the mood.

He shook his head slightly. 'I knew her quite well. We'd become friends.'

Just friends? But she didn't ask the question. Perhaps she didn't want to know. Not for certain. She stood staring at him, waiting for him to continue.

'When we first moved here you were so busy. I'd been working on the house, commuting north to project-manage the building at weekends, still keeping the day-job in Islington. You know how it was.'

She knew how it was. Manic. Exhilarating. The sense that they were at the start of an adventure. Jumping off the edge of the world, each of them with a child in their arms. They'd thought that magically everything would change and be made right again. In a small community Christopher would get the help he needed, Daniel would have the time to write and to plan new projects, she'd find inspiration for her work. It had probably been the most optimistic time of their lives.

Daniel had started speaking again. 'Then it all stopped. When I was working on the house and travelling all the time and fitting in projects for work, I didn't have time to worry about the stress. I was coping. Then suddenly I had nothing to do and I was no one, and my world collapsed. *That* was when the stress, all those months of pushing myself, hit me. In contrast, you were a magnificent success. Of course I was pleased for you.'

'But it was hard.'

'Yeah,' he said, 'it was hard. And then last month I came home to find Dennis Gear's body. That was hard too.'

'And where does Emma fit into all this?' She tried not to sound bitter. She could have said: *How do you think it was for me, while we were living in London and you were working flat out, never home? When I was having to deal with Christopher's school on an almost daily basis and still find time for Ellie?* But it had become a habit not to challenge Daniel.

'We started talking in the playground – just chatting, you know. It was awkward, often I was the only dad there and it was good to have someone to talk to. Once or twice Emma brought Kate to the house to play with Ellie. They got on well.'

Oh, I bet the gossips hanging around the school loved that. The newcomer and the nanny going off together, the only adults in the house that they all hate.

Daniel was talking again, speaking very quickly. It seemed that now he wanted to explain, was desperate that she should understand.

'Emma hadn't had it easy. She grew up in Orkney. Her dad was violent, controlling. One day he battered her mother and ended up in prison. Emma was only fourteen. She had two younger brothers, and a mother who was a nervous wreck and could hardly hold herself together. She ended up looking after them all.'

'And what were you?' Now Helena couldn't help herself. 'A father figure?'

'Yes,' he said, with a spark of defiance. 'Perhaps I was.' He paused for a moment. 'She was only seventeen when she moved in with the Moncrieffs to help Belle out with the kids. Kate was a baby, and Emma was used to looking after small kids – she brought up her brothers almost single-handed. Robert and Belle were kind enough, but they made sure they got their money's worth, and recently they've expected her to deal with the teenagers too. Emma seemed to be caught between the adult Moncrieffs and the kids in

Deltaness. In her twenties, not really seen as a grown-up by Robert and Belle, but too old to hang out with the teens.'

'She did hang out with them.'

'What do you mean?'

'According to Christopher, she was there on the beach when they lit the bonfire and he came home in such a state.'

That detail seemed to surprise Daniel. She'd tossed it in as a weapon of defence, meaning: *Emma wasn't so lonely; she didn't need your company so much.* Now he seemed thrown by the information. 'Are you sure? She wasn't the one to bring him home.'

'No,' Helena said, knowing she was being petty and childish. 'Perhaps she didn't want to leave the party.'

Daniel didn't reply and they sat in silence. She couldn't bring herself to ask the question that had been with her since she'd seen her husband crying at the sight of Emma's body. *Were you lovers?* She didn't think she'd be able to face the answer. So she asked another, connected question instead: 'Why didn't you tell me that you'd become friends with her, that you'd invited her to the house? Why keep it secret?'

'I didn't keep it secret.' Again, he sounded petulant, like a child. 'We didn't exactly have time to talk, when we first moved to Shetland. If you were at home, you were working. Even when I came out to the studio when the kids were in bed, you could hardly shift your attention away from your designs. Mostly you were away, at trade fairs, exhibitions, meetings with retailers.'

She nodded to concede the point. She'd loved the freedom of those months, after handing the domestic responsibility over to Daniel. She'd thought she was entitled to it.

'I gave up trying to talk to you,' he went on. 'Then I got so miserable that I couldn't think about anything but myself.'

Helena heard the kitchen door open and muttered voices in the hall outside.

'Perez will want to talk to us now,' she said. 'Will you tell him about your friendship with Emma?' Not using the word 'relationship' because that was too loaded.

'Of course. If he asks. Why not?'

'Because she was murdered,' Helena said, 'and they'll be looking for her killer.' A pause. The front door opened and shut. Soon Perez would be demanding to see them, asking his questions. Now time, which had dragged when she was in the kitchen, seemed to be passing very, very quickly. 'But you're right: we had better tell the truth. Because there'll be stories already circulating round Deltaness. Gossip about you both. It's impossible to have secrets in Deltaness, isn't it? Except from me.' Then she realized that she still hadn't told Daniel about the graph-paper messages with the image of the gallows, the hanging figure. Of course there were secrets that she'd kept from him.

Chapter Eleven

Although it was still light outside, the kitchen faced east and was in full shadow. Helena switched on a lamp that hung low over the table and they sat there, as they would if Perez had been invited to an intimate supper party. She made coffee without asking if anyone wanted it, and the questions about milk and sugar, the setting out of cups and spoons, added to the impression that this was a social occasion. Perez wondered if that had been Helena's intention, then dismissed the idea. Surely the woman he'd met the day before wouldn't have been so calculating.

'Have you shown your husband the anonymous messages that you've been receiving, Helena? If not, I think you should do that now.'

Daniel looked from Perez to Helena, confused. Fleming wasn't at all what Perez had been expecting. It was irrational, but when Helena had talked about wanting to protect her husband from the unpleasantness of the anonymous cartoons, he'd imagined somebody physically weak: small, grey, insignificant. He'd been quite wrong. Daniel was tall and obviously fit. He wore jeans and a black T-shirt, and the arms resting on the table were those of a climber or someone who worked out. He would have no difficulty throwing a heavy rope over a beam and hauling a body into place.

'Anonymous messages?' Daniel was staring at Helena, waiting for an explanation.

Helena got to her feet and fetched the satchel that was tucked behind the sofa. She spread the tiny pictures on the table in front of her husband.

'This came on Friday. It's the most recent and was hidden inside *The Shetland Times*. The other drawings arrived over the last couple of weeks.'

'Why didn't you tell me?' His voice was fierce. Perez might not have been in the room.

'I didn't think there was anything to tell. A few scraps of graph paper.'

'But you told *him*.' Spitting out the words as he turned towards Perez.

'I called in to see Inspector Perez on Saturday morning.' She paused and then the words came out as a cry. 'He was Fran Hunter's partner. I thought he would understand.'

'And I wouldn't?' Daniel half-rose to his feet. Anger made him intimidating, scary. Every muscle in his face and his body was tense. He was struggling for control.

'I didn't want to worry you.' After the outburst, Helena's voice seemed very quiet.

Daniel returned to his seat, but the fury was still in his words: 'Don't *ever* pretend that you know what's best for me. I am not another of your children. And you accused *me* of keeping secrets!'

Perez wondered what secrets Daniel had been keeping from Helena, but he decided that could wait until later in the interview, or when he talked to them as individuals. The rawness of Daniel's emotion surprised him, until he remembered that Daniel had found Dennis Gear's body too. To see the hanged woman in the same place would unnerve anyone. He would still be in shock.

'Do you have any idea who might have drawn these, Mr Fleming?'

It seemed to take a moment for Daniel to focus on the question. 'Any of the small-minded people of Deltaness who resented us moving in and building this house on what was once Gear's land. I suppose Helena's right – this stuff is ridiculous and not worth bothering with.'

'You don't see any significance in the fact that there's a dead woman hanging in the barn where Mr Gear committed suicide? And that these messages have been arriving in the weeks just before she died.' Perez waited with genuine interest for the answer. When Daniel didn't answer immediately, the inspector turned to his wife. 'Helena?'

'I don't think anyone in Deltaness would kill a young woman just because they dislike a family of outsiders. Emma Shearer had almost nothing to do with us. I met her occasionally when we went for social events at the Moncrieffs', and in the school playground when we picked up the children.' She shot a glance at her husband. 'Daniel saw more of her than I did, at least when we first moved and he was doing most of the childcare.'

Perez sensed a tension, unspoken hostility, and picked his way forward carefully.

'So, you might be able to tell me a bit more about Emma, Daniel?'

The silence stretched and at last the answer came. 'She was sympathetic, a good listener. I enjoyed her company.' Perez thought that he too was choosing his words with care. 'She'd had it tough when she was a kid. I admired her resilience.'

'Did she have a boyfriend?'

Helena turned away and looked out into the darkening garden. Perez thought she was afraid her face would give away too much.

'Nobody permanent,' Daniel said. 'Some of the local boys fancied their chances. I think she went out with one a few times recently, but I didn't have the impression that the relationship was important to her.'

'Can you give me a name?'

'Magnie Riddell.'

'Any relative to Margaret?'

'He's Margaret's son.' This time Helena answered. 'Magnie works at the waste-to-power plant in Lerwick. He travels down to Lerwick every day.'

'That was where Dennis Gear worked. Before he got the sack.'

'I didn't know that,' Helena said. 'Is it important, do you think?'

Perez shook his head. 'Probably coincidence. There are only twenty-three thousand people in the islands, and most of them have some connection with each other. You'll have realized that.'

Helena smiled and Perez felt the tension in the room easing a little. He thought there was more to explore in the relationship between Daniel and Emma, but he'd do that when he had the man on his own. 'Tell me about this morning.'

'We all went out for a long walk,' Helena said, 'and took a picnic lunch.'

'What time did you leave?'

'About ten. We were home before two. I chilled out here, then went to my studio to catch up with some work. Daniel was in his office, Ellie was playing outside and Christopher was in his room. He spends a lot of time in his room.'

Perez nodded.

'Can anyone confirm your movements?'

Helena stared at him, apparently incredulous. 'You think one of us might have killed her?'

'She was found on your premises,' Perez said. 'You must see that I have to ask the question.'

'I was in my studio and Daniel was in the office. We had no visitors. No, we can't confirm our movements.' Perez was surprised by the snappy and defensive tone of her voice.

'When was the last time you were in the byre?'

'I haven't been there for days, weeks even. I know it's ridiculous, but knowing that was where Dennis killed himself, I avoided it. We got rid of the tractor and the other junk, but we haven't quite decided yet what to do with it. The kids go into the byre sometimes to play. Ellie jumps off the bales . . .' Helena's voice tailed off and for a moment she seemed distracted by their plans for the building. 'While they're still young, we thought we might turn it into a play space for the children. In the winter sometimes they spend all day cooped up indoors. No chance for exercise. We were thinking of a climbing wall at one end perhaps, and it's sufficiently high for a swing or trapeze to be fixed from the roof, if the beams are strong enough.' She realized what she'd said and fell silent.

'Daniel?' Perez looked at the man. He seemed more relaxed now.

'I was there yesterday morning. As Helena said, we're starting to make plans for the place, and I wanted to get a feeling for the space before I started working on it properly. I was walking past on my way to the hill and went inside on impulse.' There was a moment of silence. 'I didn't see anything unusual then.'

'What about today? Anything that struck either of you as out of the ordinary?'

They shook their heads, almost in unison.

Perez was thinking that Emma had probably been placed in the barn while the family were out on their walk. Stringing up the body wouldn't have been achieved quickly or easily, and the killer wouldn't have risked being disturbed while the family were in the house. If these witnesses were telling the truth, of course. If neither of them was involved in the murder.

He explained that a uniformed officer would be stationed outside the barn during the night. 'It's standard procedure, to make sure the scene isn't compromised. And to make sure that you're all safe.'

'We thought,' Helena said, 'that we were coming to the safest place in the world.' There was a moment of strained silence.

'I have to talk to Christopher.' Perez got to his feet to show that he'd finished talking to them. 'Where would be the best place to do that? Here or in his bedroom? Will he still be awake or should I come back first thing tomorrow morning? It would have to be very early.'

'Do it now,' Helena said. 'He doesn't sleep much, and it would be better to get it over, wouldn't it?' Looking to Daniel for confirmation. The man nodded. 'I'll take you up.'

Perez followed the woman up the stairs. While they were alone, he was tempted to ask about Daniel's friendship with Emma, but he knew that would require tact and again decided it should wait for another time. It wasn't a subject to be rushed while they were moving from one place to another. Instead he looked quickly at his phone; following Perez's instructions, Moncrieff had texted that Emma's car was still at the house in Deltaness.

They walked along a corridor that had glass panels, facing east towards the beach, along one side. It was as close to being outside as it was possible to be. He watched a gannet dive – sharp-pointed as a missile – into the water. Helena stopped at the last door, tapped on it and went in.

It was another extraordinary space, long and thin, stretching the width of the house, with a window at each end. Christopher sat at the west end at a desk, crouched over a computer keyboard. The last of the evening light streamed in. The opposite window looked over the shore. His bed was built as a shelf into the wall opposite the door and was reached by a ladder. Underneath was a debris of tangled clothes, crisp packets and orange peel. In the middle of the chaos stood an elaborate Lego model of a pirate ship. In contrast, his desk was tidy and uncluttered.

'He doesn't like anyone coming in to clean,' Helena

said, 'and he truly seems incapable of doing it himself. If it's in that space under the bed, he doesn't seem to see it. We've come to an arrangement that I'll do it once a fortnight, when he's at school, and I'll only take out the rubbish and the dirty clothes.'

Christopher's attention was still focused on the screen. Perez might not have been there.

'Switch off the computer.' Her voice was firm. 'You know it's much later than we agreed for switch-off. You shouldn't need me to come up to tell you.'

He switched it off, still staring until the image on the screen faded away.

'Turn around, please, Christopher. The inspector needs to ask you some questions.'

The boy swivelled his chair so that he was facing them. The hysteria of earlier in the day had quite disappeared. He was calm, interested.

'I'm sorry that you had to find Emma this afternoon, Christopher. It must have been a terrible shock,' Perez said. The setting sun behind the boy blurred the details of his face. He was hardly more than a silhouette with a halo of light behind him. 'Did you recognize Emma straight away?'

'She looked after Kate and Sam Moncrieff. And Martha and Charlie, but they're at the High School and don't really need looking after.'

'That's right. Do you know why she might have been visiting your house?'

'Not on a Sunday. She used to come with Kate and Sam sometimes after school. The days Dad picked us up. But not for a while.'

'Why did you go to the barn this afternoon? Mum says you prefer to spend time in your room.'

Christopher considered for a moment. 'The Wi-Fi was down. I was annoyed, but there was nothing I could do about it. I used to get in a rage when things like that happened, but now I try not to. Sometimes it helps to get up and walk around for a bit. I knew I was in the sort of mood when Ellie would get on my nerves, so I didn't want to play with her. I ended up in the barn instead.' He paused. 'At first I didn't know what was hanging there. I couldn't see the face. She was too high and I was looking up from below. I climbed onto the bales to get a better view.'

He stopped abruptly.

'And that was when you realized?'

Christopher nodded. 'I thought the doctor might be able to help her. I knew he'd be at the Sunday teas. That was why I ran down to the hall.'

'That makes perfect sense. You have a good view up here, out to the fields and onto the shore. Have you seen anything unusual lately? Any strangers hanging around?'

Christopher sat very still for a moment, and then slowly he shook his head.

Chapter Twelve

Sandy arrived at the Moncrieffs' house and sat in the car, looking out at the place. The house stood in the most southerly part of Deltaness, and it was surrounded by trees. This was sufficiently unusual in Shetland to make Sandy feel a little uneasy. It was large too, three storeys, L-shaped. Once it had belonged to a laird and now it belonged to the doctor. The trees must have been planted years ago to shelter the building from the road, the common people and the wind. Under the trees – mostly stunted sycamores with thick, warped trunks – bluebells were growing. The black car that had collected Robert Moncrieff from the track leading to the Fleming house was parked outside, next to a Range Rover. Sandy walked to the side of the house and saw a little red Clio.

The front door was grand, fronted by steps and framed by pillars, though the paint was peeling. In the islands the weather could do that after a couple of wild autumns, but the whole house seemed kind of scruffy to Sandy. It was as if the owners didn't care what other folk might make of it. Arrogance. He knew the Moncrieffs would have the money to tidy it up, if they wanted. The house had been inherited from Robert's father, so there'd be no mortgage, and rumour had it that Belle's family was loaded. Her dad owned a brewery and property throughout the English Midlands. That, at least, was what Sandy had heard.

He rang the doorbell and heard it echo inside. A teenage girl opened it. She had very dark hair, cut asymmetrically so that her fringe slanted. She was dressed entirely in black – black leggings, a long black baggy sweater and black ballet pumps. She had a nose-stud and a string of rings in one ear. 'Who are you?' Her head was tilted to one side.

Sandy explained.

'You'll be here about Emma. Dad's just told us. We knew already, though. You know what it's like here. Word gets out.' She seemed unmoved by the woman's death. 'Is it true that she was murdered?'

'We're treating her death as suspicious.' Sandy had never had much contact with teenage girls – not confident teenage girls from wealthy families – and he found this one scary. 'Can I speak to your parents?'

'They're in the kitchen. Mum's already on the Pinot. She's not sure how she'll cope with us all, without Emma.' The girl had started to walk away, but she continued speaking to him over her shoulder. 'I hope she doesn't expect me to step in. I've got exams in a few weeks.'

He followed her down a flagstone corridor to an open door. The girl stood just inside and held up her hands as if she was about to make an announcement. There was a small tattoo on the back of her neck, right below her hairline. Sandy couldn't see properly around her. There'd been conversation in the room, but now it fell silent. 'The fuzz is here, so watch what you say.'

A woman's voice said, 'Martha, don't be so rude.

That's not funny.' Martha turned very quickly, slipped past Sandy and disappeared. He was left standing in the doorway, being stared at by the two people inside.

As the girl had said, Belle Moncrieff had already opened a bottle of wine and sat with a large glass in one hand. The bottle was only half-full. She must have started drinking before her husband got home. 'I'm sorry, Constable, come in. Robert was just telling me.' She was a good-looking woman, dark-haired and dark-eyed, big, but with the confidence to carry it off. And the money, Sandy thought, to dress to best advantage. Today she was wearing a navy wrap-around dress, and his eyes were drawn to the impressive cleavage rather than the wide hips. 'What a terrible tragedy!'

Robert was still standing. He nodded for Sandy to take a seat. 'I asked Martha if she saw Emma this morning. Jimmy Perez seemed keen to know when she was last seen. But Martha couldn't remember noticing her at all.'

'Would Martha have seen her?' Sandy asked.

'Not necessarily. It's a big house. There are two staircases and it's a bit of a warren. Emma could quite easily have left without anyone realizing. Weekends are mad. We're all doing our own thing.' Moncrieff took a glass from the cupboard on the wall behind him and poured himself some wine. 'Jimmy said you wanted to look at Emma's room.'

'Yes, please.'

'I'll show you. It's a bit of a climb.'

Sandy followed. The house was, as Moncrieff had said, a bit of a warren; corridors seemed to lead in all directions. It was almost dark outside now and there was no natural light where they were walking. The electric bulbs seemed weak and they walked in a half-lit gloom. It seemed to Sandy that there were hazards everywhere: kids' toys on the stairs, uneven floors, small, unexpected steps. At last Moncrieff stopped outside a low door. He pushed it, but it didn't open. 'Ah, of course it's locked. Lucky that I thought to bring the spare key.' It was a simple Yale lock that would work when the door was pulled to.

'I'll take it from here, sir. I've got protective clothing. I'm sure you know how it works, you'll have seen the cop shows on TV.' Sandy tried to lighten the mood a little. 'We'll need to seal the room when I've had a quick look. Then we'll get the experts in tomorrow.'

He thought for a moment that the man would object and insist on staying, but Moncrieff only shrugged. 'Of course, if that's what you want. It's procedure, I suppose. Our life seems to be ruled by it these days.' He handed over the key.

'Is this the only spare?' Sandy thought Perez would want to know that.

'Yes. We could never quite understand her need for a lock in the first place, but she said she didn't want the children wandering in.' Moncrieff turned away and Sandy heard his heavy footsteps on the stairs.

He pulled on the scene-suit, gloves and overshoes, put the key in the lock and reached inside for the light switch. The room was built into the roof, with a sloping gable on one side and long Velux windows. During the day it would be full of light and even now, this close to midsummer, it wasn't quite dark outside, and Sandy could make out the outlines of the closest trees. They were below him now, only the tallest branches silhouetted against a paler sky.

The room wasn't what he'd been expecting at all. Emma had been twenty-four. He remembered when he'd had girlfriends in their twenties; their rooms had been scattered with make-up, dirty clothes, DVDs. And that had been the tidier ones. This felt as if he'd stepped back into a different era. There was a single bed against the windowless wall. No duvet, but sheets, blankets and a patchwork quilt. A long table under the windows held an old-fashioned treadle sewing machine, inlaid with mother-of-pearl, and a basket containing yarn and knitting needles. The machine was still threaded and a piece of gingham fabric was folded beside it. Next to the machine stood a record player – a Dansette, just like the one his parents had owned when he was a kid – and in a case under the table a pile of vinyl LPs. A jam jar of wildflowers. Two posters on the walls, one of Marilyn Monroe and one advertising a black-and-white film. Sandy had never heard of it.

There was nothing to suggest a disturbance within the room, and certainly no sign that the door had been forced. If Emma had been strangled here, she'd let in the killer and he'd pulled the door closed behind him when he left. But there had been family members coming and going in the house all day and, surely, he wouldn't have taken the risk of carrying her body down the stairs and along the corridors. This was unlikely to be the crime scene.

A white wooden cupboard in an alcove formed by the chimney breast held all Emma's clothes. Again it seemed to Sandy to be unusually neat, and again the clothes seemed unlikely for a woman of Emma's age. There were no jeans ripped at the knees, and black didn't feature. The only trousers were cropped and fitted, in pastel colours, beautifully pressed and folded. Cotton dresses hung from hangers. He looked for labels, but there were none. It seemed that Emma made all her own clothes.

In the alcove on the other side of the chimney breast there was a smaller cupboard, painted white to match. On top of it stood an old-fashioned television, square and boxy, with an aerial on top. Perez had said that Moncrieff claimed Emma was still alive the night before, because he'd heard her television. Sandy had wondered if some kind of timer could have been used to make it *seem* as if Emma had been in, but looking at the very basic set, that seemed unlikely now. Inside the cupboard there were shoeboxes holding papers: an unsophisticated filing system. Emma's passport lay on top of one. Sandy picked it up and flicked through it, but it told him nothing, except to confirm her date and place of birth. There was nothing to indicate that she'd ever travelled abroad.

A series of photographs had been propped on the shelf next to the bed. One was of a middle-aged woman who was so like Emma that it must be her mother. One of two teenage boys covered in mud, flushed but grinning, and labelled 'Da Ba, Kirkwall, New Year 2015'; and one of Emma herself, looking sideways into the camera. Sandy knew about Da Ba, a wild, rowdy ball game that took place in the streets of Orkney's main town on New Year's Day. He'd always meant to go.

In the photo, Emma looked like a film star of the early Sixties; her blonde hair was styled into a roll on the side of her head, and her eyeliner was dark and drawn beyond her eyes, making them seem long, cat-like. Her lips were very red. Seductive. Sandy found himself wondering who had taken that photo and what had happened afterwards. A laptop in its foam case was propped against one wall. Sandy slipped it into an evidence bag.

He continued his search, but there was no sign of a handbag, the woman's car keys or her phone. Despite her obsession with the past, they knew that Emma had possessed a mobile phone. Robert Moncrieff had confirmed that and given them the number. Sandy pushed open the door that led into a small bathroom. That too was clean; probably cleaner, he thought, than the rest of the house. In a small wall-unit he found a few over-the-counter cold and flu medicines. No prescription drugs. Nothing at all to suggest why Emma might have been killed.

He switched off the light, pulled the door carefully closed behind him and set off down the stairs. He might have got lost in the tangle of corridors, if he hadn't been led by adult voices. The kitchen door must have been open and although Sandy couldn't make out exactly what was being said, Belle and Robert weren't whispering. At last he reached the hall, with its flagstone floor, and knew where he was. He was still wearing the paper overshoes and they must have muffled the sound of his steps, or perhaps the Moncrieffs were so caught up in their conversation that they weren't aware of him approaching. He stood for a moment and listened.

'There is no way I'm giving up the trip to London with Helena. It's a big deal for us both.' Belle spoke just a bit louder than was necessary. Sandy didn't know if that was the wine or if she always liked to make her voice heard. 'I've done the mother-of-four domestic goddess for long enough, Robert. You'll have to take some time off and pay for a locum.'

'Hardly domestic goddess.' His voice was quieter, but the words were biting. 'The house has always been a tip, and the kids would be a complete emotional mess if it weren't for me. Emma didn't help much there, did she?' There was a sudden silence, as shocking as the words had been. Sandy walked down the passage towards them. They turned, startled, and he realized how strange he must look, still in the suit and mask. He ripped them off and pulled off his gloves. Moncrieff was on his feet, suddenly playing the host.

'Are you done up there? Anything else we can do to help? Would you like coffee? We're on the wine, but I assume we can't tempt you with that. I'm afraid you'll have to wait until the morning to talk to the kids. It was way past their bedtime, and they've got school in the morning.'

Sandy nodded. He hoped somebody else would be detailed to talk to the teenager with attitude. 'I just need to take a quick look in Emma's car.'

'Of course. You know where it is. Help yourself. It shouldn't be locked. Emma was very careful about locking her room, but her car was always left open.' Moncrieff walked with him to the big front door, keen, Sandy felt, to make sure he was out of the house.

On the gravel drive he stood for a moment for his eyes to get used to the dark. There was a chill in the air and a slim moon. Everything was very quiet. He looked at his phone and saw that Perez had left him a message: *Finished for tonight. Heading back to Ravenswick to check on Cass. Give me a ring when you're done.*

Sandy walked round the side of the house, the crunching of his feet sounding very loud. The children might have been sent to bed, but two of them were still awake – at least there were lights in two of the upstairs windows. He couldn't see Robert and Belle making much effort to check, especially tonight. The curtains in the nearest window had been pulled aside and he saw Charlie Moncrieff looking out. Backlit, he seemed almost ghostly. Sandy thought how sad he must be, to have lost the woman who'd cared for him since he was a young boy, and wondered why his mother and father weren't with him, consoling him. He thought then that he and Louisa would be very different parents. If that ever happened. If she agreed to marry him, when he finally found the courage to ask. Now, in the middle of an investigation, would probably be the worst possible time.

He found himself by the small red car. He pulled on a fresh pair of gloves. As Moncrieff had said, the vehicle was unlocked. When Sandy opened the driver's door, the internal light came on and he saw that the keys had been left in the ignition. That seemed a little unusual. He could understand her not bothering to lock the car, but it was careless to leave in the keys. He wouldn't have put it past that Martha to try a little joy-riding.

It seemed that Emma cared as much about tidiness in her car as in her room. Sandy thought it couldn't have been easy to keep it this spotless, if she had to carry those kids around. He found the torch on his phone and shone it onto the back seat. Shining it onto the floor, Sandy saw scuffed footwear prints. Vicki Hewitt, the crime-scene manager, might be able to do something with them, but he could make out little detail. They looked too big to belong to the smaller children, but Martha and Charlie were as tall as adults and the prints might belong to them.

All the same, as he straightened his back, his mind was already racing, pulling together a scenario that might explain the keys left in the ignition and the footwear prints. He saw Emma in her yellow-and-white dress slipping out of the big house and running to her car, excited maybe to be starting her day off. She'd put the keys in the ignition. But what if someone was crouching in the well behind the driver's seat. If she was distracted, lost in her own thoughts, Emma might not notice. And the killer would be in just the position to reach out and strangle her, as she took her place behind the wheel.

Sandy walked to the back of the car and clicked open the boot. It was empty and had been cleaned recently. In the light of his torch, he saw brush marks on the fabric. He closed the boot and locked the car. This was a potential crime scene and he'd leave it untouched for Vicki Hewitt, who would arrive the following day. He made his way to his own vehicle and, with a feeling of escape, drove through the trees and down the road towards Lerwick.

Chapter Thirteen

Willow had a window seat in the small plane and looked down over the islands of Orkney, trying to distinguish them. *That must be Sanday. Or could it be Shapinsay? That's certainly North Ronaldsay, so close to Fair Isle.* Leaving Orkney behind, they flew low over Fair Isle on the plane's approach to Sumburgh and she was able to make out more details than she'd ever seen before: the scattering of white croft houses to the south, two lighthouses, one at each end of the island. This was where Jimmy Perez came from. Where Fran Hunter, his lover and Cassie's mother, had been stabbed during the course of a murder investigation more than three years before. Willow hadn't been involved in that case; she'd moved to Inverness soon after. But she'd read about it, had become a little obsessed about it during her first encounter with Jimmy Perez, and had come to understand something of his sense of guilt and to know him a little better.

Now they'd be working together again, and she wasn't sure what she made of that. She'd pushed all thoughts of him to the back of her mind. It was too complicated and she was too independent. She'd not been feeling well recently, not as sharp as usual and with a lot less energy. She'd tried to persuade herself that she wasn't really ill, but that hadn't helped. It was a calm flight and she looked down to the south of Shetland mainland as the plane circled to land into the southerly breeze. And she realized that she was glad to be here; it felt a little like coming home. And no matter how awkward it might be, she was glad to be seeing Jimmy Perez again.

He was there waiting for her. She saw him through the terminal window as she walked down the plane steps – black-haired, dark-eyed, betraying his ancestors' Spanish roots. His outline was blurred and always a little untidy. Just like her. She went to greet him before collecting her bag. He seemed uncertain, but gave her a real hug and kissed her on both cheeks. She grasped him back.

'You look tired,' he said. 'Skinny. Are you well?'

'There's a compliment to greet a girl!' Because this wasn't the time for a serious talk. That would have to wait. She saw her holdall on the belt and went to get it. He was there before her and held on to it. Once she might have made a fuss, but now she was glad for him to take it. 'Where are we off to?'

'Northmavine,' he said. 'North Mainland. The settlement of Deltaness. James Grieve came overnight on the ferry and should be there already. Sandy's with him.'

'So, a bit of a road trip, Jimmy.' She thought that was good, because it would take a little while for her to tell him her news. 'I read your email before I left, but you can fill me in with the details on the way.'

'Vicki's not with you?'

'She had stuff to finish off this morning and will be in on the next flight. She's arranged to pick up a hire car.' Willow waited, expecting more questions, but Jimmy accepted the explanation. He opened the boot of his car and lifted in her bag. Cassie's booster-seat was fixed in the back. Willow thought for a moment that the child was like her mother's ghost. Always there, in one way or another.

'That's good then,' Perez said. 'So, I'll have you to myself.'

I'm not quite sure, she thought, *that we're ever really alone.*

They drove north along the road that was familiar to her now. Perez was talking about the victim and the two other families involved in the case so far: the Flemings and the Moncrieffs, one old-school Shetland and the other incomer. It seemed that this was all about families. Willow tried to concentrate and to ask the right questions. 'It sounds as if the victim was more like a childminder than a nanny, if all the kids are at school now.'

'Yeah, but she lived in, helped out with the shopping, driving the kids to sports clubs and music lessons. You know the sort of thing. Belle Moncrieff sees herself as a supermum, but since the youngest two were small, she's depended on Emma. Belle's working again too now, as a freelance publicist. She and Robert are having some sort of domestic meltdown because they're not sure how they'll cope without Emma.' He turned and grinned at her, showing that, as a single parent, with a job without regular hours, he knew about domestic chaos.

They'd come to Ravenswick and Willow looked up the bank to the house where Perez lived with Cassie, and then down towards the sea past the Hays' farm with its polytunnels and neat fields. This was the place that still featured in the worst of her nightmares.

'Apparently Magnus's house has been sold,' Perez said. Perhaps he guessed at her memories and was trying to pull her attention back inland to happier things. 'I haven't met my new neighbours yet, though.' He paused. 'The woman who lives in the place in Deltaness where the body was found came to see me on Saturday morning. I thought that was why she was there: because she was moving in.'

'What *did* she want?' Willow found herself engaged in the conversation again, grateful to be distracted.

'To tell me that she'd been getting anonymous messages, strange little cartoons on graph paper of gallows and hanged men. We've collected them all, of course, and the paper's been sent for fingerprinting.'

'And the next day a woman is hanging in her barn. That must have freaked her out, big-style.' They were driving through Cunningsburgh; Perez had slowed down as they passed the school. In the playground mothers were waiting with buggies and prams while their children played chase and kicked around a ball. A bell rang and the children ran towards the door, pulled like iron filings to a magnet.

'Ah well, there's an added complication in the fact that a man committed suicide there not long ago. He'd once owned the house where the Flemings stay.' Perez paused for a moment before adding: 'Besides, I'm not sure that Helena is the sort to get freaked out.'

'Helena Fleming, the designer?'

'You've heard of her?' Perez seemed surprised.

'What are you saying, Jimmy? That I've got no style?' She couldn't help teasing. Her style was frayed jeans and baggy sweaters. Wild hair. Boho without the chic. 'She featured in one of the Sunday newspapers a couple of weeks ago and I noticed, because of the Shetland connection. Why did Helena come to you for help? Don't they have a community bobby out there in the wilds?'

'She knew Fran,' Perez said. 'I couldn't turn her away.'

'Oh, Jimmy . . .' His kindness was a curse, and one of the sexiest things about him.

They sat for a moment in silence and he turned off the main road towards Scalloway, to avoid driving though Lerwick.

'Why did you ask me to be on my own when I picked you up?'

She was surprised by the directness of the question. Often Perez was cautious around her, worried about hurting her feelings or being hurt himself. She took a deep breath. 'There's something we need to talk about.'

'You're not leaving the force?' He kept his voice light, jokey. 'Getting married and moving to the other side of the world?'

'Not quite that dramatic.'

'You're ill. I knew you weren't looking well.' He spoke with absolute certainty. They'd turned onto the road that led east back towards the main road up the spine of the island. Willow had an idea of the geography of the islands now. They were close to the Ting Loch, where once the Viking parliament had met, and in the distance there was a bare hill, laden with massive wind turbines. He pulled into the lay-by where car-share drivers left their vehicles and switched off the engine. She wanted to reach out and touch him.

'No, Jimmy, I'm not ill, though in the last few weeks it's felt as if I am.' She paused. 'I'm pregnant.'

He stared at her. There was no response. He could have been chiselled from stone or very hard wood.

'You're the father. That's what I'm telling you. There wasn't anyone else. Not for ages. I told you I wasn't the sort for a recreational shag with a stranger. Or even with a friend. Not now I'm grown-up.' He still didn't speak and she continued, turning away so that she wasn't able to see him, hating the blankness of his face and the tension in his body. 'I've decided to have it. Keep it. When I found out, I knew I wanted this more than anything in the world. I won't make any demands, Jimmy. I promise. I can manage fine by myself. But I wanted you to know.'

She wasn't sure what she'd expected or hoped for. Maybe in her wildest dreams, late at night, that he'd take her into his arms and tell her that it was the best news in the world. That he'd ask her to marry him and move to Shetland to be with him and Cassie. That they would be a real family. This was Jimmy Perez, after all: emotionally incontinent, spreading his compassion to everyone he came into contact with. But not, it seemed, to her. Not this time.

'Why didn't you tell me before? You must have known for a while. You were here at the beginning of February.'

'I don't know,' she said. 'I wanted to wait until I was ten weeks and miscarriage was less likely. No point making a fuss if nothing was going to come of it.' Then she told herself that this was Jimmy she was talking to, and he deserved more than that. 'Really? It was cowardice. Because I was still confused, after all that happened then. Because it was hardly something to do over the phone or put in a work email.' A pause. 'I thought you might be happy for me, Jimmy. I wanted a child. So much.'

'I'm very glad I was a satisfactory means to an end.'

The words winded her like a punch in the belly. 'No!' She thought this was going as badly as it could possibly go. 'It wasn't planned, what happened between us. There was nothing calculated in it.'

A silence. She turned back so that she was facing him, was aware of tears streaming down her cheeks and at that moment hated her weakness and the hormones that were making her so woolly and confused. Cars and lorries streamed past towards Lerwick on the road ahead of them. 'I don't lie, Jimmy. If you know me at all, you know that about me.'

'I'm not sure I know anything about you.' He was as cold and closed as when she'd first met him, soon after Fran's death. For a while no cars passed. An oystercatcher called overhead. One of Jimmy's hands was still on the steering wheel and she was desperate to reach out and put hers on top of it. To have some physical connection with him. But she knew how hurt she'd be, if he pulled his away.

'What are we going to do?' Her voice seemed to be spoken by someone else. Someone old and serious and lonely.

Another silence. 'We're going to work,' he said at last. 'We're going to find a killer. That's what we do.' He started the engine. Before he drove off, he looked at her and she had a brief moment of hope, which was dashed as soon as she heard the anger in his voice. 'Does anyone else know about this?'

She shook her head. 'Not even my family. A couple of the women in Inverness nick might have guessed. I've been kind of rubbish at work lately. All over the place. Always tired. But you had to be the first person to know.'

He nodded briefly, as if to say that at least on that score she'd done the right thing, and then pulled out into the road.

Chapter Fourteen

Sandy was early to the ferry terminal and was there to see the NorthLink make its way up Bressay Sound and tie up to the dock. The professor would have had a smooth crossing, but Sandy thought James Grieve wasn't the sort to get seasick anyway. And if he did succumb, it would take more than a bit of nausea to trouble him. He cut up dead bodies for a living, and he'd let slip after a few drams that he'd been part of the investigative team in the Balkans after the war in the former Yugoslavia. 'The body of an elderly man, arthritic bones and a bullet hole in the back of the head . . . I think we could say that was a war crime, not the result of legitimate combat.'

Grieve was the first person off the ship and, when Sandy saw him, he was walking down the stairs, not taking the lift.

'So, you're my taxi driver for the day?' The man had started speaking as soon as he reached the bottom step. He had a voice that could have been honed on the parade ground, and most of the waiting passengers turned to stare.

'Jimmy asked me to take you straight to Deltaness, where the body was found.' In contrast Sandy waited until the pathologist was close enough for him to keep his voice low. News of the woman's death would be all over the islands by now, but it seemed disrespectful to discuss it in front of the people streaming off the ferry.

'But you don't think that's where the victim died?' Grieve slung his bag onto the back seat and climbed into the car.

'It's possible, but unlikely; there must have been a lot of careful planning if she was killed there. It's certainly not suicide, unless someone came along afterwards and took away whatever she was standing on while she tied herself to that beam. I wondered if she could have been killed in her own car.' Sandy described the footprint, the scenario that he'd conjured in his head.

Grieve nodded. 'It sounds possible. If it was manual strangulation, we should be able to tell from the marks on her neck whether the murderer stood behind or in front of her.'

When they got to the Fleming house it was still too early for the children to have left the house for school. Sandy parked in the courtyard as close as he could get to the barn. The constable from the night before was still there. Someone had taken him a chair and there was a flask of coffee on the floor beside him. He was eating a bacon sandwich, still hot, the grease seeping into the kitchen towel that was wrapped round it.

'The family's been looking after you then?' Sandy thought it hadn't been such a hard night for the man after all. Not wet and not cold.

'They seem fine people.' His mouth was still full of bacon and bread.

Sandy wondered what he'd say if one of the fine

Flemings turned out to be their killer. He gave the man James Grieve's name for the log. 'You can get off now and grab some kip.'

The constable stuffed the remainder of his sandwich into his mouth, picked up his belongings and set off. Grieve climbed into his scene-suit, but even when he was ready, he stood for a moment at the barn door, looking inside.

'Did you bring a stepladder?' he said. 'I need something so I can see her *in situ*, and obviously I can't use anything belonging to the Flemings. We don't want contamination, do we? And even though they've been feeding up the local constabulary, and my wife would pay a fortune for one of Helena's creations, one of them could be the killer.' He paused. 'Can you get hold of Annie Goudie?' Annie was the funeral director based in Lerwick. 'Jimmy says there are children in the house. Let's get her lads here this morning, so we can get our victim away and off to Aberdeen on the ferry tonight. This one would haunt my nightmares, I hate to think what she'd do to a sensitive eleven-year-old.'

Sandy left the barn and walked to the front of the house. Helena was just leaving with the two children. The boy was in shorts and a T-shirt, sandals on his feet, a small rucksack with a cartoon superhero on his back. His back was very straight. He showed no curiosity about Sandy. The girl was dark-haired too, younger and it seemed she was unable to keep still. Again Sandy wondered what it would be like to have kids. He supposed it was a kind of lottery, and you wouldn't know whether you'd get a daft one or a calm one until they arrived. But surely parenting had something to do with how they turned out? Louisa was a teacher and she worked with children all day. She was kind and patient, so if anyone was going to be a good mother, it would be her. Helena Fleming was tying the lassie's hair up in pigtails.

'You two can go on,' she said, when she'd finished. 'I'll catch you up. Wait for me at the road.' She pulled a face at Sandy. 'I'm not looking forward to the school playground this morning. The gossips will be there, full of questions and speculation. I was even wondering if the kids were old enough for me to send them on their own, but decided against it. Christopher would be OK, but Ellie's a bit crazy and not a big fan of school. It wouldn't surprise me if she spent all morning on the beach. Anyway I wouldn't put it past the gossip vultures to start on *them*.'

'I'm just going to contact the undertaker in Lerwick,' he said. 'Her boys will come later this morning to take down the body. Emma should be gone by the time the bairns are back from school.'

She breathed heavily. 'Good,' she said. 'But *this* won't be over, will it? The talk. The gossip. The investigation. This will go on until you've found out who killed her.'

'We will find out,' Sandy said. 'Jimmy Perez is a brilliant detective.'

She looked at him, a little surprised. 'Yes,' she said. 'I'm sure he is.' And she set off down the track, almost at a run, to catch the children up.

Sandy had put on his own scene-suit to carry the step-ladder into the barn. James Grieve had moved a little closer to Emma Shearer and was talking into his Dictaphone. He clicked it off and turned to the detective.

'You're quite right, Sandy, I don't think she was killed here. No shoes, you see. If the killer had arranged to meet her here, she'd surely still be wearing her shoes. Unless the killer had a good reason to take them off her. But why would he do that?'

'Surely she'd have been wearing shoes if she was in her car.' Sandy wasn't quite as scared of Grieve as he'd once been. He was happy now to express his own opinions.

'Depends on the shoes.' Grieve was still staring at the woman, almost talking to himself. 'They could have been knocked off as she was bundled into a boot to bring her here. And I don't see this as a woman who'd be out in walking boots or good strong brogues. Not with that outfit.'

'Why do that? Why risk being caught bringing her up here? The family was only out for the morning, and no one could have guessed how long they'd be gone.'

Grieve set up the stepladder, positioning it carefully. He took a couple of photos and the unexpected flash made Sandy blink. 'I suppose it could be someone who enjoys risk,' Grieve said. 'Someone who's turned on by that. Or perhaps the killer is sending a message.'

'A message to the Fleming family?'

'Maybe! But it's your job to consider that, Constable. It's not mine to speculate.' Sandy held onto the steps and watched Grieve climb up. 'Can you take her weight for a moment?'

Sandy held the woman around her legs and thought how light she was. After all, it wouldn't have been so difficult to bring her here and string her up. Her skirt rose up as he grabbed her and he caught a glimpse of bright, white underwear. He found himself fascinated, but turned his head; he didn't want to be caught staring.

While Sandy took her weight, the pathologist pulled the rope away, so he could see her neck. More photos. 'That'll do, Sandy, you can let her go now. Gently, though.' As Sandy released the body, it started to swing, slowly, and turned so that Emma was facing him. Grieve's camera flashed again and he saw the red lipstick and the heavy eye make-up that she'd been wearing in the photo in her room. This must be her signature look. Seeing the woman from this angle, her cheekbones seemed even sharper. Sandy thought she was different from any other woman he'd seen, and suddenly found the idea ridiculous. How could he fancy a dead woman? It was as crazy as Perez getting obsessed with that woman they'd found in the croft in Ravenswick, after the landslide earlier in the year.

Grieve had already started talking again. 'I think this could fit in with your theory. There are marks of manual strangulation, and I'd bet anything you like that the killer was behind her when she died. There are no signs that she struggled, so I'm guessing that he surprised her.'

Outside there was the sound of a car coming up the track. Sandy was glad of an excuse to turn his back on Emma Shearer and go outside. It felt like breaking a spell. Inside the byre he hadn't been able to take his eyes off her. 'It's Jimmy and the chief inspector,' he called back to Grieve. 'They've made pretty good time from the airport.'

He was pleased that Willow had made it safely into Shetland. She and Perez made the best possible team and when she was there, Sandy felt less responsible for lifting his boss's mood. He went out into the sunshine and waited for the car to reach the house.

But when the pair arrived, Sandy could sense at once the tension between them. Willow greeted him warmly enough when she climbed out, but she looked grey and tired. Perez sat where he was, staring ahead of him. His car window was open and Sandy shouted in to him, 'The professor is here, Jimmy. He's got some thoughts about the cause of death. I think you should speak to him.'

It took Perez a while to answer. This was how he'd been immediately after Fran's death. There'd been times then when Perez had been so wrapped up in his own grief that Sandy had been driven crazy, when he'd wanted to yell at Perez, to tell him to stop being so rude and selfish. So bloody childish.

'Willow's here now. She can deal with Prof. Grieve.'

Willow looked back at the vehicle, and Sandy thought she was about to cry. When he'd been growing up his parents had rowed occasionally. His father was a stubborn man with a temper on him. Then, Sandy had felt like this: confused and distressed. As if his world was falling apart.

'What are your plans, Jimmy?' Willow asked, very quietly. Before, there'd been jokes between them. She'd tease Perez for taking charge when she was supposed to be the senior officer. But now neither of them was joking.

'I'm going to Deltaness,' Perez said at last. 'I want to track down a man called Magnie Riddell. Apparently he was the dead woman's boyfriend.' He paused for a beat. 'I'm not sure how long I'll be. Why don't you get a lift back to Lerwick with Sandy? He can drop you at your B&B. I've booked you into the same place as last time.' Then he started the engine and drove away.

Chapter Fifteen

Perez drove too fast down the hill, loathing himself for his display of petulance, for his cruelty to Willow, for his inability to disentangle his emotions. In the end, it was too much for him to think about. Her child. His child. He shut it at the back of his mind, with all the other stuff he couldn't bear thinking about: guilt, grief, the flashbacks that still came out of the blue and made visits to his parents in Fair Isle so painful. All that would have to wait. He would focus on this investigation, on Emma Shearer. At least a dead woman wouldn't betray his trust.

He drove past the school and the hall and came to the new building that held the community shop. Inside, a woman in a purple sweater with a patterned yoke was stocking the shelves and an elderly man stood next to the counter. Perez could tell that he'd been there for a while. He wasn't waiting to be served – he already had a recycled carrier bag with a newspaper and loaf of bread at his feet – but he was lingering for the company and to chat. Inside, it seemed dark and cool, a little dusty and disordered, but it contained everything that the people of Deltaness might need. The shop was run by volunteers.

Perez took a bottle of water and a Mars bar from

the shelves and carried them to the counter. The woman in purple straightened and joined him. 'It's Jimmy Perez, isn't it? You came once and gave a talk to the bairns in the school.'

'You've got a very good memory.' He made himself smile. He didn't want to think about sitting on a small desk, answering questions from the children in the class. The eager faces. It took him back to Willow and the ideas he was trying to forget. 'That must be ten years ago.'

'Well,' she said, 'I've seen your photo in the paper since then too.' She leaned towards him. 'You'll be here about that business in Dennis Gear's old place. The lassie that died.'

He nodded. 'Did you know her?'

'She came in here with the Moncrieff children from Ness House a couple of times a week. On their way home from school. Sometimes she'd buy them a few sweeties. Sometimes it was ciggies for her.'

'She smoked?' Perez put the water and the chocolate into his jacket pocket.

'On the sly. I don't think Belle and Robert ever knew.' A pause. 'But then I think she got up to quite a lot that Belle and Robert didn't know about.'

'Oh?' He tried not to sound too curious.

'She was young when she arrived at the big house. Just out of school. The Moncrieffs treated her a bit like a big kid. But even then, she had a way with her. She dressed older than her years . . .'

'In a provocative way?' Perez didn't want to put words into the woman's mouth, but he didn't want to be here all day. Not with the elderly guy listening to every word, hoovering up information to spill out at a later date.

'Not quite that. I mean not tarty. Not skirts like a pelmet and bosoms hanging out, like some of them. She wore the sort of clothes they went for in the Fifties and early Sixties. Like the old movies they used to show on the telly on Sunday afternoons. It didn't seem right on a lassie of that age. There was something . . .' she struggled to find the right word and in the end relished the Gothic nature of the situation, 'grotesque about it. Like she was a little girl dressing up in her mammy's clothes. I thought it was kind of creepy.' She paused for a beat. 'The men seemed to go for it, though.'

'Any specific man?'

But it seemed that question was too direct. She shrugged. 'They all seemed to be taken in by her.'

'I heard she had a boyfriend. Magnie Riddell. Margaret's son. Works at the waste-to-power plant.'

Perez thought the last two pieces of phrases had been unnecessary. The woman knew exactly who Magnie Riddell was. But it didn't hurt to let her know that he already had information about the community.

'I did hear they were hanging about together.' She looked directly at Perez. 'But that was a while ago. I hadn't seen them together recently.'

'Where can I find him?'

'He'll be at work.' As if the question was daft and the answer obvious. She was fidgeting now. Any pleasure in the conversation was long over. She'd probably gone to school with Margaret, and Perez could see how the two women might be pals.

'But he still lives with his mother, doesn't he? You can tell me where Margaret lives.'

The woman hesitated and the elderly man answered, not even pretending that he hadn't been listening. 'She's in one of those houses that the council put up when the oil came. Next door to her sister Lottie. It's the one with the blue door and the fancy knocker. She should be in; it's not one of her days for Brae.'

Perez thanked them and walked out of the shop. He left his car where it was and walked along the shore to the double row of houses that ran along the bank parallel to the water. They were small, grey, the concrete stained. There'd been nothing pretty about them when they'd first been built in the early Eighties, put up to house the growing population of people who'd come to Shetland to work in the oil industry. Now they were ugly, a blot on an otherwise beautiful landscape. But people had to live somewhere and the islands had never been a theme park for tourists.

He found the house with the blue front door. Perez knocked and the neighbour's net curtains twitched. He wondered if the people of Ravenswick behaved like this. Would a stranger walking around the settlement where he lived be scrutinized in the same way? Perhaps he would after a murder, Perez thought. It would have been like this after Fran found Catherine Ross's body. Murder made everyone tense and curious.

The door opened and the woman who'd been talking so loudly at the Deltaness Sunday teas opened the door to him.

'Mrs Riddell?'

'Yes.' Wary. She looked down the street to see if anyone was about. The place was empty.

He introduced himself.

'You'd better come in.'

In the distance there was the sound of a bell and children's laughter. It must be mid-morning playtime at the school. She showed him into a small but spotless front room. The furniture was slightly too big for it and he had to squeeze between a sofa and an armchair to find a seat.

'When I was still married, we had a bigger house in Voe.' The words were full of bitterness, but also a kind of apology. 'We had to sell when the divorce came through. I wanted to come back to Deltaness, but this was all I could afford.' She looked at him. 'You were at the Sunday teas. Did you know something like this was going to happen?'

'No!' he said. 'That was just chance. Coincidence.'

'Will you take something? Tea? Coffee?' The invitation was grudging, but she knew what was expected when anyone came into her home.

'Tea would be lovely.' He thought her coffee would be dreadful, but she would make a good cup of tea. And suddenly tea, comforting and familiar, was exactly what he needed.

She nodded and disappeared into the kitchen. He heard the kettle being switched on and the rattle of crockery, tried to focus on that and the facts of the case, to squeeze out the other thoughts that were battling to come into his mind. Margaret Riddell returned with a tray – a teapot, two cups and saucers, a milk jug and a plate of home-made shortbread. Proving to the inspector that she knew how to behave, even if she'd ended up here, in a former council house. She poured his tea and waited for his questions, sharp eyes set like currants in a doughy bun, looking out at him.

'I understand that your son was friendly with Emma Shearer,' he said.

'I don't know who told you that.'

He didn't answer the implied question.

There was a silence, which eventually she filled. 'I think he took her out a few times. Then he saw through her.'

'What do you mean?'

'Magnie's a good man. He's had his problems in the past. You'll have checked and you'll know that he has a record. He got in with a bad crowd when he first started working in Lerwick and he couldn't control his temper. He had his own flat there and nobody to keep an eye on him. But he's changed, now that he's back in Deltaness. He works hard and he likes things simple. She messed with his head.'

'In what way?'

This time she was the one to avoid the question. 'It wasn't her fault. She'd had a bad time as a youngster. Her father died in prison and her mother was ill for most of her life. Emma was left to bring up her brothers. She had too much responsibility when she was a bairn. No wonder she decided she was going to look after number one, once she left home.'

'Are you saying she was selfish?' Perez asked.

Margaret Riddell thought for a moment. 'Maybe self-centred would be a better way of putting it.'

'I'm not sure what the difference is.'

'I thought her life was a kind of performance. She needed people to look at her and admire her. Like she was a star. Everything was a drama. Magnie couldn't deal with that. He likes to know where he is with folk. He's not one for games.' Margaret poured more tea and helped herself to another slice of shortbread.

'So, he was the one to end the relationship?'

'If there was a relationship. Magnie fell for her, and she liked the admiration. The flattery. He earns good money at the plant and he was always wasting his money on her, buying her daft presents. I'm not sure she really felt anything for him.' There was another pause. 'For anyone.'

'How did she get on with family she worked for?'

'Well enough, I suppose.' Margaret sniffed. 'They're wild, those children, allowed to do as they please. You'd think a doctor would know better. Emma could keep them under some sort of control, at least.'

'You'd have known Robert Moncrieff since he was a boy,' Perez said, 'if you grew up in Deltaness.'

'I'm a bit older than him, and his father didn't like him mixing with the local kids. We weren't good enough.'

None of her answers were straightforward. It was almost as if she was speaking in a sort of code that Perez was supposed to decipher for himself. 'I was at school with Robert,' he said, in an attempt to make a connection.

'He went south to university, and he only came back after his father died.' Another answer that carried a weight of meaning behind it. 'And then he had Belle with him. She was very glamorous. Not what we were used to at all. That caused a bit of a stir. I wasn't sure that she'd settle.'

'But she has done?'

'Yes.' Margaret sounded almost surprised, but at least it was a direct response.

'I might come back later and talk to Magnie when he's home from work.' Perez was wondering if there was some way of seeing Magnie away from this house and his mother's oppressive presence. 'Or maybe I'll catch him in Lerwick before he comes back.'

'He won't tell you anything different from me!'

'All the same, if he went out with Emma, he might know a little bit about her and anything will help. We haven't been able to track down any close friends.'

'She didn't really have women friends,' Margaret said, bitchy until the end. 'Maybe they saw through her. Maybe they realized that if you got through the style and the make-up, there was nothing there.'

He stood up and was out of his way through the door into the hall when he turned back, remembering the conversation he'd heard between Margaret and her sister at the Sunday teas. 'What do you make of the people who've moved onto Dennis Gear's land?'

The question surprised her. He caught a fleeting expression on her face that surprised *him*. Tenderness? Longing? It was gone before he could decide, but it had made her more human, more sympathetic. 'They seem alright,' she said. 'They've built a weird kind of place up there, and the lad's not right in the head. Not his fault, but I'm not sure he should be in the school with the normal kids.'

He thought of Helena Fleming, who'd had to put up with this bile since she'd moved to Shetland, and any sympathy he'd felt for Margaret Riddell disappeared. The islanders he knew were welcoming to strangers.

Then he remembered that Margaret's husband had left her for an incomer, and her son had gone off the rails for a while. She hadn't had it easy, either. He realized his response to her was shifting with every word she spoke, and thought that was nothing to do with the woman herself. His emotions were all over the place. He needed to focus again.

'You work in the bank in Lerwick?'

'I used to. It's too far to commute from here. It's all right for Magnie; he seems not to mind the drive and he works long shifts and earns good money. I'm at the Co-op in Brae now.' She frowned. He could see how Brae would be less exciting and the job less important. He thought she would probably miss the bustle of Lerwick and the chance to catch up with her friends. 'I'd hoped I might be thinking of retiring by now. My ex-husband is manager of the bank, where I used to work. Another reason for resigning. When we were together, I only worked to get out of the house. Now I need the money.' She blushed, suddenly embarrassed that she'd given away so much of herself. 'Is that everything?'

He nodded and left the house. Standing in the street, he saw that the curtains in the next-door house were being pulled aside again. A face stared out and he recognized Lottie, Margaret's sister. She realized that he'd seen her and quickly the face disappeared. He was left with an impression of sadness and of isolation.

Chapter Sixteen

Helena hoped that Jimmy Perez would still be there when she returned from taking the children to school. The situation that she was facing now terrified her. She'd thought she could cope with stress; it was what she'd always done. Now she felt as if her own sanity was unravelling and that her world was spinning out of control. The possibility that Daniel had had an affair with a woman less than half his age was far more distressing than the fact that the woman, the object of his desires, was dead. Because Helena was convinced that Daniel had been consumed with desire, that Emma Shearer had been the subject of his passion – infatuation – even if there'd been no physical relationship. Now she wondered if *she* had become infatuated too, with the scruffy, dark policeman who lived with a little girl in Ravenswick. As she walked back up the track to the house, she thought that if Perez was there, calm and understanding, everything would be well.

But when she approached the house she saw that the detective's car had not come back. Putting off an encounter with Daniel, she crossed the courtyard and walked down the path towards the barn. Crime-scene tape blocked her way and she was about to go into her studio, to lose herself in work, when a woman called out to her, 'Hello! Are you Helena?'

The voice was a woman's, but there was no other way to determine gender. She was dressed in a white suit, hood and mask. As if she were an alien, or as if the barn and its surroundings were radioactive, toxic.

'Just hang on.' She took off the mask and the hood, and Helena saw a long tangle of straw-coloured hair, a wide mouth, freckles. 'My name's Willow Reeves. I'm Senior Investigating Officer.'

Helena had thought Jimmy Perez was that, but decided it would be rude to say so. 'I was wondering if you'd all like some coffee.' She could hear men's voices in the barn, so she realized there must be at least two more of them.

'I'm not drinking coffee at the moment, but tea would be fab. And the two in there are caffeine addicts.' Willow smiled, but Helena thought she looked exhausted. What must it be like to spend your life working with other people's tragedies? 'We're nearly finished. The undertaker will be along to take away Miss Shearer's body soon, but there will be other intrusions, I'm afraid. Would you allow us to do a search of your house? If you invite us in it'll be quicker, save us the need for a warrant.' The detective's tone was conversational, almost apologetic. She might have been inviting herself to dinner. 'You might prefer to be out while we're doing that.'

'Could you get it done today? While the children are still at school? This has been upsetting enough for them.' Helena imagined how horrified Christopher would be if he had to see strangers inside the house, going through his things.

'I don't see why not. Vicki Hewitt, our crime-scene manager, has just landed in Sumburgh and she's on her way now. At least they can make a start today.'

'You think our house is a crime scene?'

'A young woman has been killed and her body was found on your property. We should have started looking last night, but Inspector Perez didn't want your son disturbed.' Another smile to soften the words. 'Besides, it's a nightmare getting our people into the islands. We wouldn't have been able to do much until the flights started this morning anyway.'

Helena found Daniel in the kitchen. They'd gone to bed together, but there'd been no real contact. They hadn't talked. He seemed to fall asleep immediately, but she suspected he was pretending, to avoid confrontation. She'd been restless, had drifted off for a couple of hours and then woken at dawn, suddenly, knowing she'd been in the middle of a nightmare but with no memory of the details.

'I've just spoken to the person in charge of the investigation. It's a woman. She flew in from Inverness this morning. She seemed kind enough, but you wouldn't want to stand in her way.' Helena switched on the kettle, wondered if she'd make do with instant coffee for the men in the byre, then thought she'd give them the real thing. Irrationally, she wanted them to like her.

'What happened to the bloke that was here last night?' Daniel's antipathy to the detective was obvious.

'Jimmy Perez? I don't know. I suppose there are leads they have to follow.' She reached into a cupboard for a teapot. 'They want to search the house. I asked them to do it now, while the kids are at school. I think they want us out of the way.'

'What do they think they're going to find here?' Daniel was angry now. She could feel the tension in him again, as she had when Perez had been interviewing them. Distant and icy. She'd always imagined depressed people as soft and weak, sitting in corners and crying all day; she hadn't expected these sudden outbursts of temper. Because she saw now that Daniel was depressed. He was so different from the man she'd married.

'I don't know! Evidence that Emma has been in the house. Fingerprints. They'll probably want to look at our phones and computers to see how much contact we've had with her.'

He was still, frozen.

'What will they find, Daniel? I'd rather you told me than I find out from them.'

'You know she's been in the house. I explained that she brought the Moncrieff children to play after school sometimes. What's suspicious in that?'

'Where in the house, Daniel? Will they find evidence that she's been in the bedroom? Our bedroom?' Helena wanted to scream recriminations at him: *After all I've done for you! I'm keeping this family together, while you wander round taking pretty pictures. You can't even load the dishwasher. And you fall for some woman hardly out of school, with no education, because she tells you a hard-luck story. And because she's got a nice bum.* Hearing in her head how petty and ridiculous she was being, knowing that she was blowing the small irritations of domestic life out of all proportion, but somehow not being able to stop them mattering.

'You don't understand,' he said. 'It wasn't like that.'

'Then tell me what it *was* like. We'll go out. Walk.

All the way up to the cafe at Henwick, and by the time we get back to pick up the kids I want to know everything. You know, I do want to understand.'

He nodded and walked away. She made coffee and tea and carried it outside, left it just outside the scene tape and shouted into the barn that it was there. Willow Reeves appeared from behind the house. Now she'd taken off the rest of the white suit. She had a mobile phone in her hand and it seemed she'd been making calls. She waved the phone at Helena. 'You've got good signal up here. I wasn't expecting it.'

'It comes and goes,' Helena said. 'Daniel and I are going out. We'll walk north to Henwick and be back in time to collect the children from school. The house is unlocked. Help yourself to more coffee and tea.'

'How old are the children?'

'Christopher's eleven and Ellie's seven.' Helena wondered why the detective was taking an interest in the kids. Why would she need these details? It felt like an intrusion.

'Enjoy your walk.' Willow Reeves turned away.

They headed up the hill behind the house. It was hard striding over heather and through bog and the slope was steep, so there was no chance to talk. Helena was glad of the exercise, the pull on her muscles and the sun on her face. She felt a quick moment of joy, which came close to gloating: *At least I'm alive.* Immediately afterwards there was survivor's guilt: *What right have I to feel this good, when a young woman's dead?*

Daniel spent more time on the hill and he was fitter than she was and she found herself struggling to keep up. She wondered if this was how he felt now, in comparison to her: a little inadequate and in her shadow. He'd always been the successful one, the winner of prizes. Since the house was completed, he'd taken a back seat. There'd be few projects as big as this in Shetland and he'd decided to try something new. Photography, or a book about the islands perhaps – about the art that it had inspired. She'd had the limelight, and she'd basked in it, hadn't she? The new opportunities, the photos with celebrities. No wonder he'd felt jealous and resentful. She'd probably have been the same. As she plodded after him, fighting for breath, she thought envy was the most destructive of emotions. It ate away at your guts and your brain and it stopped you thinking straight. Envy and jealousy.

At the top, they stopped. A huge pile of driftwood, empty fish boxes and pallets stood on the crest of the hill and close to the edge of the cliff, which was high and sheer here. They'd watched it grow over the previous weeks, brought there by tractor and quad bike from the other side where the slope was gentler. On midsummer's eve at midnight it would be lit, along with other beacons along the coast, a chain of light to mark the solstice. There would be a party. The children were already excited.

Daniel took off his jacket and spread it on the heather, so they could sit in comfort. They were forced to sit very close together. The house was spread below them, a child's toy from this distance, with plastic vehicles and plastic figures. There seemed to be more people, a lot of activity. Helena found it hard to believe that the scene below had anything to do with her. It no longer looked like their home. She couldn't remember the last time she and Daniel had been alone together away from the house.

'Was it a mistake?' she asked. 'Coming to Shetland?'

'No!' His response was immediate. 'Look at all this. I couldn't go back to the city.' There was a pause. 'We've made mistakes, though. And we've been unlucky. The old man killing himself on our property. We couldn't have done anything about that.'

Helena wondered about that. Perhaps they could have been kinder, invited Dennis Gear to see the house once it had been finished, made him feel he still had a place in it. They'd known his family had lived there for generations. He'd turned up once, some pretext about collecting tools from the byre. She'd been in the middle of cooking tea for the kids and she'd been waiting for an important phone call from the US. She hadn't been rude exactly, but she'd been impatient to see the old man go; she'd kept him on the doorstep while they'd been talking, not invited him in.

'Maybe we could buy in some childcare for the kids,' Daniel said. 'Not every night, but a couple of evenings a week and occasional weekends. So we have more time together.'

'A nanny like Emma? Someone young and beautiful.' The words came out before she had time to think about them, hard and spiteful.

He looked as if she'd hit him. 'I'm sorry. It was just a thought. To give us a bit of breathing time, so we can enjoy all this.'

'No, I'm sorry.' She reached out and took his hand, squeezed it. 'Tell me about her.'

Still holding her hand, he stood up and pulled her to her feet. 'Not here,' he said. 'Not in view of all that.'

He nodded down towards the house. 'Let's walk on for a bit.'

They crossed the back of the hill and walked down towards the long sweep of Suksetter, the pebble beach where Daniel spent hours, watching otters. He'd become entranced by them. She supposed that he wanted to show her the animals, but instead of heading for the shore he took her a little way inland. The land here was very low, separated from the shore by dunes and irregular fields where sheep grazed; there was a series of freshwater lochans, with iris and marsh marigolds at the fringes, everywhere the call of lapwings and oystercatchers. A breeze blew the flowers and nothing seemed fixed. Everything was moving: feather, reed, water. Helena felt as if she'd stepped into an Impressionist painting of blurred lines and splashes of colour. Hesti, with its police officers and forensic scientists, could have been on a different planet.

Someone had built a basic bench, just a plank on a couple of big flat stones, close to the largest loch. Scratched into the wood was Dennis Gear's name. Then 'RIP' and the years of his birth and his death. So, after all, Helena thought, there was no escape.

'I only saw it when I came here a couple of weeks ago,' Daniel said. 'It's a memorial to him. Sometimes there are flowers. Always fresh.'

They looked down – both of them, it seemed, unwilling to sit on the name etched into the wood. Daniel took off his jacket again and they rested on that, looking out at the water. Daniel pulled a couple of bars of chocolate from his jacket pocket and offered one to her.

'We should tell the police about this,' Helena said.

'It's probably not important, but they should know that someone's trying to keep his memory alive.'

'I don't know. I want as little to do with them as possible.' His face was set, stubborn.

'This is a murder inquiry, Daniel. And at the very least it might draw attention away from us for a while.'

It occurred to her then that *that* was what he was trying to do, by bringing her to the loch and showing her the tribute to Dennis Gear. He was trying to distract her, to stop her asking awkward questions about Emma Shearer.

'Whoever made it must be fit! It's quite a walk from the end of our track.'

Daniel shook his head. 'You can drive in from Henwick and park just behind the dunes. Most people who come to look for the otters do that.'

'Did you ever bring Emma here?' She realized that she was shouting, but she was worried the words would get blown away by the breeze.

He was still looking out over the loch, following the path of a group of waders flying low over the water.

'Look at me, Daniel. I want to understand.'

He turned slowly towards her.

'I mean, I really can't quite see it. This isn't really the place for kitten heels and a dirndl skirt.' Because humour had always held them together and although this was pretty pathetic, it was all she could manage. 'Or did Emma have designer wellies?'

He gave a quick, sharp smile and she saw that at least they were communicating. 'I brought her in the car. She could manage the path up from the dunes.'

'Why here?'

'Because it's private,' he said. 'Nobody comes much midweek.'

'Were you having an affair? Is that what you're telling me?' Helena felt quite calm now, because at least they were talking. Daniel was facing her and he'd lost that icy, frozen stare that shut her out completely.

'No!' Now he was the person shouting. 'No.' A pause and then came the confession. The admission of betrayal. 'I wanted to, but she wouldn't. We kissed a couple of times. Nothing more.'

'So, she was a prick-tease?' Helena wanted to hurt him. 'She took the adoration and the car rides into the country, but she gave nothing back.'

'I don't think she could.' He stood up suddenly.

She followed him and they began to walk back towards the shore. Suddenly she realized that she was starving. She couldn't remember the last time she'd eaten properly, and if they didn't get to the cafe at Henwick for lunch soon, they wouldn't get back to pick up the kids. 'What do you mean?'

'Emma was damaged. She wouldn't talk about it much. She said she didn't deserve affection.'

Helena was tempted to mock him. *And you believed her? The gallant Daniel Fleming rode up on his charger to make everything better.* But she didn't mock, because that was what had drawn her to Daniel. The fact that he was gallant and honourable, in an old-fashioned way, as well as being very, very sexy.

'She didn't make any demands,' he said suddenly. 'She didn't want anything from me. Just my company.'

They came to the path that ran along the shore. Helena could see the cafe, a battered Portakabin, at the end of the bay, and was distracted for a moment by the thought of sausage, egg and chips with lots of ketchup and a hunk of home-made bread.

'She sounds quite a screwed-up kid.' Helena liked the fact that she could be patronizing about Emma. She thought she'd almost stopped hating her. And she wasn't here any more, was she? She couldn't fuck up their lives when she was dead. Their boots crunched on the shingle. Daniel didn't say anything, but he didn't pull away from her. She took his hand. 'What will the police find on your phone and computer?'

'Emails and texts.' Another pause. 'Lots of emails and texts. For a while I was obsessed with her.'

'What will they say, these emails and texts?'

He took a moment to reply. She caught all the background sounds: waves breaking gently, wading birds calling, sheep. 'That I loved her. That I would struggle to live without her.'

She stopped in her tracks. It was as if she'd never move again. Had Daniel ever said things like that to her? Not for years. Not since the children had arrived and they'd had more to think about than their own pleasure and their own feelings. He must have sensed her anger.

'It was a sort of illness, Helly.' His pet name for her. She hadn't heard that for years, either. 'I can see that now. I thought she could save me.'

But I've been the one to save you! Always! Since we were students together, I was the one who kept you sane. I protected you from the stress and the worry, all the domestic crap. Until we moved here and I got a life of my own.

'How did it end?' She stopped and faced him. 'It *did* end?'

'Yes,' he said bleakly. 'It did end.'

'When?'

'About three weeks ago.' She thought he'd probably be able to give the exact date if she pushed him. The exact time. 'I met Emma at school and asked if she wanted to bring the kids back to play. She said it wouldn't be a good idea. People were already talking. "Don't get in touch again, Danny." That's what she called me. "You've been lovely, but it'd be a bit weird if we kept on seeing each other. It's about time I started mixing with boys of my own age." That was the last time we had any sort of conversation.' He paused. 'It was as if she wanted to hurt me.'

'And that was the night the kids found you crying in the bedroom.'

'Yes,' he said. 'I thought my world had come to an end.'

'But it hadn't. You survived. And we'll survive this.' Helena thought she was doing what she always did in a crisis. She was taking charge. Reassuring. But this time she wasn't sure she meant any of it. Daniel's world might not have come to an end, but perhaps hers had.

He was walking on ahead of her towards the cafe. He must have realized that she wasn't following, because he stopped and turned to face her. He smiled. 'You are an amazing woman.' Then: 'What do you think I should do now?'

In her cold, detached mood, she wondered if the flattery was premeditated, just a way of getting her back onside, but the habit of taking control was too strong for her to question it now. 'We'll have lunch. A very large lunch. Then we'll walk back. I'll go to school and collect the kids, and you'll ask to speak to the detective in charge and you'll tell her everything.'

Daniel nodded, compliant, waited until she'd caught up with him and put his arm around her shoulder. She tried not to shrug him away.

Standing in the playground, squinting against the bright sunlight, Helena was aware that the waiting parents were watching, but she wasn't frightened. There was no panic. Daniel had gone into the house to find Willow Reeves. The body of the woman had been taken away. Life had been as bad as it could get, but whatever happened now, she would survive it. She was back in control.

Chapter Seventeen

Jimmy Perez left the row of concrete houses where Margaret Riddell and her sister lived and stood looking out at the sea for a moment. He tried to concentrate on the case and plan his next move, but thoughts of Willow intruded. Willow, pale and hurt. Willow, whose decision to have a child would force him to make uncomfortable choices, would push him to a place he wasn't ready to be. But, he told himself, he didn't have to make those choices yet. Now he had an investigation to run and a murder to solve. He was tempted to leave Deltaness altogether and put some physical distance between Willow and him. He had an excuse. He could drive to Lerwick and pull Magnie Riddell out of work at the power plant. He could talk to him there about his relationship with Emma Shearer.

Then he thought that wouldn't be fair. If he asked to see Riddell at work, the rumours would start. Folk would see Riddell as a suspect, and before long he'd be down as a killer. Even if they found another culprit, there'd still be a taint of guilt around him. Perez thought he could wait and see the man at home. Instead he picked up his car at the community shop and drove south a little way to Ness House. He'd been there once before. It had been a birthday party. Robert

Moncrieff would have been twelve or thirteen and all the boys in their class had been invited. Perez wasn't sure why he'd been included, because he'd been a year or two younger than the others. Perhaps because the woman in charge of his boarding house had felt sorry for him and pulled some strings.

It had been summer and Robert's father had organized a cricket match on the lawn behind the house. Perez had never played before, had been out first ball and had dropped a catch. The whole afternoon had been as alien as if he'd been shipped to a foreign country. For a while he'd sat on the grass and talked to Robert's mother, who seemed frail and insubstantial, very English in a dress and a straw hat. For tea, there'd been little sandwiches that disappeared in a mouthful, and shop-bought cakes.

Now Perez drove through the trees and parked in front of the house. He saw that Emma's car had been taken away. Sandy must have organized that. He rang the bell, not really expecting an answer, but Belle opened the door. She was wearing leggings and a long black top. Her hair was tied back in a red-and-orange silk scarf.

'Jimmy, come in. Are you alright in the kitchen? Sorry about the mess. It was such a shock last night and I'm afraid we polished off a couple of bottles of wine between us, once we got the kids to bed.' Hardly pausing between sentences.

He followed her into the large, rather dark kitchen. Automatically she pushed the kettle onto the hot plate of the Aga, then started to clear plates and pile them into the sink. 'I'll stick them into the dishwasher later.' A pause. 'Since all the kids started school and Emma had more time during the day, she did a lot of the housework stuff. We've been spoilt.' She turned to him. 'I was about to have some lunch. Will you join me?'

'If it's not too much trouble.'

'I suppose you've got lots of questions. I'm not sure how much I'll be able to help. Emma was a very private person. Self-contained. Even though she was so young when she first arrived, she never confided in me. I was never any kind of mother substitute.' Still, it seemed, Belle couldn't stop talking. Perez wondered if she was always like that, or if his presence was making her nervous.

She made coffee, rinsed a mug under the hot tap and poured it out for him, then put a couple of plates, a loaf, oatcakes and a plate of cheese on the table. 'Help yourself. I expect you've had an early start. You must be starving.' She cut several slices of bread and pushed the board towards him, then, apparently unable to sit still, she jumped up to fetch butter and a bowl of tomatoes from the fridge.

'Tell me about Emma,' he said, once she'd taken her seat again. 'She's lived in your house for seven years. Even if she was a very private person, you must have got to know her very well.'

'She fitted in extremely well,' Belle said. 'Right from the beginning. I'm not sure what I expected of a seventeen-year-old – that she'd be in Lerwick every weekend partying, or that she'd bring unsuitable boys back into the house – but she seemed very steady, very mature. In lots of ways she was more grown-up than we were. We were the ones with a hangover on a Saturday morning while she was up taking care of the children.'

'She was good with the bairns?' Perez was distracted for a moment after asking the question. He supposed that Willow would need to organize some form of childcare because, surely, she was planning to go back to work. How did that come about? How would you be sure that you'd found the right person? He hoped Willow would check references; she had a tendency to be impulsive.

'Yes, she was. Emma could do the consistent thing that parents find so hard, because we're emotionally involved. If she said no, she meant it, and they soon learned that. So they didn't play her up, whereas they'd take no notice at all of me.' Belle gave a little laugh. 'The monsters.'

'Wasn't that hard for you?'

'Not at all. They didn't *love* her, you see. That would have been difficult, but there was no competition. I'm not even sure they liked her very much. Occasionally they'd come and moan about Emma to us. That she was too strict, that they were too old to need her now, but as I said, she'd made herself pretty well indispensable and we wouldn't have considered getting rid of her, at least until Kate moved on to the high school.'

'How did she get on with . . .' Perez tried to remember the conversation he'd had with Robert at the Sunday teas about his oldest daughter's exams. 'Martha? She must think of herself as almost adult now. There must have been some friction between her and Emma.'

Belle was trying to spread butter straight from the fridge onto her bread and paused, knife in the air. 'It could get a bit tempestuous occasionally, but I think it had settled down lately. They'd even had a couple of girly nights out to the cinema at Mareel.' She gave up on the butter and cut herself a lump of cheese. 'To be honest, Jimmy, I've been so busy lately working with Helena Fleming that I've hardly been here to see what's been going on.'

'Had you noticed any change in Emma recently?'

'No. But really, Jimmy, I'm not sure that we would have noticed. I'm afraid that we took her for granted. She was reliable, quiet, always there. You know.'

Perez thought that wasn't so different from the time when this was the laird's house, and the servants who made life bearable for the master and his wife went unnoticed and unrecognized.

'She was going out with Magnie Riddell, I understand.'

'Yeah, I think they hung out together for a while. There aren't that many young people in Deltaness. He came to call for her a few times to take her into Lerwick. All dressed up in his Sunday best. It was rather sweet.'

'But not serious, you think?' Perez felt that Emma was sliding away from him. He couldn't picture her other than as a corpse, lifeless and without personality.

'I think *Magnie* was serious. It was impossible to tell with Emma. She never gave anything away. She was inscrutable. All we saw was the retro style, the Fifties dresses and the make-up. That defined her for everyone.'

'What about girlfriends? Lasses she might have confided in?' Perez hoped there was someone. He hated to imagine Emma, alone in her room at the top of this house. He wanted to picture her laughing with her mates, texting, sharing stupid photos on Facebook.

'I'm not sure. She probably had friends in Orkney – there was one girl who came to stay. But there was nobody close in Shetland. I can't think of anyone she brought back to the house.' Belle paused. 'It must have been hard, coming to a small community at the age that she did. The kids would all have been to school together; friendships would have been formed. Emma must have felt like an outsider. She was from Orkney, another islander, but that wouldn't have mattered. It would still feel as if she'd come from the other side of the world.' There was another silence before Belle continued, 'Besides, Emma never made any effort to fit in. I had the impression that she didn't really need anyone. She was like the animal in the Kipling story: she was the cat that walked alone.'

Perez thought Emma had done what she'd needed to, in order to survive. She'd come from a troubled home to a place where she'd known nobody. He thought of her now as a cat, slinky and elegant, going through life in her own way and on her own terms, choosing companionship carefully, keeping her distance. But the self-reliance hadn't been able to protect her in the end. She'd been the cat who walked alone, and it seemed she'd died without friends too.

'As I said, there was a lass from Orkney who came to stay once,' Belle said. 'Emma asked if it was OK. She was lovely and they seemed very close. I offered her the spare room, but she slept on a mattress in Emma's room in the end.'

'Do you remember her name?'

'Claire,' Belle said. She got to her feet to fetch the

coffee pot from the Aga, waved it at Perez, who nodded. 'Can't remember her second name, but they'd been to school together in Kirkwall, so I'm sure you'll be able to track her down. She had curly red hair, the kids adored her and she laughed a lot. Robert and I talked about that afterwards. About how we'd never really seen Emma relax until Claire was with her.'

'When did you last see Emma?' Perez asked. 'I know you heard her television on Saturday night, but when did you last see her?'

'During supper on Saturday. It was a bit of a bonkers meal. Robert was out with some NHS colleagues in town and I was frantic. I'd been baking all afternoon for the teas, and trying to catch up on some work for Helena too. One eye on the laptop for emails, and the other on the oven for scones. For supper, I just dug a few burgers out of the freezer and Emma made a salad. The kids were hyper – this time of year, when the nights get lighter, they seem to be perpetually wound up. Emma managed to calm them down a bit, but Sam and Kate were still giggly, as if they had some mischief planned. Martha hardly said anything, but that's how she is at the moment. Moody.'

'And what happened after you'd eaten?'

'Emma took the little ones up for a bath and got them ready for bed. Martha slunk up to her room. Charlie was out with a mate and didn't come back until later.'

'But you didn't see Emma again?'

Belle thought carefully about that. Perez thought she was running through the events of the evening in her head. 'No, I didn't see her. She shouted down the stairs to say that Katie and Sam were in bed and ready for a story. If I'm at home I always like to read to them before they go to sleep. Then she said that if I didn't need her for anything else, she'd head up to the attic. That's usually the deal. When the little ones are in bed, the time's her own.'

'What time would that have been?'

'About eight-thirty. A bit later perhaps. Robert got home at ten and we were in bed by eleven.'

Perez imagined Emma retreating to her room, glad to escape at last the messy house and the manic children. It would have been peaceful there. Nothing on that Saturday seemed to have been different from any other. So what had happened to make things change, to persuade someone that the young woman would have to die? He got to his feet. 'Thanks for the lunch.'

'I'm sorry,' Belle said. 'I haven't been very helpful, have I?'

'You've painted a picture of a very private person. A bit austere, perhaps.'

'Have I?' She sounded surprised. 'Perhaps I have. And that sums her up, actually. Emma was very private and a bit austere.'

Perez was walking from the house when his phone rang. He looked at it, wondering if it might be Willow, with more explanations, more excuses. Half-hoping that it might be, because a call from her would always excite him. And because he knew that he'd overreacted. At some point they would need to talk. But it was Sandy.

'Where are you?'

'Still in Deltaness,' Perez said. 'I've just been talking to Belle Moncrieff at Ness House.'

'You might want to come back to the Flemings' place.' Sandy paused and Perez could hear muttered voices behind him. 'We've found Emma's handbag.'

Chapter Eighteen

Willow was sitting outside Hesti, her face turned to the sun. She was drinking tea and nibbling the biscuits Sandy had brought up from the community shop, stealing a few moments to herself. She was thinking about Jimmy Perez. There was nothing unusual about that; she often found herself thinking about Jimmy Perez. Today, though, was rather different. She was contemplating a life without him. She was nurturing the spark of defiance that she'd need to carry her through the investigation with the man as a colleague. If Perez couldn't accept their child, let him stay in his house in Ravenswick, let him keep it as a shrine to his lost love. Let him wallow in guilt and self-pity. Willow was a strong and independent woman and she would manage without him. If he found it impossible to move on from Fran's death, she would be better off on her own.

She was still sitting there, this time trying to untangle the strands of the case – two hangings: one suicide and one murder; two educated families, with no motive for killing the woman who'd had dealings with their children – when Daniel Fleming found her.

Willow thought he looked very much like his son. She'd seen photographs of Christopher and Ellie all over the house, and Daniel and the boy had the same dark good looks, the same rather haughty stare that gave them an aura of arrogant self-belief.

'I need to talk to you,' Fleming said. It came across as a demand. There was no sign of Helena, who must be doing the afternoon school run. Willow thought he must have come to her straight from the walk. He looked hot and a little dishevelled.

'Is there somewhere we can use to chat? My colleagues are still in the house and we might be disturbed out here.' If she had to act the part of senior detective, Willow thought she'd struggle, sitting here on the grass.

'We could go to Helena's studio.'

She got to her feet, brushing biscuit crumbs from her sweater. It had never bothered her before that she might seem unprofessional, but now she felt she had to prove herself. She would show Perez that she could work well as a pregnant woman, without his support.

The studio faced onto the courtyard and had been converted from a smaller outhouse. The byre was to the east of it, closer to the shore. If a killer had dragged Emma Shearer's body to the barn on the afternoon that it had been found, surely Helena would have heard them passing, even if she hadn't seen them. Willow made a mental note of that. There was no spectacular view from here, but the huge windows in the roof let in light, a vision of clouds as thin as smoke against a blue sky. It contained a drawing board on an easel, a big pale-wood desk with a sophisticated computer. On the walls, photos of people Willow vaguely recognized wearing Fleming creations. She took the seat by Helena's desk and Daniel sat beside her, as if he were the client.

'What is it that you want to tell me?' He looked so serious, so intense, that she half-expected a confession. She wondered if they should be doing this in the police station, where the conversation could be recorded. She saw the possibility of her escape. If Daniel Fleming admitted to the murder of Emma Shearer, she could fly home and get on with her life and let Jimmy Perez get on with his.

'I was obsessed with Emma Shearer. You'll see that from my phone calls and emails.' A pause. 'I thought I was in love with her.'

'Are you saying that you stalked her? Made her life uncomfortable?'

'No! No, I wouldn't have done that.' He seemed shocked by the suggestion. 'When she asked me to stop seeing her – stop contacting her – I did.' He paused. 'And in the beginning, she responded to me. I thought the relationship was reciprocal. I never put any pressure on her.'

Oh yeah, even though she was less than half your age, you're married with two kids, going through some kind of mid-life crisis and she was a damaged young woman.

'When did this start?' Willow kept her voice gentle, sympathetic even.

'Soon after we moved here. Helena's business suddenly took off, big-style. Something to do with the romance of living in the islands adding to her image, perhaps. And I was left looking after the kids, doing the boring stuff. It wasn't what I was used to. After the excitement of building the house and the move, hardly sleeping, living and breathing the project, everything seemed very flat, meaningless. Maybe I had some sort of breakdown.'

Or maybe you just found out how tough it is to do the domestic stuff, the boring grown-up chores that keep things going.

'And that was about a year ago?'

'Less than that. We moved in at the end of last summer.'

So, Willow thought, Emma would have been twenty-three, a lot younger than Fleming, but still an adult. A relationship with her might have been foolish, but not a crime. 'Tell me about it. About her.'

He sat with his hands on his knees. 'Now, I think I turned her into my dream woman. Young, stylish, undemanding. I needed someone to be excited about.' He looked up and for the first time he smiled. 'Pathetic, huh? Classic mid-life-crisis stuff. I thought Emma might make me feel alive again.'

Willow thought he was hoping for understanding – a rebuttal to the statement that he was pathetic – but she couldn't give that. 'And what did she make of you?'

'Her family was troubled. She grew up with domestic violence, later with a father in prison and a mother who couldn't cope. She lived in Orkney and had only been to the Scottish mainland a couple of times. I don't know. Perhaps I represented excitement for her too. Broader horizons. I lent her books about art and architecture, occasionally we watched a film while the kids were here playing. I liked that, playing her teacher.'

'Her guru?'

Willow had grown up in a commune and she understood the power of a charismatic leader and how easy it was to give up responsibility to someone who claimed to have all the answers.

Daniel looked at her. Willow could tell he was wondering if she was mocking him. In the end, he ignored the comment. 'She did have real style, you know. She made all her own clothes, not using bought patterns, but her own designs. I thought she was wasted working for the Moncrieffs, dealing with their brats and cleaning up their mess. I thought she should go to art school.'

'Was that what Emma wanted?'

'I think she liked the idea of it, but she lacked the confidence.'

Willow considered that. She'd hoped Daniel Fleming would bring Emma Shearer to life for her, but the young woman seemed even more enigmatic. It still felt as if Emma had no personality or character of her own. She became what other people wanted her to be; she reflected back their dreams and desires. Did that indicate a lack of confidence? Perhaps. Or someone who was supremely manipulative.

'Did you have a physical relationship?'

'No,' he said. 'It wasn't what she wanted.' He paused. 'It was a kind of intense friendship. Passionate, but we never made love.'

'Idealized?' Willow thought the act itself would probably have disappointed. Nothing could live up to his expectations.

'I suppose so. I suppose I idealized her. It didn't seem like that at the time.'

Willow heard footsteps on gravel. They'd brought in all available officers in Shetland to help with the search of the house and it seemed they were moving outside. They trooped past the window.

Daniel appeared not to notice them and he was speaking again. 'It seems a bit ridiculous now. A kind of madness. I have everything I need here – a wife who loves and understands me, two children, a beautiful home. Why would I consider putting all that at risk for a fantasy? But at the time Emma seemed the most real, the truest thing in my life. I would have been prepared to give up everything for her.'

'Did you kill her? Because she refused to be a part of that fantasy?'

'No,' he said. His voice was calm. 'I was mad for a while, but I was never that crazy. And the infatuation had passed by the time she died. Things were starting to settle down, to get back to normal. I could see a future for myself again. Most of the locals in Deltaness dislike the house that we've built here. They would rather we'd put up a Scandinavian kit-building, or just left Dennis Gear's house as it was. But some Shetlanders love it. I've had enquiries and I'm thinking of setting up my own practice again. Nothing too stressful. One design at a time – bespoke buildings for people who appreciate what I'm trying to do. I haven't spoken to Helena about it yet, but it's been in my mind for a while, and I think she'll support me.' He looked up and there was another smile. 'Perhaps we can even think about employing someone to help with the children. But it won't be a young woman like Emma. I won't be losing my mind again.'

'Did your wife know about the relationship?'

'No!' he said, shocked. 'No! I only told her this morning.'

'And Emma wouldn't have said anything to Helena?' Willow imagined the younger woman dropping hints, gloating, enjoying the power she had over the man. How would a wife react to that?

'No!' Daniel said again, but this time he sounded less certain.

'Do you have any idea who might have wanted her dead?'

There was a moment of silence, filled, as always here, by the sound of gulls and sheep.

'I didn't know much about her life away from me,' Daniel said. 'She talked occasionally about work – how the children could be difficult. Belle and Robert weren't very helpful. They spoilt the kids and then got annoyed when they were demanding and disobedient. But Emma wouldn't leave. I don't know what was keeping her in Shetland. At the beginning, I was deluded and persuaded myself that *I* was the reason she stayed, but I see now that it can't have been that. She'd been living there for years before I became a part of her life.'

'Another man?'

'Perhaps. When she broke off all contact with me, she said something about needing to find friends of her own age.'

Willow thought back to the conversation she'd had with Perez in the car about the case. 'I understand she was seeing someone called Riddell.'

'Magnie Riddell. Yes, I'd heard that rumour too. I was the person who gave his name to the inspector. The gossip in this place spreads like wild fire.'

'Do you know him?' Willow imagined the gossip there'd be when Shetlanders discovered that she was pregnant. Would they consider her a scarlet woman, that she'd led Jimmy Perez on, so she could have a child before she was too old? *And is that what I've done? Maybe, subconsciously.*

'Not well,' Daniel said. 'I've met him a few times at village dos. His mother and his aunt live here too. I know *of* him. I've heard the talk.'

'And what are people saying about him?'

'That he went a bit wild when his parents split up. His mother had ambitions for him. College, a job with the council. That wasn't what Magnie wanted. He moved away from home and got a flat of his own in Lerwick. He was on drugs, apparently. He couldn't hold down a job. There was a fight in a bar. He appeared in court and got put on some sort of community-service order. One of the conditions was that he move out of town and stay with his mother.'

So, he was someone else who needed saving. Emma seemed to go for that kind of man. What did that say about her?

'He's a very good-looking lad,' Daniel said. 'I can understand why all the girls are after him.'

Willow had been scribbling notes throughout the conversation and now she put down her pen. There was something about Daniel Fleming that she found smug and self-centred, and in her present mood she thought she'd spent enough time with him. She needed time to assess his relationship with the victim, and she wanted to re-join her team to see what they'd found in their search of the house.

'There's something else,' Daniel said. 'It's probably not important.

'Yes?' Willow tried to contain her impatience.

'Someone's made a bench by the loch of Suksetter on the other side of the hill. It's a memorial to Dennis Gear. At least his name is carved into it, and I've seen fresh flowers there. If you think the two deaths are linked in some way – because of the hanging and the anonymous drawings – we wondered if it might be significant.'

Willow scribbled another note and stood up. There was the sound of footsteps on gravel again. This time they were made by one person running. A moment later, Sandy Wilson knocked at the door and threw it open, tried and failed not to sound excited. 'Could I have a word, Boss?'

'Just a minute, Sandy. We're nearly finished here.' She shook Daniel's hand and went outside with him. She watched him go back to the house, his creation. Looking down into the valley, she saw Perez's car making its way up the track, and far in the distance three figures walking along the shore from Deltaness. They must be Helena and her children on their way back from school.

It occurred to her that from this vantage point she could see everything that went on in the community, even as far as the trees that surrounded the big house where Belle and Robert Moncrieff lived. It would be a great place for a gossip to live. And yet, of all the people who lived in Deltaness, the Flemings probably didn't care what their neighbours were up to. They were used to an anonymous life in the city. In her jaundiced mood, she thought Daniel Fleming probably didn't care about anything but himself.

'What have you got for me, Sandy?' Turning away,

so she wasn't watching the progress of Perez's car up the track.

'I think it's the dead woman's handbag. We haven't touched it, of course, but it would be a bit of a coincidence if it belonged to anyone else.'

'And you let Jimmy know? I see he's on his way.'

'Yeah, you were tied up with Fleming and I thought . . .'

'You were quite right, Sandy, it could be important.' *And besides, Perez will always be the person you turn to first.* 'So where did you find it?'

'There's a building at the bottom of the field, close to the shore. It was in there.'

Willow followed Sandy round the house. This part of the garden, sloping away from the house towards the coast, was clearly the realm of the children. The grass had been roughly cut and hardy bushes had once been planted along the boundary wall to provide a windbreak, but there had been no attempt to grow flowers or vegetables. A wooden climbing frame had been built and a trampoline had been tethered to the ground with ropes and large rocks to stop it blowing away. Beyond the wall, a field uneven with cotton-grass and bog fell away to the coast. A few sheep grazed there. A stile had been built over the wall and the grass was flattened into a footpath on the other side.

'This is all Hesti land,' Sandy said, 'but when Gear stopped crofting, he let it out for grazing. The arrangement still stands.' He was already on his way down the footpath, but Willow stopped at the top of the stile to look down at the sea. This was the very north of the long, shallow bay that stretched along the settlement of Deltaness. The hill at the back of the Flemings' house curved into a headland that provided some shelter for this part of the shore. There were high, sheer cliffs and, even from here, she could hear the seabirds calling.

The path took them to another wall and another stile, this one leading onto a patch of wind-blown grass. There was no shingle bank here to separate land from sea, but a flat pebble beach, where a rough jetty had been built. A pile of lobster pots stood on the grass.

'Dennis Gear kept a boat here,' Sandy said, 'but he sold it when things got tough. He couldn't have got much for it.'

Willow remembered that Sandy had been called out to Gear's suicide. On the grass beside the lobster pots a shed had been built. It had stone walls and an upturned yoal for the roof. That took Willow back to her first investigation in Shetland: a traditionally built boat, known in the islands as a yoal, had been found drifting in Aith marina with a dead man inside. This one would never have stayed afloat. Willow could see how the planks were warped and gapped. It had been covered with tar now, to make the building weatherproof. There was one window, dusty and covered with cobwebs, and a plank door.

Willow pulled on a scene-suit. Vicki Hewitt was inside, but she moved away to let them in. 'I could do with a break and some fresh air.' Her voice was strange through the mask. 'There *are* fingerprints in the place, though. A number of different individuals. And yeah, I know. We'll get them checked as soon as we can.'

Inside, the building smelled of wood, tar and

damp. The floor was made of beaten earth. On one wall there was a shelf with tins of nails and screws, fish hooks and coils of rope.

'Could the rope that was used to string up Emma have come from here?' But Willow had already turned away from the wall with the shelves, her attention caught by the rest of the space. Here the floor was covered by a rug. There was a low, long sofa made from a row of fish boxes, the seat and the back formed by cushions with red-velvet covers. A larger crate was turned into a coffee table and on it stood a candle stuck with wax onto a saucer. The place had the feel of a child's den, except that this had obviously been used by adults. A couple of empty wine bottles stood in one corner. In pride of place on the table, next to the candle, was the handbag.

Willow could see why Sandy had thought it might belong to Emma. It was rather glamorous, in an expensive, understated way. Not Helena's style at all, and certainly not something they might have picked up in a charity shop for Ellie to play with. This was shiny patent leather, black and sleek.

Willow pulled her head back and straightened. 'Let's let Vicki get on with things, shall we? When she's done, we'll have a look inside the bag and see what it can tell us about the mysterious Emma.'

Walking back towards the house, past the children's playthings, she half-expected to see the dark figure of Jimmy Perez loping over the grass towards her. After all, his car had been on the track when they set off towards the jetty. But there was no sign of Perez. Instead she noticed a movement in an upstairs window and saw Daniel Fleming staring down at them.

Chapter Nineteen

Magnie worked the early shift at the waste-to-power plant. He watched the giant claw lift household rubbish into the furnace, keeping an eye on the instruments that kept the system running, to provide hot water for half of Lerwick, the schools and the hospital. But he worked like a robot, ignoring the banter and noise all around him. He thought this was a job you could do in your sleep, once you got used to the smell. At clocking-off time, he got his stuff from his locker and hung about until everyone else had gone. He didn't want to answer his colleagues' questions about the murder in Deltaness. They didn't know of his connection with Emma, but they were curious. It had been the subject of gossip during the breaks.

'You live there, don't you, Magnie? Give us the low-down. What was she like? Did she kill herself, like Dennis Gear?'

For the first time since he'd moved back to live with his mother, Magnie felt the need for something to take the edge off his pain. He was tempted to go into town and find one of his old pals. They'd hole up in the Thule bar and drink themselves stupid, then go back to a room somewhere and he'd smoke weed until he could dream that nothing mattered. That Emma had not mattered. But the robot in him led him to his van, made him start the engine and begin the drive home. That took less thought and less effort than making his way into Lerwick and tracking down a friend. He'd been awake for most of the night and felt edgy, sandy-eyed through lack of sleep and too much caffeine at work.

Coming into Deltaness, he arrived at Ness House. He couldn't face his mother just yet and pulled the van into a lay-by opposite the entrance to the garden. The trees blocked his view of the ground floor, but he could see the windows of Emma's room in the roof above the branches and he tried to conjure up the only time he'd been there. He'd re-created the scene in his head many times, embellishing it, adding touches from the porn he watched when his mother was out of the house, turning the memory into an everyman fantasy. Now, he thought the memory was spoilt, had perhaps been spoilt before the picture of her body swinging from the beam in the Flemings' byre had been branded into his imagination. It had been tainted by another image, that of Emma's face lit by the flames of the bonfire as she watched Christopher Fleming, his hands over his ears, his eyes shut, while the crowd yelled at him.

Chapter Twenty

The team sat around the desk in Helena's studio. Perez had asked the designer's permission to use it as a base while they were working at the house. He'd expected some resistance; this was her place of work and she had a living to earn. But she'd been relaxed about the idea: 'Of course, Jimmy. Anything to help get this sorted out quickly.' The woman had seemed stronger, more confident. Standing at the top of the track, Perez had watched her walk back from school with her children. She'd placed herself between them, their school bags over her shoulder, so she could hold each of their hands. She was swinging their arms in some sort of game. As they got closer he could tell that they were all laughing.

Now the handbag stood in the middle of the desk. Helena had confirmed that it didn't belong to her or to Ellie, though she had recognized the designer's name.

'Very flash,' she'd said. 'That wouldn't have come cheap.'

'Do you think Daniel might have bought it for Emma?' The question had come from Willow.

Helena had frowned for a moment. 'No. That wouldn't have been his style at all.'

Perez hadn't been sure if she'd meant the bag or the gesture.

James Grieve had gone to Lerwick to catch the ferry back to Aberdeen. The same ferry that was taking Emma south, so that the pathologist could carry out a post-mortem. Vicki Hewitt, the CSI, was still working in the shed by the shore. Perez had gone to see it for himself. Christopher had tried to follow him across the field, suddenly full of questions, not about Emma and the murder but about Vicki and what she might be doing there, about fingerprints and DNA.

'Mum says she's a CSI. Is that right?'

Perez had sent him home. Willow had described the place as a love nest: 'I bet Emma and Daniel met there. He didn't tell us anything about *that*.' It didn't seem right that the boy should see inside, even if Vicki had finished her work.

Now, there were only the three of them, the old team. Sandy, Willow and Perez. Sandy must have sensed the tension between his senior officers because he was awkward, talking too much. He'd checked out Magnie Riddell's record and spoken to the officer supervising the order.

'I remember the case now, don't you, Jimmy? One of those lads who just seems to lose his way in the last few years of school. Bored and not academic. And at the same time his parents were going through a very public separation. They were a bit of a laughing stock. His father was something high up in the kirk and fell for that Latvian lass working at the Kveldsro Hotel. Margaret must have been mortified. They had to sell their grand house in Voe and she moved back to Deltaness. Everyone was talking about it behind their backs. Enjoying the story, because they'd both been a bit pompous. But the lad must have hated it.'

'I was planning to talk to him this evening,' Perez said. 'I'd like you to be there, Sandy. It sounds as if you've got the background covered. Willow can take your car back to Lerwick and I'll give you a lift home.'

Willow shot Perez a look, but he turned away and reached out to open the bag. He was wearing gloves, but he could feel the quality of the workmanship through their thin skin.

'How could Emma have afforded that?' Willow said. 'I assume she didn't get paid much, as a mother's help.'

'Margaret Riddell said Magnie bought her expensive presents.' Perez looked inside. The contents were ordered – there was no tangle of used tissue, half-finished lipstick, loose change, the detritus found in most women's bags. 'Perhaps this was one of them. We still have to rule out Daniel Fleming, though – we only have Helena's word that it wouldn't have come from him.'

'If it came from Magnie, he was a generous boyfriend,' Willow said.

'Or he was trying to buy her affection.'

Perez felt into the bag and pulled out a purse. Inside there were sections for credit cards, and a driver's licence. 'This was definitely Emma's bag.' He showed them the licence, the tiny photograph that could have been anyone; the name: Emma Louise Shearer. 'She passed her test in Shetland, but she gave the family home in Orkney as her permanent address. Is that significant, do you think? She never intended to settle here?'

'Well, the job wasn't going to last forever.' Willow's voice was suddenly sharp. 'The kids would grow up eventually and Emma wouldn't be needed.'

'I suppose so. And I think Belle's getting a bit old to be planning another.' Perez regretted the words as soon as they were spoken. He felt out of control, a ventriloquist's dummy, and that someone else was speaking for him. He and Willow were sending barbs of aggression at each other and it seemed there was nothing either of them could do to stop it.

There was a silence while he avoided looking at the woman by his side. 'Emma's credit and debit cards are still here and there's about thirty pounds in cash. I don't think we ever saw this as a burglary gone wrong – it's much too staged – but this proves it.'

The others nodded their agreement and Perez reached in for Emma's phone. 'The battery's flat. Let's get that sorted, Sandy, and we'll check out all the recent calls. Let's see if Daniel Fleming was telling the truth when he said he'd stopped hassling her.' Willow had described her interview with Fleming when the three of them had first got together. He knew she'd been inclined to believe the man's story, but Perez wanted to see the evidence. 'Have we got anything back on Emma's laptop yet?'

Sandy shook his head. 'I'll chase that up when I've finished here.'

There was a make-up bag. Every item was clean, lids on, no smears from lipstick or mascara, no powder from eyeshadow. Apart from that, nothing. Perez tipped up the bag to make sure, but there were no scraps of paper, sweet wrappers, supermarket receipts: nothing to suggest that it had been owned by a real human being.

'Do you think the killer went through it already, before leaving it in the shed?' Sandy clearly couldn't believe anyone could be that tidy. Even Louisa, who was neat and ordered in every other way, had a bag that looked like the contents of a waste bin.

Perez shook his head. 'If there were anything to hide, wouldn't it be on the phone? And that's still there.'

'Perhaps the bag was new,' Willow said, 'and it hadn't had time to get mucky.'

'Aye, that's possible, I suppose.' Perez looked at his watch. 'Sandy, let's go and see if the man's home. He was on the early shift, so he should be back by now. I don't want to spend all evening here. Maggie's picked up Cassie after school, but I'd like her to sleep in her own bed tonight. The bairn needs a bit of routine.'

Across the desk, Willow was looking at him. During their conversation in the car, after picking her up from Sumburgh, she'd seemed lost. All the fight had gone out of her. Now she seemed more her old self. Challenging. Fierce.

'You'll be tired,' he said, 'after the early start this morning. Go to the B&B and ask them to get you some supper. Have an early night.'

She nodded but said nothing.

Magnie Riddell opened the door to them. His mother had obviously warned him that they would be turning up, because he didn't seem surprised to see them. She was behind him, clattering pots in the kitchen. Perez ignored her. 'Is there somewhere we can speak in private?'

Magnie took them into the room where Perez had talked to Margaret. A grey cat sat on the back of one of the chairs. It stretched, jumped from the chair and walked slowly out of the room. Magnie shut the door behind it. The television was on, some game show that Perez thought his mother had been watching. Magnie turned it off.

'You're here about Emma.' He was big, a Viking of a man, with white hair that curled around his collar. Perez could imagine him marching in the Jarl's squad in the Up Helly Aa parade. He'd changed out of his work clothes and smelled of soap and shampoo.

'My mother said you were here this morning.' Magnie wasn't friendly but he wasn't overtly hostile, just a little wary. Tense.

Perez and Sandy sat in the overstuffed chairs and watched him. Perez nodded at Sandy to begin the conversation. Sandy was closer to Magnie's age and might be less threatening.

'We heard you were friendly with Emma, but Margaret tells us the relationship was over.'

'My mother would have liked it to be over.' Now there was an edge to Magnie's voice and Perez could see how he might have drifted into trouble. This was an angry young man, rootless and restless, with something to prove.

'But it wasn't?' Sandy hit just the right tone, implying that parents could be interfering pains and sometimes, of course, you weren't going to tell them everything.

'No,' Magnie said. 'It wasn't. We were taking it easy. No rush. And no need for the whole world to know about it.'

'It's hard to keep anything secret in a place like Deltaness. I know, I'm from Whalsay. Sneeze – and all the old gossips will be talking. As for any sort of love life . . .'

'Tell me about it!'

'But you managed, you and Emma,' Sandy said. 'I mean you managed to get together sometimes, without anyone knowing.'

'Yeah.' Magnie seemed close to tears and Perez thought he was glad to have the chance to speak about the dead woman. Even if he'd been the one to kill her. Love and hate, other sides of the same coin. His mother wouldn't want to hear his memories of Emma. In this house, he'd have no chance to grieve. 'I picked her up sometimes when she'd finished work. I never went right up to the house, but I'd wait on the road and send her a text to say I was there. That was what she wanted. There was a staircase that no one else much used, and she could get out without the family seeing.' Perez thought Magnie was going to add something more, but he closed his mouth tight.

'Where did you go for a bit of privacy?'

'Oh, we managed to find places we could be on our own.' Magnie shifted in his seat and Perez saw the red flush of a blush creep up his neck. Clearly he was embarrassed by the idea of Sandy probing into his sex life.

Perez was puzzled. Didn't most young men enjoy boasting about their sexual exploits these days? He'd heard them joking and shouting in the bars in town.

There was no reticence or discretion. It struck him then that Magnie was embarrassed for exactly the opposite reason: like Daniel, he'd never made love to Emma and he'd find that hard to admit.

Sandy, though, had already moved on. 'Did you ever go to the boatshed down by the Hesti jetty? *It* would be private enough.'

Magnie looked confused. 'The place that Dennis used to keep his stuff in? No, we never went there.'

'How did the two of you first get together?'

'It's kind of boring, being stuck all the way up here in Northmavine, and the court order stopped me going to town in the evenings. The local kids hang out in the community hall on a Friday night. Sometimes there's music, sometimes they just stick up a couple of pool tables. No bar, but the kids all have booze hidden away outside. It was something to do, at least a way of getting out of the house. If the weather was fine they might have a bit of a party on the beach.'

'And that's where you met Emma? In the community hall?'

He nodded. 'Sometimes she was there with Martha, the oldest Moncrieff girl; sometimes she came down on her own. I think she felt the need to escape too. It couldn't have been much fun, living on the job. You'd feel you were always working.'

'So she came down to the Deltaness Hall and let her hair down?'

'Not when Martha was there. She was always professional then. But yeah, sometimes.' Magnie smiled to himself and Perez could see that he was reliving the memory. 'Sometimes she'd have vodka in her bag, and we'd sit outside and just drink and chat, you know.

And Emma was a great dancer. You couldn't stop looking at her. We had some good nights.'

'But really it was a youth club. You must have been older than most of the other people there.'

'A bit, maybe. But like I say, there's not much to do in Deltaness in the evenings, and a couple of folk of our sort of age drifted down. In the end it became quite a cool place to hang out.'

Perez thought Emma and Magnie would have had something to do with that, with changing the young people's attitude to the place. They'd have made a stylish couple.

'Were there any adults supervising?'

'The hall committee take it in turns to keep an eye. Some of them can't be bothered to stay all evening. They open up and let us get on with it, then come back later to lock up.' Magnie looked up. 'I don't understand why you want to know about this? What can it have to do with Emma being dead?'

Perez answered before Sandy had a chance to speak. 'It's all background. I want to understand her, and it seems you knew her as well as anyone.' He paused. 'When did you last see her?'

'Over a week ago. Down at the hall. The Friday night. Then the weather was so good that the kids went down to the beach and lit a bonfire, listened to some music.'

'Not since then? Not last weekend?'

Magnie shook his head. 'Like I said, we were taking it easy. I had some overtime at work.'

'Were you working on Sunday?' Perez realized he'd taken over the questioning now, but Sandy seemed happy enough to stand aside for him.

'No.' He must have realized where this was leading, but Magnie volunteered no information.

'What *were* you doing?' Perez looked at him. 'We are asking everyone who knew Emma these questions. It doesn't mean you're under suspicion.'

Magnie nodded. 'I was catching up on my sleep,' he said. 'It had been a hard week.'

'And your mother will confirm that?'

'My mother will tell you anything she thinks you want to hear.' The reply was quick and bitter, but then he gave a little shrug. 'She's protective. You can't blame her. I'm all she has now.' A pause. 'I was here all morning, but she wasn't. It was the Sunday teas and she was down at the hall, helping to set up. She'd been baking all week.'

Perez looked at the clock on the wall. Suddenly he just wanted to be back in Fran's house in Ravenswick with Cassie. 'Had Emma been scared or anxious in the last few weeks?'

Magnie shook his head. 'She didn't seem any different from usual.'

'Is there anyone who might have wanted to harm her?'

'Apart from my mother?' It was an attempt at a joke, and Perez smiled to be kind. 'No. No one.'

Perez stood up then and it was Sandy who asked, on their way out, 'Did you give her a fancy handbag as a present?'

Magnie shook his head again. 'I did give her presents. I earned so much more than she did, and she loved having nice things. But not a handbag.'

Perez would have left it at that, but Sandy persisted. 'It was big. Shiny leather. Did you see her with something like that?'

'No. She kept her stuff in a bag that she'd made herself. It was made of fabric, pale pink-and-blue stripes. You'd have never known it was hand-made.'

At last Sandy was ready to leave. They stood briefly in the cramped hall to thank Magnie and shake his hand. Margaret, still in the kitchen, stared at them.

Chapter Twenty-One

Christopher was in his bedroom at the top of the house. When they'd got back from school there'd been people here, strange cars parked outside, the kind of break from routine that usually troubled him. He'd asked his mother what was going on and she said they'd been searching the hill for traces of Emma.

'For clues?'

She'd given a strange little laugh, though he couldn't understand what was funny. 'I suppose so. There's a Crime Scene Investigator in the old boatshed near the jetty.'

Christopher had wanted to see that. He'd wondered if it would be like the television show, but had suspected it wouldn't be quite the same. The detective with the dark hair had turned him away and he'd wandered back to his room, disappointed.

Now most of them had gone. He couldn't see the track down to Deltaness from his room, but he had a view of the yard and the vehicles, and he'd heard the engines starting and seen them move away. Now only one unfamiliar car remained. There were no unrecognizable voices. No noise at all. Even the sea was quiet. He switched on the computer and tried to lose himself in a game.

Today, the magic of the screen didn't work, though. He was still troubled, not by the break in routine, but by pictures that came into his head, blocking the familiar images on the screen, so he found it impossible to concentrate. This had never happened before. He got to his feet and began to pace backwards and forwards across the bedroom floor, from one window to the other, in an attempt to shake the pictures loose, to send them on their way. It didn't work. Whatever he did, Emma Shearer was lodged in his head.

He walked quicker and tried to order the images, to control them. He decided to treat them like the Pokémon cards he collected. He liked to place the Pokémon characters in the order in which he'd collected them. He'd lay them out on his floor, shifting them occasionally, angry with himself if he thought he'd got the order wrong. So he allowed the pictures of Emma Shearer to flash through his head and he sorted them chronologically.

His first day at the new school. Emma in the playground. Christopher had been allowed out with the other children then and had seen Emma talking to his father. He'd liked the way she looked. The shape of her. Small and thin, like a kid herself. Not scary. Not then. Standing with her head on one side, having to look up at her father, because he was so much taller. Listening to him, her face concentrated, as if what he was saying was the most interesting thing in the world.

Emma in their garden. Kate and Sam had been there too, playing with Ellie. On the trampoline and the climbing frame. Christopher didn't really like being outside and had watched them from his room. Part of him jealous because he hadn't been included in the games, and part of him feeling superior, because they were being so childish. Emma had been lying on one of the white wooden chairs that Mum said reminded her of a deckchair on the *Titanic*. Dad had brought her a drink. Not tea and not wine. Something in a big glass, with lemon and ice. It had been earlier in the year, sunny, but not very warm, and Dad had tucked a blanket round Emma, so she'd looked even more like a passenger on a big cruise liner. Kate had fallen from the trampoline and Emma had gone to help her. But she hadn't wanted to go. The picture Christopher remembered was of Emma's face, as she set aside the glass and the blanket and got to her feet. He tried now to think of a word to describe her expression. Annoyance? That wasn't quite right. Fury.

He was satisfied that he'd pinned down the way Emma had looked that day, and moved on to the next image. The night of the bonfire. Would he have gone if he'd known Emma would be there? Oh yes! Because he hadn't been thinking about anything but the flames and what they would feel like, how the sparks would be flying up into the night. The fire had been irresistible. Now, in his bedroom, he felt a sudden urge to fetch matches and paper and create a fire for himself. Then, he hadn't seen Emma at first. He'd sat at the top of the bank and watched the wild bird shapes of the flames and felt the sharp, stinging heat. Then they'd turned and seen him. Emma had laughed with the rest of them. Her thin face turned towards him, sharp-edged. She'd looked like a bird herself, pecking towards him, mocking.

Christopher stopped for a moment and rocked, backwards and forwards, remembering the way he'd felt, the centre of their attention. He'd wished the fire had spread, that the monster flames had opened their mouths and eaten the people all up.

And that brought him to the last picture, the final card in the pack. Emma hanging by a rope in the barn. Their barn. He wondered if he'd caused it, if it had been his fault. Sometimes that happened. He misread signals and got things wrong, caused hurt when he hadn't meant to. Often he was just being truthful. How could he upset people when he was telling the truth? Mum said he should try to be more tactful. Of course he shouldn't lie, but there was no need to cause offence if he could help it. Now, he thought again that the truth was that he was glad Emma Shearer was dead. It had been a shock to see her, hanging there. A shock because he'd dreamed of her dying, and it was almost as if his wishes had caused her to be killed. That was what had sent him running down the hill to the hall to fetch Dr Moncrieff. A kind of guilt.

He supposed now that he shouldn't tell anyone he was pleased Emma was dead. That wouldn't be tactful; Mum wouldn't want him speaking the truth in this situation. She wouldn't want him causing offence. He started walking again, but more slowly now. He felt calmer, that his thoughts were in order. He landed up at the window, looking down towards the sea. He could see the trampoline and, close to the house, the two white wooden loungers where Emma and his father had sat. A woman was standing on the lawn staring out towards the water.

She had very long hair that was tangled and curly. He thought it would be very painful to brush the hair and perhaps that's why she hadn't bothered to do so.

She wore jeans and trainers and a long, loose jumper. She could have been one of his mother's artist friends, though the ones who came to stay occasionally from London were usually smarter than that. He'd seen her talking to the detective, though, standing in the yard before he drove off, so he assumed she was part of the police team. Christopher wondered if she would want to speak to him. He thought that would be OK, as long as she came to his bedroom to do it.

But it seemed she'd made up her mind to go. She turned away from the sea and started to make her way round the house to where the car was parked. For a moment, her face was turned towards him and he saw that she'd been crying.

Chapter Twenty-Two

Willow planned to park Sandy's car outside the police station, where he could pick it up later. She could walk to her B&B. It wasn't far. Then she remembered she had a heavy bag and exhaustion took over. She'd leave the car at the top of the bank, close to the guest house, and Sandy could collect it from there in the morning. Or she'd drive it back to Deltaness, if that was where they were going to base themselves. Perez probably wasn't in the mood to be offering her a lift.

The Sheriff's House was where she'd stayed when she'd last been in Shetland. That had been February, grey, with torrential rain, apart from a couple of sparkling and frosty days. The couple who ran the place had been expecting a baby, and that had made her broody. Had her hormones, her sudden and inextinguishable desire for a child, made her careless? Perhaps Perez was right and she'd used him to get what she wanted, without thinking about his feelings or the consequences. Lifting her bag from the back seat of the car, Willow thought she was too tired and too close to the problem to reach a conclusion. She hadn't been physically sick during the pregnancy; rather, all her energy had drained away, leaving her limp and listless. She'd allowed herself a few tears at

Hesti once she'd been left on her own, but now she was ready to carry on fighting. Bugger Perez, with his principles and his pomposity! She'd be happier dealing with this child on her own.

The guest house was reached from one of the narrow lanes that ran up from Commercial Street. It was big and solid, three storeys and a basement kitchen. Willow pushed open a gate and walked into a walled garden, saw a washing line filled with baby clothes. The door into the house was ajar. She rang the bell and went inside; she heard voices in the basement below and shouted down, 'Hiya!'

'Come on down. The kettle's just boiled.'

They were English and had moved to Shetland in search of a better life. Like Daniel and Helena Fleming. Willow wondered if it caused resentment: these confident, educated incomers, buying up the nice houses, subtly changing the character of the place. She'd always thought Shetlanders were certain enough of their own culture, hospitable enough, not to mind too much, but now she wasn't so sure. Wouldn't it feel like an invasion? She left her bag where it was and wandered down.

The baby was sitting in a bouncy chair. He was soft-skinned and content, with downy hair and serious eyes. Willow had seen him the day of his birth and had been so jealous of Rosie that for the first time she'd understood how women could steal newborns from a hospital ward.

'What did you decide to call him in the end?'

'Michael,' John said. 'We thought he looked like a Michael.'

Willow drank tea and listened to the couple chat.

They offered her a meal, but she made do with a bannock and a slice of cheese and some home-made ginger biscuits. Soon she'd had enough of their company. She said she'd go up to her room; there was no need for them to show her, if it was the same as last time. It was jealousy again that sent her away. She knew that even if Perez had welcomed the news of her pregnancy, they would never have this sort of relationship: tender, calm, unflustered. There would always be something to come between them. Work, or Cassie, or Fran Hunter's ghost. Her child would never live up to Cassie, in Perez's mind, and she would never live up to Fran.

In the room, she wondered if she should call Perez to find out how the interview with Magnie Riddell had gone. On any previous investigation she would have done that, or she'd have gone round to see him late in the evening, once Cassie was in bed. They'd have sat, with coffee or beer, talking over the details of the case. Instead she phoned Sandy.

'How did it go? Did you get anything new?' There was a moment of silence and she knew Sandy was wondering why she was calling *him*. 'I know Jimmy will be tied up with Cass. I didn't want to disturb them, and I was curious.'

Sandy launched into a story about the Deltaness young folk hanging around the community hall, how Magnie and Emma had been part of the crowd. Willow knew what it was like to live in a place where there was nothing for young people to do. She'd grown up in a commune in the island of North Uist. Now she could appreciate the beauty of the Uists, which seemed to be formed only of water and light. Then she'd been bored silly. As a kid, she had drunk too much and played dangerous games, just for the kicks. To feel that she was alive. But today everyone had talked about how mature Emma Shearer had been, old before her years. She'd had a tough childhood and all she'd wanted from her new life in Shetland was stability. Willow couldn't imagine Emma taking crazy risks to relieve the boredom.

'Anything else?'

'Magnie doesn't have an alibi for Sunday morning, and you can tell he was obsessed with the lassie.' Sandy paused for a moment. 'He's got a history of violence.'

'So he's got to be a suspect. Did he give Emma the handbag?'

'He claims not. He says he's never seen her with anything like it.'

'It must have been a recent present, if Magnie didn't recognize it.' Willow wondered if there was another admirer. Or perhaps Daniel hadn't been telling Perez the truth, and he was still obsessed by the young woman. He wouldn't be the first middle-aged man with a shaky marriage and mental-health issues to stalk an attractive young woman and shower her with expensive presents. 'Let's see if we can track down where it came from; I don't suppose anywhere in Shetland would stock it?'

'We've gone upmarket these days,' Sandy said, 'and we have some very classy shops. I'll check.' He paused. 'What's the plan for tomorrow?'

Willow had a brief moment of panic. In the past, she'd never had problems making decisions. 'Briefing in the police station at eight,' she said, and thought she sounded quite like her normal self. 'I'll bring your car along then, if that's OK. Can you pass that on to Jimmy? I had an early start and I'm knackered. I'm ready for my bed.'

'Sure,' Sandy said. But there'd been a moment of hesitation. Perhaps she didn't sound so like her normal self after all.

Willow wasn't certain that Perez would be there when she arrived, but his car was parked outside when she got there. He was pouring water in the coffee machine in the ops room. She stood for a moment in the doorway, not sure that she could face him. She wondered if the wisest course would be to plead ill health and get the first plane home. But then she'd always hate herself for her cowardice.

Perez must have sensed her watching him, because he turned towards her and seemed about to speak. Then they heard footsteps on the stairs and Sandy was there, breathless, mumbling an excuse about having slept through his alarm. Perez gave her a brief grin: a shared moment of contact and humour, because Sandy was always sleeping through his alarm. She smiled back and walked into the room, took her place at the head of the table and started the briefing. Thinking: *I might be crap at ordering my personal life, but this is what I'm good at.*

'Our victim is Emma Shearer, aged twenty-four, childminder to the Moncrieff family. Their father is Robert, local GP; mother Belle, freelance publicist now working for Helena Fleming, textile and knitwear designer. The victim was found on the Flemings' property. Fully clothed, apart from her shoes, and we know it's a priority to find them. No immediate sign of sexual assault, though we should know more when James Grieve has completed a post-mortem. No definite info on where Emma was killed. Sandy suspects the killer was hiding in her car and killed her there, but let's keep an open mind on that.'

She paused. 'We need to be sensitive here, because there are children in both families. The Flemings' eldest son, Christopher, is high-functioning autistic. Very bright, but given to obsessions and he's been the subject of some discussion within the community. Jimmy?' Willow turned to the man.

He shrugged. 'Sounds as if folk overreacted to some problems at the school. He set fire to some waste paper in the playground. There was no damage and no further action was taken. The Flemings seem to have attracted resentment, and Christopher's behaviour is just another excuse for complaint.'

'Could Emma's murder be linked to the anonymous notes the Flemings have been receiving?' Willow asked.

'Maybe. It's certainly a coincidence that they show a hanged man and that Emma was strung up after being strangled. I'm not sure if we can link the cartoons to the victim, though. It's *possible* Emma was behind them: she was a knitter and might have had used graph paper for her designs. She would have heard the stories about Dennis Gear.' Perez leaned back in his chair. 'But I'm not sure *why* she would have sent the drawings to the Flemings.'

'To send Daniel a message? Or to intimidate his wife?'

'Maybe.' Perez shrugged.

'Emma and Daniel had a relationship,' Willow said. 'Not an affair, if Daniel is to be believed, but he was certainly obsessed with her. We've had a report back on her laptop and phone, and for a while there was a constant email and text exchange between them.' She paused. 'But not recently. Recently there was no contact at all, so it seems Fleming was telling the truth. About that, at least.' She turned to Perez. 'There are four Moncrieff children. You know the family, Jimmy. Fill us in.'

'Martha aged sixteen, Charlie fifteen, Sam ten and Kate eight.'

Willow nodded her thanks. 'Emma is originally from Orkney and came to work for the family when Belle was pregnant with Kate. She had a troubled childhood, had to take responsibility for her brothers, and was taken on by the Moncrieffs as a favour to her own GP in Kirkwall.'

'According to Robert Moncrieff,' Perez said. 'We still need to check that out.'

'Can you do that this morning, Jimmy? I'd like an opinion about her from someone who's not involved in the case.'

'I was wondering if I should go to Orkney.' Perez looked at her, his voice tentative. 'I could talk to the brother too. Local officers have notified him of Emma's death, but like you, I have no sense of Emma. Even the two men who seem to have been obsessed with her – Daniel Fleming and Magnie Riddell – can't really describe the attraction. I'd need only be away for a night.'

Are you running away from me, Jimmy?

'Good plan,' she said, her voice brisk. 'Can you sort out someone to look after Cassie?'

'Duncan's back at last. Cassie needs to spend more time with her father and we'd arranged for her to stay with him this week anyway.' He paused. 'I thought I'd go down to Kirkwall on the lunchtime flight. I should easily be able to get everything I need and be back by tomorrow evening.'

'Speak to some of the other professionals involved with the family. There must have been a social worker, if there was domestic violence and the father got sent away. Emma was only seventeen when she started working for the Moncrieffs, so there should be a teacher who remembers her.'

He nodded. 'What about you?'

'I'm going to be a radio star. I think we need to work out if the cartoons sent to the Fleming family really had anything to do with Emma and the murder. I suspect they were triggered by resentment against the incomers, not as a warning that a young woman was about to be strung up. If I can persuade the person who sent them to speak to me in confidence, it might save us time following up leads that don't have any importance.'

'You're doing an interview with Radio Shetland?' Perez allowed himself a smile.

'Exactly. Fame at last!'

'Don't dismiss those drawings altogether.' Perez paused. 'I thought they were creepy, a bit weird.'

Willow looked at Sandy. 'Have we had the fingerprints from them back yet?'

'They could only find Helena Fleming's.'

'So the person who drew them was wearing gloves.'

'Unless Helena sent them to herself,' Perez said, 'and that's hardly likely. Why would she do that?'

Willow didn't answer. She thought Perez was blinkered, where Helena was concerned. It was the celebrity-designer thing making him star-struck, and Helena's connection to Fran. Not that Willow was jealous, of course. It was clear that Perez was now a free man, and he could fall for whomever he liked. As long as it didn't get in the way of the investigation. Daniel Fleming had been obsessed with a younger woman. And, in Willow's opinion, that gave Helena a very good motive for murder.

Chapter Twenty-Three

On the flight to Kirkwall, Perez found himself sitting next to a man he'd grown up with; he was now a vet in Orkney and he'd been visiting home. They chatted about friends, family and the pull of the islands.

'I thought I was going to break away,' the vet said, 'see something of the world. And I did travel a bit when I was a student, but in the end I didn't move very far, did I?'

'And I came home to Shetland.'

Perez considered how things might have turned out if he'd stayed in Aberdeen. He'd joined the police service in the city and he'd first worked there as a detective. Maybe it had been a mistake to come home after his divorce. At the time it had felt like running away, cowardly. Now, he thought people were wrong when they considered Shetland a place of escape. In the islands, there was nowhere to hide.

Perez saw Willie Milne as soon as he walked into the terminal. Willie had grown up in Orkney in a farming family and looked more like a farmer than a detective: round, red-faced and comfortable in his considerable skin, a laugh loud enough to turn heads in the street. He had joined the service in Glasgow and now, like Perez, he too had come back. That pull of the islands and home.

Seeing the man across the building was enough for Perez's mood to lift. Willie yelled a greeting, put an arm around his shoulder and led Perez outside. In the car, he swept a pile of sweet wrappers from the front seat of his car onto the floor. 'I promised Steve I'd give up smoking, but now I'm addicted to sherbet lemons. Bugger, huh?'

Willie's partner was a merchant seaman, a senior engineer on cargo vessels travelling the world. He was away at sea for months at a time and then came back to Orkney for long periods of leave.

Willie started the engine. 'Where are we going first, Jimmy? I'm your chauffeur for the day.' The accent sounded strange to Perez, lilting. All day he would feel as if he was in a foreign country, partly because of the unfamiliar rhythm of the voices around him.

'I need to talk to David Shearer, our victim's brother. I assume he'll be at work.'

'The Watermill, the restaurant where he's a chef, won't be serving lunch today, only dinner. I checked for you. So maybe we should go there straight away, because he'll be busier later.'

'What do you know about the Shearer family?'

'I was still in Glasgow when the father got sent down, but I've been asking around. Seems as if he was a real bastard. He beat up the mother in secret for years. Nobody was sorry when he died. Except maybe Caroline, the mother, who was still making excuses for him. Even when he was in prison, her husband was in her head, playing games with her mind. You know how that works sometimes, Jimmy, when the men are really controlling.'

Perez nodded. The car was travelling through a landscape that was softer and greener than he was used to. There were the same low horizons and enormous skies, but in this part of Mainland at least the place was less bleak. It gave him an odd feeling of disconnection, as if he'd wandered into a dreamworld that was familiar, but not quite the same.

The Watermill was in a valley that led inland from the coast. They drove through a patch of mature woodland, then out into bright sunlight and around a small pool to the entrance of the hotel, which was marked by two stone pillars. Again, Perez had the sense this wasn't quite real; the reflected light on the water was too startling and the shadow too sharp. The building was like nowhere he'd expect to find in Shetland; the old three-storey mill remained, but a glass-and-wood extension looking over the millpond housed the dining room. It looked very sleek, very elegant, and it occurred to Perez that this could have been a Daniel Fleming design. Apart from an elderly couple walking hand-in-hand through the garden, the place seemed deserted. There was nobody in reception and Willie went to ring the bell on the desk. Perez shook his head to stop him. He didn't want to have to explain why they were there.

They found David Shearer in the kitchen on the ground floor at the back of the building, a place of stainless steel and quiet. He was the only person there and he was chopping parsley with a fat, long-bladed knife, hitting the top of the blade with the palm of his left hand. There was no other sound. Perez could see the family resemblance to Emma; he had the same sharp features, the same cat-like eyes. He must have been expecting them.

'You want to talk about my sister.' Not a question. He set the knife aside reluctantly to give them his attention. There was nowhere for them to sit, no offer of refreshment. He wanted this over as soon as possible.

'It must have come as a shock. We're very sorry.' Perez knew from his own experience that these words would mean nothing to a bereaved individual, but they were a ritual that had to be gone through.

'Maybe we're used to shock in our family. A quiet life with nothing going on would be more unusual for us.'

The response was unexpected; in Perez's experience, platitudes came more easily.

'But you seem to have survived the difficult childhood. All three of you had done well.' David said nothing and Perez continued, 'Adam's at university and, according to Willie here, this place has a terrific reputation. Emma seemed settled enough with the Moncrieffs in Shetland.'

There was a moment of silence. The mill walls were very thick and no sound came from outside. Perez thought it was the kind of dense silence you might find in a monastery. At last the young chef answered. He'd turned away, so Perez couldn't see his face.

'I'm happy enough at work – it's great to have found something that I'm good at – but it's the only place I *am* happy. I don't have any kind of life away from here. If I'm not in the restaurant, I'm in my flat, too scared to go out to face folk. Adam's in therapy for anxiety and depression, hanging on to his uni place by his fingernails. And I'm not sure about Emma. She always seemed fine on the surface, but she never spoke about her feelings. She created a fantasy world set in the past. You'll have seen the clothes she wore. All that retro shit. That wasn't something she did because it was fun. It was a reality better than the one she'd been landed with.' There was another moment of silence. 'She was the oldest. She must have realized what was going on with our parents before we did. It was worse for her.'

'Did any of you keep in touch with your father when he was in prison?'

'My mother visited him! After all he'd done to her, she'd make the trek south to see him.' Even now that his mother was dead, David sounded furious.

'But she didn't take you or the others?'

The man thought for a moment. 'I think Emma might have gone once.'

The silence settled again, like dust.

'Did Emma talk to you much about her life in Shetland?'

'We spoke on the phone once a week, but that was a kind of duty thing. More pretence. Playing happy families. She'd talk about what the kids she was looking after were up to. I'd tell her about what I was cooking. But there was nothing real, nothing important.'

Perez thought about these three siblings, still very young and very lonely. Isolated by geography and the experience that might have brought them together.

'Are you closer to Adam?'

'Yeah, I guess so. When he phones, he's usually kind of desperate. Or pissed. But at least I know what he's really feeling. It was impossible to tell with Emma. All she could do was the big-sister thing. Concerned for us, but not willing to talk about herself or her own problems.'

'So you wouldn't have been able to tell,' Perez said, 'if she was especially worried or anxious recently?'

'No. She phoned the week before she died. Sunday night. That was the usual time, because she had Sunday off and the restaurant's closed after the lunchtime service. We talked about the usual stuff. She was banging on about a fancy new handbag. She was thrilled about that. I didn't notice anything else different about her mood, though.'

Perez thought the shiny patent-leather handbag seemed to take on a greater significance, to become a symbol of the perfect, glittering image that Emma had tried to create for herself. He told himself he was being fanciful again. Since he'd landed in Kirkwall his perspective had become warped. He was losing his grip.

David continued speaking, his voice bitter. 'When she didn't phone this Sunday, I was relieved. For myself, because it was always an effort thinking of something to say to her. But for her, too. I thought finally she might be getting a life of her own. But of course she wasn't. She was already dead.'

'She had a friend when she was still living in Orkney,' Perez said. 'Claire somebody. She went to stay with Emma once in Shetland. Any idea who that might have been?'

'Claire Bain? Yeah, I think they were good mates at one time.' He paused again and closed his eyes for a moment. 'If Emma ever really did have a mate. I'm not sure she actually trusted anyone. I can't.'

'Is Claire still in Orkney?'

'She went away to art school, but she's back now. She works in a gallery in Stromness. Local paintings and crafts. It's right on the harbour, close to the library.' Perez shot a look at Milne, who nodded to show that he knew the place.

They drove straight to Stromness. The small town had a carnival air. There was a huge cruise ship moored in the harbour, and Perez watched passengers flooding the narrow streets in waves as the tenders brought them ashore.

'What did you make of David Shearer?'

Willie shrugged. 'Pretty screwed up. Very sad.'

When they arrived at the gallery, the place was packed with elderly Americans, who were admiring the textiles and the glass, standing in front of the paintings, talking. Perez recognized Claire Bain as soon as he walked into the gallery. She was just as Belle Moncrieff had described her – red-haired and full of laughter.

The three of them sat in a quieter upstairs room, looking over the water.

'Had you heard that Emma was dead?' Perez suddenly caught sight of one of Fran's paintings on the wall and was distracted. He was pleased that she was still selling – the price seemed extortionate – but it was a shock, like finding a piece of her handwriting or hearing a recording of her voice. It made her seem alive again. Reincarnated. Another bizarre moment in this strange day. He forced himself to look back at Claire.

'Of course. She was Orcadian. The news was the first item on the local radio. It seems so unfair.' Claire paused. 'As if violence was following her around. Stalking her.'

'You knew her well? Before she headed north to Shetland.'

'We lived close to each other. Her parents kept the shop in Stenness and my folks have a small hotel there. There weren't so many other children around. We went to the primary school together, before moving on to Kirkwall when we were eleven.'

'Did you have any idea what was going on in the Shearer family?' Perez wasn't sure how this was relevant, but he was curious. How could such violence take place without the rest of a tight community knowing, or at least guessing? 'Before Shearer was arrested, I mean.'

'Not at all, not until the police came to take him away. Then, though my parents tried to protect me from what had happened, of course I heard all about it. From other kids at school. Listening in to the staff in the hotel. But I was only thirteen when that happened, a very young thirteen. Sheltered, an only child, doted on.' She looked up at them. 'In a way, we all enjoyed the drama. Do you know what I mean?'

Perez nodded. In a place where nothing very much happened, Shearer's arrest would have seemed like a grand form of entertainment.

Claire was still talking. 'I knew Kenneth was strict with Emma and the boys, and he had the reputation of having a temper. There were never any fights, nothing like that. He was considered very respectable. Upright. But he'd come into the bar of my parents' hotel sometimes and the regulars would keep a distance. When we were young, Emma would always come to my place to play. I was hardly ever invited there, and even when once I was, my mother made some excuse. She said later there was something about him that scared her.'

'And Emma never told you what was happening at home?'

'No,' Claire said. 'She was often very quiet, and some mornings she was so tired that she'd fall asleep in the bus on the way to school, but I had no idea what that was about. Later, she told me she was too frightened to tell anyone. Her father had threatened that he'd kill them all, if she told what was happening at home.'

'Did she get any help when her father was arrested?' Perez was wondering what that would do to you. Carrying such a huge secret around would be like having a heavy weight strapped to the shoulders. It would drag you down and stop you functioning properly.

'You mean counselling or something?'

'Yes, I suppose so.'

'The family had a social worker,' Claire said. 'Some bloke. But soon after her dad was sent away, her mother got ill and Emma ended up having to look after the boys. They were younger than her, still in primary school. People offered their support, but she said she wanted to do it.' Claire gave a little laugh. 'I just didn't get it. I mean the boys were quite cute, but it can't have been a barrel of fun, clearing up after them.

And there were times I could tell Emma resented it. Resented them. The fact that, because they were younger, they didn't have the same responsibility.' She paused. 'I didn't see so much of her then. She stopped coming to school after the standard-grade exams, and I *was* into fun. Big-style. Boys and partying. And my art.'

'But she asked you to go and stay with her in Shetland?'

'Yeah. We'd got together on Facebook, started texting and emailing. And suddenly I got this invitation out of the blue. I was home from college and it was easy enough to get the ferry up. I'd never been to Shetland, which is bonkers.' Claire leaned forward, her elbows on her knees. Outside the window one of the cruise ship's tenders was carrying a group of passengers back to the boat. 'It seemed like an excuse to see the place.'

'How did it go?'

'Well, it was a bit weird. That big house and the mad kids, and the parents taking no notice of them and leaving it all to Emma. I couldn't imagine why she stayed.'

'Did she seem happy?' Perez waited for an answer. Hoped it would be positive.

'Yeah. Yeah, she did, I suppose. I mean, I think it was what she wanted. Her own space. No one on her back. The parents let her get on with the job and never interfered. Maybe that was what she needed. I was surprised she stuck it out for so long, though.'

'You just went once?' Perez said.

'Yeah, she never invited me back, and I never asked to go. I'm still not quite sure why she wanted me to go. Perhaps to prove that she *did* have a friend, that she wasn't some odd loner. I saw her a couple of times when she came back to Orkney when her mother was dying. My parents still run the hotel in Stenness. We didn't have much to talk about. I was so crap at keeping in touch – I still had a head full of my own life, my friends and my work. I did go to Caroline's funeral. Emma had all that to organize. There were no other relatives to help out. Folk in Stenness turned out to pay their respects, but nobody else.'

Perez wondered who would organize Emma's funeral and where it would be held. Orkney or Shetland? He wanted to ask Claire if she would turn out for that too, if she would be a mourner at Emma's funeral. But another group of tourists came into the gallery and Claire said she would have to go.

Chapter Twenty-Four

Willow sat in the BBC Shetland studio opposite the presenter, a microphone on the table in front of her, and forced herself to leave thoughts of Perez behind and to concentrate on the matter in hand. Of course she'd give no details of the little drawings that Helena had received. That way they could check the authenticity of any information that came through as a result of her appeal. Helena and Daniel were adamant that they'd told nobody about the hangman cartoons. And she'd try to make it clear that the person who'd sent them wasn't necessarily a suspect in the murder investigation. She'd simply ask anyone who had any information about messages delivered to the Fleming family to come forward in confidence. She would be bland, prosaic, boring even. The last thing she needed was to generate more hysteria.

In contrast, the journalist opposite seemed determined to bring as much excitement as he could to the interview. He looked very young. Very ambitious. The drama of the young woman's death seemed to be feeding him, raising his energy level until she thought he might explode. He fidgeted like a hyperactive child on a diet of brightly coloured sweeties while he checked her sound level. Willow could tell he was itching to ask her if Emma had been sexually assaulted.

It seemed very hot and airless in the small room and there was no natural light. Willow felt a moment of claustrophobia and panic. The presenter looked at the producer in the corner and gave a little nod, to show he'd got the message that they were ready to go. 'I understand that you'd like to read us a statement, Chief Inspector, about the Deltaness murder. I wonder if I could ask you some questions before you begin.'

Willow smiled and took a breath. At times of stress the yoga exercises she'd been forced to learn as a child came in useful.

'Why don't you wait until you hear what I have to say, John? Then your questions might be relevant.'

He seemed so taken aback that he failed to reply – perhaps most people who appeared opposite him in the studio were more easily intimidated – and in the moment of silence she began to read from the sheet of paper that she'd already placed on the table in front of her:

During our investigation into the death of Emma Shearer, it has come to our notice that three messages were delivered to Hesti, the house in Deltaness where the body was discovered, shortly before her death. We would ask that the person responsible for these messages – or anyone who knows anything at all about them – should contact us immediately. I'd like to stress that this person has committed no crime and we're not linking the messages to the murder of

Emma Shearer, but we think the writer might have valuable information. Thank you.

With the last two words, Willow smiled. She'd once been sent on a media course and had been told by the tutor that a smile could be communicated even by radio. The tutor had said a lot of other stuff that Willow had considered ballocks and had immediately forgotten, but for some reason that piece of advice had stuck. She hoped she'd sounded sufficiently warm and welcoming for the anonymous sender of the hangman messages to contact her.

She folded the sheet of paper and smiled at the interviewer too. 'Now, John, do you have any questions about my statement? I'm afraid it's impossible for me to discuss other aspects of our inquiry any further at this early stage, though of course if any of your listeners saw anything unusual in the vicinity of Deltaness, late on Saturday night or on Sunday morning, I would ask them to come forward. They can talk either to me or to one of the officers based in Shetland, who might be more familiar to them.'

While John was still forming any possible question in his mind, she continued: 'No? Then thank you very much for letting me come to speak to you today. We are all very grateful for your assistance.' She stood up, nodded towards the producer and left the studio.

Outside, the weather had changed. There was little wind, but the sun was filtered by a mist that seemed to get thicker, even as Willow walked up the lane to the street that led to the police station. There was no warmth in it now – any breeze that there was came from the north – and Willow was tempted to return to the B&B for a thicker sweater or a coat. But she just walked more quickly and ran up the steps to the police station, suddenly feeling more energetic than she had for months. Sandy was still in the ops room, on the phone. He gave her a little wave and she switched on the kettle and dropped a camomile teabag into a mug. When she turned back, he'd finished the call.

'Did Jimmy get off OK?' She was worried that the mist might have stopped the flight.

'Yeah, fine. It's clear at Sumburgh. The forecast's not great, though.' He looked at her. 'Are you two alright?'

'Of course,' she said and then, thinking he deserved more than that, 'just a couple of things we need to sort out. Sorry, it must be awkward for you.'

'He's not an easy man,' Sandy said. There was a long pause that he clearly hoped she'd fill with more information. When none was forthcoming, he added, 'But if anyone can handle him, it's you.' Another pause. 'You brought him back to us, after that business with Fran. I'll always be grateful for that.' He turned away from her, suddenly embarrassed by the intimacy of the comment. Only the beetroot tinge to the back of his neck stopped her from becoming emotional herself. But seeing his awkwardness, it was a struggle not to laugh.

'Did you get anywhere tracking down Emma's bag?' she asked and he faced her again, apparently glad that the moment was over.

'They don't sell it anywhere in Shetland. Not even the classy new place in Commercial Street that I thought might stock it.' Sandy looked down at his notes. 'The woman was helpful, though. She thought there were a couple of sites you might get it online and have delivered to the islands. I've written them down.'

'Maybe get the techies in Inverness to work on that one.' Willow thought she wouldn't know where to start finding a real person to answer their questions. 'What next, do you think, Sandy? You've met most of the people involved with both families. Anything we've missed?'

'I think it would be worth talking to the Moncrieff kids,' he said. 'The older ones, Martha and Charlie. Emma was closer in age to them than she was to the parents. We know, from Magnie Riddell, that Emma and Martha used to hang out socially on occasions.'

'How would we go about that? Go back to Deltaness and catch them after school tonight?'

'I was thinking a more . . .' he paused, struggling to find the right word, 'unorthodox approach. If I know anything about teenagers, they're not going to tell us what they were really getting up to at the community hall, or at their parties at the beach, with the parents listening in.'

'What are you suggesting then, Sandy? Go and see them at the school?'

He shook his head. 'Then the teachers would feel obliged to contact the parents. And even if we could persuade the school that Robert or Belle didn't need to sit in, they'd want to be involved.'

'So?' She loved Sandy to bits, but sometimes it took him hours to get to the point.

'They don't come across to me as swotty kids. Not the kind to stay in school in their lunch break, eating the healthy choice in the canteen, followed by a trip to the library to make a start on their homework . . .'

'Where would they go then?' She was starting to follow his drift.

'There's a caff not far from the school. It was there even in my day, and it was where all the older guys went. They did brilliant saucermeat sandwiches. And cheap. The kids would come in waves. And the owner had the food all prepared, wrapped up in serviettes, ready to take away, so you didn't have to wait hours. There wasn't much room inside and we'd sit on the wall, looking down towards the water. Weather like this, you'd be glad of a nice warm car to sit in, if you just happened to meet a grown-up – someone you knew – who also fancied a saucermeat sandwich.'

'Shame that I'm veggie,' she said. 'I think this is something for you, Sandy. You're more their age anyway. And they know you.'

He looked suddenly horrified. 'I was thinking we should both go. It'd look bit dodgy if it got out: one male officer in a car with two kids.' A pause. 'And I wouldn't know what to say to them. They might have been born and brought up here, but they're not really island bairns. Do you know what I mean?'

Willow nodded. She knew exactly what Sandy meant. She'd never really been an island bairn, either. Her father had been an English academic and her mother had made silver jewellery. The talk in the commune had been about history and philosophy, not the price of sheep or fish.

'Come on, then.' She got hold of her bag. 'I expect the caff would do me a fried-egg sandwich. I'm bloody starving.'

Chapter Twenty-Five

By the time they'd parked outside the caff close to the school, the mist was so thick that Willow wasn't sure Sandy would recognize the Moncrieff teenagers even if they appeared. The street was quiet when they got there. An elderly woman with a plastic rainhood and long mackintosh pulled a shopping basket on wheels, but nobody else was about. Perhaps the kids had decided the weather was so unpleasant they would have lunch in the school canteen after all. But it seemed that the draw of sugar and fat was too great. Willow heard them before she saw them; there was a high-pitched buzz of conversation first, and then she made out good-natured banter and individual shouts. As Sandy had said, they came in waves. The first group consisted of older boys, bag-swinging, mock-wrestling, yelling obscenities as if they were the generation to invent them.

'I've seen Charlie Moncrieff around,' Sandy said. 'He's sporty. One of those kids who seem to win without any effort. In *The Shetland Times* every other week because he's got some medal or other. I think I'd know him. I've only met the girl once, though, on Sunday night when I went to look at Emma Shearer's room.' He sat with his nose to the window as a giggling gang of younger girls swept along the pavement, then leaned back once to wipe away the condensation with his hand.

In the end, it was easy to make them out because they were walking together, apart from the other students. Sandy nudged Willow as the pair emerged from the mist, though there was no need for silence; they wouldn't have heard any sound inside the car. Besides, they seemed preoccupied, deep in conversation. The boy's shock of white hair stood out from the shadow, but the girl seemed to be lost in it. She wore a black waterproof jacket, black jeans, black DMs.

'How do we play it?' Sandy was still whispering, enjoying the drama of the situation.

'We wait until they're in the queue. Then you go in just behind them, start a conversation, see if you can lure them in for a chat.'

He nodded.

The kids walked past the car and disappeared inside. Sandy jumped out and followed them. He turned back as he was about to close the door. 'Were you serious about the fried-egg sandwich?'

'Yes! I told you. I'm starving.'

They took so long to come out that Willow wondered if Sandy had decided to talk to them on his own after all. It was impossible to see inside the cafe, which seemed packed with kids. She sat back in the passenger seat and tried to relax, but she was thinking of Perez in Orkney, his attempts to find out more about the dead young woman. His attempts to come to terms with the fact that he might soon be a father. In all her dealings in Shetland, she thought, the personal and professional had clashed.

She was surprised from her daydreaming when at last they appeared on the pavement. They were clutching enormous bread buns, the grease already seeping onto the napkins that were wrapped around them. Lerwick was a grey town at the best of times, and the mist had sucked the colour out of it. She thought the teenagers and Sandy looked like characters from a black-and-white film, moody and a little sinister. Sandy opened the back door to let the Moncrieffs inside. 'I've found a couple of folk needing shelter from the weather. You don't mind?'

'I don't mind anything as long as you've bought me some food!' Then: 'You did tell them I was veggie. This hasn't been fried in bacon fat?'

'Yeah, of course I asked them.' Sandy looked back at the kids, rolled his eyes and then winked. They sniggered. Willow thought he already had them hooked.

'Are you fuzz too?' This was Martha, leaning forward towards Willow.

'Yep!'

'You don't look like a policewoman,' Charlie said.

'I'm a police *officer* and I'm *his* boss.' Willow thought Martha was just like she was at that age. Trying too hard to gouge out an identity, to separate herself from parents already well known within the community. She wasn't sure about Charlie, who seemed more settled but less mature than the girl.

'What made you join up?' Martha again.

'Honestly? To piss off my parents,' Willow said. 'They always thought the police were the enemy of the people. They claimed to be anarchists. I grew up in a commune.' A pause. 'But there were other reasons; I'm easily bored. I knew I couldn't spend the rest of my working life stuck in an office.' Another pause. 'Though that's how I seem to spend most of my days now, so I got that wrong, didn't I?' She took a bite of the sandwich. 'Are you interested in joining the police?'

'God, no!' The response was violent and immediate.

'You think they're the enemy of the people too?'

Martha looked over her sandwich, suspicious that Willow was mocking her. 'I wouldn't want to be in a position where I'm bossing people about.'

'But that's not what policing's about.' This was the last conversation Willow had expected, but there was something touching about how lost the girl seemed and, besides, she couldn't help getting preachy about work. 'It's about bringing a bit of order to the chaos. And standing up for the people who are being bossed about.'

'Like finding out who killed Emma,' Charlie said.

Willow tried not to grin. If she'd scripted the interview, this couldn't have worked out better. Now they were definitely back on track. 'Yeah,' she said. 'Stuff like that.' She paused. 'What was Emma like? You're probably the people who knew her best.'

'She was alright,' Charlie said.

'She was alright to you.' Martha still had her sandwich in her mouth, but it didn't stop her speaking. 'She liked *you*.'

'Didn't she like you?' Willow was thinking it might be quite hard to like Martha, who seemed so spiky and who took offence so easily.

Martha seemed to be regretting her outburst already. She wasn't so unconventional, it seemed, that she was comfortable speaking ill of the dead. 'I think she was one of those people who get on better with men. Charlie and Sam could twist her round their little fingers, but Kate and I could never get anything right. And Emma definitely liked Dad better than Mum.' Again she seemed worried that her words might be misinterpreted and she added: 'I don't mean they were having an affair or anything like that. Just that sometimes things were a bit tense between Emma and Mum.'

'It must have been a bit hard when you were younger,' Willow said. 'Was it like having two mums?'

'No!' Again Martha responded without thinking first. 'Emma was nothing like a mother.' And again she seemed concerned that she'd given the wrong impression. 'Even when Emma first arrived I didn't really see her as a grown-up.'

'You were only nine, though. I mean I can see that as you got older she must have seemed more like a sister than a mum, but then it must have felt different.' Willow finished the sandwich and wiped her fingers on the paper napkin.

'We'd had teenager babysitters before,' Martha said. 'Girls from Deltaness to look after us when Mum and Dad went out for the night. I saw Emma more like that. I didn't realize she'd be staying.'

Willow wondered about that. Surely Belle and Robert would have explained to the kids that a stranger would be living in the house and taking care of them? But perhaps it had been a chaotic time, with a new baby in the house, and a nine-year-old's memories wouldn't be entirely reliable.

Martha must have sensed Willow's surprise. 'We're not exactly a functional family. People think we are:

big house, doctor-father, rather glamorous mother. But it's all actually a bit of a mess. We don't communicate. At least we all talk, but nobody really listens.'

Charlie seemed uncomfortable. 'Come on, it's not that bad.'

The girl stared at him. 'Isn't it? Then why do you spend so much time at your mates' homes in town. Or playing bloody football.'

There was a moment of silence. There was condensation on all the windows now, and that and the mist made it feel as if they were cut off altogether from the outside world.

'We should get back,' Charlie said. 'We'll be late for afternoon school.'

'No rush.' Sandy's voice was easy, relaxed. 'We can give you a lift.'

'Who did Emma talk to?' Willow asked. 'It must have been lonely for her.'

'She had a friend to stay once,' Charlie said. 'Claire. I liked her.'

'And she had her men.' Martha gave a little smile. 'Her admirers: Magnie and Daniel Fleming.'

'Any others?'

Martha seemed to consider for a moment and Willow thought she was going to come up with another name, but in the end she said nothing.

'Did either of you see her on Sunday morning?'

'Nah,' Martha said. 'I stayed in bed until nearly lunchtime and then I got the bus into town. It was mad in the house. Mum doing her best Nigella impression, Dad sniping at her. I couldn't stand it.'

'Did you notice if Emma's car was there when you went out?'

Martha thought for a moment. 'No. Sorry.'

'Charlie, did you see Emma?'

'No,' he said. 'I had football practice.' He scowled at his sister. 'Look, we need to get back.'

'Sure,' Sandy said. He started the engine. He switched on the windscreen wipers, but the visibility was still so poor that they couldn't see to the end of the street. Which, Willow thought, was a perfect metaphor for the way the investigation was going.

Chapter Twenty-Six

Willie Milne insisted that Perez stayed with him and not in a guest house or hotel. 'We've masses of space, man. You'd be doing me a favour, keeping me company.'

The house was new, a large white bungalow built to Willie and Steven's specification, a boys' fantasy palace with a sauna, a room that they'd filled with Lego and Scalextric and a home cinema. Willie loved every inch of it and Perez thought the main reason for the invitation was so that he could show it off. Perez trailed after the big man into room after room and tried to summon the enthusiasm that Willie so obviously expected. The house stood not far from the hotel run by Claire Bain's parents. It looked north over the Loch of Stenness across flat land towards the famous Neolithic standing stones.

'Do you fancy walking down to the hotel for a beer?'

'Why not?' Perez thought perhaps here he'd have a sense of the real Emma Shearer. This was where she'd spent her childhood. That word lingered in his head: *childhood.* Suddenly he had an image of *his* child, growing up without him, and felt a sense of longing and desolation. Walking down the bank to the bar, with

Willie rattling on about the wedding he and Steve were planning, Perez tried to unpick his emotions. Why had he reacted so violently to the idea of being a father? Because it felt like a betrayal, to Fran and to Cassie. Because he didn't deserve a second chance. So Willow wasn't to blame at all, but she'd taken the brunt of his guilt and his anger. Now he felt guilty all over again.

In the end, Emma Shearer was as elusive in Stenness as she'd been in Shetland. On the main road, the shop where she'd lived was no longer in business – a petrol station stood in its place – and two young students were manning the hotel bar, so he couldn't ask Claire's parents about the girl they'd once invited to play.

Back in the house, Willie heated a casserole that his mother had cooked and opened a bottle of wine. Later, the Highland Park whisky appeared. At one point towards the end of the evening, stretched out on a white leather sofa, a glass in his hand, Perez was tempted to tell Willie about Willow and the baby, but even drunk, he knew that would be a mistake. This was something he had to sort out alone.

He woke the next morning to a hangover and thick fog.

'Looks as if you'll be staying a bit longer than you expected.' Willie nodded towards the grey, almost invisible garden. 'There'll be no planes out today. The forecast is dreadful.'

'What about the boat?'

'Aye, maybe you should book onto the ferry tonight. The forecast is bad for a couple of days.'

'I'll have to let the team in Shetland know.' Perez

thought a slow trip north was just what he needed. Time to deal with his confusion over Willow and the child. He watched Willie pile bacon onto his plate and helped himself to coffee.

Willie had meetings in Kirkwall, but he offered Perez the loan of Steven's car. Driving along the narrow road in the fog, Perez felt calmer. It was good to be anonymous, hidden and alone in a place where he wasn't known.

His first call was to the health centre in Stromness, to talk to the GP who'd recommended Emma as a nanny for the Moncrieffs. Perez sat in the waiting room, where pregnant women queued to see the midwife. He found himself listening to conversations that seemed entirely alien, intrigued by words he'd never heard before, until the receptionist called him through to the doctor.

The man was called Alan Masters and he was younger than Perez had expected, younger than Robert Moncrieff, or aiming at least to give that impression. He wore jeans and a sweater and was tapping on his computer keyboard when Perez walked in.

'I can't believe that Emma's dead.' He swung round in his chair, abandoning the screen. 'I suppose if I hadn't asked Robert to consider taking her on, she might still be alive.'

'Why *did* you ask him to take her on?' If the man wanted absolution, Perez didn't feel he could give it.

The doctor took some time to answer. 'I was the Shearer family doctor. I was very young, new to general practice. New to Orkney. Too gullible, I suppose. I'd bought into the idea of the islands as a place of paradise. When Caroline came to me, presenting with problems of anxiety and depression, I saw the bruises. She had a story ready – it had been a cold winter and she said she'd fallen on a patch of ice. The explanation seemed almost plausible, but not quite. I wondered if she might have had problems with alcohol – that would fit in with the depression. I thought she could have tripped because she wasn't steady on her feet. Domestic abuse never occurred to me. Her husband seemed very good to her, caring and gentle. He came with her to the surgery. Of course that should have rung alarm bells. I should have insisted on seeing her on her own. But I didn't.'

'Did you see the children?'

'Occasionally. I made a point of visiting Caroline at home a few times. Again, looking back, perhaps I should have contacted social services, but until the severe attack that put Caroline in hospital and Kenneth in prison, there was no real cause for concern. The kids seemed a little quiet and withdrawn, but well fed, cared for.' He looked up at Perez. 'But they were living in that nightmare for years. And now Emma is dead.'

'Tell me about the attack.' Perez thought of his own childhood. His father had been a little strict perhaps, a bit narrow-minded, but home had always felt safe. *His* insecurities had started with the move to the Anderson High School in Lerwick, the homesickness and petty bullying. He couldn't imagine what it would be like to be scared of his own family.

'Kenneth almost killed his wife,' Masters said. 'He was trying to strangle her when Emma came home early from school and found them. If the girl hadn't turned up, Caroline would have died. She was already unconscious.'

'So, Emma called the police?' Perez said. 'She finally found the courage to accuse her father?'

'She called for an ambulance. The cause of the injuries was obvious and they told the police. Kenneth went on the run for a while, but they found him trying to get on a ferry south. Caroline was still making excuses for him, even at the trial. It was Emma's evidence that put him away.'

There was a moment of silence, before Masters continued speaking. 'Caroline had always been emotionally frail and even before she was diagnosed with cancer, Emma ended up as the main carer in the family. When the boys became teenagers and more independent, I really thought Emma needed to get a life of her own. The job with the Moncrieffs seemed ideal: a supportive family not too far from home.'

'How well did you know the Moncrieffs?' Perez wasn't sure that he would have described them as a supportive family.

'I'd never met Belle, but I'd come across Robert at meetings. He seemed sympathetic. I explained Emma's background and he said he was happy to give her a go.'

But only because nobody else applied for the post.

'Did you ever hear from Emma, once she'd started in Deltaness?'

'No.' The man seemed surprised. 'Of course I asked Robert how she was getting on, when I met him. He said it was all going brilliantly. So, Brownie points all round for me.' The doctor seemed to be ignoring his role in sending Emma to her death and failing to recognize a deeply troubled family. His words at the beginning of the interview had been an attempt to disarm, not to accept responsibility.

'You didn't contact Emma herself?'

'No.' He was suddenly defensive. 'Why would I? She was no longer my patient.'

Perez said nothing.

Emma's former class teacher was prickly too. Perez felt all the professionals who had been involved with the Shearers were anxious to slide away from blame, to find excuses for their lack of action. The woman had recently retired from teaching and lived in a neat whitewashed house in Finstown, with a yappy dog and a silent husband. They sat in her living room. Perez looked out of the window towards the garden and the sea, but could see nothing but fog.

'There was nothing to indicate that there was trouble at home.' She was probably a kind woman. She stroked her dog as it lay on her lap and was clearly fond of it. 'Emma was quiet and well behaved. Well turned-out. Never late.'

'Her friend said she often fell asleep on the bus into school.' Perez tried not to sound judgemental.

'I wouldn't know about that. Why would I? I'm sorry, Inspector, but the court case happened ten years ago, and what had gone on in that family surprised us all.' She had tight grey curls, so similar to the dog's hair that Perez found himself staring.

Before he could ask another question, she started talking again: 'Emma was thirteen at the time of the court case. She completed her education when she was seventeen. Really, I don't know what her school life in Orkney can have to do with her murder in a different place so much later. It must be a tragic coincidence.'

Perez said nothing. He thought the woman was probably right. What connection could there be between Emma's dysfunctional family and her murder in Shetland? Her parents were dead and he'd checked flights and ferries: her brothers hadn't left home on the weekend that Emma had died. Perez stood up, thanked the teacher for her time and left. He felt suddenly heartbroken for the teenage girl who'd survived such stress and responsibility, only to be killed when she was still a young woman, with the possibility of a happier life ahead of her.

The social worker reminded Perez of some middle-aged police officers he'd known: cynical, worn-out, but still secretly passionate about the job. Uninterested in promotion away from what he considered real work. He had yellow smoker's fingers and a creased grey jacket, a beer belly, and he carried with him the smell of cigarettes and fried food. His name was Billy Samson.

'Of course I remember the Shearer family. It was a bloody disgrace that we weren't called in earlier.' They were in a cramped office, with mounds of files on the desk. Samson, it seemed, preferred paper to the computer. The light was on because it was so grey outside. 'She was a weird little thing. Very tight and closed. I'm not sure she confided in anybody.'

'You worked with the family after the father was arrested?'

'Aye, that was the first time we had any idea there was a problem. The mother had been to A&E lots of times, complaining of strange symptoms, but everyone put it down to the fact that she was neurotic, and when there *was* a real injury – a broken elbow, bruising – they thought she was a piss-head and had fallen over.' He looked up. 'The GP started that rumour. No proof.' He paused. 'She *was* bloody neurotic, mind. She drove me crazy. I'm not sure how Emma coped with her.'

'So you thought it was a good idea when Emma got the job in Shetland?' Perez was pleased there had been somebody at least who'd been engaged with the family.

Samson looked up. His eyes were sleet-grey. 'I thought it suited some people to get her away from Orkney.'

'Why?'

'I said Emma was very tight and closed in, but there were a couple of incidents just before she went away. She lost it. Lashed out at some kid who'd been mocking her mother. Was caught with some older guy she'd met in a bar. Now, maybe, I'd say it was PTSD. All that time watching her father inflict violence on her mother must have screwed her up, big-style.'

'She didn't get any support? Counselling?'

Samson shrugged. 'She was offered it immediately after the father got sent down, but for some reason it never happened. Later, according to the other professionals, all was well. The father was out of the picture and the family seemed to be coping fine. It didn't quite fit the narrative when she started getting into fights and picking up strange older men. If she'd stayed, who knows, someone might have noticed and insisted on an inquiry into the events leading up to Kenneth Shearer's arrest.'

Perez wondered if Samson had been pushing for that inquiry. There was something personal in his description of events. Perez understood that. He took his work personally too. 'Did you keep in touch with her when she moved to Shetland?'

'Sure. Not as much as I should have done – even in a place like this, we're stretched – but I phoned every so often. I met her when she came back for her mother's funeral.'

'How did she seem?'

Samson stared out of the window into the gloom. 'Controlled. There were no tears at the funeral. She said she was happy with the family in Shetland. There was no reason for her to come back to Orkney. Adam was at university and David was old enough to manage without her.'

'But you didn't believe her? That she was happy?'

Samson shrugged. 'I didn't know what to believe. But there was nothing I could do. She was an adult and I had to respect her decision.' He paused again. 'But it was a case that haunted me. You know how some of them get under your skin? You know you shouldn't get too involved, but you can't help it. Emma Shearer is one of the kids who keep me awake at night.'

Chapter Twenty-Seven

Christopher was disturbed by the fog. He couldn't see the beach from the window to the east, and the view to the west was limited to a line of darker shadow that was the hill. He felt that his room was no longer anchored to the rest of the house. It was as if he was floating in a grey bubble. Of course he could go downstairs and sit with his mother and sister in the kitchen. They were baking together and soon there would be good things to eat. But there was a tension in the house that was all about Emma. He couldn't see why her dying should make his mother and father so awkward with each other. Ellie was too young to notice the strange atmosphere, but he could feel it, just as he'd felt the dampness of the fog on his skin when they'd walked back from school.

He wondered if his mother and father planned to separate. In the old school in London lots of the kids had parents who lived apart. They'd boasted sometimes about the treats they'd got when they were staying with the absent father. It usually was the father who moved out. Christopher pondered that. If his parents separated, where would Dad go? His father had seemed happier in London, but if he moved back to the city, how would Ellie and Christopher see him?

Would they fly south or go on the boat? How would they manage if their father didn't come to collect them? In his mind he saw himself and his sister, holding each other's hand, wandering around a big airport. Lost. Ellie crying. The idea troubled him and he pushed it out of his mind.

Although he usually kept his bedroom door shut tight, today he'd left it open. There was something about the fog making him feel trapped. Because it wasn't closed, he heard a knock on the front door and then the murmur of voices in the hall. He hadn't heard the sound of a car and that was odd, because he still had his window wide open. Christopher wondered if the detectives were back. He didn't mind the detectives. Talking to them made him feel important. He walked out into the corridor until he could see down the stairs to the adults still talking just below him.

His mother was there with Margaret Riddell. Christopher recognized Mrs Riddell. He knew she was Magnie's mother and that she worked in Brae. He hesitated for a moment to work out how he knew those things, then remembered that she'd been at the Deltaness community hall when there'd been a craft fair. She'd had a stall next to his mother's and had been selling her knitting. Not classy stuff like his mother made, but old ladies' jerseys, hats and mittens. He couldn't imagine many people wearing them because the wool would be very itchy. Christopher hated the feeling of wool next to his skin. He'd pointed out how uncomfortable that would be, and his mother had got upset and told him not to be rude. She'd said that she made clothes out of wool too. Mrs Riddell had pretended not to hear the comment, but later he'd heard her talking about him to her friend. She'd been much ruder about Christopher than he'd been about her knitting.

Now he wasn't quite close enough to hear what they were saying. He could see his mother's wild hair, looking from this distance like one of the wire scourers used for scrubbing burnt stuff from pans. Mrs Riddell was wearing an anorak and he thought it was as if winter had come back again, with everyone wrapped up in coats and hoods. He hadn't been able to tell it was her until she'd taken off her hat, a knitted bonnet shaped like a mushroom. His mother seemed agitated, angry even. He could tell by the tone of her voice and the fact that she hadn't invited the woman into the kitchen for tea or coffee. Everyone in Shetland expected to be offered tea or coffee, and usually home-made biscuits or cakes as well. His mother had been baking with Ellie, so there would have been something to give the woman, but Mum seemed determined to stop her coming further into the house. Christopher moved closer to the top of the stairs.

'I'm not sure why you've come to tell me this.' His mother's voice was shrill and loud enough now for him to hear every word. 'It's just malicious gossip.'

'I thought you would want to know what folk are saying.'

'I have no interest at all in what people are saying.' His mother's voice clear and loud again. Christopher wasn't sure that was true; even if it was, he was certainly interested. He liked grown-ups' conversations much better than the chat of people his own age. That he found largely inane. 'Inane' was a new word for him and he was proud to have found a use for it.

'Maybe I should go then,' Mrs Riddell said. It sounded like a challenge. Or a threat. Christopher wondered where his father was. He should be there, helping Mum deal with the batty old woman.

'I think that would be for the best.' His mother walked out of his sight-line and he heard the front door being opened.

Then Margaret Riddell disappeared from view, and Christopher was left with the sound of his mother muttering swear words under her breath.

Chapter Twenty-Eight

During the day, there were a few responses to Willow's radio broadcast. Mostly nutters, Willow decided. An older woman claiming to have the gift of second sight and promising to give the police information about the sender of the messages to Hesti, but only if Willow showed them to her. An excitable young man, more interested in gaining knowledge about the investigation than in passing it on. Then, just as Willow was thinking she'd call it a day, go out for food before heading back to the B&B, an officer on the desk buzzed up with a name that she recognized. Magnie Riddell.

She went to collect him and saw him before he saw her. He was sitting in the one plastic chair in the front office, hunched into a big leather biker's jacket. He had soft blond hair that reached his collar, blue eyes, big hands. Hands big enough to strangle a slight young woman like Emma Shearer. He turned his head slowly and Willow thought he wasn't a man for quick movement. Everything about him would work at half-speed, as if he thought slowly too.

He seemed surprised to see her. 'I thought it might be the other one. Jimmy Perez.'

'He's not here,' she said. There was still a stab of

excitement at the sound of his name. 'I can find a local officer, if you'd rather.'

'You were the woman who spoke on the radio.' Not a question.

She nodded. 'Do you want to come through? We'll find somewhere to chat. Maybe some tea.'

He hesitated, and for a moment she thought he'd say it was all a mistake and that he'd slide back into the fog. But he got to his feet and followed her. She took him to a meeting room, not the interview room next to the cell. She didn't want him to feel he was any kind of suspect. He was, of course, because he'd been close to the victim: a man with a temper, infatuated with the woman, liable to lash out if he sensed rejection. But now Willow wanted Magnie relaxed. She made him tea, without asking again if he wanted it, giving him time to settle.

'You wanted to know about messages sent to the folk at Hesti.' Magnie looked at her. He was holding the cardboard cup in his fist and she thought the tension would make him squeeze it and spill the tea all over the table.

'You have some idea who sent them?' She paused. 'Was it you?'

'No!' It came out as a shout and, as he looked around him, he reminded her of a large caged animal. Any minute, she thought, he'd start pacing.

'So not you. But someone you know?'

'Were they small?' he asked. 'Little scraps of paper with squares? The graph paper that women use for plotting out their knitting patterns.'

She nodded. Now he'd started talking she didn't want to interrupt him. He didn't speak for a moment and she heard the sounds outside the room: the wheezing of an old printer, someone laughing.

'I think it could have been my mother,' he said. 'Margaret, my mother.' There was another pause, more noises off. 'She got strange ideas about those folks at Hesti. Got kind of obsessed about them, after Dennis Gear killed himself.' He looked up at Willow. 'But she wouldn't have murdered anyone. Really. She might not have been over the moon that I was seeing Emma, but she didn't hate her.'

'Not like she hated the Flemings?' Willow said. Magnie's silence was an answer of sorts and she continued: 'What sort of strange ideas did she have about them?'

'She had all sorts of strange ideas after my father left us.' A flush of embarrassment rose from his neck and spread across his face. 'She got it into her head that Dennis Gear was the love of her life. He'd been a childhood sweetheart, she said, and they were meant to be together. She kind of pestered him for a while. He was still at Hesti then.'

'What did Mr Gear make of that?'

'They saw each other a few times, I think, but when Dennis realized my mother didn't have enough cash to bail him out of the financial mess, he dropped her. It would never have worked anyway. He was pretty screwed up by then. Drinking too much. You'd catch him in the bar in Brae most days, crying into his beer. Soon afterwards, he lost the house and it was sold to that family from London.' Magnie looked up. 'My mother got it into her head that it was all their fault that he hanged himself. That, somehow, they'd ripped him off to buy the house. But he'd lost the house way before they came on the scene. She was just telling herself stories to make herself feel better.' He was silent for a moment. 'I thought it was a mean thing to do: to kill himself there, where a bairn might have found him.'

A bairn did *find Emma Shearer. But surely Margaret Riddell wouldn't have killed to get her own back for the death of an imagined lover.*

'What makes you think your mother sent those messages?'

'I saw one. I got in earlier than I expected from work and she was in the lounge, making dots in the tiny squares of the paper to make a picture like a hanged man. At first I thought she was planning a new piece of knitting, but she always uses traditional designs.' He looked up and for the first time gave a little smile. 'I don't think a gallows features in most Fair Isle knitting.'

Willow smiled back. 'Maybe not. But then I'm no knitter.'

'I asked her what she was doing,' Magnie said. 'At first she wouldn't answer, then she said: "That family needs to know they're not welcome here." Nothing I said would make her see reason. It wasn't just about Dennis. It was Helena Fleming having such success with her business. Mother ranted about that too. There was nothing rational about it. It was as if the obsession about Dennis Gear and the jealousy were burning her up inside, making her ill.'

'What did you do?' Willow ached for the man. Crazy parents were always a nightmare. In a small community like this, where there was little else to do but gossip, having a mother like Margaret would seem horrendous.

'Nothing.' Magnie looked straight at her. 'I didn't know that she'd actually sent the messages. I hoped I'd made her see sense.' He paused again. 'I should have asked my mother if she'd got rid of them, or warned the family up at Hesti. But I couldn't face another row.'

'Is there anything else I should know?'

He paused. 'I think she watched folk.'

'What do you mean?'

'She parked her car where she thought nobody would see and watched what they were doing. She told me things about Emma that she could only have known if she'd been snooping. It was the same with the family at Hesti. Sometimes she followed them. It gave her a buzz. Knowing secrets always gave her a buzz.'

'Maybe you should move out,' Willow said. 'Get a place of your own.'

'Aye.' She thought that he'd already considered the idea and dismissed it as impossible. 'But then how would she be, rattling around in that place with no company? That's not going to help her get back to normal.'

'Doesn't she have a sister?'

'Lottie,' Magnie said. 'She lives next door, but she just agrees with everything my mother says. Humours her.' He shook his head. 'It's me my mother needs. No one else will do.'

Willow showed Magnie out and stood at the police-station entrance, staring out at the blurred outline of the town hall. Her phone buzzed. A text from Perez: *No planes today because of the weather. Booked on tonight's ferry. See you in the morning. Hope all's going well.* The message seemed conciliatory, almost friendly. She was tempted to phone him to tell him the latest news, had scrolled down to find his number, then stopped herself at the last minute. She couldn't push him. Instead, she went inside to seek out Sandy. He was in the ops room in the middle of a phone conversation and the interruption seemed to throw him. He made embarrassed apologies to the person on the other end of the line and ended the call.

'When do I get to meet her?'

He seemed confused.

'That *was* Louisa you were talking to?'

He gave a sheepish smile. 'Her mother's not been too good. I wanted to check that everything was OK.'

'Talking of mothers . . . I've just had Magnie Riddell in to shop his.'

'For the murder of Emma Shearer?' Sandy's face was a picture.

'No,' Willow said, 'for sending those strange little anonymous notes to the Flemings. Magnie says she's been stalking them too. And Emma. He reckons his mum's a bit of a nut job.'

Sandy seemed to think about that. 'I don't know her well, but I would say she's sane enough. Full of malice and gossip – one of those people who can't speak a good word about anyone – but if that makes the woman a nut job, then I've met a fair few who could do with being locked away.' He slipped his phone into his pocket. 'Is it relevant to Emma Shearer's murder, do you think?'

'I'm not sure.' Willow looked at her watch. It was already eight o'clock. 'Do you fancy something to eat?

It seems a long time since that egg sandwich with the Moncrieff kids. My treat. I'll drive, if you fancy going somewhere out of town.' She couldn't face going back to the B&B, where Rosie and John would be playing happy families with their baby. And the phase of needing to sleep for twelve hours a day seemed to have passed.

'Why not? If you're paying.'

Willow looked at him for a moment, suspecting pity, then she decided she didn't care anyway. She needed company.

They ended up in Fjara, a cafe bar still in Lerwick but a little way out of the town centre and close to the water. The place was unusually quiet. A group of women, dressed up for a night out without their kids, were squabbling cheerfully about the bill, each insisting on paying. Willow and Sandy found a table close to the window. The mist shifted for a moment and there was a view of two seals hauled up on rocks staring back at them, so close they could see the detail of whiskers and eyelashes, before everything was grey again.

'Just as well Jimmy's booked on the ferry,' Sandy said. 'I don't think there'll be planes any time soon.'

The women trooped out in a cloud of laughter and perfume, and Willow and Sandy had the place to themselves. A waiter brought the menu. They ordered.

'What do you want to do about Margaret Riddell?' Sandy was drinking fancy lager from a bottle with a piece of lime in the neck.

'We'll talk to her tomorrow. I want to go back to

Deltaness anyway; that's where this all started. And she's got a sister. Let's have a word with her too.' She stopped talking as the waiter brought their food. 'I haven't met the adult Moncrieffs yet.'

'Have you heard from Jimmy? How's he getting on in Orkney?'

'He's keeping me posted by email.' Her voice was light. She felt like a parent in a loveless marriage, putting on a brave face for the children. 'He's spoken to Emma's brother David and her friend Claire, to some of the professionals involved with the family. He has a sense that they were all keen to get Emma away from Orkney, that the case was badly handled and she hadn't been given the support she needed.'

'I can't see how that could have anything to do with her murder so many years later.' Sandy was eating lamb shank and some of the sauce had dripped onto his chin. Willow took her napkin and wiped it away and then felt awkward. She wasn't actually his mother after all. He seemed unbothered.

'Unless Emma had suddenly decided to sue them for negligence, or go to the press about the way she'd been treated,' she said. 'Perhaps Daniel Fleming gave her the idea.'

He grinned. 'I can't imagine a posse of teachers and social workers coming north to stop her talking.'

'Nah, it does seem a tad unlikely.' Willow gave a little laugh. 'Emma's social worker suspected she was suffering from Post-Traumatic Stress Disorder. Odd that Moncrieff didn't pick up that she might have been affected by the violence she witnessed when she was younger.'

'I think Robert was just happy to have someone

take the kids off his hands,' Sandy said. 'Like Martha said, the whole happy-family image seems to have been a bit of a sham. I'm not sure he *would* have noticed.'

The cafe staff were starting to clear up around them. Chairs were being put onto tables. It wasn't so much a hint it was time for them to leave that it had become rude, but Willow got the message. Some of the employees might live out of town and the drive home wouldn't be much fun in this weather.

'Shall we have an early start?' she said. 'I'll pick you up.' She got to her feet and Sandy followed.

'We could get Jimmy from the ferry on the way,' he said.

'Why not?' Because she was an adult and what else was there to say?

Outside the streets were empty. Each street light was an orange blur and the buildings were only shadows. There was nothing substantial. She dropped Sandy off at his flat and parked at the top of the lane as close as she could get to the Sheriff's House. She was glad the place was already in darkness and she could make her way to her room without speaking to the owners. In her room, Willow checked to see if there was an email or a text from Jimmy Perez, but there was nothing and she went to bed. The moan of a foghorn in the distance drifted in and out of her dreams.

Chapter Twenty-Nine

Helena Fleming watched Margaret Riddell stamp out into the fog and felt murderous. How dare the woman come here, spitting her bile, revelling in every accusation. How dare she suppose that Helena would be glad to hear it.

Daniel appeared from the door of his office. 'Who was that?'

Helena directed her anger at her husband. 'Couldn't you tell? You must have heard her. Classic that you hid away in there, leaving me to deal with her.'

He blinked and for a moment she thought he was going to cry again. She wondered what had happened to the strong, fun, energetic man she'd married. The one who'd stayed up all night with her, planning their future together, bursting with ideas about design and art and shared adventures. How had he turned into this grey, cowardly shadow?

But I was different then too. I admired him and shared his ideals and promised to work with him to make things happen. I wasn't obsessed with my own work, my own life, my strange kids.

'I didn't think it would help,' he said. 'I knew I

would only wind her up. You seemed to have it covered. And honestly, I didn't hear any of the detail.'

'She claims that you and Emma had an affair. She thought I should know that everyone is talking about it. She seemed to think she was doing me a favour by telling me.'

Unbidden, Helena had a picture of her and Daniel on holiday soon after they'd married. Not a honeymoon. Honeymoons were clichés and everyone had one. They'd told themselves and their friends that this was different, just an escape from London after a long, cold spring. They'd found themselves on an island in Greece. Unplanned and a moment of madness. After scraping together money for the flights and the ferries, they'd found an elderly woman willing to let them use a room in her house, which was surrounded by olive trees and birdsong. In the end it had probably cost more than a hotel, but they'd loved it. The heat and the light, the dreaminess that came with little sleep and too much rough Greek wine. Now she wondered if they could rebuild their marriage by running away again.

'I told you the truth,' Daniel said, breaking into her thoughts. 'About Emma. We knew there would probably be gossip.'

'Do you think we can stick it out here?' she said. 'Make a go of it, after all that's happened?' *And the long, dark winters and the fog. People spreading rumours just for the thrill of it.*

They looked at each other in silence.

'Yes,' he said in the end, 'if you want to. I couldn't do it on my own, though. You were always the strong one. Let's show them, shall we, that we won't be intimidated? Let's face it out.'

She wondered if Daniel knew what he was asking of her. She would be seen as the wronged wife, the woman standing by her man, even as he was being suspected of murder. She would be pitied and humiliated. She thought it might be easier to be considered a killer. 'I need a drink,' she said. 'Let's open that bottle of champagne we were saving for a special occasion.'

'Is this a special occasion?' He closed his office door and came towards her, stroked the back of her neck with his thumb.

'No,' she said, 'it's a muddle. But perhaps that's what grown-up life is like and we have to get used to it.'

'So, that's what we're drinking to? Muddle?' He seemed to understand.

'Perhaps to life not being perfect. And to coming to terms with that.' The dream of the perfect holiday in the sun was slipping away from her. She remembered now that they'd argued on that holiday in Greece too.

In the kitchen, she watched him open the wine while she got the glasses. The room seemed to have retained the heat of the previous days. She thought of winter days here, the house being battered by wind, the four of them safe and warm inside. Wondered if that was a dream of the perfect too. She took a glass from him, enjoyed the feeling of bubbles on her tongue, pushed away the memory of Margaret Riddell, of Emma Shearer in this house, somehow persuading her husband that she was special.

Daniel raised his glass to her. 'To muddle and

confusion,' he said. 'And coming through it stronger in the end.' She touched her glass against his, but didn't speak. She thought that was easy enough to say. It would be much harder to do.

Chapter Thirty

Sandy woke early and spoke to Louisa. He imagined her lying in bed in the bungalow in Yell that she shared with her mother. She'd be propped up on her elbow, drinking tea from a big yellow cup. It was the bed she'd had as a teenager – she'd had a great teaching job in the south and had only come back to the islands when her mother was diagnosed with dementia. Sometimes he stayed overnight with her, and it was a terrible squeeze in the single bed. Each time they giggled about it and said they'd have to get something bigger, but they never did. Perhaps they knew that Mavis was getting more and more ill and, even with regular carers, a time might come when she'd have to move into a home. Or that she'd die. Then Louisa would need to come to a decision about where she wanted to live and work. Sandy wasn't sure what would happen then. He didn't like to presume that he'd be part of Louisa's plans.

Willow was waiting for him when he arrived at the end of the lane, close to her B&B. She was standing on the pavement and drops of moisture from the mist clung to her long, tangled hair. She could have waited in her car, but seemed happy enough outside.

'Listen to that!' She turned her face to him and it seemed full of wonder, a child's face.

He was suddenly aware of the blast of birdsong. There were trees and bushes in the sheltered town gardens, home to garden birds that were more scattered elsewhere on the islands. The sound lifted his spirits and made him optimistic. He thought they would find the killer of Emma Shearer, Willow and Perez would become friends again, and he and Louisa would marry and build a family.

'What's so funny?' Willow must have seen him grinning.

'Nothing. I've just got a good feeling about today.'

They arrived at the terminal in time to see the ferry pull in. Because of the cancelled flights there were lots of passengers, but Jimmy Perez was one of the first people off. He seemed preoccupied, but not quite as tense as when Sandy had last seen him. These days Sandy was tuned into the man's moods. Perez nodded to Willow, a kind of acknowledgement at least.

'So, what have you got organized?'

'I'd like Sandy to talk to Moncrieff,' she said. She turned to him. 'I've left a message saying you'll be there to talk to him before morning surgery. That starts at nine, so we'll drop you off on the way through.'

'You're sure you want me to do it?' Sandy disliked the man. Perhaps, he thought now, that was because the doctor scared him. He'd always been intimidated by men like Moncrieff. Educated people who used long words and made references that Sandy didn't understand. He'd even been frightened of Louisa when they'd first met. 'Wouldn't he be better talking to you or Jimmy?'

'Not at all. He'll be more cautious with either of us. Folk always underestimate you, Sandy. That's a strength, not a weakness. Talk to him about Emma again. Why didn't he see that she was suffering from PTSD? Did the doctor in Orkney warn him of the extent of the trauma she'd been through? Had any of the professionals there contacted him to see how she'd settled? Don't let him bully you.'

Sandy remembered that Perez had told him exactly the same thing. Did everyone think he was such an easy target?

The surgery was in a small, modern health centre close to the school and the community centre. All three buildings would have gone up when oil was flowing into the terminal at Sullom Voe, not very far to the south. That had been a time of affluence and optimism, but the atmosphere in the islands had changed as the oil had dried up and interest rates had fallen. Shetlanders had become used to getting just what they wanted for their community, and some were struggling to come to terms with the new reality. It was hardly austerity, but the easy access to cash and good public services was over.

Sandy watched Willow drive away and walked inside. The place seemed empty, apart from a cleaner mopping a corridor floor in the distance and a woman behind the desk in reception. With some relief, Sandy recognized the receptionist as Nettie Gill, a friend of his mother's. She wasn't a Whalsay woman, but they'd been at the high school together and remained good pals.

'I'm afraid you might have a bit of a wait. Robert doesn't usually get here until fifteen minutes before surgery starts. Will you take some tea? Come into my office and I'll put on the kettle.'

He sat on one side of a clear, uncluttered desk, drinking tea while she looked at her computer. When it seemed that she'd finished dealing with overnight emails, he began to talk again.

'You must have known Emma Shearer. She'd have come into the surgery from time to time.'

'Oh, she wasn't a patient,' Nettie said. 'Robert's the only GP based here and maybe he'd have thought it might be awkward for her. A young lassie wouldn't want her boss to know everything about her. She came to the dentist and picked up prescriptions from the pharmacy sometimes.'

'Of course.' Sandy was quiet for a moment, thinking. 'Did Robert ever talk about her?'

Nettie looked up at him. 'Are you asking me to gossip about my boss, Sandy Wilson?'

'I want to feel that I know her,' he said. 'At the moment she's like a shadow. I can't get any sort of hold on her.' He paused and it felt as if it was his mother sitting opposite him, Nettie was so easy to speak to. 'It seems so sad, a young woman like that, and it's as if no one's missing her. The bairns don't seem bothered. The Moncrieffs miss her as a worker, but not as a person. Maybe Magnie Riddell is upset that she's gone, but I can't find anyone else who was friendly with her.'

'You know there are rumours flying around the place.' Nettie held his gaze. 'I hear all sorts in here. It's as if I'm not a person, sitting behind the desk. Folk just ignore me.'

'What sort of rumours?'

'That Emma wasn't a very . . .' Nettie hesitated, 'nice young woman. That she was cold and hard with the bairns, that she set her cap at the men with money and power.'

'Like Robert Moncrieff? Was the gossip that she set her cap at him?'

'Some folk said that. I can't believe it was true. Certainly not that she succeeded, even if she did have designs on him. Seemed to me that he wanted her for a skivvy. I never saw any evidence that he had feelings for her.'

'What about Daniel Fleming?'

She didn't seem surprised by the question. 'Ah, you've heard those rumours too. Margaret Riddell's telling anyone who'll listen that they were having an affair.'

'You don't think it was true?'

A silence. The sound of a vacuum cleaner in the distance. 'I know that I saw Emma and Magnie on the beach one night after youth club in the hall. Magnie staring at her as if she was the answer to all his prayers. As if he was besotted. Margaret wouldn't have liked that. He's all she's got, after her man left her for a younger woman in Lerwick. She'd have preferred to believe that Emma was a scarlet woman chasing after Mr Fleming.'

Sandy thought he wasn't learning much new here, but it was good to have confirmation of the things they'd already been told. 'Is Margaret a patient?'

'Aye, most of Deltaness come here.'

He was trying to put together the words to ask about the woman's state of mind, when they heard footsteps crossing the reception area and Robert Moncrieff's voice. 'Nettie? Where are you?' Impatient. Sandy thought the man could have been calling a wayward dog. Nettie rolled her eyes. It seemed there was little love lost between her and the doctor. She got to her feet slowly. 'I'm in here. There's a detective wanting to speak to you. Sandy Wilson.'

The man paused a beat. He hadn't realized he'd been overheard and his voice became more conciliatory, more polite.

'Ah yes, I got his message. Send him into my room, would you, Nettie? I'll see him before I start surgery. I'm sure it won't take long.'

Sandy sat in an orange chair on the other side of the doctor's desk and felt as he had as a small boy, dragged along by his mother to see the doctor in Lerwick. Nervous and awe-struck, as if he was in the presence of the Almighty. 'Emma Shearer wasn't one of your patients?'

'No. I suggested she register with the GP in Brae and she followed my advice. If you need information about her medical history, you can check with the practice there.'

'Emma's social worker thought she was suffering from Post-Traumatic Stress Disorder,' Sandy said. 'Does that make any sort of sense to you?'

Moncrieff made a noise that was a cross between a sneer and a laugh. 'I never saw any evidence of it. She always seemed a remarkably stable young woman to me. Of course social workers have no medical training.

Really, I wouldn't take an amateur's opinion too seriously.'

'The doctor in Orkney didn't mention anything of that sort?'

'No,' Moncrieff said, 'and I'm sure he would have done, if he'd had any suspicions of PTSD. He knew Emma would be working with vulnerable children.'

'Did he get in touch with you to find out how Emma was settling in?'

'Really there was no need for him to do that.' Now Moncrieff was becoming impatient. 'He knew we'd look after her. It was in our interests to make sure she was happy.'

Sandy thought of the young woman who'd spent most of her spare time alone in the attic room in Ness House, making old-fashioned clothes, dreaming that she lived in the past. That wasn't his idea of happiness. He said nothing.

Sandy's silence seemed to increase Moncrieff's ill temper. 'And I must say that I take a very dim view of you interrogating my children in the street. That was highly inappropriate. If it weren't for my wife, I'd be making an official complaint.'

'We bumped into Martha and Charlie while we were buying lunch.' Sandy's voice was mild. He was feeling more confident now, wondering what the doctor might have to hide, what he was scared that his children might have given away. 'And we gave them a lift back to school.'

'I'd be grateful if you'd keep away from them in the future. If you have any questions, ask me or their mother.' Moncrieff glanced at the clock on the wall. 'I think you should go now. My first patient will be waiting.'

'Were you having an affair with Emma Shearer?'

There was a shocked silence. Then fury. He could tell that Moncrieff was struggling to keep his temper, and Sandy was half-scared and half-hopeful that the man would hit him. In the end, the doctor regained a measure of control. The words came slowly, with equal emphasis on each syllable. 'That is a foul accusation. When she came to us, Emma was scarcely more than a child. We took her into our home and cared for her. We did not exploit her.' Moncrieff stood up. 'Now you must go. I have more important things to do than listen to your ridiculous stories.'

On his way out, Sandy waved to Nettie. He hoped the other professionals working there were more pleasant than Moncrieff. Otherwise it must be a miserable place to spend her day. Outside the weather seemed brighter. Sandy stood for a moment, wondering where he should go next. Willow and Jimmy would be talking to Margaret and Lottie. The children were already inside the school and the community seemed very quiet. He was thinking that Moncrieff was rattled, which was an interesting thing, and that there was more than one way for a young woman to be exploited.

Chapter Thirty-One

Helena woke to the memory of the champagne they'd drunk the evening before, the sense of some kind of reconciliation. Daniel was still asleep, breathing easily. He stirred, opened his eyes and smiled at her. The mist was still there outside the window but it seemed less dense. White, not grey, and shimmering, rather beautiful, as if there was light behind it.

In the school yard there was no noticeable difference in the parents' response to her. Belle was there before her with her youngest children, and made a beeline for Helena as soon as she came through the gate. 'You do know they're all talking about us.' She turned to wave to a group of mothers who were trying not to stare. 'Have you got time for a coffee later? I've got some questions about that trade fair in Birmingham. And the London press has got hold of your connection with the murder. We should talk about our response.'

'Do we need to respond?' Helena could think of nothing worse. She'd already been bothered by Reg Gilbert from *The Shetland Times* – he seemed to have tracked down her personal mobile number – and she'd hung up on him every time. The thought of her name being linked to Emma Shearer's in whatever context was a nightmare.

'I think we could turn the publicity to our advantage, if we handle it properly.' Belle watched Kate run towards the school door as the bell went. 'I must say, she doesn't seem particularly traumatized by Emma's death. What about your two?'

Helena thought about Christopher's statement that he was glad Emma was dead. 'I don't know. It's hard to tell.'

'So, you're free for coffee?' Belle was already walking towards the road with her car keys in her hand. 'About eleven? Shall I come to you? I hadn't realized just how much we'd come to rely on Emma and how much we took her for granted. Our house is a total pigsty without her. I'll have to sort out a cleaner, even if I don't get extra childcare. Robert's being useless.'

'Sure,' Helena said. 'Come to me. I'll show you those new designs I was talking about. The ones using the patterns I found in the museum in Fair Isle.'

'Fabulous.' Belle was already in her car and driving away. Her house was closer to the school than Hesti, but Helena had never seen her walk.

Instead of heading straight back to the house, Helena climbed the pebble bank and looked out to the sea. She could hear gulls, but couldn't see them. They were lost in the white light that seemed to be filtered through gauze or the finest knitted lace. Sliding back down to the road, she waited for a car to pass. Willow Reeves was in the driver's seat.

'Want a lift?'

'Are you heading up to the house?'

'Not yet,' Willow said. 'Maybe later, but I can give you a lift, if you like. Won't take a minute.'

'No, thanks. I'm enjoying the walk.'

Willow didn't push it. 'It's kind of eerie, isn't it?' She started the engine. 'This weather. But in quite a lovely way.' It seemed an odd comment from a woman who spent her life working with criminals.

Belle arrived early, before Helena was quite ready for her. The doctor's wife was dressed for action with full make-up and a slinky black top, loose black trousers that had probably cost a fortune. Perhaps she'd hoped that the press would already be here. It occurred to Helena that the weather had done her and Daniel a favour. There'd been no planes into the islands since the previous morning, and she supposed journalists would be reluctant to take the boat.

Daniel had gone into Lerwick to talk to a businessman who was considering commissioning a green hotel in the south of Shetland mainland. The truce of the night before had lasted over breakfast, when he'd explained his plans for the new venture, looking at her eagerly, wanting her support. He'd set off excited at the prospect of a new project.

'It'll be a big deal, Helly. A showcase for sustainable development.' She hadn't seen him so happy for months and she thought that Emma's death had released him from some sort of spell; after the initial grief, he seemed like a newly freed man. The implications of that she pushed to the back of her mind.

Just before Belle arrived, there was a phone call from Willow Reeves.

'Did you get a visit from Margaret Riddell last night?'

'Has she been to *you* with her rumours and foul accusations?' Helena felt the anger of the previous night return.

'Nothing like that. So, she was with you? That's all I needed to know.'

And that was it, the end of the conversation, and Belle was at the door, shouting that she was letting herself in. Helena made coffee in the kitchen and then the women walked across the courtyard to her studio. The mist was lifting slowly from the north, and Helena too was losing the feeling of being trapped. They talked for a while about Belle's ideas for overseas promotions, the trade fair, Helena's new designs. Helena thought Emma Shearer was hovering between them, not so much the elephant as the ghost in the room.

At last Belle tackled the subject head-on. 'I've been thinking about what you said in the playground about our response to the national press. You were quite right, of course. We should keep a dignified silence while the investigation is continuing, but then I don't see anything wrong with negotiating an exclusive with a national, once it's all over. An interview with you – wearing one of your own creations, of course – talking about the trauma of finding a body in your home.'

'Oh no!' Helena was horrified. 'I couldn't. It would be as if I was profiting from Emma's death.'

Belle pretended not to hear. 'It would be a good way to put an end to all the rumours spreading here. A way to show them that your family has nothing to be ashamed of, that you're prepared to go public on it.'

'My family *has* nothing to be ashamed of. Emma's

body was found in our byre, but she worked for *you*.' Helena regretted the words as soon as they were spoken. This sounded like a scrap between children, not between grown women who were supposed to be friends. 'I'm sorry. That was unforgivable. It's the stress, I suppose, making us all lash out. Of course I didn't mean that you were in any way responsible for the murder.'

Belle stared at her for a moment, not moving. 'I'm not sure that the police would believe that,' she said at last. 'They want to speak to me again today.' Suddenly the glossy make-up and the bravura performance seemed rather desperate. 'Do you know they talked to Martha and Charlie yesterday? Caught them at lunch-time outside the caff where all the kids go for lunch. Pretended it was a chance meeting. We wouldn't have found out about it, if Charlie hadn't let something slip. Robert's furious, he's threatened to get lawyers involved to make an official complaint. I've told him he should just let it go. If we make a fuss, it'll look as if we've got something to hide.'

This is how rumours start and suspicion spreads, Helena thought. *One woman's death is tragedy enough, but everyone who knew her is affected. We all become victims.*

Chapter Thirty-Two

Willow saw Helena Fleming as a silhouette in the mist at the top of the shingle bank, backlit and strange in the filtered white light. She was recognizable because of the curly hair and the distinctive long jacket. Willow had dropped Sandy at the health centre and Perez was still sitting beside her. She'd stopped the car on impulse. Helena was an obvious suspect – she could easily have found out about Daniel's infatuation with Emma, and jealousy was always a strong motive – but Perez refused to consider it, just because the woman had been a friend of Fran's. Helena refused the offer of a lift and there was nothing for Willow to do but drive on.

She parked on a bit of scrubby grass close to the shore and turned to Perez. 'I'm going to talk to Margaret Riddell about the anonymous notes. Do you want to come along?'

'If it won't cramp your style.' On previous investigations she would have taken that as a joke. Now she wasn't sure. It could be a barbed insult.

'You don't mind walking for a bit? I could do with some exercise to clear my head.'

'That's fine,' he said. Not hostile, at least. She supposed that was the best she could expect.

They walked towards the street where Margaret

Riddell lived. Willow thought there was nothing attractive about these houses. Margaret had made an effort with fresh paint, but the effect was gaudy and unconvincing. Her car was parked outside her home, but when Perez knocked there was no answer. She couldn't be at work in Brae; she'd need her car for that, surely. Perez knocked again and this time a door did open, but it was the neighbour's.

'I think she must be ill.' The woman was still in nightclothes, a long old-fashioned nightdress under a candlewick dressing gown. She stood inside her house with her head poked forward and turned uncomfortably towards them, obviously embarrassed to cross her threshold not properly clothed. 'It's Margaret's day for Brae and usually she'd be gone by now.'

'You must be Lottie,' Willow said. She moved along the pavement so the woman could talk to her more easily.

'Aye.' Lottie shuffled back inside the house. There was little light inside and she became no more than a shadow. 'I was just starting to worry about her, but I don't know what to do. Magnie's been in Lerwick and he's not back yet.'

'Should we go and check, do you think? I suppose you do have a key?'

Lottie disappeared without speaking and Willow followed her into a gloomy hall and the world of the 1970s. A downmarket stage set for *Abigail's Party*. The carpet was highly patterned with swirls of orange and the walls were covered with painted woodchip wallpaper. Perez waited on the pavement, knowing that an older woman wouldn't want him in the house while she was still in her nightclothes.

'Have you always lived here?' Willow thought the place couldn't have been redecorated since it had been built.

'It was our parents' house.' The hall led to a kitchen, also captured in time. Lino floor, Formica units and table. Orange featured here too. Lottie took a key from a hook on the wall. 'I moved in to look after Mother when she was ill after my father died, and I stayed. It seemed the best thing.' A pause. 'Margaret thought it was for the best.'

Willow thought that probably summed up the relationship between the sisters. According to Perez, who'd seen them together, Margaret was the strong personality, the one who took all the decisions. 'Would you like to come next door with me?'

'Not like this!' Lottie seemed horrified. 'What would Margaret say? You go along in, and I'll follow once I've made myself decent.'

Perez knocked on Margaret's door again before using the key, but there was still no reply. Willow thought Lottie was overreacting; the whole community would be jittery after the murder of Emma Shearer. The sister had probably taken a day off work, had wandered down to the shop for milk or a paper. But it was a great opportunity to get into the house. If they found evidence that Margaret had sent the anonymous notes to the Fleming household, they could keep Magnie out of any discussion.

The layout was a mirror image of Lottie's home, but it was lighter and cleaner. The kitchen was full of appliances that had probably come from the former marital home – a microwave, food processor, sleek black toaster. The living room was packed with oversize furniture, not to Willow's taste, but solid and expensive.

Perez shouted up the stairs, 'Mrs Riddell? Are you there?' No response. Willow was tempted to look through the drawers in a sideboard that fitted into an alcove, but she thought that would have to wait. Just in case Margaret *was* lying unconscious in a room above them.

Perez followed her up the stairs, so close behind her that Willow could smell the soap he'd used that morning. She pictured turning, taking him into her arms and burying her face into his hair, then imagined his reaction: horror, embarrassment. She continued walking.

The first door led into Magnie's room. It was surprisingly tidy. The duvet and pillows had been straightened, and dirty washing had been placed into a wicker laundry basket. The surfaces had been recently dusted and still smelled faintly of lavender polish. It was a strangely anonymous room – there were no books or posters. A large TV screen was fixed to the wall and faced the bed. Willow wondered if Margaret had been in here since he'd set off for work the day before, or if Magnie looked after it himself. She looked out of the window, expecting to see Margaret walking up the street with a bag of shopping, but there was no sign of her or of Lottie. The mist was definitely lifting. Now it was possible to glimpse a line of sunlight on the water.

Back on the landing, Willow could see through an open door to the bathroom. Everything white, and again everything spotless. Perez was knocking on the remaining door that was firmly shut. 'Mrs Riddell, are you there?' He waited for a moment, then let himself in. Willow stood beside him, just inside the room.

The bed was large and took up most of the space. It had a curved headboard and purple cushions were propped against it, so it looked as if it belonged in a pretentious hotel. There was no sign of Margaret Riddell, except that her image stared out of a large studio photograph of her with her son. The picture had been fixed to the wall in the same space as the television in Magnie's room. The bed was made, and floral pyjamas were folded on the pillow. If she'd slept there the previous night, she'd tidied the room before leaving. Willow took another look out of the window, saw again that the street was empty and opened the wardrobe. On one side, dresses, skirts and jackets hung in a neat row. On the other, a rack of shelves contained underwear and jerseys. All folded.

'Wouldn't you think,' Perez said, 'that this was the product of an ordered mind? Not someone as obsessed as Magnie described.'

They'd left the front door open for Lottie, and now Willow heard tentative sounds below. 'Just a moment. I'll come down.'

Lottie had pulled on a pair of shapeless trousers and a jersey made of some man-made fibre in snot-green. She was still wearing the slippers. She looked up as Willow walked down the stairs towards her. 'Is she there?'

Willow couldn't tell if the anxiety in her voice was caused by worry for her sister's health or about Margaret's reaction if they'd been caught snooping. 'No,' she said. 'Everything's fine. She must have gone out for a walk.'

'Margaret doesn't walk! Not unless she has to.'

'Maybe someone gave her a lift into work.' Willow wanted Lottie out of the house, so they could look in the sideboard drawers. Perez was still upstairs. Willow wondered if he'd gone into Magnie's room, checking that she'd not overlooked something important.

'I can't mind who that might be.' The woman still hovered just inside the door as if she felt awkward about intruding.

'Why don't I have a quick look round and see if I can find any clue as to where she might be? You could go home and try phoning her.' Willow would have bet that this woman didn't own a mobile. 'And I would love a cup of tea.' She smiled. 'Maybe you could put the kettle on?'

As soon as Lottie had left, Willow moved quickly to the living room and opened the sideboard drawer. There was a thick file labelled 'Divorce': a pile of correspondence between solicitors, acrimonious words about details that seemed to Willow to be petty – ownership of furniture and household goods, a dispute about who had contributed most to the deposit for the house in Voe, to the largest car. There was another file relating to the purchase of Margaret's Deltaness home. Willow flicked through it quickly, aware that Margaret could return any moment and assuming that there would be little of interest.

She heard Perez's footsteps on the stairs and was aware of him coming into the room, but her attention was focused on the file. At the back was a brown envelope, unlabelled. Willow pulled out the contents and found letters that went back more than three decades. The handwriting was as clear and round as that of a studious child, and Willow found them very easy to read. She saw almost immediately that these were love letters. Love letters from Dennis Gear, the man who'd committed suicide in the Flemings' barn. Writing to a young Margaret, they were all addressed to 'my peerie Tammie Norrie', the Shetland dialect word for puffin. The words were playful and excited, making plans for trips to Lerwick to see a favourite fiddle player, and then talking of a dance in the Vidlin Hall:

> *What a splendid night that was! All those folk dressed in their finest and you the bonniest of them all, and so light on your feet. I felt the luckiest man in the world.*

Without a word, Willow passed them one by one to Perez. At the back of the pile there was a note, very sad and apologetic. Willow thought it must have come after Margaret had announced her engagement to Neil Riddell:

> *Of course I can't blame you for your decision. I haven't treated you as I should in the past, and Hesti will hardly provide a living for one man, let alone a family. But know this. No other man will ever love you as much as I do.*

Willow passed that on too and looked at Perez, waiting for a reaction, thinking: *No other woman will ever love you as much as I do.* He read the letter, but said nothing. His face was impassive. She returned to the file.

Along with the letters was a small piece of graph paper. Spots within the tiny squares formed a gallows and a noose. But Margaret had made a mistake – a spot in the wrong square – and the image was spoilt, not perfect. She must have started again, but kept the faulty message.

'So Magnie was right. Margaret did send those notes.' Willow stood in the overcrowded room and felt the weight of Margaret's disappointment as a physical pain, a headache, not a heartache. Margaret had chosen Neil Riddell for his prospects, only to be abandoned by him for a younger woman. It was clear that Dennis Gear had cared for her, at least at the beginning. That hadn't been a figment of her imagination. His death would have made her reassess every important decision she'd made in her life. There would have been regret that she'd chosen the wrong man, bitterness and, above all, there would have been guilt. At her betrayal of Dennis when she was younger, and that she hadn't prevented his suicide. No wonder she'd needed someone else to blame.

There were footsteps outside the front door. Willow stuffed the papers back into the file and closed the drawer. She turned round, thinking quickly of the words she'd use to explain her presence in the house. *Lottie let us in. She was worried that she hadn't seen anything of you today.*

But it was Lottie who was standing there, obviously distressed. 'Margaret's not answering her mobile. And I phoned her work. They were expecting her in today and she hasn't been in touch. I don't know what to do.'

'Let's go back to your house.' Willow's head was still full of the love letters from Dennis Gear, so touching and undemanding. 'We'll have that tea, shall we? And see if we can track her down. We'll leave Jimmy here, in case she turns up.' She felt only sympathy for the missing woman, imagined her lonely and desperate somewhere, and then the thought intruded that this was no way for a police officer to respond. Margaret could be a suspect, and she needed to keep some emotional distance.

There was orange patterned wallpaper in Lottie's living room, but it had faded, so it blended into the beige carpet and brown furniture. Everything here had faded. Willow thought nothing in the house had been changed since the death of Lottie and Margaret's parents. She wanted to ask about the family. It was clear that Lottie had retired, because there had been no mention of her being employed, and the room was littered with signs that she spent most of her time in this room – a knitting basket overflowing with yarn, a pile of library books, half-open women's magazines. Lottie was someone with time on her hands. But now the priority was to find Margaret.

'Have you contacted Magnie? He might know where your sister is.'

Lottie shook her head. 'I don't have his number. He was always Margaret's boy, you know. Even when he was a peerie boy, she didn't like to share him.'

Again, Willow thought this was a very strange thing to say, and again she was intrigued by the odd relationship between the women, by Lottie's willingness to be dominated, her refusal to fight back.

'I have his number,' Willow said. 'We'll try that, shall we?'

The women were still standing. All thought of tea had been forgotten. Lottie was at the window, staring through a gap in the net curtains as if she hoped Margaret would suddenly and magically appear. Her body was tense, frozen and she seemed close to tears. Willow had put Magnie's number in her phone and was scrolling through her contacts list.

'There's no need!' Lottie moved away from the window and almost ran across the room and to the front door.

'Ah, so she's here,' Willow said. 'All that worry for nothing.' But when she walked to the window, expecting to see the reunion of the sisters, hoping from the encounter to get a better idea of the relationship between them, she realized that Margaret hadn't returned at all.

It was Magnie's van that had pulled up outside the house, and Margaret's son that Lottie was talking to. She'd stretched out and was gripping his arm, her hand hard and white like a claw.

Chapter Thirty-Three

Perez thought that Magnie Riddell looked exhausted; he'd probably been working the night shift at the power plant. Perez had seen the van arriving and had made his way out into the street before Willow.

'What's going on?' Magnie stood by the side of his vehicle, looking around him. He seemed confused by the attention he was getting – his aunt, stick-thin and yelling, grabbing hold of his arm; the two detectives on the pavement, staring.

'We're not sure where your mother might be,' Perez said. He kept his voice easy and unhurried. No need to spread panic. 'Do you have any idea?'

Magnie shook his head. 'I thought she'd be at work.'

'Come in,' Willow said. 'Let's all go into your aunt's house, shall we? Lottie was just putting the kettle on. I'm sure there's an obvious explanation.'

Magnie followed her. Perez thought he was like a child, glad to have someone else take charge. Perez sat next to him on the brown fabric sofa and they both looked towards Willow. Lottie was back by the window, twisting a piece of net curtain in her fingers.

'Margaret's not at work and her car's still here,' Willow said. 'She's not in the house. Can you think where she might be?'

Magnie shut his eyes for a moment. 'No,' he said. 'I haven't seen her since yesterday afternoon. Before I came into Lerwick, to the police station, to talk to you. She wasn't working yesterday.'

'How did she seem then?'

'Kind of restless. I was on my way out and she was rattling on about something. I wasn't really listening to what she was saying. It was foggy and I wanted to get away, to allow more time than usual to get into town.'

'There must be something.' Willow's voice was kind enough, but firm. Perez thought how good she was at this, at pulling information from sensitive witnesses.

Magnie closed his eyes again as if he was trying to remember the threads of the conversation. 'She was talking about putting things right. She couldn't just sit at home, when people didn't realize what had been going on.' He paused. 'She said she was going to go to Hesti. She wanted to talk to Mrs Fleming. There were things she should know.'

'Was she going to drive there? Lottie told me she never walked anywhere.'

'She didn't like driving in the fog,' Magnie said. 'She had an accident when we were living in Voe and it knocked her confidence. She might have walked this time.'

Willow left the room. Perez thought she was phoning Hesti to check if Margaret had been there. She wouldn't want to be overheard. While she was gone, he turned to Magnie. 'Where were you last night? Working the night shift?'

Magnie paused. It occurred to Perez that he might be about to lie. 'No,' he said at last. 'I was out with friends.'

Perez was going to push for details, but Willow came back into the room.

'Margaret *was* at Hesti,' she said. 'I've just checked with Helena Fleming. Did you see her after that, Lottie? She would have left there at about eight.'

Lottie shook her head. Her eyes were still fixed on the road outside.

'It wasn't only the Hesti folk Mother was ranting about,' Magnie said. 'She had things to say about the doctor and his family. I wasn't listening properly, though. I just wanted to get away.' He paused, turned to Willow. 'I'd made up my mind to talk to you and I was kind of nervous.'

'Is there anywhere Margaret goes when she's feeling a bit low?' Willow asked. 'Maybe a favourite place to remember Dennis—'

Lottie interrupted before Magnie could speak. 'She goes to Suksetter, just over the hill from Hesti. Dennis used to take her there when they were courting. Away from prying eyes.' She paused. 'But I think he probably took all his lasses there.'

Perez was surprised by the tone. It seemed a bitter thing to say when they were all so anxious about her sister.

Willow seemed not to notice the resentment and only asked another question: 'Could Margaret have walked there from the Flemings' house? Wouldn't it have been a stretch, and a bit dangerous in the fog?'

'She was very agitated yesterday,' Magnie said. 'Restless. I can see that she might have decided to walk it. And the ground's uneven on the hill. She might have tripped, broken an ankle.'

Perez thought about that. 'I could get a search team

out,' he said, 'but that would take time. And if she's had an accident, or just wanted a bit of time to herself, maybe Margaret wouldn't want a fuss. People talking about her. Perhaps we should take a look first. See if we can find her.' He looked across at Willow, who nodded her approval. *So, we can still work together. At least I haven't ruined that.*

Magnie nodded. He still seemed lost, confused.

Willow was already on her feet. 'Will you stay here, Lottie? In case there's nothing wrong at all and Margaret comes back. I'll give you a card with my mobile number. Phone me if she turns up.' She stood by the door, expecting Perez and Magnie to follow. 'We'll take my car, shall we? You must be shattered, Magnie, after working all night.'

Perez was going to say that Magnie hadn't been working, but Willow was already outside, waiting for them to get into the car. 'Is Hesti the nearest place we can drive to?'

'No, there's a road that leads behind the dunes. Families park there to get to the beach, and further along there's a cafe at Henwick.'

Magnie directed Willow Reeves to take the inland road that curved around the hill and back towards the sea. The mist was still lifting; they drove into patches of sunlight and then back into the haze. Perez felt a little disorientated. The boat had been so full that he hadn't managed to book a cabin. A group of young people had taken over the ferry bar, playing their music, and he'd stayed up watching them until the early hours. One lad with long hair and a frayed Fair Isle jersey had leapt onto a table with his fiddle and played like a demon. His skill and energy had reminded Perez of Roddy Sinclair, a young musician who'd been part of another murder investigation. That had been midsummer too. Fran had still been alive. Perez thought he'd always considered Shetland as unchangeable and solid, but in the last few years his life had altered at a crazy speed. Now he felt a desperate desire to slow down events and stop them spinning out of control.

He knew this place on the coast. He'd come here a number of times with Fran for Sunday-morning walks along the shore to Henwick. She'd made a painting here, all water and sky. He'd loved it and asked her not to sell it. It still hung on the wall of the bedroom that he'd once shared with her. Ahead of them were the dunes, tall enough here that there was no view of the sea. Behind them a series of lochs, almost invisible because a pool of mist had collected over the water. He could hear the wading birds, make out fronds of reed and tall grass that surrounded the loch closest to them.

'What should we do?' Willow asked. 'Is there a footpath over the hill towards Hesti? Should we try that first?'

'If my mother wants to remember Dennis Gear, I know the place she'll be sitting. I made a bench for her there. Just a plank and a couple of rocks, but it was a kind of memorial to him.' Magnie was looking away from the beach towards the nearest pool.

Willow seemed to know what he was talking about, and Perez remembered what Daniel had told her about the memorial. 'OK,' he said. 'Let's look there first. We can try the hill if there's no sign of her there.'

Magnie led the way. The further inland they walked, the patchier the fog became. At last they came to the point of the long loch and it spread ahead of them, the light milky and still shifting. Perez was following Magnie towards the promontory at the other end, when there was a sudden break in the cloud and a shaft of lemon sunlight shone through like a spotlight. He was reminded of a picture he'd seen in a book at Sunday school. It showed Ascension Day and there'd been shafts of sunshine just like this, shining through a cloudy sky onto a white-robed Jesus. Now the bench Magnie had made was lit up in the circle of light, when the land all around it was still in shadow, hazy. Perez saw a figure lying there, curled up, apparently asleep.

He sprinted ahead, shouting at the other two to stay where they were. This was a crime scene and Magnie was a suspect. The last thing they needed was for the man to contaminate the area. He turned briefly and saw that Willow was taking the man's arm, gently as if she was supporting him, not holding him back.

As he got closer Perez recognized the woman at once. Margaret Riddell was lying on her side with her head on the bench, but twisted so that her legs were on the floor. On her head was the woollen hat that she'd been wearing at the Sunday teas, squashed now. Perez knelt beside her and felt for a pulse, knowing that he wouldn't find one.

He looked up at Willow and saw that she was already on her phone. She still had one arm linked through Magnie's, and the man stood beside her compliant, unmoving. Perez stepped away from the body and returned to the couple. Willow released Magnie into his care and turned away to make more calls. When she finished speaking she swivelled back so that she was facing them again. For a tall woman, all her movements were graceful. Perez thought she'd be a great dancer, imagined her for a moment in the Fair Isle hall, stepping out with his father, who was a splendid dancer too.

'What's happened?' Magnie said. He still seemed dazed now, as if he hardly knew where he was.

'We're too late, Magnie,' Willow said. Her voice was very gentle. 'Your mother's dead.'

Perez was watching the man's face and saw one sudden and blinding look of relief. Of freedom. Then Magnie closed his eyes for a moment and, when he opened them, his face was blank once more, without expression. 'What was it?' he asked. 'A heart attack?'

'No,' Perez said, his eyes fixed on the man. 'She's been strangled. Your mother was murdered, Magnie.'

'Just like Emma,' Willow added.

Perez thought that, for Magnie, this was nothing like Emma. He'd appeared heartbroken by Emma's death. But it seemed to Perez that Magnie Riddell would struggle to grieve for his mother at all.

Chapter Thirty-Four

They sent Magnie back to the car to wait and stood where they were, blocking the path in case stray walkers wandered in, and waiting for Perez's team to turn up and secure the site.

'He wasn't at work last night.' Perez was looking up towards the sky; the mist seemed to be rolling back fast. With any luck, James Grieve and Vicki Hewitt would get a plane in today. 'Magnie, I mean. When I asked him, I thought perhaps he was going to lie about it, but he would have known we'd be able to check.'

'So, where was he?'

'He muttered something about being out with friends.'

'Well,' Willow said, 'we'll be able to check that too.' She paused. 'You see Magnie as a suspect then?'

'Don't you? He has a history of violence, and I can imagine Emma Shearer playing with him, provoking him. A cat with a pathetic little mouse. It's clear he was obsessed with her. Maybe she told him she had another man and something snapped.'

'And his mother?'

'I only met her a couple of times, but she was a bitter old witch.' Perez remembered the bile that the woman had spouted about the Fleming family at the

Sunday teas. 'If she'd found out that her son killed Emma, she'd use that to keep him with her for the rest of her life.'

'She might have been a bitter old witch, but she was very sad too. Keeping those love letters from Dennis Gear all those years, regretting so much the decision she made when she was younger . . .' Willow stretched and Perez saw again how supple she was. 'I think Helena Fleming's a more obvious suspect. After all, look at the two victims here: a younger woman who seduced Fleming's husband, and the person who'd been sending her poisonous anonymous letters.'

'No!' For some reason the idea horrified him. How could the woman who cared so deeply for her family, who was so patient with her autistic son, commit murder? 'I don't see it.'

'Why's that, Jimmy? Because Helena came to you, a damsel in distress, seeking your aid? You've never been able to resist that. And after all, she's so much more sympathetic than Margaret Riddell. Or is it because she was a pal of Fran's?'

There was a moment of silence. Perez was tempted to walk away, but he stayed where he was. He suspected Willow was right: his judgement was clouded by guilt and grief, and he'd been flattered that a famous designer had asked him to help her.

'Jimmy, I'm sorry.' Willow stretched out a hand, but couldn't, it seemed, bring herself to touch him. 'That was crass.'

Perez shook his head. 'You're right. Of course we have to keep an open mind about them all.' There was a silence broken by bird call and the sound of the breeze in the long grass. He chose his words carefully. 'How have you been while I've been south in Orkney?'

She didn't answer immediately. 'I'm fine, Jimmy, honestly. Feeling much better. I actually seem to have more energy.' A brief pause. 'I think Shetland must agree with me.'

They agreed that Willow would go to Deltaness with Magnie, to talk to Lottie, and Perez would take Sandy's car, when he arrived, and prepare the ops room in Lerwick for the second murder investigation. The easy camaraderie of earlier investigations was missing, but the crackling tension had gone.

When Perez phoned James Grieve, the pathologist was already at the airport waiting for a flight into Shetland.

Perez filled him in on the little he knew. 'Our new victim's a fifty-eight-year-old woman called Margaret Riddell. I think she was strangled too. We'll arrange for a car to meet you at the airport and take you to the scene. Sandy will be there. We'll join you later.'

'That's fine, Jimmy.' He paused. 'Have you seen my post-mortem report on Emma Shearer? I sent it off to Willow late last night.'

'Not yet,' Perez said.

'Are the two of you no longer communicating? What's going on there?'

Perez ignored the question. 'I've been in Orkney. Digging into the background on the first victim. I only got in on the ferry this morning, and now we have another victim.' He paused. 'I doubt Willow's had the chance to take in all the details of your report herself yet.'

'Just a minute, Jimmy. This is important. Let me find somewhere I'll not be overheard.' Grieve's phone went dead for a moment, and when he started speaking again, the background chatter had faded. 'Am I right in thinking that Kenneth Shearer was only charged with abuse against the mother, not the children?'

'Yes. The children were witnesses, but not victims.'

'I found a couple of untreated fractures.' The pathologist kept his voice even, but Perez remembered again that Grieve was a father of four children. 'It would suggest that Shearer lashed out at Emma as well as the mother.'

'But nobody noticed. And she never spoke.'

'Fear, maybe. Or guilt. Abused children often blame themselves.'

Perez thought that would explain the wariness behind the eyes, and Emma's reluctance to get too close to any of her admirers. He wished now that he hadn't described her to Willow as a cat playing with a pathetic mouse. That had been cruel, unnecessary. The professor's findings might also explain the Orkney professionals' desire to find a new home for her. Perhaps she *did* confide in them, once her father was safely convicted, but they had no enthusiasm for revisiting the case. He still couldn't see how the new information was relevant to her murder in Shetland, but it was important to *him*.

James Grieve, still on the end of the line, was growing impatient. 'Are you there, Jimmy?'

'Yes, just trying to work out what that might mean for our investigation.'

'Ah,' the pathologist said. 'That's a decision for you, not for me. I'll see you later today.'

Perez sat at his desk, trying to get a handle on Margaret Riddell, digging into her past. Lottie was the older sister, but Margaret had been the achiever, with good exam grades. She'd got a place at teacher-training college in Aberdeen, but hadn't completed the course and had come back to Shetland and to her parents. She wouldn't have been the only hopeful student to find life away from the islands harder than she'd expected. On her return to Shetland, she'd started working in the bank in Lerwick and there she'd met Neil, her boss and future husband. Perez gleaned most of this information from online issues of *The Shetland Times*; a wedding photograph showed her in traditional white, standing beside a tall, rather stern-looking man. The only mention of Margaret in connection with Dennis Gear was in a much earlier report of a music festival in Lerwick. They were standing together in a photograph of young people, but the image was so blurred that it was impossible to pick out any of the individuals.

Magnie's birth was announced in the newspaper too. He'd been baptized in the church where Neil was lay-reader. Of course there was no mention of the Riddells' divorce, of Neil setting up home with a Latvian housekeeper, or of Margaret leaving her job in the bank to work part-time in the Co-op in Brae. It would have been talked about, though. There was nothing a gossip liked more than a tale of the mighty fallen, a respectable family breaking apart.

Perez phoned the Deltaness health centre several times and spoke to the receptionist there. He was interested to know if Margaret had visited Ness House on the evening of her death. If Magnie was right, she'd talked about going there as well as Hesti. The only information he received was that Dr Moncrieff was out for the afternoon on home visits, and the receptionist had no idea when he would be back. Nettie was sympathetic – Perez supposed that news of Margaret Riddell's death would have seeped, like osmosis, into the community – but she said that she couldn't give out any medical details without the doctor's permission. The last time Perez called, there was only an automatic answering-machine message. He tried phoning Ness House, hoping to speak to Belle, but that call went unanswered too.

On his own in the ops room, Perez tried to pull together his thoughts. He'd felt at first that Emma Shearer's death had something to do with a hatred of outsiders. There was a poisonous atmosphere in that community, a horrible mix of gossip and prejudice. A local man had committed suicide and it was if everyone wanted to shift the blame onto the newcomers. But Margaret Riddell had been born and brought up in Deltaness. She seemed to be at the heart of all the muck-spreading and rumour. So perhaps he'd got the whole thing wrong and he needed to start again from the beginning.

Chapter Thirty-Five

Willow left Sandy standing guard over the reclining body of Margaret Riddell and walked back to her car. Perez had already headed back to Lerwick. There were just ribbons of mist now, caught by the sunlight and blown by the breeze back out to sea. As she'd thought he might be, Magnie was asleep in the passenger seat. He didn't stir, even when she started the engine and the car bumped over the rough track back to the road and Deltaness.

Lottie was waiting for them, still at her post at the window. Willow decided not to disturb Magnie. She'd rather talk to Lottie alone. The front door was ajar and she let herself in, met Lottie in the hall.

'You didn't find her then?' Lottie seemed even more distraught than when they'd left. 'I've had no news, either.'

Willow put her arm round the woman's bony shoulder to shepherd her back into the living room, and waited until they were both seated before speaking. Lottie made no protest and asked no further questions.

'We *did* find Margaret,' Willow said. 'She was on the bench that Magnie made for her in memory of Dennis.'

'Has she been there all night? She'll have caught her death in all the fog. Where is she now?'

'She's dead, Lottie.' Willow waited for a beat, to make sure the words had sunk in. Sometimes relatives shut out the truth, heard only the words that they wanted to hear. 'She was strangled. Murdered, like Emma Shearer.'

There was a moment of complete silence. Lottie was still facing the window, as if waiting for her sister to appear at the end of the street.

'Did you understand, Lottie?' Willow made sure that her voice was gentle and clear. 'Somebody has killed Margaret. I need to ask you some questions. It'll be hard for you, I know, but we have to find out who killed your sister. I need to know why anyone would want to do that.'

Lottie turned her head slowly, so that she was facing Willow. 'I'm not stupid.' The words hard and sharp. 'Margaret sometimes treated me as if I was stupid, but I'm not. I knew something was wrong when she didn't leave for work this morning. I knew something has been wrong with her for weeks.'

'Since Dennis Gear killed himself?'

'No,' Lottie said. 'Maybe not that long ago.'

'Do you have any idea what might have upset her?'

'She didn't like me and the Shearer girl becoming friends.' Lottie sat back in her chair now and shut her eyes for a moment.

'You were friends with Emma?' Willow found this astonishing. What could the stylish young woman and Lottie, in her Crimplene slacks and ugly sweaters, have in common?

'I found her once, when I was on my way back

from the shop. She was sitting on the bank, looking out to the beach. She was crying. I asked her into the house for some tea. I'd just bought biscuits, so we had those too.'

'Did she tell you why she was upset?'

Lottie shook her head. 'And I didn't ask. Not my business, and she'd tell me in her own time if she wanted to. We talked about Deltaness. She wanted to know what it was like growing up here, all the old stories.'

'You've lived here all your life?'

'Oh no!' Lottie seemed shocked by the idea. 'I was born in the South Mainland. Dunrossness. We moved to this house when it was new, when the oil came. My father found a job at Sullom Voe. My mother never settled. She said it was the back of beyond, but I liked it well enough.'

'Did Emma come and see you quite often, after you found her crying on the beach?'

'Every week on a Monday, before she collected the little children from the school.' A pause. 'Margaret was always at work on a Monday. She'd never taken to Emma since she started seeing Magnie.'

'But your sister found out somehow that you and Emma had become friends?' Willow wasn't sure where this was going, but she was curious.

'I let it slip one time. I couldn't stand Margaret ranting on about what a poor influence Emma was on her son.' Lottie shut her eyes again. She seemed to be replaying the encounter in her head. 'I told her I thought Emma was a fine young lassie and Margaret should be pleased that the boy had found someone. Did she want Magnie to be as lonely as we were? And then she wouldn't let the matter go. That was Margaret all over, prodding and prying until I told her Emma came to tea with me every Monday afternoon.'

'Did Emma ever confide in you?' Willow asked. 'She had a tough time growing up in Orkney. Did she talk about her parents? The things that happened to her family?' She thought Lottie would be an easy person to talk to. Unthreatening. Unselfish.

'We didn't talk about anything important,' Lottie said. 'That was why we got on so splendidly. It was just tea and chat. And maybe sometimes a bit of bitching about her bosses. We had that in common, you see. Working for the Moncrieffs.'

'You used to work for the Moncrieffs?' Again, Willow was surprised. She hadn't pictured Lottie as having any paid employment. She'd seen her as a carer to her parents in their later years, but hadn't considered what she might have done before that became necessary.

'Not for Robert and Belle,' Lottie said. 'I worked at Ness House long before they got together. I wasn't clever, like Margaret. I never passed any exams. When we lived in the south I got a job in the Sumburgh Hotel, cleaning the rooms and helping in the kitchen. Then my parents moved to Deltaness and I couldn't do that any more. It was too far to travel and I didn't want to live in. So I got a job with Robert's parents, Donald and Lucy. "Housekeeper" they called me, but that was a grand name for it. Skivvy more like. They paid a pittance and treated me like dirt. But it got me out of the house for a while and the money was a bit of independence.'

Willow nodded. She could see how the women

might get on, sharing grievances, mocking their employers. 'And you never did find out why Emma was crying that day you first invited her back?'

Lottie shook her head. 'I put it down to the Moncrieffs.' She paused. 'I cried a fair bit while I was working at Ness House too. Robert and Donald were cut from the same cloth. Robert's all charm and concern on the outside, but he has a mean way with him. And Donald was a bastard.'

'Do you have any idea who might have wanted to kill Margaret?' Willow thought the past was fascinating, but she couldn't see how Lottie's experience of working for Robert Moncrieff's father had anything to do with what was happening in Deltaness now.

'My sister wasn't an easy woman to get on with,' Lottie said. 'She could hold on to a grudge longer than anyone else I know. She said the Moncrieff bairns were monsters because they played a trick on her when they came guizing for Hallowe'en. They threw eggs at the house and it took an effort to clean up all the mess. Emma wasn't with them that time, but she still got into trouble when Margaret went and complained to the parents.' There was a pause. 'Margaret only behaved that way because she was hurting. She thought she was settled for life with Neil, in that big house in Voe. She'd sacrificed a lot to get it.'

'Dennis Gear?'

'You know about that? Yes, she loved the bones of him when they were younger. By the time she moved back here and tried to get together with him again, he was a different man. Depressed and drunk. She thought she could save him, but it was too late and he didn't care for her. Besides, by then, Dennis was beyond saving.'

They sat for a moment in silence.

'You said Margaret was disappointed that you'd made friends with Emma. Had you noticed any other change in her recently?'

'She'd taken against that new family in Hesti, but you know all about that. She'd made no secret of it.'

Willow said nothing. She had the sense that there was more to come.

After a brief pause, Lottie continued: 'Margaret said they'd as good as killed Dennis.' There was another hesitation. 'She called them the hangmen.'

'Did you know she'd been sending them anonymous notes? Little drawings of gallows.'

'No, but I knew she'd become obsessed with that family.' Lottie turned to stare at Willow. 'Easier, I suppose, than blaming herself.'

'Magnie thought she was losing her mind a bit. What do you think?'

Lottie gave a sharp, hard laugh. 'I think she was as sane as the rest of us, except that maybe she couldn't let go of a grievance. She let it burn inside her until it gobbled her up. Then she did what she felt she had to – lashing out at people she thought had hurt her – just to survive. But she didn't survive, did she? All that bad feeling was wasted. Now she's gone.'

When Willow left Lottie's house to rouse Magnie, he was already waking up. He stretched awkwardly in the front seat of the car and for a while seemed not to know where he was. Willow opened the passenger door. 'We'll go inside, shall we? I need to ask you a few more questions.'

Inside he wandered through to the kitchen and put on the kettle as if he was sleepwalking. Willow thought that would be what he'd do when he came home from a night shift. He'd be working on autodrive. The smell of coffee, which had turned her stomach in the first few weeks of pregnancy, seemed suddenly delicious and when he offered her a mug, she accepted.

'Where were you last night, Magnie?' Because he might be acting as if he'd been on the night shift, but he'd told Perez that he'd been with friends.

He shifted awkwardly.

'Just out with a few pals.'

'I'll need their names, Magnie. You do understand that. And you were out all night. I need to know where you were staying.'

'I stayed with my dad and his new wife in Lerwick.' He looked up, stubborn now. 'He'll tell you I was there.'

Will he? Willow thought. *And even if he does, will I believe him? Even a good man, guilty about deserting his wife, might perjure himself to protect his son.*

She nodded. 'I'll give your father a ring later.'

Magnie stood, leaning against the kitchen bench. 'What happens now? To my mother, I mean.'

'The pathologist will want to see her at the locus – where we found her. He hopes to be on a flight this afternoon. Then he'll need to take her back to Aberdeen to do a post-mortem. We won't be able to release her body until then.' Willow paused. 'Of course you'll be able to bring her home to bury her.'

He nodded and she saw that he was overwhelmed

by the responsibility, the things that would need to be done, rather than by the loss of the woman he'd lived with.

'Are you sure it was murder?' he asked. 'She didn't kill herself?'

'No, I don't think that she can have done that. Why would someone have moved her body to the side of the loch?' Willow paused for a moment. 'Are you saying she was suicidal?' Lottie hadn't implied in any way that Margaret had considered taking her own life.

Magnie thought for a moment. 'No,' he said. 'I don't think she was. But she was angry and confused.'

'Have you any idea who might have wanted to kill her?'

He took his time answering, drinking the coffee until only the dregs were left, then setting his mug on the bench. The silence stretched. 'She wasn't an easy woman,' he said at last, repeating almost exactly the words Lottie had used. 'She stuck her nose into other people's business and then she gossiped about them. There will be folk in Deltaness who won't be sorry to see Margaret Riddell dead, but none of them would have killed her.'

'What about your father and his new wife?'

'My mother made their life hell when they set up home together in Lerwick. She sent letters to the paper, to the bank's headquarters, to the minister of the kirk. Complaining that my father's hypocrisy made him unfit for work and for his office in the church. But that had all calmed down. She must have seen that she was making herself look ridiculous.' He looked straight up at Willow. 'I never blamed my father for leaving her. They weren't content for as long as I can remember. It was time for him to find some happiness.'

'Emma was your girlfriend, and Margaret your mother.' Willow was feeling the shock of caffeine after the weeks of abstinence. Her thoughts were racing and she wasn't quite sure where they were leading. 'Now the two women in your life are dead. Is there anyone who would want to hurt you so much that they might be prepared to kill the people closest to you?'

Magnie looked at her as if she was crazy. 'That sounds like a horror movie, not real life.'

'I suppose it does. I'm just thinking aloud here. I can't think what else they might have in common.'

'They had nothing else in common,' he said. 'It must be some madman, mustn't it? Some stranger who enjoys strangling women.'

Willow didn't answer. She couldn't see that the case was as easy as that. There'd been no stranger in Deltaness. And she thought there must be some logic to the killings, in the mind of the murderer at least. 'What will you do?' she asked. 'Will you go to stay with your father for a while?'

The man shook his head. 'I'll tell him what happened, before he hears from someone else. But this is my home. If you need me again, this is where you'll find me.'

As Willow was leaving the house she felt her phone vibrate in her pocket. Sandy.

'We've got cover here until the prof. arrives later this afternoon.' Sandy sounded breathless, as if he was walking into the breeze. 'What would you like me to do now?'

'Meet me at the Flemings' house,' she said. 'Daniel

spends a lot of his time filming the wildlife close to where we found Margaret. And Hesti is the nearest house to the body. I can't help feeling that the family is involved.' *Whatever Jimmy Perez thinks.*

As she opened her car door she looked up and saw that Magnie was closing his bedroom curtains. Again he was doing what he always did when he arrived home, after being away all night. She wasn't so sure that she would sleep so easily if her mother had been murdered, even if she was as tired as he was.

Chapter Thirty-Six

Helena and Daniel had just sat down to a late lunch when the two detectives arrived at Hesti. Belle had stayed, chatting in the studio, for more than an hour. Helena hadn't been quite sure what she'd wanted in the end. Perhaps to get out of the big, untidy house, which must still hold the ghost of Emma Shearer for her. Or perhaps she'd arranged the visit because she was as curious as everyone else in Deltaness about Emma's death. Belle had certainly been listening to gossip, because at one point she'd asked, as if she was genuinely concerned, 'Is Daniel very upset about what's happened? I had the impression that he and Emma were great friends.'

'We're *all* very upset,' Helena had said, her voice flat. She still thought that had been an inadequate response and wished she'd had the courage to tell Belle to ignore the gossipmongers and mind her own business.

The reply must have disappointed Belle, because soon afterwards the doctor's wife had made an excuse and left.

Now Willow Reeves and Sandy Wilson stood in the kitchen, insisting that Helena and Daniel continue eating. The woman detective seemed brighter today, but there was still something feral and unkempt about her; it was the tangled hair and the charity-shop clothes. Helena thought it must take courage for a senior police officer to dress like that. She wished Jimmy Perez had turned up on their doorstep instead. He would be easier to talk to, easier to convince.

'We can explain why we're here while you finish your lunch, and then we can ask you some questions afterwards.'

But Helena leapt up to fetch plates and cutlery. There was only cheese and salad and bread from the Walls Bakery, she said, but there was plenty to go round. She hated the idea of eating with the two strangers standing and watching. As if she and Daniel were animals in a zoo at feeding time. Besides, the officers were hungry. When they'd first come in, she'd seen the envy in their eyes when they'd seen the meal laid out on the table. She wondered when they'd last eaten.

So now they were all sitting together and Sandy was hacking at the bread, which Helena knew would drive Daniel crazy. Daniel was pleased by symmetry and order – that was what made him a fine architect, his attention to detail and his love of clean lines. Sometimes Helena wondered if he was on the autistic spectrum like Christopher, but not diagnosed. Although she didn't want more bread, she took the loaf next and cut a slice to tidy it up. Daniel shot a grateful glance across the table at her.

Willow Reeves explained why they were there, before she started eating. 'There's been another murder. Margaret Riddell. She was strangled too and left on the bench by the loch on the other side of the hill.'

She reached out for a tomato. They were very sweet and small. Helena had called in at the Hays' farm shop to buy them, when she was in Ravenswick to talk to Jimmy Perez. That seemed a very long time ago.

'Why was Margaret here?' the detective asked. 'Was it a social occasion? I didn't have the impression you were that close.'

'We didn't invite her,' Helena said. She was imagining Margaret Riddell as a supper guest, at the same table as Robert and Belle Moncrieff, and couldn't help smiling. The idea was ridiculous. Then she thought what a snobbish cow she must seem and tried to explain. 'Margaret turned up out of the blue, out of the fog. She said everyone in Deltaness was talking about Daniel and Emma, saying they'd been having an affair. She thought I should know. Of course that was nonsense. She just wanted to spread her poison.'

'What time was that?'

Helena looked at Daniel. 'Can you remember? The fog made it seem much later than it probably was. It seemed late for a social call. She didn't stay long. I didn't invite her in.'

'Had she driven here?'

'I didn't see a car, and that was odd too. I've never seen Margaret walk anywhere. She even drove down to the community hall for teas and meetings and that's no distance from her house.'

'Perhaps,' Sandy said, 'someone gave her a lift to the bottom of the track. Or she left her car there. Did you notice headlights? Before or after?'

Helena shook her head. 'But I wouldn't have done. The fog was so thick and the house doesn't look out that way.'

'How did she seem?' Willow was focused on spreading butter on an oatcake and only looked up at Helena when the question had been asked.

'Agitated. Very wound up. I'm not sure what she wanted from me. Gratitude, perhaps, or company. I had the sense that she'd expected to be made welcome. But she disgusted me. The way she wanted always to see the worst in people. There was no kindness or understanding.'

'Don't you think that made her sad?' Willow asked. 'The fact that she'd made herself so unpopular.'

It seemed such a strange thing for a police officer to say that Helena was shocked into silence, and it was Daniel who took up the conversation.

'It was hard for us to feel sorry for Mrs Riddell,' he said. 'She made life very difficult for us. From the moment we moved in, it was clear that she resented us. After the old man killed himself she was even more unpleasant.'

'She'd loved Dennis Gear when she was a girl.' Willow brushed crumbs from her fingers and then, almost without pausing, she continued speaking. 'We've found evidence that Margaret was the person who was sending you the little drawings of gallows and hanged men.'

'I suppose it had to be her.' Helena wondered why everyone hadn't come to that conclusion before. 'I can't think of anyone in Deltaness who would be quite so spiteful.'

'Now she's dead, you won't be bothered by them again.'

Helena felt as if Willow had slapped her very hard on the face. 'You can't think we're pleased that she's dead.'

'I'm pleased,' Daniel said, and again Helena thought how like Christopher he was, saying whatever came into his head, not worrying what other people would make of it. 'Now that she's gone, it might be possible for us to settle here and become a real part of the community.' He turned calmly towards Willow. 'I didn't kill her, though, if that's what you're suggesting. I didn't hate her as much as that, and I wouldn't risk all that we have here. A court case. Prison.'

There was a moment of silence.

'You're familiar with the bench where Margaret's body was found. It was dedicated to Dennis Gear.' Willow wasn't asking a question of Daniel, but he answered as if it was one.

'Yes, it's one of my favourite places. I love photographing the otters on the beach and the waders in the pool.' He paused. 'But the last time I was there was when Helena and I went for a walk over the hill, and that was the morning after Christopher found Emma's body. I didn't leave the house last night. We were all in together.'

'We were!' Helena turned to the detective, desperate to be believed.

'And early this morning?' Willow asked. 'Did either of you leave the house then?'

In her mind, Helena ran through the events of the morning. Daniel had been up before her – he'd said he wanted to continue planning his new project.

She hadn't seen him until after she'd taken the kids to school, but she was sure he'd been working in his office.

'I walked the children to school,' she said. 'Otherwise, neither of us left the house.' She looked towards Daniel, who just nodded his agreement.

'I think that's all for now.' Willow was on her feet, walking towards the door. 'Thanks for lunch.'

Helena walked outside with the detectives. For the first time in two days she could see all the way down to Deltaness and in the other direction to the hill, with the beacon stark on the skyline. There was the smell of salt, cut grass and wildflowers. The air seemed clearer. She thought again of the night before, Daniel and herself drinking champagne, toasting muddle and compromise. With Margaret no longer stirring up trouble for them, perhaps Daniel was right and life here would be easier. The dreams they'd had for the place no longer seemed quite so impossible.

In the school playground that afternoon, the talk was all about Margaret Riddell. Helena could tell there was no real information. People knew that the woman was dead, but the rest was speculation; there were wild stories of a dark stranger who'd been arrested as he boarded a plane in Sumburgh. The police had been at Lottie Marshall's house for hours and had taken Magnie away for interview, but he was back at home now. Helena found herself listening and even joining in the conversation. She had concrete information to pass on, after all.

'Margaret was strangled,' she said. 'Just like Emma.'

'How do you know?' The parents gathered around her, heads forward. Geese pecking at grain.

'The police were at ours this afternoon. We gave them lunch.' She added the last sentence because somehow it proved their innocence. The police surely wouldn't eat with anyone they suspected of murder. She became aware of Belle Moncrieff, on the edge of her sight-line, running late as always, joining the other parents.

'Did the lovely Jimmy Perez have lunch with you?' someone asked. Even here in the playground, the atmosphere seemed lighter and more frivolous. Helena no longer felt intimidated.

'No, only the woman and Sandy Wilson, the guy from Whalsay.'

Another voice from the crowd joined in. 'Jimmy's been in Orkney. My man's pals with Duncan Hunter, and he's looking after the peerie lassie. You know, Fran Hunter's daughter. Jimmy couldn't get back until last night's ferry because Sumburgh's fog-bound.'

'What was he doing there? Do they think the killer's from south?'

'He's surely been looking into Emma Shearer's background. That's where she came from, isn't it?' The speaker was an older woman, a grandmother, not a mother. She turned to Belle. 'That's right, isn't it, Mrs Moncrieff? Emma came to you from Orkney?'

'Yes.' Belle, who was usually so comfortable being the centre of attention, seemed awkward. When the bell rang and the children started running out, she took the opportunity to move away from the group.

Helena waved to Ellie and then waited for Christopher and the support worker to emerge. She thought of what Willow had said at lunch. Nobody in the playground had expressed any regret at Margaret's death. Rather, they were revelling in it as a source of entertainment and drama. Willow had been right; it *was* rather sad that the woman had nobody to mourn for her, that she was as lonely in death as she had been in life. But Helena still found it impossible to grieve for her.

Chapter Thirty-Seven

Magnie Riddell lay on his bed. The curtains were thin and the light came through. There was more than enough light to read the numbers on his phone and for him to get through to his father's mobile. He'd be at work, but usually his father answered and he did so immediately today.

'Magnus.'

'Dad, something's happened.'

Silence. In the past, when they were all living together in the big house in Voe, there would have been angry questions: *What have you done this time? What bother are you causing us now?* But Neil Riddell no longer saw himself as a saint. He was a sinner like the rest of the world, and he was enjoying the benefits of his new status. He was more tolerant, kinder. 'What is it, Son?'

'Mum's dead.'

'How?' His father wasn't a man to waste words.

'The police were here when I got back from work. They say she was murdered.'

'Are you alright, Son? Would you like to come and stay here with me and Krista?

'I'll be fine.' Because the last thing Magnie needed was to be around his father and Krista. They still radiated happiness and romance. Neil floated through the flat with a constant smile on his face, and Krista fluttered around him like a moth drawn to a flame, all light kisses and touches. His mother had said the woman must be faking it. 'She wants a British passport. After Brexit, she's worried she'll be sent home. What could she see in Neil Riddell?'

Magnie could feel that the affection was genuine, though. In their company, his relationship with Emma had always seemed half-hearted and unsatisfactory.

'I told the police I was with you and Krista last night, Dad. I don't have any kind of alibi, and they seemed to think I was a suspect. First Emma, and then my mother. The two women in my life, the detective said.'

There was a silence at the other end of the line and Magnie waited for the old recriminations.

'Did you kill her, Son?'

'No!' Because what else could Magnie say?

'Then when they ask, we'll tell them you were with us. And you know when you're ready to talk to us, we're here.'

Magnie switched off his phone. He lay back on the bed and tried to sleep, but images of the bonfire on the beach returned. The flames wild and untamed, the young people drinking and jeering. The poor Fleming boy screaming, with his hands over his ears. Emma beside him, watchful and unmoved. And his mother, who must have scrambled onto the shingle bank, standing there, looking down at them all, judging them.

Magnie wondered again if he should tell Willow Reeves about that night; she might find out anyway and then how would it look? He felt more ashamed of how they'd all behaved, sneering and screeching like gulls around a piece of leftover food, than he did about the worse things he'd done. The image of his mother, staring down at him, drifted in and out of his dreams all night.

Chapter Thirty-Eight

The next day in Lerwick, the sun was shining. The cloud had rolled back over the sea and hovered there, a warning that it would return. They met early in the station; Willow had suggested a discussion there before they headed back to the scene at Deltaness. A cruise ship was anchored in Bressay Sound, waiting to disgorge its passengers, but now the town was quiet, catching its breath before another busy day.

In the ops room there was a smell of coffee. Willow had arrived first and was looking at a pile of paper. Sandy had been standing at the window looking out towards the town hall, but now he joined them.

'This is James's post-mortem report on Emma Shearer,' Willow said. 'We didn't have the chance to discuss it properly yesterday.'

'James told me about the untreated injuries.' Perez had been thinking about that ever since he'd heard about them. What would it do to a child, not just physically, but emotionally and mentally? A father should protect his children, not terrify them. Not hurt them so badly they would carry the scars for the rest of their lives.

Sandy looked up from his coffee. 'It made me want to weep.'

Willow continued talking. 'It seems your theory about Emma being killed in her car still holds up. She was strangled from behind.'

'It would take some nerve,' Perez said, 'to kill the woman, drive her to Hesti, string her up in the byre and then return the car to Ness House.' He paused. 'Nerve or desperation.' He thought the murderer *must* have been desperate. Killing Emma had been more important to them than getting away with the crime; they'd considered it a risk worth taking.

Willow set the post-mortem report aside. 'I spoke to Neil Riddell. He confirms that Magnie was with them the night Margaret disappeared.'

'Magnie told me he was out with friends.'

'According to Neil, he had a few drinks with his pals, decided he wasn't fit to drive home and turned up at their place at about midnight. Magnie was a bit awkward about it because, according to the court order, he wasn't supposed to be spending time in the town centre.'

Perez supposed that might be true. 'I'd like to find some other witnesses to confirm that.'

'I've found out how Emma got hold of her designer handbag.' Sandy had been itching to pass on the information. He looked at them, eager for approval, a schoolboy who'd completed his homework without being prompted.

'And?' Perez thought it seemed like a long time since they'd found the bag in the boatshed on the shore at Hesti.

'She paid for it herself, bought it from a specialist site on the Internet.'

'Something like eBay?'

Perhaps the bag had been a bargain buy; that might explain the purchase and Emma's glee in owning it.

'No! She bought it from the designer and paid full price. Five hundred quid. Seems we should take up childminding, eh, Jimmy? I couldn't afford something like that for Louisa.'

'Have we checked out Emma's bank account? Any unexplained payments?'

'What are you thinking?' Willow said. 'Blackmail?'

'Maybe.' Or, Perez thought, perhaps it was subtler than that: professionals in Orkney with a conscience, thinking Emma deserved compensation because her case had been so badly handled. He wasn't sure how that would have worked, though, unless they'd helped her to access some charitable funding. 'Of course she could have won the lottery, or got a handout from a wealthy relative.'

'Do we know if Emma's mother owned her own place?' This was Sandy again. 'Perhaps Emma could have inherited, if a house was sold when the woman died?'

'I checked that while I was in Orkney.' Willie had filled Perez in with the information, the night they'd got drunk on Highland Park whisky. 'The shop was sold when Kenneth Shearer was sent to prison. The family rented a house in Kirkwall after that. So there'd have been no big payout on the mother's death.'

'So where was Emma getting the money?' Willow leaned forward across the table. 'If we can trace that, perhaps we have our killer.'

Soon afterwards, they drove north to Deltaness. Willow had gone ahead with James Grieve, and Sandy was driving. Perez said little. He couldn't stop thinking about Emma Shearer. Claire Bain had talked of violence stalking Emma throughout her life and now it seemed that was true. As they passed Tingwall Airport, one of the small inter-island planes took off, silver and gleaming in the bright light. It wheeled south and Perez thought it could be heading for Fair Isle. They drove on in silence, past the township of Brae where Margaret Riddell had worked, and on through Mavis Grind, the narrowest point in the Shetland mainland. It was said that Vikings had dragged their longboats across the gap to save rowing around the top of the island and that here you could chuck a rock from the Atlantic into the North Sea. Perez had never tried, but he thought it'd have to be a pretty powerful throw.

Turning down the narrow track towards the sea, it was as if they'd wandered into another country, a low-lying place of water and sunshine. The bare hills were behind them. Sandy parked at the foot of the dunes and they got out, pulled on scene-suits and headed up the path, past the daisy chain of lochans. A uniformed female officer nodded to them as they went past. 'This is the agreed access route,' Sandy said. 'There's been someone here all night. This morning we're having to turn away the dog-walkers and joggers. And the nebby souls who think there's something exciting about a dead middle-aged woman.'

Perez saw Willow, dressed in a white scene-suit that hid any early sign of the pregnancy. She must have heard their car and seen them walking up the path towards her, but she seemed lost in thoughts of her own. She stood, watching James Grieve from a distance. It seemed that they were getting on well enough to work together, but there was no intimacy and Perez realized now how much he missed it. He should apologize for his first reaction to her news, but something – pride or resentment at the demands being made upon him – made it impossible.

James Grieve was already at work. Perez and Willow walked together towards him.

'Do you think this is where she was killed?'

Willow shrugged. 'Let's wait until James has worked his magic before we make a judgement about that. I'd say she might have been dead when she got here, though. She'd be heavy to carry all this way, even for a fit and healthy man, but I thought there were drag marks in the shingle at the car park and on the path.'

'So, what's the plan for today?

'Come with me to speak to the Moncrieffs. I haven't met the parents yet and, according to the kids, it's not the happy family everyone thinks. Let's see if they've had any contact with Margaret recently. She enjoyed a moral crusade, it seems. If they had a secret they'd rather keep hidden, and Margaret found out about it, that would be a motive.' A sudden breeze caught Willow's hair and she pushed it away from her face.

'You think one of them killed Emma, Margaret suspected and they killed her to stop her speaking?'

There was another quick grin. 'Or Robert and Belle worked together? That makes more sense logistically. It's only a theory, but it's possible, don't you think?'

They found both adult Moncrieffs at home. The house seemed to have descended even further into chaos.

There was a pile of damp washing in a plastic laundry basket at the bottom of the stairs and the kitchen floor was sticky and covered in crumbs. Belle was stirring soup in a pan at the stove.

'Jimmy, you always seem to catch me at mealtimes.' She nodded to the table. 'You'll be welcome to join us. Robert always works from home on a Friday afternoon.'

Moncrieff had opened the door to them and stood now, openly hostile, leaning against the wall. He wouldn't have made the invitation.

Perez shook his head. 'You'll have heard about Margaret Riddell? We have a few questions.'

'This isn't convenient.' Moncrieff's words, sharp and arrogant, made Perez feel like an ignorant island boy again. A servant in the big house. He kept his temper and his voice even.

'A formal interview in the police station would be even less convenient, I'd have thought. There's already a gang of reporters camping out in Lerwick, eager for news on the case. This is a little more discreet. But your choice, of course.' He nodded towards Willow. 'This is Chief Inspector Reeves from Inverness. She's the senior investigating officer and she wanted to meet you.'

There was a silence.

'I'm sure lunch can wait.' Belle's voice was conciliatory. She seemed calm, unflappable. Perez remembered that she worked in PR; she'd have been in uncomfortable situations before. 'We'll go through to the sitting room, shall we?'

The room was high-ceilinged and rather grand, in a battered country-house sort of way. Furniture that might be antique and worth a fortune or picked up in a charity shop – two sofas covered in green fabric with a design in white showing hunting scenes, a desk with a leather top, a large sideboard, elaborately carved, holding glasses and decanters. The long window looked out to the garden and the sycamore plantation. The room would always be dark, and even today, with bright sunshine outside, it was gloomy. Robert and Belle sat on one sofa, Willow and Perez on the other.

Perez waited for Willow to begin the conversation. This was her shout. Besides, despite himself, he felt again the old childhood sense that he was an impostor here.

'Margaret Riddell was your patient?'

'You know she was.'

'Had you formed any opinion of her mental health?'

'Are you saying she committed suicide?' Moncrieff leaned forward. 'She didn't consult me at all. I couldn't have predicted such a severe depression.' Covering his back.

'You thought she was depressed?'

'No! I knew she'd become obsessed with the family at Hesti and she blamed them for the death of Dennis Gear.'

'What form did that obsession take?'

'As far as I could make out, she was an old-fashioned gossip. She was lonely and bored and she took an unhealthy interest in other people's affairs. That doesn't amount to a psychiatric illness, in my book.'

'When did you last see Margaret?' This time Willow's question was directed to both Robert and Belle.

'I haven't seen her since the Sunday teas,' Moncrieff said. 'My God, that's less than a week ago. It feels as if this nightmare has been going on for an eternity.'

'Mrs Moncrieff?' Willow turned to his wife.

'I saw her on Wednesday night,' Belle said. 'The night of the thick fog. I was upstairs, saying goodnight to the youngest children and drawing their curtains, and she was standing outside. There's a small length of pavement just outside the house and she was there. It seemed odd.'

'She was watching the house?'

Perez thought Willow seemed particularly interested in this.

'That would have been very weird, don't you think?' Belle gave a little laugh. 'Why on earth would she? No, she seemed to be waiting for someone. Perhaps she'd arranged for a lift. Robert and I went out that night. Some friends in Hillswick had invited us for dinner. We decided to organize a taxi so that we could both have a drink. We thought Martha could mind the children for the evening. It would do her good to take some responsibility. When the taxi arrived ten minutes later, there was no sign of Margaret. I'd forgotten all about it until now.'

'What time was that?' Willow was leaning forward so that Perez could only see Robert Moncrieff on the adjoining sofa. He was giving nothing away.

'I can't be precise,' Belle said, 'but the taxi was booked for eight-thirty, so sometime before that.' A pause. 'Was I the last person to see her alive?'

Willow didn't answer. 'What time did you get back from your friends in Hillswick?'

'Not late.' Robert answered this time. 'We weren't

much in the mood, actually. We were certainly home by eleven. Belle went straight to bed. I watched a bit of TV and I wasn't very much later.'

'And there was no sign of Margaret then?'

'No.' They answered together, united at least in this.

Chapter Thirty-Nine

They bought food from the Deltaness community shop – rolls from the Walls Bakery, cheese, crisps and fruit – and sat on the beach side of the shingle bank in the sun to eat lunch and talk about the case. On the horizon, the bank of cloud still lingered. Willow had decided this was better than going all the way back to the ops room in Lerwick, or commandeering the community hall and causing a fuss. Sandy listened while she and Perez talked about their meeting at the big house and then he had a question of his own.

'You didn't ask about Emma's childhood injuries?' He was still haunted by the thought of that, wondered how he'd manage in a city force where he'd come across similar horrors all the time. 'Moncrieff almost laughed when I mentioned PTSD.'

'No.' Willow bit into an apple. 'I wanted to keep that little bit of information to myself for a while.' She paused, changed tack. 'Did you notice, Jimmy? It was only Belle who saw her in the fog that Wednesday night. Robert didn't see her. Or so he says.' She tucked the apple core carefully into a brown paper bag and put it into her jacket pocket.

'You think Margaret might have been waiting for Robert?'

'It's a possibility, don't you think? And perhaps she came back later, once he got home.' Willow sat for a moment then, staring out to sea, so focused that Sandy was expecting some great revelation at the end of her reverie. But it seemed she was only thinking through practical matters.

'I'd like you to go and see Lottie this afternoon, Sandy. Magnie will be out at work and I've asked his permission to go through Margaret's things, so we can pick up those old love letters from Dennis Gear. Get Lottie talking about those times. She'll speak to you. You talk the same language.'

'So does Jimmy!'

'But Jimmy would scare her.' She shot a quick look at Perez. 'He has a manner about him that can be a bit cold and intimidating at times. You don't.'

And so Sandy found himself standing outside Margaret's door to search for a pile of ancient love letters. He couldn't see how they could be of any meaning to the current investigation. Willow seemed to have a fascination with history; she said tensions and problems of the present could be traced back to events of the past. He couldn't see how that could work, when Emma Shearer hadn't even been alive at the time of the love affair.

The dead woman's house had been sealed, and a constable he didn't recognize stood at the door. He'd been pulled in from Inverness and just seemed desperate to get home to his family. Sandy could understand that. He couldn't wait to get back to Yell and Louisa. He realized he'd never written love letters to her, only boring texts. Maybe he should write something – a letter that they could hang on to, show their children. But he wouldn't know where to start.

Vicki's team had already been in for a first sweep. Sandy could see fingerprint powder on the window ledges and the kitchen worktops. He found the letters where Willow had said they'd be and read them carefully, before slipping them into a clear plastic envelope. Then he went outside and took off his gloves before knocking at Lottie's door. He found that his hand was shaking as he gripped onto the envelope. He felt under pressure to get something interesting from Lottie. Willow had put her faith in him.

The woman who opened the door to him was thin, with wispy white hair and a frightened gaze, but he could see some resemblance to her sister.

'You're the policeman from Whalsay.'

'Yes,' he said. 'There's nothing to worry about. I'm just here for a chat.'

She sat him in her living room and he heard her in the kitchen making tea, opening a tin for something she'd baked. When she returned, it was with mugs, not a pot on a fancy tray. She set them on the table and came back with a quarter of a fruitcake. 'I made this for Emma, but then she never came, of course, and I've been eating it ever since. It's saved me having to cook. It'll not have dried out, being in the tin.'

'I'm sure it'll be splendid. A good fruitcake improves with keeping.' He paused, feeling his way. Lottie had brought up the subject of Emma, so perhaps he should follow her lead. 'Did she speak much about her time in Orkney?'

'Not very much. She wasn't happy there.'

'Was she happy here?'

'They're not an easy family, the Moncrieffs. Your boss will have told you I worked for Robert's father?'

Sandy nodded, but said nothing. Perez had taught him the value of silence.

'He was a hard man. He expected too much of the boy. If you get bullied, you're likely to turn into a bully yourself.' Lottie stared out of the window. Sandy wondered what her parents had been like with her. And with Margaret.

'Did Robert bully *his* children?'

She shook her head. 'According to Emma, he didn't really see them enough to bully them. Not when they were tiny. Once they were old enough to be proper companions, he was around more. But he's a competitive man. He needs them to succeed. Charlie is a great sportsman and Robert's there for every competition, cheering him on. But not always in a good way, you know? He hates it when Charlie loses. And Martha rows for the Deltaness Ladies in the regatta now. I'm not sure Robert cares so much about that. It seems Charlie is the important one.'

'So, Robert never hit the children?' The question was tentative and Lottie took a long while to consider. In the end Sandy added: 'Because Emma was beaten herself, you see. Nobody realized at the time, but Professor Grieve found old injuries when he did the post-mortem.'

'I don't know,' Lottie said at last. 'Robert's father hit *him*, but that wasn't so strange in those days. As I said, Robert wasn't around so much when the children were small. Not his fault maybe; he'd have been busy with work.' There was a moment's silence. 'And then he and

Belle are often out in the evening. They're great ones for dinner parties. I'd say Robert is cold rather than cruel.'

There was another silence. Companionable, not awkward. Sandy cut another slice of the cake, out of politeness.

'We need to talk about Margaret,' he said after several mouthfuls.

'She was an unhappy woman.' Lottie might have been continuing the same conversation they'd had about Emma and Robert. 'Never content. She looked back at her marriage to Neil as if it were perfect, but all the time she was with him she complained about him.' A pause. 'Poor man, I wasn't surprised when he left her to find some joy in his life.'

'Did you ever say that to Margaret?'

There was a sudden quick grin and the thin, grey face lit up. He saw for a moment how she would have looked as a girl. 'I would never have dared,' she said. 'We were all frightened of Margaret. She had such a sharp tongue on her. It would cut you in two.'

He smiled back and put the plastic envelope on the coffee table between them. 'It seems she was happy with Dennis Gear. She kept his letters at least.'

The woman opposite stared at him as if he were mad. 'Margaret told you that Dennis wrote those letters to her?'

'Well, they were in her house.' Sandy felt himself floundering now. The woman who had seemed so frail and kind was suddenly hard, angry. He wasn't quite sure what he'd said to hurt her.

'She stole them,' Lottie said. 'Dennis wrote those

letters to me.' Another pause. 'And she stole him from me too. All those years ago.'

'Why don't you tell me about it?'

'I was working in Ness House for Robert Moncrieff's parents. Keeping the house for them and looking after Robert too. His mother was a nervy woman. She didn't like Shetland from the start. I think they gave her tranquillizers to keep her calm. Some days she was hardly herself at all. Hardly awake. That was the year Margaret was south, training to be a teacher. Dennis and I became friendly. You know how it is in a place like Deltaness. You bump into each other in the kirk or at weddings and parties, and suddenly you realize it's more than friendship. He was making a go of Hesti then. The oil terminal was being built and he got work there too and the pay was good. He was a young, strong man and he was willing to work.'

'I see.' Sandy wasn't sure he did understand, but he wanted the woman to tell the story in her own way. He imagined himself as Dennis Gear, back in the Seventies, with a croft and extra work with the oil, good money coming in. Of course he'd want a woman. Someone to share his life with, work with him on the land and give him bairns. Lottie had kept house for the Moncrieffs and looked after their son. She had an even temper and a sense of humour. He could see how Dennis might be attracted. 'And that was when he wrote those letters to you?'

'He was a soppy thing on the quiet. Romantic.' She softened for a moment before her back straightened again. 'Then Margaret came back from the south, with new fancy clothes and on the hunt for a man of her own. She always wanted what someone else had.'

'And she wanted Dennis Gear.'

'For a while. Until someone better came along. And Dennis allowed himself to be swept away with her plans for his house and her talk of new ideas. What was I? A skivvy in the big house. Not worth bothering with.' Lottie looked up and there were tears in her eyes. 'He'd had a taste of something different from his new friends at Sullom Voe. I was just boring.'

'But Margaret dumped him for Neil Riddell.'

'Of course! He was an assistant bank manager, with prospects and a chance of a cheap mortgage. That seemed better than the life of a crofter's wife, animals to care for and peat to cut.'

'So, Dennis Gear was free again. He must have come to his senses and come back to you.' Sandy thought of Lottie, all alone except for her elderly parents.

'Oh, he did that! Dressed in his fine Sunday clothes, knocking at this door and saying what a mistake he'd made and asking me to take him back.'

'But you wouldn't?' Sandy knew the answer already. He could tell by the fierce look in her eyes and the straightness of her spine.

'I might have been a glorified housemaid, but I had some pride. And he'd deserted me once. How would I know that he wouldn't do it again? I suppose I was like Margaret. I thought I could do better.' She sighed. 'And I didn't want her cast-off.'

'Only nobody came along?'

'There were one or two, but no one who would write soppy love letters. And by the time I came to my senses, Dennis was already courting somebody else. He got married not long after.' Lottie paused. 'They seemed settled enough.'

'And after she died?' Sandy wished he could change the history of the couple. He would have loved a happy ending.

'He was a different man by then. Drinking too much. The centre of a party, wherever he went. He'd always been a fine musician, but now it was all about performing. He wasn't playing for the music itself. There was a kind of desperation about him, a need to be admired. I wouldn't have wanted to be with a man like that.' She set down the mug she'd been clinging to.

'But Margaret would?' Sandy asked.

'I told you – Margaret always wanted whatever other folk had, and what she couldna have.'

They sat in silence.

'You were still friends with Margaret? After what she did to you?'

Lottie looked up, surprised by the question. 'We were family. And maybe she did me a favour. Maybe Dennis would have turned out that way – kind of stupid and demanding – even if I'd married him.'

'Magnie thinks Margaret was obsessed with the new family at Hesti. That it had become a sickness. We even wondered if she was stalking them. After all, she took your letters and pretended they'd been written to her.' Sandy nodded to the envelope that still lay on the table.

'I don't think Margaret was sick,' Lottie said, 'unless envy is a kind of sickness. She saw that grand new house, a happy family, the wife famous for her knitting – and Margaret was always known here for her fine knitting – no money troubles at all. And Margaret hated them for it. It was the same with the letters. She was jealous that Dennis had written them to me, not to her. That was why she took them. Envy was burning inside her.'

Sandy wondered what it would be like to be consumed with jealousy. He thought that might turn your mind. 'She was seen outside the Moncrieff house on Wednesday night. That was the night she disappeared, the night of the fog. Do you know why she was there?'

Lottie shook her head. 'I have no idea.'

Sandy got to his feet. 'What will you do with yourself, now she's gone? She must have been company at least.'

'I'll be able to please myself, won't I? And Magnie will still need looking after.'

Sandy moved towards the door, but Lottie stood in his way.

'Do you have a woman in your life?'

'Yes, she lives in Yell. Teaches in Unst.' He couldn't help smiling just at the thought of Louisa.

'Don't let her escape,' Lottie said, playful and serious all at the same time. 'Hold on to her and don't let her go.'

Chapter Forty

Helena was loading the dishwater after dinner when the phone went. It was Belle Moncrieff, and Helena paused for a moment before answering, worried that Belle would be hassling her again about doing a press piece or needing more information for London Fashion Week in September. But it seemed that Belle didn't have work on her mind.

'The forecast tomorrow is brilliant. We wondered if you felt like a day on the beach. An escape from Deltaness. We're going to head out to Burra and thought you might fancy it too. Let the kids run wild for a bit. Take a picnic. You know, real *Swallows and Amazons* stuff. We don't get the weather to do that very often.'

Helena's first thought was that she'd have to leave Christopher at home with Daniel. He hated the outside. Even more he hated the beach; the texture of sand on his feet and the constant noise of the waves seemed to blow a valve in his brain. Then she thought she couldn't take the decision for Christopher. He might enjoy it, or at least learn to tolerate the new experience. Perhaps he'd feel left out if he wasn't included in the party. Sam and he got on well enough and he'd once told Helena he thought Martha was cool. He could sit on a rug, keep on his shoes and socks. Helena would charge his iPad and he could plug himself in, with headphones to block out the sound of the wind and waves.

'Sure,' she said. 'Sounds brilliant.'

The next day felt like an adventure and, as Belle had said, like an escape. *Let the police and the forensic scientists do their dirty work*, Helena thought. For one day the Fleming family could at least try to forget about murder. She packed up a picnic and they loaded the car with so much kit that Daniel asked if they were going away for a fortnight. But even Daniel looked the part in shorts, T-shirt and espadrilles. Helena remembered again the holiday in Greece, Daniel's body, brown and strong. He seemed himself again, light-hearted, joking with the children as he drove down the track, leading them in some daft song that Ellie had learned at school. By the time they left Northmavine and headed south down the long, thin spine of Shetland mainland, they were singing at the tops of their voices, even Christopher. They followed the Moncrieffs' people-carrier and there were always glimpses of the sea, of mussel buoys and salmon cages and distant uninhabited islands.

At Scalloway they crossed the bridge to the isle of Trondra and then another to Burra. Two new islands. This was unexplored territory for the Flemings, gentler than they were used to and more fertile. They followed Robert into a small car park and piled out. Soon they were all heading down a narrow grassy path towards the sea, the adults loaded with surfboards and windbreaks and wetsuits, and the younger children charging ahead, whooping and laughing. Charlie and Martha sauntered between the groups, followed by

Christopher with his tight robot gait. At first the teenagers seemed to consider themselves above the childish behaviour, but they became wilder and more enthusiastic the closer they got to the water. There were some stone steps cut into a shallow cliff and they were there, at a perfect cove that looked, to Helena, more like Cornwall than Shetland.

They set up base above the tideline, where there were flat rocks to sit on, rock pools for the young ones and white fine sand. Helena had brought Christopher his own rug and he sat there, a little apart from the others, tucked behind the windbreak, his knees to his chest. Not happy exactly – he needed to have his discomfort recognized – but not anxious or flapping. Helena thought this was just what they needed: air that seemed more intoxicating than wine, the laughter of the children carried from the water's edge, the companionship of friends.

They didn't mention the murders or the police investigation. There had been no formal agreement beforehand that the subject was off-limits, but it seemed that none of the adults wanted to be reminded of Deltaness with its claustrophobia and gossip, with its army of police officers and scientists and press. Instead they shared indiscretions of their youth, talked about the travelling they'd done, and finally they came to Daniel's commission for the eco-hotel.

'Of course you'll need someone to manage publicity for you . . .' This was Belle, only half-joking. 'If we get the word out properly, you'll have enough work to see you through until retirement.'

Daniel had rolled onto his side, his head supported by his hand. 'Hey, how old do you think I am?'

'It doesn't matter! You could still be working until you're eighty. People will be queuing up for commissions.'

'Yeah, yeah.' Mock-dismissive, but Helena could tell he was loving the flattery and the banter. He seemed happier than she could remember. Happier perhaps than at any time since the kids were born.

People don't tell you what children can do to a relationship. They make it all sound so easy.

Today, it *did* seem easy. The children scattered, forming small shifting groups, poking in rock pools, building castles, only returning to base for food and drink. The teenagers slid into wetsuits and went into the sea, lying on surfboards, idling and waiting for the perfect wave, then powering into shore as sleek as seals. When they came out they were shivering with cold, but joyous. They pulled on jeans and jerseys and gathered together the young ones for a game of rounders. Christopher pulled out his earplugs and turned round to watch, clapping occasionally at a particularly good hit.

Helena wondered if it had taken the murders to make them appreciate this. Would the children have played so well, so uncomplainingly, if they hadn't lived through almost a week of parental tension and anxiety? Usually outings like this one seemed a wonderful idea in prospect, but often ended in disappointment and tears.

Time passed without her really noticing. She lay on her back on a towel, reading and dozing. The tide came in and afternoon turned to early evening. Robert decided this was the time they should all go in the sea. He stood up and stretched and would take no opposition. The water had crossed the warm sand, he said, and surely couldn't be as chilly as when they had first arrived. Part of Helena resented his attempt to take charge, the male arrogance that assumed they'd all fall in with his plans, but the water looked inviting and, in the end, wasn't it just a bit of fun?

Most of the other families had left the cove, clambering in groups up rough steps and along the path to the road. The Moncrieffs and Flemings climbed into swimming costumes, with much joking and pretend horror.

'No wetsuits!' Robert said. 'That's cheating.'

They spread out, holding hands, so they were like a string of beads across the mouth of the bay. Their shadows were long on the sand. Helena was at the end of the line, standing next to Charlie. He seemed like a Viking prince with the sun on his face, very tall and strong. Daniel was in the middle of the group with Ellie on one side and Belle on the other. Helena heard the sand shift behind her and Christopher was there, stripped to his underpants, reaching out to take her other hand.

She was going to ask if he was OK, if he was sure he wanted to do this, but he was staring towards the water and she could tell he was looking forward to the iciness of it, the sharp tingle of the cold on his skin, so she just grinned at him. Robert had taken charge again and was counting down from ten. They all joined in. 'Go!'

They ran forward in a ragged but unbroken line and jumped the small waves until the adults were knee-deep, gasping with the shock of the cold, splashing. Beside her, Christopher started giggling, the sound loud and unrestrained, as he jumped high and hard. Helena let go of Charlie's hand and swung her son into the air. She saw the drops of water from his body in slow-motion as gold sparks in the sunlight. Ice and fire, she thought. He loves them both and probably feels them as the same sensation.

Even when they were all dry and dressed, they didn't want to go home. The picnic food had been eaten and they'd already decided they'd stop for fish and chips in Frankie's in Brae on the way back to Deltaness. But Belle produced a couple of bags of marshmallows, and Robert started scavenging for driftwood and called the children to help. They found three chunks of pitch pine and a twisted branch that looked more like bone than wood, because it had been in the water for so long. The colour was seeping from the grass at the top of the cliff and from the sea, and the scene looked like a sepia photograph. Helena thought Ellie at least would be asleep before they got to Brae, but the idea of a bonfire and roasted marshmallows was exciting and kept even the young ones going. Christopher stuck by Robert and, when the fire was lit, sat as close to it as he could get, seeming not to care about the sand in his shoes or the background sound of the retreating tide.

Chapter Forty-One

At first Christopher hadn't been sure about the fire. He was afraid it would remind him of his confusion when he'd wandered down to the beach at Deltaness, the noise and the big kids jeering. But he found he loved it. It was smaller than the one Charlie and his friends had built on the shingle beach at Deltaness, but still he was drawn into it; he could feel himself a part of the flames and the heat. He was hardly aware of the others, saw them as shadows, heard them as faraway whispers.

Charlie had found wire, part of a disintegrating lobster pot that had been washed up on the rocks. He'd twisted the wire until it snapped into long pieces, and the others were threading marshmallows onto the ends and holding them towards the fire. Christopher would have preferred to be alone here, but he reined in his irritation. He could cope with them. When someone offered him a marshmallow he shook his head, trying to be polite, but too resentful to quite manage it.

The light had almost gone now and that made the fire more dramatic. He watched the sparks that flew from it until they disappeared, until they seemed to join the stars that were just starting to appear in the sky above him.

He needed a pee. He'd known for a while that he'd have to go, but pissing in the open air always freaked him out. Now it was dark, it wasn't so scary. Nobody would see. He stood up and backed away from the fire, his attention still drawn to it, then turned slightly and saw his mother's face, half golden and half in shadow. Two-faced. He whispered to her what he was planning and she nodded to show him that was fine.

Away from the bright contrast of the fire, it didn't seem so dark. He could make out where he was going, once his eyes got used to the strange half-light. He stood tucked into a crack in the cliff, so nobody would see him, even if they were very close, and pissed, being careful not to drip onto his clothes or his feet. He was still not wearing shoes, still getting used to the feeling of sand and small splinters of shell on his bare feet. It felt brave to be standing here like this. He could hear the liquid splash against the rock. Then there was a sound behind him, like a footstep in the sand, and he wondered if someone had followed him – Charlie perhaps, intent on making fun of him, or one of the grown-ups come to check on why he was away.

He turned quickly, had a sense of movement on the beach in front of him, but his sight was restricted by the rocky outcrop and, when he moved further out, everyone still seemed gathered around the fire. They'd built it just below the high-water mark, with its kelp and shells, so the ash would be carried away by the sea on the next high tide. He could see the whole party as a group silhouette and it was hard to make out individuals. Nobody was moving much now.

It was as if they were all as mesmerized by the flames as he had been.

He didn't head straight for the fire, but for the edge of the sea. He thought he'd walk along the shore towards the rest of the group. The water would feel good on his bare feet. He was looking out to the horizon, to a big ship, fully lit, moving slowly south, when he tripped on something. He thought it might be a bucket or spade left behind by the littlies. His mother would be pleased if he picked it up and took it back. They'd packed everything up, ready to take home, and Robert and his father had already carried most of the things into the cars, so there wouldn't be much to do when they decided to leave. Christopher hoped they'd leave soon. Now he was ready for his room and his computer screen. He'd socialized enough for one day.

He bent down and saw a pair of shoes, made of leather, shiny like the kind of sandals Ellie wore to parties. But these were too big for Ellie; they belonged to a grown-up. They'd been placed carefully as a pair, the toes facing the water. They had pointed heels. One of them had fallen on its side, where he'd tripped. He bent down and looked more closely at the shoes and the sand around them. There was too little light to make out the colour, but they were pale and he thought they might be yellow. Emma Shearer had owned yellow shiny shoes with pointed heels. She'd often worn them with the dress she'd had on when he found her in the barn. He couldn't see how the shoes could be here, so many miles from Deltaness. That idea – the distance, the space they'd covered that morning in the car and his memory of Emma, twisting at the end of the rope in the Hesti byre – made him dizzy. He began to panic. He didn't feel brave any more. He put his hands over his ears and screamed for his mother.

Chapter Forty-Two

When Perez arrived home on Saturday evening, the house seemed quiet and empty. Cassie was still at her father's. Perez stood just inside the door and allowed himself a moment of self-pity. This was Fran's house. She should be here, sitting at the kitchen table, her glasses, always too loose, slipping down her nose as she worked at her laptop. He could picture the scene exactly. She would look up and smile, still a bit distracted.

'Had a good day, Jimmy? Have you set the world to rights?'

And he would talk to her. They would share a bottle of wine and some food, and then they would share the bed where he now slept alone.

But honesty made him admit it hadn't always been like that. There'd been arguments. When Fran was working on a painting she was engrossed by it. It was at the centre of her mind for days. He and Cassie might not have existed. He could be equally self-obsessed. He'd thought some of her arty friends pretentious, and she'd considered that some of his colleagues were bores. He'd thought himself in love with Sarah, his first wife, but when she'd struggled to have children, he hadn't been there to give her the support she needed. Or so she'd said. Perhaps his relationship with Fran would have disintegrated too, fallen apart when his work took over.

He was glad when his phone rang. It did no good brooding. As he picked it up, he wondered if it might be Willow, asking if she could come over, wanting to talk not about the case, but about *their* relationship. He would put her off. He wasn't in the mood. He felt too brutal, too cold. But it was Duncan.

'Is it Cassie?' Perez had a moment of panic. 'Is she ill?'

'She's fine,' Duncan said. His voice was a little slurred. Perez thought the man had been drinking. 'She's fast asleep. But there's something I need to tell you.' He paused. 'I'm planning a move away from the islands. The business in Malaga has taken off. I need to be there.'

'What about Cassie?'

'She stays with you. Obviously, she stays with you. Soon she'll be old enough to come out for the holidays, and I'll come north to see her when I need to be in the UK.' Duncan paused again. 'You're a better father than I could ever be.'

The line went dead and then rang again immediately. This time it was Helena Fleming on a very bad line.

'Jimmy, I'm speaking from Burra, from the beach there. I think we've found Emma's shoes.'

Perez was still absorbing Duncan's words and it took him a moment to realize what she was telling him. Helena continued before he could answer. 'I mean the shoes that she usually chose to wear with the dress we found her in. The dress that she died in.

They're yellow, patent leather.' Another pause before she added, 'Daniel identified them. He would know them, I think.'

'Are they above the tideline? Will they be safe for a while?' He thought Helena might be imagining things; she was as obsessed as he was by Emma Shearer.

'Yes,' she said. 'They're below high-water line, but the tide's going out.'

'I'll come along. Will one of you be able to wait for me?' He could hear children's voices in the background and wondered what they could have been doing there on a beach in the dark, felt a prickle of disapproval and then of suspicion.

'Just a moment.' There was a murmured conversation. 'Will you be able to give me a lift home to Deltaness? Daniel will take the children back and I'll wait.'

'Sure.' He was glad that Helena would be the person waiting for him and not Daniel. 'I'll be there as soon as I can. Twenty minutes.' He paused. 'Have you touched the shoes?'

'Christopher tripped over them in the dark. It freaked him out, big-style. He recognized them. Apart from that, no. We were about to leave anyway.' A pause. 'We were here with the Moncrieffs. They've already headed back for Deltaness. They didn't say, but I could tell they think I'm making a fuss over nothing.'

He'd already pulled on his coat and had his car keys in his hand. 'No,' he said. 'Definitely not a fuss over nothing.'

By the time he pulled into the car park there was a moon, full and white, and he didn't need the torch he was holding to make his way down the path. He'd been here a couple of times with Cassie the summer before. Hardly ever before that. This was a place for families. Local families; it was off the usual visitor route. He saw Helena as he turned to walk down the steps cut into the cliff. She was sitting on a rock, staring out at the sea, but she must have heard him coming because she stood up and looked his way.

'I'm sorry to have kept you waiting. Are you cold?' Compassion his default mechanism. Willow had once called it his secret weapon.

'No, I came well prepared for Shetland weather. The forecast was good, but I'm starting to realize you can never rely on it.' She was in a sweater. Maybe one of her own creations.

'Four seasons in a day.' The Shetland cliché. He felt awkward standing here, next to her, though he wasn't quite sure why. 'Where are these shoes?'

She pointed and now he did use his torch. The shoes stood just below the tideline where the shore was damp and hard. It should have been perfect for footprints, but the sand had been churned by too many feet and he thought it would be impossible to make out any individual marks. Helena must have guessed what he was thinking. 'I'm sorry! When Christopher screamed, we all rushed to see what was the matter. We didn't touch the shoes, though. He'd backed away from them and was pointing down at them. Our focus was on him at first.'

The shoes were caught in the torch beam. As Helena had said, they were yellow patent leather –

what Perez thought might be called a court shoe. Plain, elegant, with a small heel. They hadn't been washed here at high water. They were clean and dry and stood together facing the horizon, perfectly aligned, except that one was tipped on its side, where Christopher had kicked it. They matched exactly the colour of Emma's dress.

'Were there other folk here when you found them?'

'No. Lots of people around earlier in the day, but they drifted away over the afternoon. We built a fire, roasted marshmallows with the kids. It was good to be away from Deltaness for the day. I don't think any of us was in a hurry to get back.' Helena paused. 'But then Deltaness came to us, didn't it?'

'Whose idea was it to make the trip here?'

'Belle's. She phoned last night and suggested it.'

'Could the shoes have been there all day?' Perez knew that wasn't possible. They would have been disturbed by the water. But he wanted to hear what she would say. He thought she was too intelligent to lie to protect her family and friends, but when they were stressed, people did strange things.

'Absolutely not. We were sitting just here. One of us would have noticed. Anyway, they're below the tideline.'

There was a moment of silence when they both considered the implication of that. The shoes must have been arranged as they were, either by one of the Moncrieffs or one of the Flemings. Or by some stranger who'd been hiding in the shadows. And that seemed pretty unlikely.

'Christopher thought he saw someone just before

he fell over the shoe.' Helena must have realized she sounded desperate because she added, 'He doesn't make stuff up.'

'Did anyone else know you were planning a visit to Burra?'

She shook her head.

Perez took photos of the shoes and the scuffed sand. The flash seemed to startle Helena; she started shaking and wrapped her arms around her body as if she was very cold. He thought she might seem to be holding everything together, but she was scared, struggling. He pulled on gloves and scooped up the shoes into an evidence envelope. There was nothing more to be done here. And in the morning any evidence would have been washed away. 'Let's get you home.'

'I'm sorry. It's such a long drive for you. Perhaps I could get a minicab.'

'Really, it's not a problem at all.' He thought she didn't relish the idea of spending time with him as they drove north. 'Besides, at this time on a Saturday night, you could wait ages for someone to come out here to pick you up.'

He lit the way for her up the steps. At the top, before turning back towards the road, they stopped for a moment and looked back at the beach, black sea and waves breaking white in the moonlight. Peaceful and perfect.

They talked little on the drive back. Helena sat beside him, but shrank into the corner next to the passenger door, wrapped into her jersey. He thought she still seemed a little shaky. He was about to ask about the children – how Christopher was getting on at school, if there been more incidents with matches – when words suddenly seemed to spill from her.

'It seemed so staged. The shoes on the beach. Like someone's idea of installation art. Or as if someone was playing games with us.'

'Any idea who might want to do that?'

'I don't know,' she said. 'One of the Moncrieff children? If they found the shoes in their house and thought it would be a good joke? Something to scare us. A kind of tasteless prank that when wrong when Christopher was the person to find them. Maybe they couldn't admit they'd done it when they saw how upset he was.'

Perez thought about that and decided it could be a reasonable explanation. He wondered where the shoes had been found, though. A search team had gone through Ness House. There would be one way to find out for sure if this was an elaborate childish hoax – they should be able to check the shoes for fingerprints. He wondered what Moncrieff would say when he asked to take Charlie and Martha's prints and found himself looking forward to the confrontation. As he drove, his mind was wandering. If Emma had worn the shoes without tights or stockings, might there be a possibility of finding DNA on the insole? He would like to be certain that they belonged to her.

When they got back to Hesti, Daniel was still up, waiting. Helena had invited Perez in for coffee. Her husband didn't seem overjoyed to see him, but he was more relaxed than Perez remembered.

'Did the kids get to bed OK?' Helena was at the sink, filling a kettle with water.

'Fine. Ellie was asleep by the time we hit the bridge to Scalloway. I carried her into her room. She'll be a bit sandy . . .'

'No worries, she can have a bath in the morning. What about Christopher?'

'Still awake. Glued to his computer. I thought it was better not to make a fuss.'

'Yeah, no school in the morning.'

The ordinary domestic conversation touched Perez more than he would have thought possible. He stood and waited while the coffee was being made. They sat in the kitchen, drinking coffee, the shoes in the clear plastic envelope on the table between them.

'You think these belonged to Emma?' Perez directed the question to Daniel.

'She certainly owned a pair just like that.' He paused. 'She liked things matching, tidy, and they're exactly the same colour as her dress.'

'Do you happen to know her shoe size?'

'Four.' No hesitation. The blush came a moment afterwards. It must have seemed a very intimate piece of knowledge. Perez wondered how he would explain it to his wife later.

He turned the envelope upside down. The size was clearly marked on the sole along with the maker's name. Four.

'Can you explain how the shoes came to be there?' Perez tried to keep the question light, conversational, but thought it still sounded like an accusation.

'Helena and I were talking about it. We wondered

if it could have been one of the Moncrieff kids. Their idea of a sick joke.'

Perez nodded. He could see this would soon become the accepted story. 'Is that their style?'

'I don't know the older ones so well. But don't all teenagers want to cause a stir? Disturb their parents.'

'Maybe.' But Perez thought he'd never been like that. He'd upset his parents at times – they'd always wanted him to stay in Fair Isle, take over from his father as skipper of the *Good Shepherd*, the island's mail boat, work on the family croft – but he had never meant to.

There was a silence. Perez knew he should go. It would be late by the time he got back to Ravenswick and he should probably leave a message for Willow and tell her about the shoes. She was still in charge of the investigation. But he felt a kind of lethargy. It wasn't a pleasant prospect to go back to an empty house.

'Could Martha or Charlie have brought the shoes to the beach? Were they carrying their own bags?'

'We were all carrying bags,' Helena said. 'That's how it is for a day's outing to the beach with kids. You take so much stuff. Food, towels, spare clothes.'

'A bag they kept an eye on? Or that the rest of the family wouldn't look inside.'

'They had personal rucksacks. Martha seemed to have brought schoolbooks, but I didn't see her look at them.'

'Big enough to fit the shoes in?'

The Flemings looked at each other. 'Yeah,' Daniel said. 'I guess.'

Perez thought they would have agreed, whatever

the size of the bag. It was a convenient way of tying up the story. And even if the teenagers denied the stunt with the shoes, who would believe them, once the story had become established? That was how gossip worked; like fake news, it undermined the truth and left everything uncertain.

Chapter Forty-Three

Willow woke early and stretched for her phone. An automatic response when she was working. It was Sunday, a week since Emma Shearer's body had been found in the Hesti byre, and still, it seemed, they were no closer to finding the killer. Traditionally a day of rest in Shetland, but there'd be no time off for her. She sat up in bed and, looking down past the steep town roofs to the harbour, saw that the sun was shining again. There was a text message from Perez, sent the night before at eleven: *Looks as if we've found Emma's shoes*. No further information. She felt an irritation that verged on anger. Any other subordinate and she'd be straight on the phone, demanding details and to know why he hadn't made more of an effort to contact her the night before. With Perez these days, though, she had to be careful and weigh her words.

In the basement kitchen Rosie was feeding the baby. She'd already set out breakfast for Willow. 'Just help yourself.' Then, as Willow poured orange juice and ate some muesli: 'What's Jimmy P. been doing with himself? We've hardly seen him this time. Have we done something to offend him?'

Willow forced a smile. 'Ah, you know how it is in the middle of an investigation. No time to breathe.'

Back in her room in the attic. she pushed the window open and looked down on the Lerwick lanes. Two elderly women in Sunday-best coats made their way slowly up the steep slope towards the early service in the Methodist chapel. Willow went through her regular morning yoga exercises, but found it hard to lose the tension that had been the result of the text message, her preoccupation with Perez. In the end, she gave up and phoned him.

'Jimmy, tell me about these shoes.'

She listened to his explanation. 'And do you buy it? That the older Moncrieff kids somehow found the shoes and put them on the sand as a kind of joke?'

'Maybe.'

'But . . . ?' Because she could hear the hesitation.

'I don't know. Perhaps it's just too simple. It makes life too easy for them all.'

'But why would an adult do it? If the killer had kept the shoes for some reason, or they fell off Emma by mistake during a struggle, why not get rid of them? Why make a show of leaving them where two families were having a party? And when we'd assume that one of those people must have murdered Emma?'

There was a silence. 'Perhaps that's *why* they were left there,' Perez said at last. 'To point us towards the Moncrieffs or the Flemings.'

'You really believe in this mysterious, shadowy stranger seen by an eleven-year-old child? An eleven-year-old with behavioural problems.' There was no immediate answer and she continued: 'How would this stranger know that they'd be there? The families only decided the night before that they were going on the outing.'

'They live in Deltaness.' His voice was patient. 'Where neighbours see things and talk. Someone would have noticed Belle buying picnic food in the community shop, or seen Robert driving away with surfboards on the roofrack. After that, it would be easy to guess where they were heading. Burra's where Shetlanders go for a day on the beach.' He paused. 'There are very few secrets in the islands.'

'So, what do we do now?' She thought suddenly that she couldn't live in a place like this, where people thought they knew you from the purchases you made in the community shop, or the company you kept. She didn't want to be anonymous, but she needed more privacy than this. Perhaps Perez had done her a favour by not welcoming the news of her pregnancy. Now she could choose her own place to bring up her child.

'I think we should talk to Martha and Charlie, don't you? As you said, a teenage joke is the most likely explanation.'

'So, we head out to Deltaness?'

'No,' Perez said. 'I think a more formal interview is in order. I'm not suggesting we charge them. Nothing like that. But let's invite the parents to bring the kids down to the police station. I don't see why we should be running after them all the time.'

'I don't know, Jimmy. Moncrieff was already talking about complaining through his solicitor.' She remembered that Perez had been to school with Moncrieff and thought there might be some lingering antagonism. His judgement might be slightly flawed.

'If Robert Moncrieff wants his solicitor present, that's fine. At least the kids will take us seriously.'

'Will he get a lawyer on a Sunday?'

'Oh, Robert Moncrieff usually gets what he wants, whatever the time or the day.'

It was almost lunchtime before they all gathered at the police station. There was no Belle. She was at home, playing the good wife.

'Someone has to look after our younger children.' Robert Moncrieff's voice was self-righteous and a little too loud. He had dressed in his meeting wear of shirt and jacket, to remind them of his professional status.

Martha and Charlie looked younger than Willow remembered, freshly scrubbed. Charlie seemed watchful; his mouth kept twisting into a nervous grin. Martha was sullen. The solicitor was a middle-aged mainland Scot in a suit and tie. Perez seemed to know him and nodded when he came in. 'So, Inspector,' the lawyer said, 'how do you think we can help you?'

'We'd like to talk to Martha and Charlie.' Willow interrupted before Perez could speak. 'Nothing formal. Just a chat, away from the distractions of home, in the hope that they'll remember things better.' A pause to make sure he'd understood that she was the person in charge. 'I'm sure nobody wants to be here longer than needed. We've all got better things to do on a Sunday. So, I propose two separate interviews that can be conducted at the same time. That way, nobody's hanging around twiddling their thumbs. I'll talk to Martha, and Inspector Perez here will chat to Charlie. And as you've kindly agreed to come along to help, we can have a responsible adult in each room with the young people.' She looked up. 'I take it everyone agrees?'

Willow sat in a small, overheated room with Martha

and the solicitor. He'd told her his name, but she'd forgotten it immediately. He was that sort of person. They sat round a coffee table, not across a desk. Willow had arranged both rooms that way. She'd made it clear that this was a serious matter, by dragging the family all the way down to Lerwick. No need to turn it into an interrogation. The girl was already tense, defensive.

'You were there when Christopher found the shoes on the beach.' Willow leaned back in her chair, felt a flutter in her stomach and for a moment she forgot where she was. *It's probably wind. Hunger. It was a long time since breakfast.* But knowing it was the baby's first movement. A spark of joy.

Martha nodded and stared down at her black Converse sneakers.

'What did you make of it?'

'When he screamed, I just thought it was Christopher doing his thing. I know he can't help it, but he's weird. He makes odd noises, gets freaked out by small stuff.'

'But the shoes,' Willow said gently. 'What did you make of those?'

'They looked like the sort of shoes Emma might wear.' Martha shrugged. 'Yeah, they might have been hers.'

'And how do you think they got to the beach? You must have thought about it.'

Martha shrugged again and said nothing. Willow thought of herself at that age; her reluctance to communicate, in a family that talked everything through in the tiniest and most emotional detail, must have driven her parents crazy. It still felt like surrender to tell them anything important about her life. She wondered when she'd build up the courage to pass on the news that they were about to be grandparents. They wouldn't be dismayed by her becoming a single parent. They'd never bothered about convention. But they would be astonished that she'd decided to allow a child into her life. They'd always considered her entirely selfish. Willow dragged her attention back to the overheated room and continued the one-sided conversation.

'Because the shoes didn't just float there on the tide. They were there as a sign. A message. Or a joke.'

At the last word, Martha raised her head and looked Willow in the eye for the first time. But she allowed Willow to go on talking.

'Not a very good joke, maybe, but sometimes when things are stressful we look for ways to release the tension a bit. And I can see that a pair of posh yellow shoes belonging to a dead woman, on a beach, might do that. In a kind of surreal way.'

Still Martha held her gaze without speaking.

'Or at least it might stir things up.' Willow leaned back in her chair again and allowed the silence to stretch. 'Make things happen.'

'Why would I want to stir things up? The last week has been a fucking nightmare. It's been disturbed enough as it is. All I want is to stick out school, pass my exams and escape.'

The solicitor didn't wince, but Willow could sense his distaste at the language. She thought if he wasn't here, he'd be at church.

'So, you didn't find the shoes somewhere at home

and put them on the beach as a kind of joke? Because that's our most likely scenario at the moment.'

'No!' The word came out as a howl. Willow hoped it couldn't be heard in the room where Perez was talking to Charlie. The last thing she needed was Robert Moncrieff appearing, demanding to know what was going on.

'What about Charlie? Is it the kind of thing he might do?'

'Maybe. With his mates after a few drinks. He's easily led. But not with Mum and Dad around.' She rolled her eyes to show her disdain for her brother's cowardice.

'But you don't care what your mother and father think?'

There was a moment's pause. 'I think parents have to earn your respect.'

'And you don't think Robert and Belle have done that?'

The question made the solicitor shift uncomfortably in his seat. Willow ignored him and waited for Martha to answer.

'Actually no. I think they're pretty crap parents. Now Emma's not around, I hope they'll spend more time with Sam and Kate than they did with Charlie and me when we were growing up. But I wouldn't bank on it.' She paused. The solicitor seemed inclined to speak, but Willow glared at him and he changed his mind. Martha continued. It seemed as if years of rancour were finally spilling out. 'Mum likes the drama of being pregnant and having babies – the attention – but she can't really do the boring bit of looking after her kids. It's probably not her fault. She was spoiled rotten as a child. She never learned to be bored. Whereas we've had lots of practice.'

'And your father?' Willow didn't have to pretend to be interested.

'Ah, his parents were quite different. Cold and hard. I remember them, you know, though they're both dead now. My grandparents. There was nothing kind about them. They were like characters in a fairy story. Evil. Dad was an only child too. Perhaps that's why he wanted so many kids. He didn't want us to be lonely.'

'When was the last time you saw Emma wearing the shoes Christopher found on the beach?' Because this analysis of the family was fascinating, but Willow thought it wasn't getting them anywhere.

'I can't remember. Probably the last time she went out with Magnie. Or went up to Hesti to see Daniel. Emma liked dressing up for her men.'

'Were there any other men in her life?' Willow wasn't sure where the question had come from, except that she could tell Martha was holding back information. The girl might be prepared to bad-mouth her parents about their parenting abilities, but there was certainly something she was reluctant to pass on.

The question shocked Martha too. 'What are you saying?'

'That you mixed socially with Emma once you got older, and you probably knew her as well as anyone else. If she was seeing another man, you would know. You spent time with her, didn't you, in the youth club at the community hall?'

'Oh, that!' Martha was dismissive. 'Yeah, sometimes she'd hang out with the kids there.'

'And she was there when Christopher got upset at the bonfire. His mother told me about that.'

Martha was more wary now. 'Yeah, I think she was there that night.' A pause. 'Christopher really lost it.'

There was a moment of silence. The sun flowed through the window and suddenly Willow felt unbearably hot. She heard a door open, then Robert Moncrieff's voice outside. Perez must have finished the interview with Charlie.

'Is there anything else you'd like to tell me, Martha? Anything that might help clear this up, so you can all get back to normal.'

For a second, Willow thought Martha would confide in her. But she glanced across at the solicitor, caught his eye and shook her head. Willow wrote her mobile number on a scrap of paper and slid it across the coffee table. 'If anything comes to you, please give me a ring.'

Martha stared at the paper as if it might be too hot to touch, then she scooped it into her pocket, stood up and walked out of the room.

Chapter Forty-Four

Perez wished Willow had chosen Moncrieff to be present at her interview with Martha and that she'd left John Munro, the solicitor, for him. He could sense the doctor's hostility as they walked through the door into the small, hot room and thought this would be a complete waste of time. Charlie was clearly intimidated by his father and would give nothing away in his presence.

Perez had put a jug and three glasses on the low tables and now he poured out water.

'Tell me what happened yesterday. I want to know all about it.'

'Really, Jimmy.' Moncrieff jumped in immediately. 'What is this all about? I've already explained that we had a day at the beach. We needed a bit of time away. What more is there to say?'

Perez ignored him and turned to the boy. 'Take me through your movements.'

'Mostly I was chilling out with Martha.'

'You get on well, the two of you?' Perez asked.

'Yeah, I mean she's really cool. For a big sister.'

'So, you confide in each other?'

'Yeah, I guess.'

'Has she got a boyfriend?' Perez was feeling his

way. Didn't most sixteen-year-old girls have boyfriends?

Charlie looked at his father and shook his head. 'She's got mates at school and I know there are people who fancy her, but I don't think there's anyone special.' A pause. 'She's a bit of a loner.'

'And you *would* know, wouldn't you? Because you're very close.'

'I suppose.'

'So, you were chilling out on the beach. Did you see anyone there you knew? Anyone other than the Flemings and your own family, I mean.'

Charlie thought for a moment. 'I saw a lad from school. He was there with his folks, but they left not long after we got there.'

'Did you notice anyone after the bonfire was lit?'

This time Charlie responded immediately. 'No. By then it was just us on the beach. Everyone else had gone.'

'Had you noticed the shoes before?'

Charlie shook his head. 'They definitely weren't there when we were looking for driftwood for the fire. I went that way and I would have noticed.'

'It seems to me,' Perez spoke very slowly, 'that you're telling me one of your group must have placed the shoes where Christopher found them. If they weren't there when you built the fire and nobody else was on the beach, I can't see any other explanation.'

The wariness on Charlie's face was replaced by panic. He glanced again towards his father.

'Look here, Jimmy.' Moncrieff's face was red. It was the heat and a restrained fury. 'What are you implying?'

'I'm trying to understand what happened yesterday. I'm not implying anything.' Perez paused and looked across at father and son. 'Did either of you see someone put Emma's shoes on the beach, just below the tideline? I understand it was getting dark, but you were all there together. It seems odd that the shoes suddenly appeared. As if by magic.'

'We don't even know they were Emma's shoes!' Moncrieff said.

'Are you saying you didn't recognize them?'

There was a moment of silence.

'All this fuss about a pair of bloody shoes!' It seemed that Moncrieff could contain his anger no longer.

Perez ignored the outburst and turned back to Charlie. It pleased him to see Moncrieff so rattled, and he thought that perhaps Willow had been right after all to put them together. 'We thought it might have been some kind of joke. That you and Martha might have thought it funny to bring the shoes out like that. It would be a silly thing to do, but not criminal, you understand. Not something you'd get into major trouble for. Not if you tell me now. We've been looking for the shoes that Emma was wearing when she was killed, and if you or Martha found them somewhere in the house, it would be really helpful to know.'

The sun was shining on Charlie's face, lighting him up, as if he was caught in a spotlight. A reluctant star of a reality-TV show. He was sufficiently good-looking to be the member of a boy band.

'Sorry,' the boy said at last. 'I don't know anything about them.'

Perez asked more questions, but got nothing useful at all out of the interview.

They sent the Moncrieffs back to Deltaness and sat in the ops room eating the sandwiches Sandy had bought in the Co-op on his way in. They were made with soft white bread and there was a very limited veggie option for Willow, but the food disappeared quickly enough. Lack of any positive information had made them hungry. For a while there was no sound but the opening of plastic wrappers and the crunching of crisps.

Perez was imagining himself on the beach at Burra. No light but that coming from the moon and the bonfire. Would it have been possible for one of the party to slip away and put out the shoes without being seen? Maybe. The smaller kids would never be still, and the parents would be wandering off to check on them. It wouldn't take long to pull the shoes from a beach bag when nobody was looking. The alternative was some elaborate conspiracy, and he didn't believe in conspiracy theories.

'Martha's hiding something,' Willow said. 'Maybe protecting someone.'

'Her parents?'

'I don't think so. She wasn't exactly complimentary about them.'

'Her brother?' Perez thought of the boy, his face lit by the sun. Good-looking, amenable, adoring. He could imagine that Martha might feel the need to protect *him*. He would be her validation.

'Perhaps,' Willow said. 'But from whom? Do we

really think that lad killed Emma and Margaret Riddell? Because I don't see it.'

Nobody had an answer.

'So, what now?' Sandy was impatient. He always struggled with the detail of an investigation. The boring checking of facts that inevitably came in the middle of a case.

Perez waited for Willow to answer. In the past they would have joked about that. The fact that she was his boss. Today she was businesslike.

'The shoes are already on the plane south to go to the lab in Aberdeen. They'll look for DNA on the insole, fingerprints, and I've asked Lorna Dawson at the Hutton Institute to take a sample from the sole too. We know we'll find sand, but there might be soil or pollen trapped below that. It could give some indication of where Emma was walking before she died – though if she was killed in her car, as we suspect, that won't help much.' She paused. 'Sandy, why don't you have the afternoon off? Go and spend a bit of time with Louisa. We'll see you back here first thing tomorrow morning.'

Sandy almost ran from the room. Perez looked after him. 'I never knew he could move that fast.'

'What about you, Jimmy? What are your plans for the rest of the day? I expect you could do with some quality time with Cassie.'

He looked up sharply, not sure whether that was some kind of dig; did she resent his preoccupation with Fran's daughter? But it was hard to tell from her face what she was thinking.

'Cassie's been with her father this weekend. He's keeping her until the middle of the week. After that, he's away on another of his business trips and we're not sure when he'll get to see her again.'

She nodded to show she understood. He expected something more, a question or a comment about joint parenting. They were on their own now and this would be the time to discuss her pregnancy, but still the subject was wedged between them, a barrier. Solid and apparently impenetrable. He thought the longer the silence on the subject continued, the harder it would be to break, but he couldn't find the words to start the conversation.

'I thought I'd head up to Deltaness,' she said. 'Since Christopher Fleming found the shoes we've been concentrating on Emma Shearer, but I'd like to talk to Magnie and Lottie again. Margaret Riddell might have been a screwed-up old gossip, but she was a victim too.'

'Would you mind if I tagged along?' He wasn't sure where those words had come from. He didn't need an afternoon of awkward silences. It was habit maybe. He'd become used to seeking out her company. And still he loved being with her.

'Sure, Jimmy. If you want to see how this policing business is done, I'd be happy to show you.' Then she gave that grin that made his stomach flip, before leading him out of the room.

There was no answer when they knocked at Lottie's door, but when they moved on to Magnie's house, both aunt and nephew were there, standing in the narrow hallway, apparently on their way out. Magnie, Viking-big, seemed to take up all the space. Lottie looked even thinner, even less substantial. A strange couple: opposite but somehow complementary.

'We were planning a trip to Suksetter,' Magnie said. 'To where my mother died. To pay our respects.'

Perez saw that he was holding a bunch of flowers. The boy would have bought them from the supermarket in town. They were ready-wrapped with a giant bow formed with gold ribbon. Celebratory and inappropriate.

Magnie added, 'My auntie wanted to see where it happened.'

'Maybe we could come along?' Willow's voice was sympathetic, but she allowed Magnie no choice in the matter. 'We'll bring our own car. Then we can leave you to spend some time on your own there.' A pause. 'We'd like to pay our respects too, wouldn't we, Jimmy?'

'Of course.'

Perez thought they made a strange procession, walking from the car park inland from the shore, past the chain of lochans to the spot where Margaret Riddell's body had been found. The sun shone into his eyes and he felt too hot, uncomfortable. In Shetland, they weren't used to dry weather lasting as long as this; to this warmth. He felt for a moment that the world had gone crazy: elderly women shouldn't be so full of hate that they ended up dead; a bonny young woman shouldn't be found swinging in a dusty old byre. And the sun shouldn't still be shining.

When they reached Dennis Gear's bench, they

stood in an awkward group. Magnie laid the flowers on the wooden plank. Lottie was the first to speak.

'Is this where Margaret was killed? All the way out here?'

'We think maybe she was killed somewhere else and dragged here,' Willow said. 'But we don't know yet.'

'She was a heavy woman.' Lottie paused. 'And she didn't walk much, either. She was never terribly active, but since she had the arthritis in her knees . . . You're right, I can't see that she would have made it over the hill from Deltaness.'

'We think perhaps someone brought her body to the end of the path and pulled it from there. That's not so far.'

There was a moment of silence. 'I used to come here with Dennis too.' Lottie sat on the bench. 'Maybe it was where he brought all his lady friends.' She gave a dry chuckle. 'He didn't have much imagination, it seems. I was probably better off without him.'

'It's a shame Margaret didn't feel that way.' Willow sat beside her, moving the flowers carefully to make room. The men stood watching, but they might not have been there, for all the notice the women took of them. 'She'd have saved herself a lot of grief.'

'She couldn't help herself,' Lottie said. 'Even when she was a girl, it was as if she was the centre of the world, and if she was unhappy it was never her fault.'

'Do you know what made her like that?'

Lottie shook her head. 'I think it was just the way she was born. And our parents probably made it worse. They indulged her because they couldn't stand her tantrums. She was bright too. Perhaps they saw a great future for her, away from the islands.'

'We know she was sending notes to the Fleming family at Hesti.' Willow spoke so softly now that Perez had to struggle to hear. 'Could she have been sending anonymous letters to other people in the community?'

There was silence for a moment. A group of oystercatchers flew, calling into the mud at the edge of the loch.

'She sent one to Emma.' This was Magnie. 'Anonymous, but we knew it must be from my mother. Who else would it be?'

'You didn't mention it before.' Willow managed not to make it sound like an accusation.

'She was my mother.' He stared out towards the shore.

'What did it say?'

'Not much that made any sense. Nothing specific. Something like: "I know what goes on in that big house when Belle Moncrieff is away. You're a dangerous woman."'

'Did Emma keep the letter?'

'No. It arrived the day we built the bonfire on the beach. The day that lad from Hesti turned up and started screaming. Emma threw it onto the fire.' Magnie shifted his feet.

'Did anything else happen that night?' Perez thought there was still something Magnie was keeping to himself about the time Christopher Fleming gatecrashed the teenagers' beach party, but the man only shook his head.

'And Margaret never sent notes to anyone else?' It

seemed Willow hadn't noticed the man's reluctance to talk about that night or she wasn't prepared to push it.

'Not as far as I know,' Magnie said.

'Was there anyone she disliked enough?'

This time Lottie answered: 'She never had a good word to say about Robert Moncrieff. She went to the surgery once, asking for a sick note when she was feeling poorly, and he sent her away with a flea in her ear.' She paused. 'But then there were very few people she *did* have a good word for, so you shouldn't read too much into that.'

They were walking back to the car when Willow asked another question. She was in front with Magnie. He'd probably thought their business was done, that he'd satisfied his aunt's request. He walked like a man who'd been let off the hook.

'What did Emma make of the Moncrieff women?'

'What do you mean?'

'Belle and Martha. They're very striking individuals. Strong characters. Three women in the same house – sometimes that's like cats in a bag. They all come out spitting.'

Magnie stopped in his tracks. 'I don't know what you mean.'

'I suppose I'm asking if the three of them got on.'

'Oh.' Perez thought Magnie sounded relieved. 'I don't think there were any problems. Emma kept her own company when she wasn't working. And it's a big enough house that they wouldn't be on top of each other.'

'So, all happy families then?' Willow had stopped too and was looking back at him.

'Happy families? Aye, I suppose so.'

Perez thought that would be the very last way he'd describe the relationships in Ness House.

Chapter Forty-Five

Helena woke again to bright sunshine. She thought her friends in the south would never believe there could be weather like this in Shetland. Any other time she'd have posted Facebook images of their perfect life, the wildflowers and the empty beaches, the children looking brown and healthy, but now she didn't feel very much like gloating.

They'd survived Sunday without any major dramas. Daniel had worked in his office for most of the morning, firming up his pitch for the eco-hotel in Lerwick. She'd felt resentful – after all, she'd stopped working on Sundays so they could have more family time together – but had said nothing. She'd told herself it was better to have her husband fulfilled and relaxed than depressed and obsessed with a younger woman. Deltaness had been quiet. It had seemed empty after the invasion of police officers and forensic workers. A tense, anxious quiet, as if the whole community was holding its breath, waiting for something to happen. The sultry lull before a thunderstorm. Sunshine before the land was covered with fog again.

Now she left Daniel sleeping in bed and went to the kitchen to make tea. It was still early, but Christopher took a lot of waking after a weekend without routine, and this weekend she thought he'd scarcely slept. She'd heard him pacing in the early hours of the morning and had gone into him, held him very tight in the way that he liked when he was upset.

'Are you still a bit freaked out about finding those shoes?'

He'd nodded so quickly that she thought that hadn't been the real problem, but when she'd asked him what else was the matter, he'd shaken his head and refused to speak.

Now she went up to his room to give him a first call and found him already awake, staring out of the window onto the shingle beach. 'You're up early!' Her voice bright and false.

'I didn't sleep.'

'Don't be daft, you can't have been awake all night.'

He didn't answer, as if it wasn't worth the bother.

When she got to the kitchen, Ellie was already there, still in her pyjamas. She'd helped herself to cereal and it was all over the floor and the table. Helena cleared it up without a word, telling herself it wasn't the time to nag. Daniel appeared, looking rested and fit, bare-chested. Since Emma's death he'd been like a different man. He made coffee and handed a mug to her and kissed the top of her head.

What's going on here? It's only a week since the woman you professed to love was killed.

'Want me to do the school run?' he asked.

'No, I'll do it.' Sometimes, she knew, she made herself into a martyr. The female means of aggression. But today she had her own reasons for wanting the walk to school. 'You get on with your pitch for the hotel.'

He seemed not to notice the bite in her words. 'Oh, thanks, Helly. You're a star.' And he wandered off to shower in peace, leaving her to prepare the kids for school and make their lunches. She didn't see him again before it was time to leave. She shouted goodbye to him, but he must have been preoccupied with his plans because there was no reply.

In the yard, everyone was still talking about the murders, but attention was no longer focused solely on the family at Hesti. Margaret Riddell's death seemed to have dissipated that. Helena didn't feel the other parents' eyes on her the moment she appeared, didn't sense their greed for news. Perhaps, because they'd lost one of their own, the police investigation didn't feel like entertainment any more. The community had had enough of being in the spotlight and wanted the whole thing over. A week had been long enough. Ellie ran off to play with friends and Christopher lolled against the boundary wall. Belle Moncrieff appeared with her two youngest, saw Helena and immediately joined her.

'The police took Martha and Charlie to the station for questioning yesterday.' The words were whispered and Belle had looked round to check that nobody else was within earshot before she spoke. 'Would you believe it? They're only kids.'

'No!' Helena was shocked of course, but she began to understand the pleasure that the playground mums took in gossip.

'It was all about those shoes. The police seem certain they belonged to Emma, but I'm not convinced.

Robert says we should just have left them on the beach for some other bugger to find.'

'Surely that would have looked even more suspicious,' Helena said. 'The detectives would have found out that we'd been to Burra.' She heard the school bell ring, but she was still thinking about Martha and Charlie being dragged in to answer questions. Perhaps that had been her fault; after all, she'd suggested to Perez that the teenagers had dreamed up a practical joke to spook the adults. She wanted to ask Belle what had happened at the police station. Had Martha and Charlie admitted anything?

'I suppose they would,' Belle said. She'd taken a make-up bag out of her handbag and was putting on lipstick, checking her face in a small mirror. 'I'm heading into Lerwick for a decent coffee and some time away. Fancy it?'

Helena was tempted for a moment. Perhaps on the way to Lerwick she'd find out more about what had happened at the police station – it seemed she wasn't immune to the pull of gossip herself – but she shook her head. 'I should do some work.' She looked round and saw that the playground was already empty. The kids were all in school. 'Have a coffee for me, though.'

When she got back there was no sign of Daniel, except for a note left on the kitchen table: *Gone for a walk to clear my head. Won't be long.*

She thought that was typical – she'd turned down the offer of a day in town with Belle to spend some time with her husband and he'd just pissed off, without thinking she might like to join him on his walk.

She knew that was unfair – work had been in her mind, not a day out with Daniel – and that for some reason she was taking pleasure in the sense of being wronged. She stuck the breakfast plates in the dishwasher and went into her studio. Finally she found she could concentrate and began to lose herself in her work.

She'd switched her phone to silent when she'd come into the studio and didn't notice the missed calls, until she decided to stop for an early lunch. She hadn't heard Daniel return, but she assumed he'd be back at his desk in the house. There had been three missed calls from the school and a voicemail asking her to call back: 'It's rather urgent.' She was annoyed rather than anxious. Messages from school were always about Christopher's behaviour and were always rather urgent. She'd known he'd be scratchy and short-tempered because he'd had so little sleep. She wondered which child he'd bitten or kicked this time and hoped that the parents would be understanding. She didn't return the call until she was in the kitchen.

'Mrs Fleming. Oh, thank goodness.' It was the head teacher, not Becky, Christopher's support teacher. The head came from the south, but had lived in Shetland long enough to pick up a bit of an accent. A pleasant enough woman, but given to drama. 'I've tried phoning your husband but he's not replying, either.'

'What's Christopher done this time?'

'Nothing. Well, not exactly.' The woman paused. 'He's disappeared.'

'What do you mean he's disappeared? I brought him to school myself.' *Though I didn't watch him go in.*

A moment of guilt. Helena wondered if guilt haunted all parents as it did her, and if it ever went away.

'Oh, he was certainly here for registration. Of course we'd have called at once if he hadn't been there for that. You're so good about letting us know if he has to be absent for any reason. We think he must have gone during morning break. But nobody noticed until half an hour ago. His class teacher thought he was with Becky, but Becky was working with another child.' Her voice tailed off.

'Had anything happened to upset him?' In London after an argument with a teacher, Christopher had once run away to a nearby park and climbed the biggest tree he could find. It had taken Helena an hour to coax him down.

'No! Really nothing. He seemed a bit tired, apparently. Quiet. Not quite his normal self. We've searched everywhere we can think of. I suppose he's not with you? That was why I've been calling. In case he just made his way home and we've been worrying for nothing. We don't want to call the police unless we need to.'

'I've been working in my studio and my husband's out. Let me go upstairs and check. I'll call you back.' Interrupting the flow, because otherwise the teacher would continue talking, making her excuses.

Upstairs everything was quiet. As Helena approached Christopher's bedroom she listened for sounds from his computer, but there was nothing. She told herself he'd be wearing headphones and there'd be nothing to hear, but now the anxiety was kicking in. She opened the door and saw that the room was empty. She could see no change from when she'd come up to rouse him hours earlier. She didn't see how he could have been here. She began going through the paper on his desk, in case he'd left a note, and came across a photo he must have printed out from the computer. The Moncrieff family with Emma, in the Hesti garden. Helena recognized the event – a barbecue. It was one of the few times all the doctor's family had come along to the house. Usually Martha and Charlie made excuses and stayed away. Here they were sitting on the terrace, on the white wooden sun loungers that Helena thought more suited to a liner cruising the Med. Their legs were stretched out and their feet were facing the camera. The younger children stood on each side of them, with Emma sitting very elegantly on the floor to one side. Belle and Robert stood behind them. Belle's attention seemed to have been caught by something off-camera.

Helena wondered why Christopher had printed out that particular photograph, then saw that Emma was wearing the dress she'd worn when he'd found her in the barn. And the yellow shoes. Perhaps he'd spent all night staring at them.

There was a noise downstairs, the front door opening and shutting. She put the photo back on the desk and opened the door.

'Christopher, is that you?' She'd run to the top of the stairs and was looking down to the space below, felt a rush of relief, which she knew would turn to anger as soon as she saw he was safe.

But it was Daniel there, just returned from his walk, pulling the camera strap over his head. In his jeans and T-shirt, he looked as if he was on holiday. The anger that Helena had planned to direct at Christopher was focused on her husband. 'Where have you been? Christopher's gone missing. The school tried to phone you.'

'You know what it's like on the hill. No reception.' His calm infuriated her.

'There have been two murders and our son has disappeared,' she said. 'And you've been out all morning taking photos of otters.' She ran down the stairs towards him. She might have hit him, but he took her in his arms and held her as tightly as she did Christopher when he was having an attack. She realized she was crying.

'I'm sorry,' he said. He made no excuses, but kept repeating the words. She saw now that he was as distressed as she was.

She broke away from him. 'Can you phone the school, tell them he's not here? I said I'd call back.'

'Sure, what are you going to do?'

'I'm phoning the police. Jimmy Perez.' Because she knew that Jimmy would take her seriously. She heard Daniel's muttered conversation with the school and walked outside with her phone, staring down the track, praying to a God she'd never believed in that she'd see her son walking towards her.

Perez answered almost immediately. 'Helena.'

'It's Christopher. He's missing.' She tried to steady her voice as she explained what had happened.

'How long has he been gone?

She tried to work that out. The morning break was at ten-fifteen. She'd spoken to the head teacher at midday. 'Two hours.'

'I'll try to drum up a search team. Then I'll be there.'

Chapter Forty-Six

When Perez got there, Helena was at Hesti, waiting outside her studio to meet him. She seemed to look through him when he approached her. He thought she'd shut down, closed off all her emotions. That would be her way of coping. During the case that had brought him into contact with Fran, Cassie had been snatched during the Up Helly Aa procession and had been missing for an evening. Perez remembered Fran's frozen panic and his own sense of helplessness. He'd felt guilty that night too. Now he thought that throughout their relationship he'd done nothing but cause her harm.

Daniel was standing beside his wife and he was the person who went through the details with Perez; he explained that Christopher had gone to school as normal, but had disappeared during the morning, probably while the kids were playing at break.

Perez checked his watch. Nearly three o'clock. 'What time do they finish school?'

'Three-fifteen. I was just going to drive down to collect Ellie. We thought it made more sense to leave her there while all this was going on. Besides, we hoped Christopher might have turned up by the time she got home.' Daniel seemed unnaturally calm, but perhaps shock had frozen him too.

Another car was coming up the drive, so fast that pebbles scattered and bounced. Sandy was driving and Willow was in the passenger seat. *Bloody fool,* Perez thought. *He could kill her, going at that speed down these small roads.*

He turned back to Daniel. 'I'll come down to the school with you. We can chat to the kids as they come out and to the parents. Everyone knows Christopher. A place like Deltaness, someone will have seen him.' The words sounded more reassuring than he felt.

Willow was already climbing out of Sandy's car. Her long hair was tied back, but bushed out from the elastic band that held it, so it looked like a witch's broom. There were sandals on her feet. She looked like no other police officer he'd ever met, more eco-warrior than detective. It came to him, the thought unbidden, that Fran had always been stylish and neat.

'Are you OK to stop with Helena?' Perez explained that he wanted to go with Daniel to the school.

'Sure,' Willow said. 'Sure.' She put her arm around Helena's shoulder. 'Let's go inside, shall we?'

Helena was walking with her into the house. She must have heard Daniel start his car's engine, because she turned back and stood for a moment, watching as they drove down the track.

In the school playground, Perez walked with Daniel from one adult to another. 'We're looking for this man's son. He's called Christopher. You know who we mean. Has anyone seen him?'

The people listened, shocked, but nobody came up with useful information. The school was hidden from most of the houses by the community hall, which was closer to the road. A mother who lived close by said, 'I always know when it's playtime because of the noise in the yard, but I can't see anything from my place.' Her neighbour agreed. Perez couldn't find anyone who'd noticed the boy or had been aware of any strange cars.

Occasionally Perez walked ahead so that Daniel wasn't with him, and then the parents' response was sometimes rather different, a little dismissive: 'Isn't Christopher the daft one that sets fires?' one man said. 'I heard he was always running off.'

Before the end of class, Perez left Daniel in the playground and went into the school. The head teacher was waiting for him just inside the door. He held out his hand to her, but for a moment the smell of bleach and floor polish took him back to his own school days. On the walls of the corridor leading to the classrooms were children's paintings. Splashes of colour against the grey-painted walls, lit by the sunshine that still streamed through the glass door that led to the yard.

'I haven't told them anything's wrong yet,' she said. 'I don't want to make them anxious.'

Perez thought she didn't want to believe that a child in her care had vanished. If she told the children, she'd be forced to believe it, but she was still hoping for a miracle.

'Was anyone on playground duty?'

'One of the classroom assistants, but she's new, only started last week. I *have* spoken to her, but she didn't see anything.' Now she was sounding defensive. 'Christopher's a very bright boy. He could run rings round most of the adults I know. If he was determined to slip out of the yard without anyone noticing, he'd do it.'

'How many classes are there in the school?'

'Three.' The head teacher took a breath, seemed to realize it was time to accept the inevitable. 'Shall we start with the youngest? I've told my colleagues to keep the kids in until we've had a chance to talk to them.'

The early-years classroom had been tidied for home-time. There was a lid on the sandpit and the picture books had been replaced in their box. A dozen children sat cross-legged on a mat in front of a motherly woman, perched on a chair that seemed far too small for her. She'd just been reading a story. She looked up when Perez and the head teacher came in. 'Now, everyone, this gentleman would like to ask you some questions. Listen carefully because it's very important.'

Perez sat on the corner of a table, so he was nearer their level. 'Does everyone here know who Christopher Fleming is?'

Hands shot into the air. Eyes were bright. In a school of this size, this was a question nobody could fail to answer.

'Good.' The hands went down. The cocky kids were disappointed that they hadn't been given the chance to show off their knowledge. 'Now Christopher's gone missing. Did anyone see him at break time?'

But it seemed the younger children had their own yard so they wouldn't be intimidated by the rowdy eleven-year-olds. Nobody here had seen Christopher since the start of the school day.

Ellie Fleming sat at a round table close to the front

of the next class, beside Kate Moncrieff. Again Perez was introduced, and again he asked if anyone had seen Christopher at break. 'What about you, Ellie? Did Christopher tell you where he might be going?'

He crouched next to her, so she could answer without the rest of the class hearing. But she shook her head. 'Christopher likes secrets. He doesn't tell me anything.'

'Does he have a secret at the moment?'

'He said he did.' Now she seemed unsure or unwilling to commit herself. Scared, perhaps, to look foolish in front of her friends.

'When did he tell you that he had a secret?'

'When we were in the car on the way home from the beach.' She looked up at Perez. 'But I don't know what it was. I was very sleepy. Even if he told me, I don't remember.'

Perez stood up. 'Anyone else see Christopher at break today?'

The kids looked at each other, but no hands went up here. It seemed that the head teacher was right and, once Christopher had made up his mind about something, he could run rings round them all. He could even make himself invisible.

Christopher's class teacher was a newly qualified male teacher. He wore a little black beard, a striped shirt and jeans. He called the children 'guys'. Becky, Christopher's support teacher, was in the room too and she seemed to be the person keeping order. Christopher's disappearance was common knowledge here and was causing excitement and chatter. Perez heard one boy talking earnestly about alien abduction.

'Quiet!' Becky banged on a table. 'This is important. The inspector has some questions for you.'

Like a warped echo behind her, the class teacher mumbled, 'Come on now, guys.'

There was an expectant silence that made Perez feel suddenly nervous, a performer just about to take centre-stage. 'Did anyone see Christopher Fleming at morning break?'

A hand went up. Perez had never seen the boy, but his likeness to Robert Moncrieff was so obvious that he knew him at once. 'You're Sam, right? And you saw Christopher this morning at playtime?'

'Kind of. He followed me out into the yard. Then I went off to play footie and I didn't notice him after that.' A pause. 'He wasn't really into games.' A couple of boys in the back row sniggered. This, it seemed, was an understatement.

'Did Christopher say anything to you as he followed you out of class?'

'No, we weren't close mates or anything.' Sam seemed anxious to emphasize this. Perez thought Christopher must have a lonely time at school, if everyone made an effort to distance themselves from him. 'But he had his bag with him and his lunch box, and that seemed kind of strange. I mean, it wasn't lunchtime and we were just going out to play. Why would you need all that stuff?'

'Did you ask him what he was doing with it?'

Sam Moncrieff shook his head. 'No, Christopher did weird things all the time.'

There were more sniggers in the back row. Becky glared at the culprits. 'You know what I think about people in this class who are deliberately unkind. And it's unkind to laugh at Christopher, even when he's not here. I won't stand for it.'

Her disapproval was echoed by another mumbled offering from the class teacher. The boys fell silent and Perez turned back to Sam Moncrieff.

'Did Christopher say anything to you about a secret?'

The boy shook his head. The children were getting restless now and Perez could see that he'd get nothing more useful from them.

'Off you go then. If you remember anything, or if you'd like to talk to me in private, ask your parents or your teacher to give me a call.' There was a sudden outburst of sound: chair legs being scraped against the floor, shouts and laughter, and they chased outside. Christopher's disappearance didn't seem to have disturbed them at all. Perez wondered why that was. If the boy had run away before, then perhaps, like the father who'd been so dismissive in the yard, they'd become used to it. Or perhaps it was because Christopher was so different that they struggled to feel empathy; they couldn't imagine him scared and alone.

Daniel was waiting for Perez outside. The yard was almost empty; the last straggling carers led their children away.

'Anything?' The man had been leaning against the wall as if he was exhausted. His eyes were fixed on Ellie, who was playing on a climbing frame in the far corner.

'I don't think Christopher was snatched,' Perez said. 'It sounds as if he planned to run away.' He explained about the lunch box and the bag. 'And he must have made an effort to slip away unseen. I think he most probably hid indoors somewhere, when the bell was rung for the end of break, and left when the youngest children were making their way inside. This isn't a huge space. Otherwise someone would have seen him go.' He paused. 'Can you think where he might be? Are there any special places where he might go? Somewhere safe, if the murders and finding the shoes on the beach had disturbed him?'

'Really his safe place was always his bedroom,' Daniel said. 'With his computer. Watching the same cartoons, playing the same games.'

'Has anything happened at home? Anything that might make it not seem so comfortable?'

'No! Things haven't been brilliant between Helena and me, but the situation's getting better. If anything, we're all more relaxed and the kids seem more settled.' Daniel called to Ellie and she ran towards him and took his hand. He lifted her into his arms and held her very tight.

Chapter Forty-Seven

Willow sat with Helena in her sunny kitchen and thought that losing a child – certainly to have a child disappear in this way – must be one of the worst things that could happen to a mother. It would be the not knowing and the guilt. You would run scenarios round in your head, wilder and wilder scenarios if you had any imagination at all, and that would drive you mad. Helena was sitting quite still, but Willow believed that her mind was racing. This was a woman who was creative; she had a lot of imagination.

'I'd love a cup of tea,' Willow said. At least if Helena was making drinks for them she might be distracted for a moment. 'Would you mind?'

Helena got to her feet, switched on the kettle, pulled out mugs and spoons. 'Shouldn't we be doing something? I mean something useful.'

'Someone needs to be here in case Christopher comes back. You wouldn't want him turning up to an empty house.'

Helena seemed satisfied with that, at least for a while. She made the tea and passed a mug to Willow.

'Are you up to answering a few questions?'

'Of course. Anything!'

'How was Christopher this morning? He'd been

upset by finding Emma's shoes on the beach at Burra on Saturday night, but he'd had a day at home to get over that. Or was he still upset?' Willow set down her mug.

'He seemed OK on Sunday. We had a lazy day, because Saturday had been pretty active and the kids were late to bed. But last night he was unsettled again. He was still awake past midnight. I heard him pacing and I went into him. This morning he was already up when I went in to wake him and he said he hadn't been asleep at all.'

'Was that unusual?' Willow asked.

'Kids on the autistic spectrum often have problems sleeping, but if it was true he'd been up all night, that was extreme even for Christopher.' Helena twisted her own mug in her hands. 'I should have asked him what was worrying him. I just gave him a hug and told him to go back to bed.'

'And he didn't give you any idea what was troubling him?'

'No.' Helena paused. 'I think he'd been on Facebook looking at old photos. There was one that Daniel had posted. I hadn't even seen it when it first went up. Too busy. Probably away pitching for work. Anyway, Christopher had printed it out.'

'Christopher has a printer in his room?'

'Yeah, an old one of Daniel's that wasn't working properly. Christopher sorted out the glitches. He's very tech-savvy.' Helena looked up and gave a grin that disappeared immediately. 'Not so savvy when he comes to reading people. He takes them on trust. If someone invites him to get into their car for a lift, he'll accept. Even though we've told him it would be a mistake.'

Willow touched her hand. 'Here, you know it probably wouldn't be a mistake. It would be someone being kind.'

'So, where is he? Who's taken him?'

Willow didn't answer. 'Tell me about the photo that seems to have caught his attention.'

'Daniel must have taken it. I remember the occasion. We had a barbecue. It wasn't very long ago. The whole Moncrieff family came along and I invited Emma too. Being selfish, I thought another adult would be a good idea to help out with all those kids. I didn't realize then that Daniel had become obsessed with her. She's there with Robert and Belle, along with the children. The thing is, she was wearing that dress. The yellow one she was wearing when she died. And she was wearing the yellow shoes.' Helena paused. 'Perhaps that was why Christopher felt the need to print it out.'

'Have you still got the photo?'

'Yeah, it was in his room. I found it when the school first phoned to say he was missing. I went upstairs to check that he hadn't come back here.' Helena was already running out of the room to fetch it.

As soon as she had gone, Willow was on her feet too, looking at the notices pinned to the fridge with puffin-shaped magnets, leafing through a pile of paper on the work bench. She came up with nothing interesting and felt shabby when Helena returned.

Helena put the picture on the table between them. The quality wasn't terrific, but good enough to make out all the individuals. Martha and Charlie, super-cool, lounging on one elbow, turned slightly towards each other. Teenage-moody. Martha in her usual black – leggings, tunic, Converse sneakers. Charlie was all in white, the sleeves of his shirt rolled to the elbow. He looked as if he'd come straight from cricket practice. Did they play cricket in Shetland? Willow made a mental note to ask Perez. In any event, the contrast between the siblings was striking and Willow wondered if the teenagers were aware of the look they'd created, or even if they'd planned it. Behind them stood Robert and Belle; Belle had her head turned slightly to one side, as if something going on in the garden had caught her attention.

Then there was Emma, with her heavily made-up cat-like eyes. She was sitting on a rug with her legs to one side. Wearing the yellow dress that made her look like a Fifties film star. And the patent-leather yellow shoes that were already in the Hutton Institute in Aberdeen, waiting for analysis. She was smiling towards the person who was taking the picture.

'Did you take this?' Willow asked

'No, like I said, it must have been Daniel.'

Of course it was, Willow thought, because the smile was seductive and who else could the photographer have been?

She stared again at the photo, this time giving all her attention to the teenagers, who could have been models in some arty ad, and to the younger children gathered around them. Christopher's face was unusually full of expression. Clearly, he didn't mind being there. He looked not just happy but rapt, totally engaged.

'This is a lovely picture of Christopher.' Willow slid it back across the table towards Helena.

'Isn't it?' She seemed less tense now.

'It looks as if he was in a particularly good mood that day.'

Helena looked at it again, more closely. 'That would have been the barbecue. I explained before, he loves fire. It was the same when we lit the bonfire in Burra. He becomes almost entranced.'

'Why do you think this photograph kept him awake all night?'

'I'm not sure that it did. He could have been worrying about something altogether different and gone onto the computer for a distraction. That's what we all do when we're anxious, don't we? We try to distract ourselves.' Helena put her head in her hands.

'What else might he do?'

'He reads. Crime fiction mostly. Books that are probably far too old for him. He started with Agatha Christie when he was about nine, but now he loves the forensics stuff. He watches endless reruns of *CSI* on TV.'

Willow didn't think this was the time to talk about the *CSI* effect, or the fact that juries were failing to convict because real-life forensic science was nothing at all like television. She looked again at the picture and a possible explanation for Christopher's disappearance began to form in her mind. She was about to suggest more tea when her phone went. A number she didn't recognize. She hit the reply button.

'Is that Inspector Reeves?'

She knew the voice. 'Magnie. How can I help you?'

'I heard Christopher Fleming's gone missing.'

'Yes.' A flutter of hope. 'Have you seen him?'

'No, it's nothing like that, and it probably won't make any difference. But I wanted to talk to you. About that night when we had the beach party. When I was there with Emma. I didn't tell you everything.'

'Are you at home?'

'Yes.'

'I'll be there. Five minutes.'

She ended the call and was aware of Helena staring at her. 'Was that news? Have they found Christopher?'

'Not yet. But it might be something that could help. I'm going to leave you with Sandy. You know Sandy, the young officer from Whalsay. And I'll be back soon.'

Driving down the track towards Deltaness felt like an act of desertion.

Lottie was standing at her window and watched as Willow approached her nephew's house. She gave a little wave, but didn't seem at all curious to know why the detective was there. Magnie was waiting for her and answered the door before she had time to knock.

'This is probably a waste of your time.' He led her into the overfilled living room. Signs of Margaret's absence were already showing, in the stained coffee mug on the windowsill, the empty beer cans in the wicker bin.

'It's obviously been troubling you.' Willow thought he'd been holding something back since the first time she'd met him. She paused for a beat. 'Is it something to do with where you were on the night your mother died?'

He shook his head. 'No! That was just like I told you.' His voice impatient, but defensive too.

'So what is it, Magnie?'

'It was when I heard the boy was missing, I thought it might help. That I'd feel like shit if it turned out to be important and I hadn't spoken about it.'

'Tell me now.'

'It's about the night the boy from Hesti wandered into the middle of the beach party.'

'I remember,' Willow said. 'He got very upset and you kindly took him home.'

'Things got ugly that night. I don't know, it was the drink maybe. But the kids were all jeering and calling him names. Chanting.'

'What did they call him?'

Magnie shook his head and for a moment she thought he would refuse to answer. 'Retard,' he said at last. 'Ignorant stuff like that. It was a kind of madness. The crowd thing. Then they started shouting something else.'

This time Willow knew she didn't need to prompt him. He would tell her in the end.

'Hangman,' he said. 'They called him "hangman".'

'I can see why he'd be upset. His father had found Dennis Gear hanging in their property not long before, but I'm not sure what this might have to do with two murders, or Christopher running away.'

'I don't think it was the kids who started that.' Magnie stared bleakly ahead. 'I think it was Emma. I've been over and over it in my head. I didn't want to believe it. Not then and not since. I told myself she wouldn't do something like that. Not to a boy like Christopher. That I'd got it all wrong. I usually get things wrong. But I was sitting next to her and I heard her. It was a whisper at first, then she got louder, until some lads standing close to us joined in. "Hangman, hangman." And once the others started shouting too, she stopped speaking and just watched. Pleased, as if it was what she had wanted all the time. That hate spreading like a wild fire on the hill.' A pause. 'It was as if she was drunk on the power.'

Willow didn't speak for a moment. She could see why Magnie hadn't told her before. He'd persuaded himself that Emma was his ideal woman and he'd wanted to preserve the image, especially after her death. Now he was admitting that he hadn't really known her at all. The notion that she'd had, looking at the photo of Emma in the Hesti kitchen, grew. Other ideas clicked into place. For the first time, she had a sense of the real Emma.

'There's something else.' Magnie interrupted her thoughts.

'Yes?' She was still trying to process the possibilities and had to pull her attention back to this room.

'My mother was there that night.'

'I'm sorry?' Willow tried to imagine Margaret Riddell, angry at the world, at a beach party full of rowdy, drunken kids.

'She must have been on duty to lock up the community hall. She'd have seen the fire and heard the noise. Somehow she got herself to the top of the bank, because when I turned round I saw her looking down on us.' Magnie closed his eyes and Willow thought he was imagining the scene.

'Was she there when Emma started the chanting?'

'I think she must have been. But she'd gone by the time I came back after taking the Fleming boy home.'

There was a silence. From far in the distance came the sound of children's voices. The school day must have ended. Soon Perez would be back at Hesti with Daniel. Willow had to talk to him. She knew now *why* Christopher had run away, but she still had no idea where the boy was. It was more important than ever to find him.

'Did you and your mother ever talk about what happened that night on the beach?'

'No,' Magnie said. 'She never mentioned it, and I wasn't going to bring it up. It wasn't something I was proud of.' A pause. 'I wanted to forget it had ever happened.'

'You did the right thing. Phoning me.'

He nodded. 'I'm sorry. I should have done it earlier.' He walked with Willow to the front door. In the neighbouring house, Lottie was still staring out of her window.

Chapter Forty-Eight

Christopher had taken matches from the kitchen before leaving in the morning. He knew his mother's hiding place. She put everything secret in a black jar at the back of the cupboard where she kept the tea and the coffee. He had to stand on the bench to reach it. He'd done that while she was talking to Dad about his work, before walking them to school. He wasn't sure why he needed the matches, but it made him feel better to know they were there, wrapped in a plastic sandwich bag at the bottom of his lunch box. They provided comfort, like the reruns of *CSI* that he watched on Netflix. Fire made him feel better. The possibility of fire was a reassurance.

The first lesson was maths. Usually he enjoyed maths, because he found it easy, and he liked being better at it than everyone else in the class. Often he could work out the answer before Mr Johnson. Today he found it hard to concentrate. Then there was music. They were practising the songs they'd sing at the leavers' assembly. He'd be leaving Deltaness school at the end of the summer too. He'd have to go in the bus to the Junior High School in Brae. That would mean getting up much earlier, and there would be other kids, new teachers. It would be a lot to get used to. He tried not to think about it.

After break it was PE. He hated PE and that was why he decided break was the best time to run away. He could have left it until later in the day, but this way he'd miss the horror of changing, of being outside on the field, of having to run.

When the bell went for playtime, Christopher collected his bag and lunch box before going outside. Sam Moncrieff noticed but didn't say anything. Sam was OK when they met outside school. Sometimes they played computer games together, built Lego. But in school he was different and never acknowledged any kind of friendship. Christopher didn't waste time worrying about that and, anyway, today Sam ignoring him worked in his favour.

During break, Christopher leaned against the school wall and watched the others chasing about. That was what he usually did. Sometimes he brought a book to read, but generally he just watched. When there were only a couple of minutes to go before the end of playtime, he moved round the corner to a narrow space, between the school and the fence that separated the early-years kids' yard from that of the older ones. He crouched down, so nobody could see him, and felt his heart racing a bit. He couldn't work out if he was nervous or excited. The bell went and everyone ran in, but nobody seemed to realize that he was missing. The gate into the road was fastened with a padlock during school time, but it wasn't very high and he jumped over it easily, even carrying his bags.

It wasn't a long walk to where he was going, but he knew nobody should see him, so he took a circuitous route, avoiding the shop, where old people often gathered to talk. The sun was shining and Christopher felt very hot. He took off his T-shirt and put it in his bag. If his mother knew what he'd done, she'd be annoyed, but the plan was that nobody would see him, at least for a while, so she'd never get to know. He was tempted to take his bottle of water from his bag to have a drink, but knew he'd be glad of it later in the day.

When he arrived at his destination, the door was open, as he'd known it would be. This was a good place to wait. By now he felt very tired. He'd been up all night, worrying that he was doing the right thing. He'd thought it had been clever to make the phone call, using the landline in his mother's workshop, so nobody in the family would hear. In the middle of the night it had seemed like a mistake. He thought it was too late to change his mind now and, in the end, he curled up in a corner and went to sleep.

Chapter Forty-Nine

Willow left Magnie's house and drove straight to the Moncrieff place. She knocked at the door, but there was no response and everywhere was locked, even the garage. She stood and listened, but had no sense that anyone was inside. She walked to the back of the house; a large garden was surrounded by a stone wall and stunted sycamores. It was laid to grass, with a full-sized football net at one end and a swing at the other. Still no sign of life. Beyond the wall there was a field of oats.

She stood for a moment and considered her options. Belle should be home by now with Sam and Kate. Her car wasn't parked outside the house, so perhaps she'd taken them out to play with a friend or to collect the older children. Willow's suspicions were based on the flimsiest of evidence. She couldn't go to the health centre and confront Robert Moncrieff with what she'd guessed, and she certainly couldn't put out a call for Belle and the kids. This was a time for patience.

But they had to find Christopher. She drove back to Hesti and saw that Perez and Daniel had arrived back from the school. Helena and Daniel were in the kitchen with Sandy. Daniel stood behind his wife and held her. It was as if he was holding her upright and keeping her strong. He seemed free of all emotion now. When Willow went in, Helena looked at her, desperate for news. She shook her head to show that she had nothing for them.

Chapter Fifty

Perez was standing just inside the kitchen door. He watched Willow come in and saw Helena's disappointment when there was no news about her son. Willow looked stiff and anxious, and Perez felt an overwhelming tenderness for her. An instant later, he knew he shouldn't feel like this. Willow was so strong that she would consider the emotion presumptuous, patronizing; after all, she was the last woman to need a man to care for her. In this relationship, it seemed, there was nothing but confusion.

She touched his elbow. 'Can I have a word?'

He followed her outside, relieved to escape the tension in the room and the parents' pain. The courtyard was busy with people he scarcely recognized – officers and volunteers were searching the outhouses now: Helena's studio, a smaller storeroom and the byre where Emma had been found.

'I don't want to be overheard.' Willow walked around the house to the paved terrace where the photograph found in Christopher's room had been taken. The white wooden loungers were still there, remnants of a more settled time.

Except it hadn't been settled, Perez thought. The family's first few months in this house had been oppressive, weighed down with resentment and jealousy. He looked out to sea. A bank of cloud, so dense that it looked solid to the touch, hid the horizon. It seemed that the fog that had shrouded the islands the week before was on its way back with a vengeance.

When they reached the boundary of the Hesti garden, Willow began talking. She confided in Perez as she'd always done, sharing her ideas about the investigation, setting aside any awkwardness. Now, it seemed, nothing mattered but the case and the missing boy. Perez listened until she'd completed the narrative.

'That makes sense, but it doesn't explain Christopher's disappearance from school or help us find him.' He thought Willow was the most emotionally intelligent person he'd ever known. In work, and in his private life, he too often let sympathy take over. He was a sucker for a sob story, but she was clear-eyed, insightful and without sentiment. He looked again at the sea and saw that the fog was closer now, rolling towards them, a giant individual wave.

Suddenly he set off at a run, leaving Willow to follow more slowly behind him. As they'd reached the end of the garden he'd glimpsed the roof of the shed formed by the upturned yoal. Surely the building would make the perfect hiding place for an eleven-year-old boy. Perez imagined Christopher inside, curled up on one of the red cushions, absorbed in a book. Pushing open the door, he was already tasting the relief of finding him safe and well. But, inside, there was no sign of the child. He stood, drained after the sudden rush of adrenaline and expectation. Willow had joined him and he sensed her disappointment too, when she saw the place was empty. He walked further into the building and crouched to look more closely, at the shelves, in the corners. The fog must have covered the sun now because, even with the door open, he needed the torch on his phone to see any detail.

'Christopher's definitely been here.'

'I know,' Willow said. 'He probably plays here all the time.'

'No. Today.' Perez lifted a wicker wastebasket onto the makeshift table where they'd found Emma's bag. Inside was an apple core and an empty raspberry-yoghurt pot. 'That was in his packed-lunch box. I asked Daniel.'

'So where is he now?'

'With the killer,' Perez said, his voice very quiet. 'That's what this is about.'

On the shore the sudden lack of light felt weird, supernatural, like an unexpected eclipse of the sun. The temperature had dropped too. Sharp edges in the landscape had blurred, and sound was muffled. Perez and Willow started to walk back towards the house. Perez thought the team must have widened their search because he was aware of movement in the fog, people no more than silhouettes shifting in and out of focus, dark shadows against the grey.

'What now?' Willow was walking beside him. The mist was damp and he could smell wet wool, wet grass.

'We don't have any proof. Nowhere near enough to make an arrest.'

'But we need to find the boy.' He could hear the desperation in her voice and thought she wasn't so detached after all. 'There might be fingerprints in the shed, if they met up there. That would be evidence of a kind.'

'Fingerprints would be in the shed anyway, from previous occasions.'

They'd climbed the stile onto Hesti land. She stopped for a moment. 'I can't believe the killer would harm Christopher.'

But Perez thought the killer was desperate, and desperate people did crazy things. *I did a crazy thing, not thinking clearly before I spoke, when you told me about the baby. Shutting off the possibility of a child of my own.*

He was trying to form the words into an apology when he was aware of a light forcing itself through the gloom. It seemed to hover at a strange angle above them, and it took him a moment to work out what it might be. At first he imagined an explosion, a fire in a small and distant aircraft. This wasn't moving, though. It was static and grounded. 'It's the bonfire on the hill. The Midsummer Beacon. Someone's set fire to it.'

'Christopher!' She was already running. 'Who else could it be?'

Chapter Fifty-One

Willow soon realized she couldn't keep up with Perez. The hill was steep and three months of tiredness, disturbed sleep and lack of exercise had left her soft and unfit. Perez was used to the terrain; he'd spent his childhood helping his father with the Fair Isle hill sheep. He understood the uneven patchwork of heather, peat bank and *Juncus* underfoot, the patches of exposed rock and the trap of crumbling drystone dyke hidden by rush and reed. She couldn't be as reckless as she might once have been. Now she climbed carefully, worried about tripping. She stopped every so often to catch her breath, frustrated by her lack of energy and her flabby, aching muscles. The fog grew thicker, the higher she climbed, and she would have lost her way if it weren't for the fire blazing wild and fierce above her. She could smell it now and hear branches snapping and cracking, though she was still too far away to feel its heat.

Eventually the slope flattened and walking was easier. She was close to the top of the ridge on a plateau that ran out towards the sea. She'd seen the cliffs from the beach below: they were steep and sheer, and water boiled at the bottom even when the weather was calm like this. The beacon had been built here simply because it was so close to the cliff edge. It would be seen from other high places all down the east coast of the islands. The mist was so dense that she couldn't see the cliff edge, but she knew it was there. As a background to the other noises, she heard the low churning of the sea below. She leaned against a rocky outcrop, glad of a moment to rest.

At first she thought she was alone here, stranded above the other life that continued below. There was no sign of Perez. Everything else seemed a long way off. She supposed that in Hesti, the team was still searching. She hoped Sandy was with Daniel and Helena, and imagined them in the kitchen there, closed in and safe.

Then she saw a figure just beyond the fire, lit by the flames, but still insubstantial in the mist. Christopher. She was about to call out to him to tell him to move away from the cliff edge, when someone else emerged from the Suksetter side of the hill.

She knew from the first glimpse that this wasn't Perez. Even blurred by the fog, she would have recognized the detective, the shape of his body and the way he moved. It was clear, even at this distance, that this wasn't a meeting of friends. Christopher backed away from the newcomer, apparently terrified. Perhaps this was the climax of a chase that had taken place across the hill. Willow thought the lighting of the beacon had been the boy's cry for help, but now she watched without speaking or moving, not running to his aid. He was so close to the edge of the cliff that she worried any sudden sound might make him fall. He must be disorientated, lost, exhausted. Her silhouette was masked by the outcrop of rock behind her; she could see *their* outlines, moving in the firelight, silent as life-sized puppets, but they couldn't see her.

The taller figure was approaching Christopher slowly. Willow was reminded of a skilled sheepdog controlling a solitary animal, moving it at will. Here, Christopher was being inched away from the fire and towards the cliff edge. The predator darted forward and Christopher stumbled. He was so close to the steep drop that Willow held her breath. An autistic boy, falling to his death in thick fog after running away from school and setting light to the beacon, would be seen as an accident, not murder. The killer turned slightly and Willow saw the flash of a blade in the fire-light. Christopher was being controlled not just by fear of the individual, but by the knife in their hand.

She left her position and, crouching low, circled the beacon towards the pair. As she moved she found herself repeating a mantra: *Please keep Jimmy away from here. Wherever he is and whatever he's doing, don't let him see what's going on.* Because Fran Hunter, Jimmy's one true love, had been stabbed to death, and Jimmy still thought he was to blame. To save the boy – whatever the danger to himself – would seem like reparation, a way of putting things right. And now, more than anything in the world, Willow needed Jimmy Perez to be alive and well, and a part of her life.

She paused for a moment. The person with the knife had their back to her and Christopher was so panic-stricken that he still hadn't seen her. The boy seemed mesmerized by the blade and unaware of the cliff edge behind him. Willow felt the heat of the fire that was still burning fiercely, the embers white-hot and glowing. She tried to think clearly and to weigh up her options. She wasn't sure she'd be quick enough to jump the predator without sending Christopher over the cliff, and perhaps Christopher was the only person now who could bring the killer to justice. Deep down, though, she knew her anxiety for the boy was an excuse: she was only concerned for her own safety and that of her baby. Willow hesitated, hating herself for her cowardice, her indecision and her inability to act. Would she stay here, watching the scene play out before her, waiting for the boy to fall to his death, too scared to move and save him?

There was a faint sound behind her. She turned her head slowly and watched Perez appear out of the fog. He made no attempt to hide. She supposed that he'd been watching the scene too, because he'd surely been here longer than her.

'Christopher!' Perez's voice seemed very loud.

The person with the knife turned towards him, and that, Willow realized, was what Perez wanted. The blade was no longer directed towards the boy. 'Just walk towards us, Christopher. Willow's here too. You know who she is – the detective from Inverness. She's going to take you home.'

Willow got to her feet. Christopher was yelping now, a strange mewing sound. Perhaps he'd been making the noise all the time, but she'd been concentrating so hard that she hadn't heard it. She walked towards him, ignoring the knife, her arms outstretched. The boy seemed incapable of movement. She almost reached him, was close enough to see that he was trembling and that his face was waxy and white, without expression.

'Come on,' she said. 'Let's get you back to Hesti.'

There was a moment of stillness and silence, as the three of them were held between the fire and the sea. Christopher began to move towards Willow. The killer waivered, shifting focus between Perez and the boy, not willing, it seemed, to attack either. Willow allowed herself to breathe again. All would be well.

Then there was a high-pitched scream and another figure, strong and agile, leapt towards them from the mist, knocking Perez off-balance. The scene came to life again: the blade flashed once more in the glow from the fire, as the killer's arm was raised high, preparing to strike. Willow pulled Christopher towards her. She felt a sharp pain on her cheek and her hand. The knife was raised again, but Willow kicked out and hit it away. Perez and the newcomer were still grappling on the ground, and Willow watched in horror as they both rolled away towards the cliff edge, into the fog and out of sight. The flames had died back to embers by now, so there was no sound but the waves breaking at the bottom of the cliff. Then there was a scream and the distant but definite noise as someone hit the rocks below.

Chapter Fifty-Two

Perez had resisted the temptation to call out to Christopher as he climbed the hill towards the bonfire. He'd hoped he'd find the boy safe, staring into the flames; hoped that the notion of a killer luring Christopher to danger was a Gothic fantasy, born in his own mind from anxiety and this strange, changing weather. But he was taking no chances. If Christopher had lit the fire to let the people who cared for him know where he was, then the killer might know too. Then Perez would need the element of surprise.

When he reached the top of the hill, he circled the fire at a distance, moving as quietly as he could, very slowly. He saw the boy on his first circuit – as Perez had suspected, Christopher was looking at the fire, apparently entranced – but for the moment Perez said nothing. He wanted this over, and the last thing he needed was for their suspect to hear him and slip away into the fog. He knew Willow was right about the murderer's identity, but they still had no evidence. The boy was safe where he was, so Perez waited.

There was a sound behind him, but he could see nothing. This was like a children's game – hide-and-seek in the dark. It could be nothing at all, or a foolhardy sheep. Still he waited, his eyes fixed on

Christopher. He'd always had the ability to be patient. Another sound, and this time there was another movement, this time in front of him: their suspect, quick and silent as a lynx. Christopher saw too and was obviously scared. Perez was about to move, when Willow slid into the picture; she must have been the person he'd heard behind him. He thought how reckless she was, how brave and very foolish, and then he walked forward, into the light of the fire, because he'd seen the knife in the killer's hand, and that flicked a switch in his brain and stopped him thinking clearly.

Everything was confusion. It was the fog and the fire and the odd sounds made by the boy. The killer's arm was raised and the blade flashed towards Willow; Perez imagined it piercing her flesh, the blood and the pain. But before he could get to her, he was knocked to the ground by a new attacker. It was the last thing he'd been expecting, though he realized immediately that he should have known. As he fell, hard on the bare rock, the case finally made sense. He tried to get to his feet, aware of Willow only yards away from him, but the assault had winded him and the attacker came at him again. They tumbled together down the steep bank towards the cliff edge, and Perez thought how foolish he'd been not to know that there'd been two people chasing Christopher over the hill. After all, the killer couldn't have been working alone.

He wondered if it would feel like flying, that moment between leaving land and hitting the water. Then he remembered Cassie and Willow and the baby, and he came to his senses. This was no time for melodrama; he had responsibilities. He stuck his heels into the soft grass to slow himself down. He and his assailant were entwined like lovers, but the person in his arms was still fighting, pushing Perez away now, in an attempt to escape. Perez came to a stop, trapped behind a scrubby gorse bush, but Charlie Moncrieff had freed himself and Perez watched, helpless, as the boy flew on to his death.

Perez scrambled back to the others. Willow stood, white and still as a statue, next to Martha Moncrieff, the young woman who had killed two people and had provoked the death of her brother.

Chapter Fifty-Three

Martha didn't speak to Jimmy Perez as they walked down the hill, arm-in-arm, following Willow and Christopher. Willow thought she must be in shock. She'd seen her brother die and must know that she was responsible. How would she live with that? Perez was holding her tight because he was frightened she might escape, though from a distance Willow thought they looked like father and daughter.

Later, in the police station, Martha couldn't *stop* talking. After so many years of keeping secrets, there was a lot to explain. The grey solicitor sat by her side, but Martha barely acknowledged him. She'd said she didn't want either of her parents there, and Willow thought Perez was too close to the case, so she and Sandy sat on the other side of the table. Mostly listening. Martha looked as if she hadn't slept for a week, and Willow wondered how Robert and Belle hadn't picked up on that, how they could be so careless, so disengaged.

'A rescue team has climbed around the rocks at the bottom of the cliff,' Willow said. 'They found Charlie's body. He would have died at once. He wouldn't have felt any pain.'

Martha looked at her. Her eyes were blank and dead. 'He shouldn't have been there. I didn't ask him.'

'But he wanted to help you. He always wanted to help you. He just couldn't find the right way.'

There was a moment of silence. Martha closed her eyes briefly and, when she opened them again, it was as if it was too hard to talk about her brother. Perhaps it was too soon for her to grieve. Instead her question was about the younger boy.

'Is Christopher OK?'

'It's hard to tell,' Willow said. 'No physical harm.'

Martha nodded. 'I shouldn't have agreed to meet him, when he phoned me. Who'd have listened to him anyway? A weird kid with a forensics fixation. But I'd kind of lost it by then. Become a bit paranoid.'

'He recognized the pattern on the sole of your trainers,' Willow said, 'from the photo of the barbecue that he'd printed from his computer. You were on the lounger, with your feet towards the camera. He'd watched the CSIs examining the prints in the barn and he'd seen your footwear marks on the sand at Burra by Emma's shoes, before everyone else rushed over to muddle them. He's got one of those memories that holds on to patterns.'

Martha looked up. Dark eyes in a white face. 'Christopher didn't think I could have killed anyone. He had a bit of a crush on me. You know.'

Willow remembered the boy's face as it had been in the same photo. Rapt. Not because of the bonfire, but because he'd been so close to Martha. The girl he'd described as cool.

Martha was still talking. 'He just wanted me to explain, but I couldn't think of any sort of reasonable explanation. Then the fog came down. I lost him on the hill until he lit the fire, and I couldn't let him go then. He knew too much. I think I was kind of crazy.'

'You took the knife with you. It must have been in your mind that you'd kill him.'

Martha turned away. 'I always carried the knife. It was a kind of comfort. I thought one day I might need it.'

'And Charlie?'

Again she refused to talk about her brother. 'I told you. I didn't want him there. It was my fight.'

Willow looked directly at the girl. 'You didn't use the knife to kill Emma?'

'No.' Martha had been nibbling her nails, and the skin around them. Now she laid her hands flat on the table in front of her. 'There would have been blood in her car then; and besides, I wanted to see her hanging in the barn where Dennis Gear killed himself. That's how I pictured it when I was planning her death.'

'You couldn't manage that by yourself, though, could you, Martha? It would have taken more than one person to string her up. Was Charlie in it from the beginning?'

'No!' Martha rose to her feet and the words came out as a scream. 'He was at football practice that morning. I was the one who killed her.'

'But later, he came and helped.'

Martha sank back into her chair. 'My brother's dead,' she said. 'Isn't that enough for you? Let them remember him as he was. Don't drag him into this.'

Willow didn't answer; she thought Martha knew exactly what she was doing. If she stuck to her story, there was no way they'd prove Charlie's involvement.

But Willow knew that even a young woman as strong as Martha couldn't have arranged the body in the byre on her own, and Charlie had probably helped to drag Margaret's body to her final resting place too. 'Why did you kill Emma Shearer, Martha?'

There was another moment of silence. The solicitor coughed and shuffled.

'Because she was evil.' Martha paused. 'I think she wanted me to kill her. She was taunting me, daring me to do it.'

Willow said nothing and waited for the girl to continue.

'When she first came, it was little things. Nips and slaps when we didn't do what she wanted. We'd been spoilt rotten, she said. We needed to learn some discipline.' Martha sat on her hands, as if to stop herself biting her nails. 'Other people had said we were spoilt too, so I thought she was right.'

'You didn't tell your parents?'

'Emma said they wouldn't be interested; they were too busy to be bothered. That seemed about right. Once or twice I *did* say something to them, but they only went back to Emma and then things got worse.' There was a moment of silence. Willow was aware of Sandy beside her and could sense his shock and horror. She thought he was too soft-hearted for this work. Martha continued talking: 'When I got older, she made my life even more of a misery. It wasn't physical then. Not usually. She pulled me apart, told me how rubbish I was, put stuff on Facebook that my friends could see. And it was unpredictable. Sometimes she pretended she was my mate, apologized for all the bad things, asked me to forgive her. And for a while I'd believe her, because I wanted it to stop so much. But it never lasted. I couldn't trust her. I couldn't trust anyone. She just said the nice things to play with my head.'

'And she demanded money from you.'

Martha looked up. 'How did you know about that?'

Willow didn't answer; she wanted Martha to continue her story. But she thought: *The handbag. Emma could never have afforded that herself.*

'Yeah, she demanded money,' Martha said. 'First she took all my allowance and then I ended up stealing from Mum and Dad, so I had more to give her. They were so wrapped up in themselves they didn't even notice the cash was missing.'

'And Emma taught you to drive?'

Martha nodded. 'On the tracks around Suksetter. That was another time when I believed things could get better, when I thought she was being kind.' For the first time she sat more upright in her seat and looked directly at Willow. 'I despised myself for not standing up to her. For not being strong enough. And she'd taunt me and tell me how pathetic I was. She was right, wasn't she? I was pathetic. The only way I could fight back was by killing her.'

'Why now?' Willow asked. 'It won't be long before you take your Highers and get away to college or uni.'

'Because I'm not the only person in that family, am I?' Martha's voice was suddenly fierce. 'Emma had already started having a go at Kate. And I wouldn't be around any more to protect her.' Only then did the tears stream silently down her cheeks. She was still crying when Willow left the room.

Chapter Fifty-Four

'Cruelty spreads, don't you think? Perhaps it passes down the generations – inherited, like blue eyes.' Willow clasped her hands around a mug of tea. 'Or like a tendency to compassion.' Her voice had been serious, but with the last words she flashed a look at Perez. A touch of humour, an in-joke that Sandy didn't quite understand.

They were in Perez's house. Although Cassie was still with Duncan Hunter, so there was no need to be quiet, Sandy thought they were unnaturally restrained, muted. It should have been like the old times: the three of them together, winding down at the end of a case; but even though he was fizzing with joy because he had a secret of his own, this didn't feel much like a celebration. Emma Shearer's murder had so much hurt at the heart of it. There was nothing straightforward about the case, and no monster to blame. Except perhaps Kenneth Shearer and, if you dug back far enough, you might find a reason for his cruelty too.

Perez was sitting at the table by the window. He was staring out towards Raven's Head, apparently lost in thought. It was already late evening, but the sun was still shining. The inspector turned back into the room.

'The cruelty ended up hard and brutal within the Moncrieff household. That was fertile ground for Emma's need to hit out in revenge for all that had been inflicted on her. She needed someone to hurt. She'd been showing signs of damage while she was still in Orkney, but the authorities couldn't see or refused to acknowledge it. Emma saw the Moncrieff kids as fair targets. In her mind, they had everything she'd missed out on.'

'I don't see how Robert and Belle Moncrieff couldn't have known what was going on. Martha said she tried to tell them at first, but they took no notice.' Sandy still didn't get that: one of their children had been so sad and screwed up that she'd been willing to commit murder to stop the bad things happening, and they hadn't realized. 'There was abuse going on right under their noses and they did nothing.'

'They were self-centred, wrapped up in their own lives,' Perez said, 'and Robert's childhood had been cold and unloving too. Perhaps he thought that was how family life was meant to be.' He turned to Willow. 'You worked it out, didn't you? You knew what had gone on. You were ahead of the rest of us, as usual.'

There was a silence.

'I think Christopher worked it out before any of us,' Willow said. 'Though he didn't want to believe that Martha could be a killer.'

'And she tried to send him over the cliff to his death!'

'I'm not sure she would actually have done that. But by then, who knows? Martha was certainly a little bit crazy by the end.'

'How did you know it was her?' Sandy thought Willow must be a mind-reader or a magician.

'It was when Magnie told me about Emma leading the chants when Christopher strayed into the beach party. Such a cruel thing. I wondered what it must be like to live with her.' Willow looked up, grinned. 'Magnie left a message on my phone a couple of hours ago. He wanted me to know where he was the night his mother died – with a woman in Lerwick. Someone he works with. A married woman. He was trying to protect her honour.'

'Start from the beginning.' Perez shifted his chair so that his back was facing the window and he was closer to them. 'Talk us through it.

'Emma Shearer arrived in Ness House not long after Kate was born. Martha was nine. Cheeky, a bit spoilt. Used to getting her own way. She wouldn't have been an easy child and, in Emma's life, violence was the way difficult behaviour was kept under control. Emma was hardly more than a child herself, damaged and out of her depth. According to Martha, the abuse wasn't extreme at first: a slap, rough handling when she was lifted out of the bath, a pinch that might have been accidental. I'm guessing that Emma was feeling her way, seeing what she could get away with. But she enjoyed the power she had over Martha. The sense of control. And as Martha got older, she strengthened her grip and the abuse became emotional rather than physical. Relentless and it went on for years.'

'What about Charlie?' Perez asked. 'Did Emma have a go at him?'

Willow shook her head. 'He was a different kind of child. Placid and eager to please. Perhaps he reminded

Emma of her brothers, and we know she'd been kind enough to them. I think Charlie probably saw what was going on, though, and felt guilty about doing nothing to stop it. That's why he helped Martha move Emma's body to Hesti and why he followed her up the hill today. It must have been hard for him, confusing. He'd been brought up to believe that men should be strong and powerful, but he was helpless to stop Emma bullying his sister. She was too controlling. He must have felt like a coward.'

'I still don't get how the girl managed to kill Emma Shearer.' Sandy thought he understood the provocation now, the motive. In the interview room he'd heard Martha's description of that Sunday morning, but he still couldn't see how this crime had been carried out, how a moody sixteen-year-old would have the nerve to plan and execute it.

'It was as you thought. She waited in the back of Emma's car on the Sunday morning. Martha knew Emma had planned a day out and would come to the car eventually. Her parents were busy – Robert had taken Charlie to play football, and Belle was at the hall preparing for the teas. Martha had overheard the phone conversation between Helena and Belle the night before. Helena had said they were planning a family walk and wouldn't be at home.' Willow turned to Perez. 'Martha said she chose Hesti to display Emma's body because Dennis Gear had killed himself there. She has a taste for the theatrical, I think. The Gothic. And she resented Daniel because he was so sympathetic to Emma. She didn't mind at all that he became a suspect. That was why she left Emma's bag in the boatshed; she knew the couple had met there.'

'She drove Emma's car up to Hesti,' Perez said.

'Yes, she waited until she could see the family on the hill, then drove up the track and tucked the car between the house and the barn, so it couldn't be seen from the community hall. By that point Charlie was back from football and Robert Moncrieff had gone to the community hall. She's a strong young woman – she rows for Deltaness in the regattas – but it would still have been too much for her to throw the rope over the beam, put the noose round Emma's neck and string her up on her own. She'll never admit Charlie's part in it, though.'

'She was lucky nobody saw her either driving up the track or while she was in the garden.' Perez was totally engaged in the conversation now. 'A place like Deltaness, where everyone's watching.'

'But somebody did see her.' Sandy found he was losing concentration and he was impatient to move the conversation along. He had other things on his mind and he couldn't wait to get back to Louisa. 'Margaret Riddell.'

'Margaret didn't see Martha at Hesti that Sunday, but we know what an interest she took in other people's business. She often watched the Moncrieff place, in the hope of catching Emma with another man. Or of seeing anything to give her ammunition to break up Magnie's relationship with Emma. She saw Martha in the back of Emma's car that Sunday morning. And Martha saw her.' Willow paused. 'Margaret was such a sad and bitter woman. If she'd just concentrated on getting on with her own life, she'd still be alive.'

'Why didn't Margaret tell us about seeing Emma and Martha together that morning?' Sandy asked.

'She wouldn't have thought it had any significance. Emma was always driving the kids around. And she would have had to explain what she was doing spying at Ness House. The sycamores hide the place from the road. She must have been standing right in the drive.' Willow paused. 'Martha thought it was important, though. She brooded over it. Every time she saw the woman she was scared that Margaret was about to threaten her with what she'd seen. Margaret was outside Ness again the night of the fog. Perhaps spying had become a habit or perhaps she was just catching her breath on her way to Hesti. It freaked Martha out, though. That night, after her parents had taken a taxi to their friends' house, she took her mother's car. We know Margaret was scared of driving when it was foggy and we know she hated walking. She'd already walked all the way to Hesti to pass on the gossip about Daniel's so-called affair, and I think she'd have been ready to accept a lift from anyone that night. But instead of taking her home, Martha strangled her and drove to the dunes at Suksetter.'

Sandy knew what had happened then. He'd sat in the interview room watching Martha fall apart, the words spewing out of her, as she'd described half-carrying, half-dragging the woman to the bench that Magnie had made in memory of Dennis Gear: *It's where she would have wanted to end up. That's what I thought. So I was doing her a favour, wasn't I, by taking her there? It was an effort, but I knew it was the right thing to do.* And the girl had stared across the table at them, begging them to understand.

'Why did she leave the shoes on the beach?' Perez asked.

Willow shrugged. 'I think that was probably Charlie. He found them in the boot of Emma's car when they got back to Ness House, and he'd been carrying them around in his school bag since then. He left them below the tideline and hoped they'd disappear with the debris of the bonfire. It must have been a shock when Christopher stumbled over them.'

Sandy was still haunted by the sight of the girl unravelling before their eyes. 'What will happen to Martha?'

'Who knows?' Perez said. 'Her father can afford the best lawyers. But Charlie, his golden boy, is dead and they might blame Martha for that. I hope her family will help her now. Through guilt, or because they want to be seen doing the best for her. Perhaps Martha will get the support that Emma never had.'

Sandy stood up. 'I need to go. Louisa's waiting for me. There's a teacher-training day in town tomorrow, so she's staying over at my place.' Then he couldn't resist telling them. He'd planned to keep his secret and save the news for a happier time, but he couldn't keep quiet. He'd never been brilliant at secrets. 'I asked Louisa to marry me this afternoon. We met up for tea after the interview with the Moncrieff girl. It seemed time for something good to happen, you know, so I plucked up the nerve.' He was aware of Perez and Willow staring at him. 'She said yes! Can you believe that? She said yes.' And then he was crying because some days he was even soppier than Perez, who could be the soppiest person he knew.

When he left the house, he looked through the window and saw Perez and Willow, deep in conversation.

Chapter Fifty-Five

It was Midsummer Day. At midnight all the beacons on the island had been lit to celebrate the solstice, an excuse for a party. Perez had gone to Deltaness the night before on impulse; it had felt the right thing to do, a way to complete the case properly. The beacon had been built again, the community glad of something to pull them together. He'd only stayed long enough to eat a barbecued burger and to watch the other bonfires lit along the coast – the fog, it seemed, had gone for good now – but he'd seen the Flemings there. The family had seemed solid enough, Daniel with his arm around Helena's shoulders, surrounded by neighbours who might become friends. Helena had given him a little hug; he'd smelled the wood-smoke on her hair.

He'd expected to see Christopher staring into the beacon, but he was standing a little way off, wary.

Helena had noticed Perez watching the boy. 'The drama on the hill seems to have cured him of that particular obsession. We should have no more trouble with him setting light to waste paper in school. He's still into *CSI*, though. Maybe he'll become a detective one day.' She'd smiled and Perez had walked away.

Now Perez was going home. Kind of. He was on the *Good Shepherd* on the way to Fair Isle and it felt as if he was already there, because he had family all around him. His father was skippering the mail boat, his last trip before retiring. His cousin was in the wheelhouse too. The chat was of sheep and the new teacher, and some strange hippy types who'd taken over one of the crofts but seemed to be making a go of it, despite the way they looked.

In the passenger cabin below there were three tourists and a young woman who would spend the rest of the season as assistant cook in the field centre at the North Light. He'd had a few words with them while they were all waiting at Grutness for the boat to come in. Beside him was Willow. Perez took her arm. 'Shall we go on deck? It's calm enough, but this old tub rolls at the best of times and I'm not the best sailor.' That was all true, but really he wanted to get her on her own. They'd talked long into the night after Sandy had left them, the day of Martha's arrest, but that had just been connecting again. No plans had been made. Willow had disappeared south the following morning and he still wasn't entirely sure how things were between them.

His invitation for her to come with him to Fair Isle had been another impulse. He'd phoned her a few days earlier, after a sleepless night when he'd rerun in his mind his panic when Willow had appeared out of the fog in search of the Deltaness killer. The possibility of losing her and the baby seemed real now too.

'I'm going to Fair Isle to catch up with my folks at the weekend. Do you fancy coming along?' Still, even then, he had no idea what he might say to her, or how the situation between them might be resolved.

There'd been a moment of silence. In the time that it took her to answer, he thought how crass he'd been and how thoughtless. He should have offered to go to her, not dragged her north again.

'That would be lovely, Jimmy,' she'd said. No questions and no drama. 'Will you pick me up from the airport? I'll get the early plane.'

The sunshine was hazy, but once the *Good Shepherd* left the shelter of Sumburgh Head, they could see the silhouette of Fair Isle, clear on the horizon.

'How are you feeling?'

'Better,' she said. 'Not exactly blooming but not perpetually tired, either.' A pause. 'I've told them at work. About the baby. That I'll need maternity leave.'

'I'm sorry about how I reacted to the news. It was wrong. Entirely wrong.'

'Ah, Jimmy, it was quite a relief to see you're human like the rest of us. Not some kind of bleeding-heart saint.' She was facing the prow of the boat and her hair was streaming out behind her, so she looked like a figurehead. Majestic. He put his arm around her and she leaned her head back against his body.

In that moment he felt lighter, as if he could soar in the air like the gannets following the boat. The guilt and indecision that had weighed him down for so many years were gone, dumped overboard into the sea between Shetland and Fair Isle. 'I want to be a part of it,' he said. 'Your life. The baby. However you want to make it work. Move to Shetland, or I'll move to you.'

She turned to face him. 'Come on, Jimmy! Would

you really do that? Move Cassie out of school and away from her dad?'

'Her dad's moving anyway,' he said. 'But yes, I'd give it all up. All this.' He waved his arm to include the boat, the family, Shetland disappearing into the distance. 'For you. And for our child.'

She turned once more, so that she was facing him. 'I've been offered a new post, once my maternity leave is over. Police Scotland want someone senior to cover the Scottish Islands – the Hebrides as well as the Northern Isles. It's the government's new thing. A nod to rural policing.' She paused. 'I've said I'll take it, if I can be based in Orkney. They must be desperate, because they've agreed.'

He looked towards Fair Isle. A group of puffins flew very low over the water. 'Then I'll come too.'

She pushed him away a little, so she could look into his face. He couldn't tell what she was thinking. She smiled, but she didn't answer and he didn't push her. For now, this was enough.

The Isle was getting closer. He could see the seabirds on the cliffs. The boat rounded the point into the North Haven and he recognized his mother's van parked near the jetty. Islanders were standing in the sun chatting, waiting to help unload the boat. He wondered what they'd make of Willow and decided he didn't care. He'd always liked things straightforward, clear-cut. From now on, he could see that his life might be messy and ambiguous. It would take some getting used to. Willow slipped her arm through his and they looked together towards the approaching shore.